LUCAS

From the Chicken House

Sometimes I can get almost too emotional about our books. This book is scarily moving. It's wild, romantic, confronting - and *dangerous.* Maybe you've read other books like it - but I haven't. The characters totally lock you in - and the action is tense and gripping. I'm still astonished by the power in these pages.
Kevin Brooks' second novel.
Astounding.

Barry Cunningham
Publisher
The Chicken House

LUCAS

kevin brooks

The Chicken House

2 Palmer Street, Frome, Somerset BA11 1DS

**For Susan –
for everything,
for ever.**

This paperback edition first published in Great Britain in 2004 by
The Chicken House
2, Palmer Street
Frome, Somerset BA11 IDS, United Kingdom
E-mail: chickenhouse@doublecluck.com

Text © Kevin Brooks 2003

Kevin Brooks has asserted his rights under the Copyright, Designs and Patents
Act 1988 to be identified as the author of this work.

ISBN 1 904442 12 9

British Library Cataloguing in Publication data available

Cover photograph © Gettyone Stone Ltd
Cover design by Ian Butterworth

Typeset by Dorchester Typesetting Group Ltd
Printed and Bound in Great Britain

High Praise for

LUCAS

SHORTLISTED FOR THE
GUARDIAN CHILDREN'S FICTION AWARD 2003
AND
BOOKTRUST TEENAGE PRIZE 2003

It was my dad's idea to write about Lucas and Angel and every-
thing else that happened last summer. 'It won't make you feel any
better,' he told me, 'it might even make things worse for a while.
But you mustn't let the sadness die inside you. You have to give it
some life. You have to ...'

'Let it all out?'

He smiled. 'Something like that.'

'I don't know, Dad,' I sighed. 'I'm not sure I can write a story.'

'Ah, now, that's nonsense. Anyone can write a story. It's the
easiest thing in the world. How else do you think I make a living
out of it? All you have to do is tell the truth, tell it like it was.'

'But I don't know how it was, I don't know all the details, the
facts—'

'Stories aren't facts, Cait, they're not details. Stories are
feelings. You've got your feelings, haven't you?'

'Too many,' I said.

'Well, that's all you need.' He put his hand on mine. 'Cry
yourself a story, love. It works. Believe me.'

So that's what I did, I cried myself a story.

And this is it.

Caitlin McCann

one

I first saw Lucas on a fine afternoon at the end of July last summer. Of course, I didn't know who he was then ... in fact, come to think of it, I didn't even know *what* he was. All I could see from the back seat of the car was a green-clad creature padding along the Stand in a shimmering haze of heat; a slight and ragged figure with a mop of straw-blond hair and a way of walking – I smile when I think of it – a way of walking that whispered secrets to the air.

We were on our way back from the mainland.

My brother, Dominic, had been staying with friends in Norfolk since finishing his first year at university the month before, and he'd called that morning to let us know he was on his way home. His train was due in at five and he'd asked for a lift back from the station. Now, Dad normally hates being disturbed when he's writing (which is just about all the time), and he also hates having to go *any*where, but despite the usual sighs and moans – why can't the boy get a taxi? ... what's wrong with the damn bus? – I could tell by the sparkle in his eyes that he was really looking forward to seeing Dominic again.

It wasn't that Dad was unhappy spending all of his time with me, but with Dom away at university I think he felt there was something missing from his life. I'm sixteen (I was fifteen then), and Dad's forty-something. They're difficult ages – for both of us. Growing up, having to *be* grown up, girl things, man things, having to deal with emotions that neither of us understand ... it's not easy. We can't always give each other what we need, no matter how hard we try, and sometimes it helps to have someone in the middle, someone to turn to when things get too much. If nothing else, Dominic had always been good at being someone in the middle.

Of course, that wasn't the only reason why Dad was looking forward to seeing him again – he was his son, after all. His boy. He was proud of him. He was worried about him. He loved him.

And so did I.

But for some reason I wasn't quite so excited about seeing him as Dad was. I don't know why. It wasn't that I didn't *want* to see him, because I did. It was just ... I don't know.

Something didn't feel right.

'Are you ready, Cait?' Dad had asked, when it was time to go.

'Why don't you go on your own?' I'd suggested. 'You can have a "father and son" chat on the way back.'

'Ah, go on, he'll want to see his little sister.'

'Just a minute, then. I'll get Deefer.'

Dad's been terrified of driving on his own ever since Mum was killed in a car crash ten years ago. I try to encourage him, but I haven't the heart to push it too hard.

So, anyway, we'd driven to the mainland and picked up Dominic from the station, and there we all were – the entire McCann family stuffed inside our decrepit old Fiesta, heading back to the island. Dad and Dominic in the front; me and Deefer in the back. (Deefer, by the way, is our dog. A big, black, foul-smelling thing, with a white streak over one eye and a head the size of an anvil. According to Dad, he's a cross between a skunk and a donkey.)

Dominic had been talking non-stop from the moment he'd slung his rucksack in the boot and got in the car. University this, university that, writers, books, magazines, parties, people, money, clubs, gigs ... the only time he paused was to light a cigarette, which he did about every ten minutes. And when I say talking, I don't mean talking as in having a conversation, I mean talking as in jabbering like a mad thing. '... I tell you, Dad, you wouldn't bloody believe it ... they've actually got us studying *EastEnders*, for Christ's sake ... something to do with *popular culture*, whatever the hell *that's* supposed to be ... and another thing, the very first lecture, right? I'm just sitting there listening to this twatty old lecturer rambling on about sodding *Marxism* or something, minding my own business, when suddenly he stops and looks at me and says "why aren't you taking any notes?" I couldn't *believe* it. *Why aren't you taking notes?* Shit! I thought university was supposed to be about choice, you know? The discipline of self-education, freedom to learn at your own pace ...'

And on and on and on ...

I didn't like it.

The way he spoke, his constant swearing, the way he smoked his cigarette and waved his hands around like a phoney intellectual ... it was embarrassing. It made me feel uncomfortable – that *wincing* kind of discomfort you feel when someone you like, someone close to you, suddenly starts acting like a complete idiot. And I didn't like the way he was ignoring me, either. For all the attention I was getting I might as well not have been there. I felt like a stranger in my own car. It wasn't until we'd almost reached the island that Dominic paused for breath, turned round, ruffled Deefer's head ('Hey, Deef') and finally spoke to me.

'All right, kid? How's it going?'

'Hello, Dominic.'

'What's the matter? You look different. Christ, what've you done with your hair?'

'I was going to ask you the same.'

He grinned and ran his fingers through his dyed-blond crop. 'Like it?'

'Very nice. Very beach bum. Is that how they all look in Liverpool?'

'Well, they don't look like *that*,' he said, flicking at my hair. 'Nice style. What's it called – the Hedgehog?'

'Hedgehogs have spikes,' I told him, readjusting a ribbon. 'These are plumes.'

'*Plumes?* Yeah, right.' He puffed on his cigarette. 'What do you think, Dad?'

'I think it's very becoming,' Dad said. 'And, anyhow, I'd rather have a hedgehog in the family than a neo-Nazi surf boy.'

Dominic smiled, still looking at my hair. '*Und was denkt deiner Liebling davon?*'

'What?'

'Simon,' he said. 'What does Simon think of it?'

'I've no idea.'

'You two haven't split up, have you?'

'Oh, don't be so childish, Dominic. Simon's just a friend—'

'That's what he *wants* you to think.'

I sighed. 'I thought you were supposed to grow up when you went to university?'

'Not me,' he said, pulling a face. 'I'm regressing.'

All the bad old memories of Dominic were beginning to

creep back. The needling, the snide comments, the constant mickey-taking, the way he treated me like a stupid little girl ... I suppose that was one of the reasons I'd been a bit wary of him coming back – I didn't *want* to be treated like a stupid little girl any more, especially by someone who couldn't act his *own* age. And the fact that I'd had a year *without* being treated like a moron only made it worse. I wasn't used to it any more. And when you're not used to something, it's harder to put up with it. Which is why I was getting annoyed.

But then, just as the irritation was beginning to set in, Dominic reached across and gently touched my cheek.

'It's good to see you, Cait,' he said softly.

For a brief moment he was the Dominic I used to know before he grew up, the *real* Dominic, the one who looked after me when I needed looking after – my big brother. But almost immediately he turned away with a shrug of his shoulders, as if he'd embarrassed himself, and good old big-voiced Dom was back.

'Hey, Dad,' he boomed. 'When the hell are you going to get a new car?'

'And why should I be wanting a new car?'

'Because this one's a shit-heap.'

Charming.

The island sky has its own unmistakable light, an iridescent sheen that moves with the moods of the sea. It's never the same, but it's always the same, and whenever I see it I know I'm nearly home.

Home is a small island called Hale. It's about four kilometres long and two kilometres wide at its broadest point, and it's joined to the mainland by a short causeway known as the Stand, a narrow road that bridges the estuary. Most of the time you wouldn't know it's a causeway, and you wouldn't know it's an island either, because most of the time the estuary is just a vast stretch of reeds and brown ooze. But when there's a high tide and the estuary rises a half a metre or so above the road and nothing can pass until the tide goes out again, then you know it's an island.

On that Friday afternoon, though, as we approached the island, the tide was low and the Stand stretched out before us, clear and dry, hazing in the heat – a raised strip of pale grey concrete bounded by white railings and a low footpath on either side, with rough cobbled banks leading down to the waterside. Beyond the railings, the estuary was glinting with that wonderful silver light that comes on in the late afternoon and lazes through to the early evening.

We were about halfway across when I saw Lucas.

I remember the moment quite clearly: Dominic was laughing uproariously about something he'd just said while patting his pockets in search of another cigarette; Dad was doing his best to look amused, tugging somewhat wearily at his beard; Deefer, as usual, was sitting bolt upright in his very-serious-dog-in-a-car pose, blinking only occasionally; and I was leaning to one side to get a better view of the sky. No ... I can do better than that. I remember my *exact* position. I was sitting just to the right of the middle of the seat, cross-legged, leaning slightly to the left, looking out through the front windscreen over Dominic's shoulder. My left arm was stretched out around Deefer's back and my hand was resting in the dust and dog hairs of the blanket on the back seat. I was anchoring myself in this position by gripping onto the surround of the open window with my right hand ... I remember it precisely. The feel of the hot metal in my hand, the rubber trim, the cooling wind on my fingers ...

That was the moment I first saw him – a lone figure at the far end of the Stand, on the left-hand side, with his back to us, walking towards the island.

Apart from wishing that Dominic would shut up braying, my first thought was how odd it was to see someone walking on the Stand. You don't often see people walking around here. The closest town is Moulton (where we'd just come from), about fifteen kilometres away on the mainland, and between Hale and Moulton there's nothing but small cottages, farms, heathland, the ranges, and the odd pub or two. So islanders don't walk, because there's nowhere nearby to walk *to*. And if they're going to Moulton they either drive or take the bus. So the only pedestrians you're likely to see around here are ramblers, bird-watchers, poachers, or, very occasionally, people (like me) who just like to walk. But even from a distance I could tell that the figure up ahead didn't fit into any of these categories. I wasn't sure how I knew, I just did. Deefer knew, too. His ears had pricked up and he was squinting curiously through the windscreen.

As we drew closer, the figure became clearer. It was a young man, or a boy, dressed loosely in a drab green T-shirt and baggy green trousers. He had a green army jacket tied around his waist and a green canvas bag slung over his shoulder. The only non-green thing about him was the pair of scruffy black walking boots on his feet. Although he was on the small side, he wasn't as slight as I'd first thought. He wasn't exactly *muscular*, but he wasn't weedy-looking either. It's hard to explain. There was an air of hidden strength about him, a graceful strength that showed in his balance, the way he held himself, the way he walked ...

As I've already said, the memory of Lucas's walk brings a smile to my face. It's an incredibly vivid memory, and if I close my eyes I can see it now. An easygoing lope. Nice and steady. Not too fast and not too slow. Fast enough to get somewhere, but not too fast to miss anything. Bouncy, alert, resolute, without concern and without vanity. A walk that both belonged to and was remote from everything around it.

You can tell a lot about people from the way they walk.

As the car got closer I realised that Dad and Dominic had stopped talking, and I was suddenly aware of a strange, almost ghostly, silence to the air – not just in the car, but outside as well. Birds had stopped calling, the wind had dropped, and in the distance the sky had brightened to the most intense blue I'd ever seen. It was like something out of a film, one of those slow-motion episodes played out in absolute silence when your skin starts tingling and you just *know* that something stunning is about to happen.

Dad was driving quite steadily, as he always does, but it seemed as if we were barely moving. I could hear the tyres humming on the dry road and the air rushing past the window, and I could see the railings at the side of the road flickering past in a blur of white, so I knew we *were* moving, but the distance between us and the boy didn't appear to be changing.

It was weird. Almost like a dream.

Then, all at once, time and distance seemed to lurch forward and we drew level with the boy. As we did so, he turned his head and looked at us. No, that's wrong – he turned his head and looked at *me*. Directly at me. (When I talked to Dad about this a little while ago, he told me he'd had the very same feeling – that Lucas was looking directly at *him*, as if *he* was the only person in the whole world.)

It was a face I'll never forget. Not simply because of its beauty – although Lucas was undeniably beautiful – but more for its wondrous sense of being *beyond* things. Beyond the pale blue eyes and the tousled hair and the sad smile ... beyond all this there was something else.

Something ...

I still don't know what it was.

Dominic broke the spell by peering through the window and grunting, 'What the hell is *that*?'

And then the boy was gone, whizzing past into the background as we left the Stand and veered off towards the east of the island.

I wanted to look back. I was desperate to look back. But I couldn't. I was afraid he might not be there.

The rest of the journey was something of a blur. I remember Dad making a curious sniffing sound, glancing at me in the mirror, then clearing his throat and asking me if I was all right.

And me saying, 'Uh huh.'

And then Dominic saying, 'Do you know him, Cait?'

'Who?'

'The droolee, the urchin ... that thing you were gawping at.'

'Shut up, Dominic.'

He laughed, mocking me – '*Shut up, Dominic* ...' – and then started on about something else.

I remember Dad changing gear and gunning the car up Black Hill with a rare burst of confidence, and I vaguely remember passing the sign that says *Beware Tractors*, only the *T* and the *R* are hidden behind a hedge, so it says *Beware actors*, and whenever we pass it one of us always makes a point of saying, Look out, there's John Wayne, or Hugh Grant, or Brad Pitt ... but I don't remember who it was that afternoon.

I was somewhere else for a while.

I don't know where.

All I can remember is a strange, buzzy feeling in my head, an intensity of excitement and sadness that I'd never felt before and probably won't ever feel again.

It was as if I knew, even then, what was going to happen.

Over the last year I've often wondered what would have happened if I hadn't seen Lucas that day. If we'd crossed the Stand ten minutes earlier, or ten minutes later. If Dominic's train had been delayed. If the tide had been high. If Dad had stopped for petrol on the way back. If Lucas had left wherever he'd come from a day earlier, or a day later ...

What would have happened? Would everything be different? Would I be a different person right now? Would I be happier? Sadder? Would I dream different dreams? And what about Lucas? What would have happened to Lucas if I hadn't seen him that day? Would he still ...

And it's then I realise how utterly pointless such thinking is. What if, what might have been ...

It doesn't matter.

I did see him, and nothing can ever change that.

These things, these moments you take to be extraordinary, they have a way of melting back into reality, and the further we got from the Stand – the further we got from the moment – the less tingly I felt. By the time we turned into the narrow lane that leads down to our house, the buzzy feeling in my head had just about gone and the world had returned to something like normal.

The car lumped and shuddered down the lane and I gazed out at the familiar view: the poplar trees, with the sunlight strobing through the branches; the green fields; the pitted driveway; then the old grey house, looking restful and welcoming in the cooling sun; and beyond it all, the beach and the sea glistening in the evening distance. Aside from a lone container ship inching across the horizon, the sea was empty and still.

Dad told me once that this part of Hale, the east side, reminded him of his childhood home in Ireland. I've never been to Ireland, so I wouldn't know. But I know that I love everything about this place – the peace, the wildness, the birds, the smell of salt and seaweed, the call of the wind, the unpredictability of the sea ... I even love this straggly old house, with its mouldy old roof and its uneven walls and its scattering of outhouses and tumbledown sheds. It might not be the prettiest house in the world, but it's mine. It's where I live. I was born here.

I belong here.

Dad parked the car in the yard and turned off the engine. I opened the door. Deefer bounded out and started barking at Rita Gray, our neighbour, who was walking her Labrador along the lane. I got out of the car and waved to her. As she waved back, a pair of Mute swans flew in low across the field, their wings throbbing in the breeze. The Labrador started after them, barking like a lunatic.

'She'll never catch them,' Dad called out.

Rita shrugged and smiled. 'It'll do her good, John, she needs the exercise – oh, hello Dominic, I didn't recognise you.'

'Yo, Mrs Gee,' Dom replied, scuttling into the house.

The Labrador was halfway down the lane now, its tongue hanging out, yapping at the empty sky.

Rita shook her head and sighed. 'Damn dog, I don't know why she – oh, Cait, before I forget, Bill said would you give her a ring about tomorrow.'

'OK.'

'She'll be in until nine.'

'All right, thanks.'

She nodded at Dad, then strode off down the lane after her dog, whistling and laughing, swinging the dog lead in the air, her red hair blowing in the breeze.

I noticed that Dad was watching her.

'What?' he said, when he saw me looking at him.

'Nothing,' I smiled.

Inside, Dominic had thrown his rucksack on the floor and was stomping up the stairs. 'Give me a shout when grub's on,' he called out. 'I'm just going to have a quick kip. I'm knackered.'

The bedroom door slammed shut.

It felt strange having someone else in the house. It unsettled me. I suppose I'd got used to being alone with Dad. Our sounds, our quietness. I'd got used to the calm and solitude.

Dad picked up Dominic's rucksack and leaned it against the stairs. He smiled reassuringly at me, reading my thoughts. 'He's just a big kid, Cait. He doesn't mean any harm.'

'Yeah, I know.'

'It'll be fine. Don't worry.'

I nodded. 'Do you want something to eat?'

'Not just now, eh? Give him an hour or two and then we'll have something together.' He leaned down and tightened one of the ribbons in my hair. 'Plumes, you say?'

'Plumes,' I agreed.

He fixed the ribbon then stepped back and looked at me. 'Very becoming, indeed.'

'Thanks,' I grinned. 'You're not too bad yourself. Did you see the way Rita was looking at you?'

'She looks at everyone like that. She's worse than her daughter.'

'She's always asking after you, you know.'

'Look, Cait—'

'I'm only joking, Dad,' I said. 'Don't look so worried.'

'Who's worried?'

'You are. You worry about everything.'

We chatted away for a couple of minutes, but I could tell he was itching to get back to work. He kept looking at his watch.

'I'm going to ring Bill,' I told him. 'And then I'll take Deefer out for a walk. I'll make something to eat when I get back.'

'OK,' he said. 'I suppose I'd better get a couple of hours in while I've still got the chance.'

'How's the new book going?'

'Ah, you know, same old stuff ...' For a moment he just stood there staring down at the floor, rubbing at his beard, and I thought he was going to tell me something, share some of his problems with me. But after a while he just sighed again and said, 'Well, I'd best be getting on – make sure you're back before it's dark. I'll see you later, love.' And he was gone, stooping into his study and shutting the door.

Dad writes books for teenagers, or *Young Adults*, as the bookshops like to call them. You've probably heard of him. You may even have read some of his books – *Some Kind of God, Nothing Ever Dies, New World* ... No? Well, even if you haven't read them, you've probably read *about* them. They're the kind of books that get nominated for prizes but never win, the kind of books that get rubbished by all the papers for being immoral, for setting a bad example, for contributing to the destruction of innocence in the youth of today. Basically, they're the kind of books that don't make very much money.

Bill was eating when she answered the phone. 'Mmyeah?'

'Bill? It's Cait—'

'Just a mm – hold on ...' I could hear the television blaring in the background, Bill chewing, swallowing, burping ... 'Right,' she said. '*Urrp* – sorry 'bout that.'

'Your mum said to ring you. I saw her down the lane.'

'Yeah, I thought she was never gonna go – just a minute ...'

'Bill?'

'That's better, dying for a ciggy. You all right?'

'Fine—'

'I saw you coming back in the car, where've you been?'

'Picking up Dom.'

'Hey, now you're talking—'

'Oh, come on, Bill—'

'What?'

'You *know* what. He's nineteen, for God's sake.'

'So?'

'You're fifteen ...'

'Girls mature earlier than boys, Cait. It's a well-known fact.'

'Yeah? Well *you* certainly have.'

She laughed. 'Can I help it if my hormones are hungry?'

'Maybe you should try going on a diet?'

'Ha!'

'Anyway, Dom's got a girlfriend.'

'Who?'

'I don't know, someone at university, I think.' I quickly formed a mental image. 'A tall blonde with long legs and pots of money—'

'You're making it up.'

'No, I'm not. Her name's Helen, she lives in Norfolk somewhere—'

'There you are, then.'

'What?'

'She's in Norfolk – I'm two minutes walk up the lane. End of story.' She laughed again, then covered the mouth-piece and spoke to somebody in the background.

I twiddled the telephone cord in my fingers and wiped a cobweb from the wall. I jiggled my foot. I told myself to ignore it, forget it, don't let it bother you ... but I couldn't. This thing with Bill and Dominic was getting out of hand. It used to be funny – *Dear Trish, My best friend fancies my older brother, what should I do?* Yeah, it *used* to be funny, when Bill was ten and Dominic was fourteen. But it wasn't funny any more, because Bill wasn't joking any more. She really meant it. And that bothered me. The trouble was, if I told her what I really thought she'd just laugh it off. She'd say – oh, come on, Cait, don't be so bloody *serious* all the time, it's just a bit of fun, girl ...

So, right or wrong, I just went along with it.

'Cait?'

'Yeah, who was that?'

'What?'

'I thought you were talking to someone.'

'Nah, it's the telly. I was just turning it down. Anyway,

are you still all right for tomorrow?'

'What time?'

'I'll meet you at the bus stop at two—'

'Why don't I come round to your place? We can walk over together.'

'No, I have to go somewhere first. I'll meet you at two.'

'The bus goes at ten to.'

'All right, quarter to, then. What are you wearing?'

'Wearing? I don't know, nothing special – why?'

'No reason, I just thought it'd be fun to spice it up for a change.'

'Spice it up?'

'You know, skirt, heels, skinny top ...'

I laughed. 'We're only going to Moulton.'

'Yeah, well ... you look nice when you get dressed up. You should do it more often. You can't wear those worn-out shorts and a T-shirt *all* the time.'

'I *don't*.'

'Yes, you do. Shorts and a T-shirt in summer, jeans and a jumper in winter—'

'What's wrong with that?'

'Nothing – all I'm saying is, you've got to make an effort now and then. Show a bit of leg, bit of belly, slap a bit of lippy on, you know ...'

'We'll see. Maybe ...'

'Oh, go on, Cait. It'll be a laugh.'

'I said maybe—'

'You never know, we might bump into someone decent ... what's Dom doing tomorrow? Bumpety bump—'

'Look, Bill—'

'Oops – gotta go. I think I heard Mum coming back and I've still got a ciggy going. I'll see you tomorrow at two—'

'Quarter to— Bill?'

But she'd already hung up.

I put the phone down and went into the kitchen. The house was quiet. Faint sounds drifted in the silence – the soft tap-tapping of Dad's keyboard, the drone of an aeroplane high in the sky, the distant cry of a lone gull. Through the window I could see the container ship drifting round the Point, its vast grey hulk weighed down with a cargo of multicoloured metal crates. The sky above it was clouding over a little but the sun was still warm and bright, bathing the island in a gauze of pale pink.

I like this time of day. When the light glows softly and there's a sense of sleepiness to the air – it's as if the island is breathing out after a long hard day, getting ready for the night. During the summer I often sit in the kitchen for an hour or two, just watching the sky change colour as the sun goes down, but that evening I couldn't settle. I'm a worrier, just like Dad. I was worried about him. I was worried about Dominic, how he'd changed so much in the last year. And the boy on the Stand ... it worried me why I couldn't stop thinking about him ... and Bill ... I wished I hadn't called her. I wished we weren't going into town tomorrow. I wished ... I don't know. I wished I didn't have to grow up. The whole thing was just too depressing.

I called Deefer and headed off down the lane.

The thing about Dad is, he's got far too much sadness in his bones. You can see it in the way he walks, the way he looks at things, even in the way he sits. When I left the house that evening I looked over at his study window and saw him hunched at his desk, staring at his computer screen, smoking a cigarette and sipping Irish whiskey. He looked so sad I felt like crying. It was that unmasked look of sadness you rarely see, the look of someone who thinks they're alone so they don't have to hide it any more.

It's Mum, of course. He's been alone with his sadness ever since she died.

It's not that he doesn't talk to me about her – he does. He tells me how wonderful she was, how pretty she was, how kind, how thoughtful, how funny she was – 'God, Cait, when Kathleen laughed it made your heart sing.' He tells me how happy they were together. He shows me photographs, reads me her poems, tells me how much I remind him of her ... he *tells* me how sad he is. But he won't take his own advice – he won't give his sadness some life.

I don't know why.

Sometimes I think it's because he *wants* the sadness to die inside him. That if it dies inside him, he's keeping it from me. But what he doesn't realise is that I don't *want* to be excluded from his sadness. I want some of it. I want to feel it, too. She was my mum. I hardly knew her, but the least he could do is let me share in her dying.

I don't know if that makes any sense.

I don't even know if it's true.

But it's what I was thinking.

Down at the creek, Deefer had ambled onto the little wooden bridge and was staring at a family of swans – an adult pair and three large cygnets. One of the adults was making a show of defending its brood, approaching Deefer with spread wings, an arched neck, and a loud hiss. Deefer couldn't care less. He's seen it all before. He just stood there staring and gently wagging his tail. After a minute or two the swan gave up, shook its head, and paddled back to its family.

The creek lies in a sunken valley that runs parallel to

the beach, stretching all the way from the middle of the island right up to the mud flats across from the Point. Between the creek and the beach there's a broad spread of saltmarsh, a pale green carpet of glasswort and purslane dotted with countless muddy pools fringed with reeds and rushes. If you know your way around, which I do, there are tracks through the saltmarsh that cut across to the beach. Otherwise you have to follow the creek path all the way up to the west end of the beach where the marshes thin out and merge into the shore, or else cut through a maze of dunes and gorse to the east and follow it round to the shallow bay beside the mud flats.

I called Deef and we cut across the saltmarsh, emerging onto the beach by the old concrete pillbox. The sea breeze was strengthening as we made our way down towards the shoreline, scenting the air with a mixture of salt and sand and unknown things that only dogs can smell. While Deefer trotted along with his head in the air, sniffing out the stories of his world, I paused for a moment and listened to the sounds of the sea. The waves lapping gently on the shore, the wind in the air, the rustling sand, the seabirds ... and beneath it all, or above it all, the faint bubbling of the mud flats beside the Point.

The Point is the easternmost end of the island, a slim finger of shingle bounded by the open sea on one side and mud flats on the other. When the tide is out you can see the remains of ancient boats that have been sucked down and lost in the depths. Like skeletons of long-dead beasts, their stripped and blackened frames emerge from the ooze, giving stark warning of the dangers that lurk in the mud. Beyond the mud flats, a tangle of stunted woodland darkens a rugged islet in the mouth of the estuary. The tiny island overlooks the shore with a haunting blend of beauty and menace, the limbs of its wizened trees twisted by the wind and tide into strange grasping shapes, like misformed hands reaching out for help.

Even in the height of summer this part of the beach is usually deserted. Visitors to the island generally keep to the west side, the village side, where the sand is soft and there's space for parking, where there's a country park (a field with litter bins), cliff walks, kite-flying, ice cream vans, a bandstand – there are even plans to open a caravan park. But that's another world. Down here on the east of the island the only people you're likely to see are locals, fishermen, dog walkers, the occasional anorak with a metal-detector, and sometimes, late on a summer's night, illicit lovers in the dunes.

That evening, though, as the light was beginning to fade, the beach was empty. A raw breeze was blowing in from the sea and the temperature was starting to drop. It wouldn't be long before the chill of night closed in, and all I had on – as Bill had kindly pointed out – was a T-shirt and a pair of worn-out shorts. So, rubbing my arms, I called Deef again and got going, heading briskly along the beach towards the Point.

Without really meaning to, I started thinking about the boy on the Stand again, wondering who he was, where he was going, what he was doing here ... making up stories in my mind. He was an islander's son, I imagined, he'd been away for a while, in the army perhaps, maybe even in prison, and now he was coming home. His father was a white-haired old man who lived alone in a tiny old fisher-man's cottage. He would have spent all day cleaning the place up, getting something nice to eat, fixing up the spare room for his boy ...

No, I thought. The boy's not old enough to have been

in the army. What is he? Fifteen, sixteen, seventeen? I pictured his face again, and – damn it – my heart actually skipped a beat. Those pale blue eyes, that raggedy hair, that smile ... I could see it all quite clearly. But the odd thing was, no matter how hard I studied the face in my mind, it was impossible to tell how old the boy was. One second he looked about thirteen; the next, he was a young man – eighteen, nineteen, twenty ...

Very odd.

But anyway, I decided, he couldn't be an islander's son, he didn't look right. Islanders – and the offspring of islanders – have a particular look about them. They're short and dark, with lidded eyes and wiry hair to combat the wind, and even if they're not short and dark, with lidded eyes and wiry hair, they look as if they should be. The Boy – I was thinking of him now as the Boy – the Boy wasn't an islander. The face in my mind wasn't worn by the wind. The face in my mind was the face of a boy from nowhere.

Maybe he's looking for work? I thought. Or looking for someone? A girl, a sweetheart – or an enemy, perhaps? Someone who's wronged him. Someone who's offended his honour. He's travelled the length and breadth of the country in search of ...

I stopped, suddenly aware of what I was thinking. My *God*, Caitlin, I thought. What the hell are you *doing*? Sweethearts? Enemies? Honour? It's Mills & Boon stuff. It's embarrassing. Look at yourself. You're acting like a dumb little girl swooning at some dopey-looking pop star in a magazine. For goodness sake, girl, get a grip. Grow up. Grow up, grow up, grow up ...

I shook my head and started walking again.

It's hard to think about growing up when you're right

in the middle of it. It's hard to know what you want. Sometimes there are so many voices in your head it's difficult to know which of them is yours. You want this; you want that. You think you want this; but then you want that. You think you ought to want this; but everyone says you're supposed to want that.

It's not easy.

I remember one time, when I was about ten or eleven, I came home from school crying my eyes out because the other kids had been calling me a baby. After Dad had comforted me and waited patiently for the tears to dry up, he sat me down and gave me some advice. 'Listen, Cait,' he said. 'You'll spend half your childhood wishing you were grown up, and then, when you *are* grown up, you'll spend half your time wishing you were a child again. So don't go worrying too much about what's right or wrong for your age – just do whatever you want.'

That got me thinking about Dad again, about his loneliness, his writing, his drinking ... and then an unexpected movement caught my eye and all my thoughts disappeared. There was someone swimming in the sea, just off the Point, heading towards the beach. And I was suddenly aware that it was getting dark, and I was cold, and I didn't know where Deefer was.

'Deefer!' I shouted, looking around. 'Here, boy! Come here, Deef!'

I waited, listening out for the jangle of his collar, then I whistled and called out again, but there was no answer. Out in the sea the swimmer had nearly reached the beach. I shielded my eyes to get a better look. It was a young, fair-haired man wearing dark swimming goggles. There was something vaguely familiar about him, but the light was unclear and I couldn't make out a face. Whoever it was, though, he was a good swimmer. As he moved closer to the shore I could hear the steady slap of his hands slicing through the water. Slap ... slap ... slap ... a strangely eerie sound.

I looked around and called out for Deefer again. No reply. I looked everywhere – back along the beach, along the fringes of the saltmarsh, over at the mud flats. Nothing. No black dog, no sign of life at all. Just me and a slightly unnerving figure in dark goggles, who at that moment was wading out of the sea and crunching up the shingle towards me. Tall, muscular, and broad-shouldered, wearing a pair of tight trunks, a fancy black watch, and nothing else. A thin-lipped, mocking grin creased his mouth, and as he got closer I noticed that his skin was smeared with some kind of oil, or clear grease. Water rolled from his skin, pearled with tiny rainbows.

'Well, if it isn't little Caity McCann,' he said, removing his goggles and smiling at me. 'What a *pleasant* surprise.'

'Oh – Jamie,' I said hesitantly. 'What are you doing here?'

As he carried on towards me, adjusting his trunks and grinning his grin, I didn't know whether to laugh or cry. Jamie Tait – son of Ivan Tait, local landowner, wealthy businessman, and Member of Parliament for Moulton East – was the closest thing to a celebrity the island has ever produced. Captain of the County Schools Junior Rugby XV, national swimming champion at sixteen, and now a rising star in his second year at Oxford University.

Jamie Tait was a Bright Young Thing.

Or, as Dad would have it, the biggest little shite on the island.

He'd stopped about a metre away from me and was flicking his goggles against his leg, breathing heavily and looking me up and down.

'So, what do you think, Cait?' he said. 'Have I still got it?'

'Got what?'

He flicked wet hair from his eyes. 'The style, the stuff ... I saw you watching me.'

'I wasn't *watching* you, I was looking for my dog.'

'Right,' he winked. 'Gotcha.'

His staring eyes gave me the creeps. Pale electric-blue, like androids' eyes, it was impossible to tell what lay behind them. I didn't like the way he was standing, either, the way he was holding his body. Too close, but not *too* close. Close enough to make it awkward to look away. Close enough to insinuate, to say – look, look at this, what do you think?

I took a step back and whistled for Deefer, scanning the beach. There was still nothing in sight. When I turned back, Jamie had stepped closer, his thumbs hooked inside his trunks. I could smell the oil on his skin, something sweet on his breath.

'Is Dom back from Liverpool yet?' he asked.

'This afternoon, he came back this afternoon. Would you mind—'

'Is he coming out tonight?'

'I really don't know. I think I'd—'

'What's the matter, Cait? Look at you, you're shivering.' He smiled. 'I'd give you something to put on, but as you can see, I don't have a lot to offer.' His eyes glanced downwards and he laughed. 'It's the cold, you know.'

'I have to go,' I said, and turned to walk away. My heart was thumping and my legs felt weak. I was half-expecting a hand to grab my arm – but nothing happened.

I don't think I was really frightened at that point, just

angry. Angry at myself for ... I don't know what for. For being there, I suppose. Angry that he'd made me angry.

After about half a dozen steps I heard him crunching along behind me, calling out in a friendly voice, 'Hold on, Caity, hold on. I want to ask you something.'

I carried on walking.

I thought I had the advantage. I had shoes on, Jamie didn't. Walking barefoot on sharp shingle isn't the easiest thing in the world. But within a few seconds he'd caught me up and was striding along beside me, hopping and grinning.

'Hey, where's the fire? What's the hurry?'

'I told you, I have to find my dog.'

'What's his name?'

'Deefer.'

'Deefer dog?' he laughed. 'That's very good. Very *imaginative*.' He laughed again, then cupped his hands to his mouth and started calling out. 'Dee-fer dawg! Dee-fer dawg! Dee-fer ...' – spinning round as he walked, like a lighthouse – 'Dee-fer dawg! Dee-fer dawg! Dee-fer dawg! ...'

I carried on, heading towards the pillbox, trying to work out what to do. There were all sorts of unsavoury rumours about Jamie Tait, most of which, according to Dominic, he'd started himself. 'Jamie's all right,' Dom told me once. 'He just needs to let off a bit of steam now and then. All this madman stuff, it's just island gossip. Jamie's a teddy bear, really.'

Well, I thought, teddy bear or not, the sooner I find Deefer and get home, the better.

I'd reached the pillbox now. A squat, circular building, half-sunk into the ground, with thick concrete walls and a flat roof, it looks – and smells – like a dirty old public lavatory. My nose wrinkled at the smell and I started to edge away, but I didn't know which way to go. Should I cut across the saltmarshes and head for home, or should I get back to the beach and carry on looking for Deefer? Which way? Saltmarshes, beach, back to the Point ...?

Jamie had stopped his lunatic wailing and was skipping along the edges of the saltmarsh poking about in the reeds. 'He's not in here,' he called out to me, stooping to pick up a stick from the strandline. 'Hey, maybe he got a whiff of Rita Gray's bitch. You know what dogs are like when they get that smell.' He swung the stick at an empty Coke bottle then started towards me. 'How's Bill, by the way? She still got the hots for your brother?'

I ignored him, looking around the beach again, scanning the shore for Deefer, but the fading light was indistinct and I couldn't seem to focus on anything. The sky was darkening, streaked with yellow and grey, and the sea had taken on a black and icy look.

Jamie came up to me with the stick yoked across his shoulders. 'So,' he said, 'what are we going to do now?' I put my hands in my pockets and said nothing. He smiled, nodding at the pillbox behind me. 'My changing room.'

'What?'

'The pillbox, it's where I get changed.' He looked down at his trunks. 'You don't think I'm walking all the way back in just these do you? I'd get arrested.'

I looked away. 'I have to get going now.'

He stepped closer. 'How's your old man, Cait? Still writing naughty books for kiddies?'

I didn't say anything.

Jamie grinned. He was still breathing heavily, but not because he was out of breath.

'I must come round some time,' he said. 'Have a chat

with the great man. What do you think? Me and Johnny McCann. Johnny Mac. We could have a drink together, a little Oirish whiskey, a little smoke ... what do you think, Cait? Would you like that?'

'Goodnight, Jamie,' I said, and turned to leave.

He moved quickly, stepping in close and bringing his stick down to block my way. A cold light iced his eyes. 'I asked you a question, Cait.'

'Get out of my way—'

'I asked you a question.'

'Please, I want to go home ...'

He pursed his lips and smiled. 'Oh, come on, Caity, let's stop messing about. You can't bring me all this way and then change your mind.'

'*What?*'

'You know what I'm talking about. Come on, it's getting cold. Let's go inside. Let me show you my changing room. I've got a bottle in my jacket. A nice drop of whiskey will warm us up—'

'How's Sara?' I asked.

Sara was his fiancée. Sara Toms. A strikingly beautiful girl, with all the social graces a bright young thing could wish for, she was the daughter of Detective Inspector Toms, the head of the local police force. She was also insanely possessive. I suppose I thought that mentioning her name was a smart thing to do under the circumstances, but as soon as I had, I wished I hadn't. At the sound of her name, Jamie froze. His pupils shrank to pinpoints and his mouth narrowed to a tight slit. For a moment I thought he was going to explode or something, but then – with an almost visible sigh – the anger left him and something else took over. Something worse. He smiled and stepped closer. Not close enough to actually touch me, but close enough to force me back against the wall of the pillbox. My head was racing, blood rushing through my veins, but I still didn't quite believe that anything was wrong. It was ridiculous, really. My instinct was telling me to kick him in the groin and run, but something else, some kind of inbred civility, I suppose, was saying – no, hold on, just hold on a minute, he's just trying it on, it's not serious, think how embarrassing it'll be if you kick him in the groin, think what the papers would make of it – *MP's Son Attacked By Local Girl*. I actually *imagined* the headline. Can you believe that?

He didn't say or do anything for a while, he just stood there breathing hard and staring into my eyes. I was still trying to convince myself that everything was OK, that there wasn't anything to worry about, that he was nothing more than a slightly unbalanced spoilt brat who needed to let off a bit of steam now and then ... and then I felt him take my hand and move it towards him.

'*No—*'

'Shut up.'

I felt bare skin, cold and oily. I tried to take my hand away but he was too strong.

'*Don't—*'

'What?' he grinned.

Kick him, I thought, *kick him* ... but I couldn't do it. I couldn't move. I couldn't do anything. All I could do was look with disbelief into his eyes as he tightened his grip and moved even closer – and then a deep-throated snarl ripped through the air behind him.

'*Shit!*' he hissed, paralysed with fear. 'What's *that*?'

It was Deefer, standing tall, with his teeth bared and his hackles up. The snarl sounded wet and bloody.

Jamie still had hold of my hand. I yanked it away.

'What is it?' he whispered, his eyes darting, trying to see behind him without turning his head.

I couldn't speak. Even if I'd wanted to, I couldn't say anything. I wanted him away from me, I wanted to push him away, but I couldn't bear to touch him. My hand, the hand he'd taken ... I realised I was holding it out to one side, keeping it away from me. My throat was as dry as a bone.

'Christ, Cait,' he said through gritted teeth. 'What the *hell* is it? Tell me!'

I was very close to setting Deefer on him. One word from me and he'd have ripped Jamie to pieces. Instead, after what seemed like an hour, but was probably only thirty seconds or so, I managed to calm down a little, get my thoughts in order, and find a voice. I told Deefer to sit. I told him to stay and guard. Then I told Jamie to move back.

'What—'

'Move back now or I'll set the dog on you.'

He took a cautious step back.

'Don't turn around,' I told him. 'Don't move. If you move, he'll bite you.'

Jamie looked at me. 'Hey, Cait, come on. Look, you don't think I was serious, do you? I was only messing around. I wasn't—'

I walked away.

'Cait!' he called out. 'Just a minute ... what are you doing? Cait? You can't leave me here, I'll freeze. Cait!'

By the time I reached the creek my calmness had evaporated and I was shaking like a leaf. I took a deep breath and yelled for Deefer. While I was waiting for him to answer, I slid down the bank of the creek and washed my hands in the running water, scrubbing until they were numb, until there was no trace of feeling left. Then I washed the tears from my face.

It's your own fault, I told myself, how could you have been so *stupid*? Stupid, stupid, stupid, stupid ... why didn't you turn around and walk away as soon as you saw him? You *know* what he's like. Why didn't you just walk away?

I knew the answer.

I didn't walk away because I didn't want to appear rude. I didn't want to appear un*friendly* ...

It was pathetic.

When I clambered back up the bank Deefer was sitting on the bridge, wagging his tail.

'Where the hell *were* you?' I said, wiping snotty tears from my face. 'You're supposed to look after me. Come here.' He lowered his head and waddled over to me, crouched low to the ground. 'Next time,' I told him, 'next time ... just come back when I call you. All right?' I patted his head. 'It's no good leaving it until the last minute – when I call you, you come back.' His tail thumped and he yawned with shame. 'And don't you dare tell anyone about this,' I sniffed. 'It's between you and me, OK? If Dad finds out, he'll kill him. I'm not joking, Deef. He'll kill him.'

The house was quiet when I got back. I went upstairs and took a shower, changed into some clean clothes, checked in the mirror to make sure the tears didn't show, then bundled up my T-shirt and shorts with a pile of dirty washing and went back down to the kitchen. I was putting the clothes in the washing machine when Dad came in.

'Hey there, Cait – what are you doing?'

'Just a bit of washing ... I was ... there was some oil on the beach ...'

'Oil?'

'Tar or something.' I shrugged. 'I got some on my shirt.'

'Oh,' he said, looking at me. 'Are you all right? Your eyes—'

I turned away. 'It's nothing, a bit of sand ...'

'Here, let me see.'

'I said it's all *right*, Dad.'

He gave me a puzzled look. 'What's the matter?'

'Nothing, I'm sorry. I didn't mean to snap at you. Honestly, it's nothing. I'm fine.' I set the washing machine and turned it on. 'Have you eaten yet?'

'I'm not really hungry, love.'

'What about Dominic? He's not still asleep, is he?'

'He went out. He had to meet some people ...'

'Where?'

He shook his head. 'The Dog and Pheasant, I expect.'

'Didn't you want to go?'

He smiled awkwardly. 'Ah, I'd only embarrass the boy. You know how it is ... we'll probably have a quiet drink together some other time ...' He crossed to the cupboard and took out a fresh bottle of whiskey. I could tell from his exaggerated steadiness that he'd already had a few drinks. He sat down at the table and poured himself another.

'Did you have a nice walk?' he asked.

'Fine ... it was fine ... a bit cold ...'

He nodded, looking out of the window. 'And you'd tell me if anything was wrong?'

'Yes, Dad. I'd tell you.'

'Promise?'

'I promise.'

He sipped his drink and looked at me with slightly glazed eyes. 'No one ever kept a secret so well as a child.'

'I'm not a child.'

'No,' he said sadly. 'That's the truth of it.'

'Dad—'

'The boy,' he said, suddenly. 'Tell me what you think of him.'

'Which boy?'

He smiled knowingly. 'The fine-looking boy on the bridge.'

'The Stand?'

He drank some more. 'Bridge, Stand, whatever ... didn't he make you wonder?'

'Wonder about what? What are you talking about, Dad?'

'Secrets,' he winked.

'I think you've had too much to drink.'

'I'm all right.'

'You don't look it.'

'Well, it's been a funny old day—'

'Yeah.'

He looked at me for a moment, his head swaying slightly on his shoulders, then he breathed in deeply and stood up. 'Well, I'd best get on. See if I can't come up with something to pay the bills ...' He smiled again, then turned and headed for the door, clutching the bottle and glass.

'Dad?' I said.

'Yes, love?'

'Don't drink too much, OK?'

'OK.'

'Please.'

'You have my word.'

He came over and kissed me, then shuffled out, back to his study. His breath smelled of whiskey and sweet tobacco.

That night I couldn't get to sleep for a long time. The air was heavy and close and I couldn't settle. The sheets were clingy, the pillows too soft, too lumpy, the mattress too hard. I couldn't stop thinking about what had happened on the beach. Jamie Tait. The feel of his hand, his creepy eyes, his greasy skin ... I knew I ought to tell someone about it, but I couldn't think who. And even if I did tell someone, what would be the point? It was my word against his. He was a local hero, an Oxford student, the son of an MP. And what was I? Nothing, just a strange little girl with ribbons in her hair, a girl who wore the same clothes all the time. The motherless daughter of a wifeless writer ...

And anyway, I kept thinking, what actually happened? He hardly touched you, did he? He didn't *do* anything ... he hardly touched you ...

Then I started crying again.

Later, as I was sitting by the open window looking out into the dark, I heard Dad singing quietly in his study. The words drifted gently in the night air: '... *Oh, I'll take you back, Kathleen ... to where your heart will feel no pain ... and when the fields are fresh and green I'll take you to your home again ...*'

I fell asleep eventually, only to be woken in the early hours of the morning by the sound of Deefer barking as a car roared down the lane and screeched to a halt in the yard. Laughter and drunken voices cracked the night.

'Yay, there! Dommo, Dommo ...'

'Watch it!'

'Woof! Woof!'

'Can't get out, man—'

'Hey, hey, Caity—'

'Shhh!'

'Mind the bleedin' *door*—'

'Ha! Yeah ...'

After a couple of minutes of slamming doors and shouting, the car revved up, squealed round the yard and screamed back up the lane. I lay in bed listening to the sound of heavy steps dragging across the yard, coughing, keys fumbling at the front door, then the door opened and clonked shut and Dominic stumbled into the hall and tiptoed noisily up the stairs and into his room. Within five minutes the sound of drunken snoring was reverberating through the walls.

I closed my eyes.

The voices ...

Hey, hey, Caity—

Shhh!

I couldn't be sure, but the one doing the shushing sounded just like Bill. And the other one, the one who called my name – that was Jamie Tait.

two

The next day I left the house around one o'clock and set off across the island to meet Bill. I hadn't got much sleep and I was feeling pretty crappy, and I really didn't fancy a Saturday afternoon in town, but I couldn't see any way out of it. It was too late to call it off, and I couldn't just not show up, could I? Well, I *could* ... but then I'd probably spend all day sitting around worrying about it, waiting for Bill to ring up and get all snotty with me, and I didn't want that. There was enough friction between us as it was.

The bus stop where we'd arranged to meet is on the west of the island, in the middle of the village. Normally I'd walk along the beach and cut up through the country park, but after the episode with Jamie Tait I thought I'd give the beach a miss for a while. So I took the long way round, following the east road as far as the Stand and then south along the island road into the village. It was a fine day for walking – hot, bright and clear, with a gentle breeze to cool the skin – but it didn't do much to raise my spirits. I was tired. Bothered. Upset. The memory of the night before kept nagging away in my mind – the sound of the car, the shouting voices, the sound of Dominic and Jamie Tait ... and Bill. I couldn't stop thinking about it. What on earth was she doing with them? Did I *really* hear her voice? Was it *really* her? At the time I could have sworn it was, but as I walked the narrow lanes towards the village I was beginning to have my doubts. Now that I was up and about, now that the day was alive, the dead of night seemed a long way away, and the memory of the drunken voices was fading with every step I took. By the time I reached the bus stop I was fairly sure I must have been mistaken. Bill might have changed, I told myself, she might have grown up faster than me, she might even get up to a bit of no good now and then – but even so ... out drinking with Dominic and Jamie and God knows who else until the early hours of the morning?

No.

No way.

She wasn't that stupid.

She wasn't at the bus stop, either.

By two o'clock the bus had come and gone and there was still no sign of Bill. I didn't really mind waiting, but I was beginning to feel a bit self-conscious about my appearance. Bill's suggestion – that I *spice it up* a bit – had totally confused me, and I'd spent a good hour or more that morning trying to decide what to wear. If I'd dolled myself up as she'd suggested, I would have felt ridiculous. Walking around town dressed like a fifteen-year-old prostitute, I would have died of embarrassment. But on the other hand, if I'd ignored her suggestion, if I'd worn my usual gear, she'd have made a big scene about it, because she'd be dressed – or undressed – to kill, and she'd make out that I was dressing down on purpose, to make her look like a tart. Of course, if we were *both* dressed as tarts, that was fine, that was all right ...

Totally confusing.

In the end, I'd made a compromise: cut-off jeans, a

cropped black top, slicked back hair, and sunglasses. But no lipstick, and definitely no heels.

I wasn't *unhappy* with the end result, in fact I thought I looked pretty good, it's just that I wasn't used to being dressed up. It made me feel strange, sort of unnatural, like I was trying to be someone else, and the longer I stood there waiting, the more I felt as if everyone was staring at me.

By ten past two I'd checked the timetable, sat down, got up and strolled around for a while, sat down again, and now, for about the third time, I was reading the Village Events poster: *Saturday 29 July* (today) – *Jumble Sale in the Village Hall. Sunday 30 July – Free Concert in the Country Park, Brass Bands + Moulton Majorettes. Saturday 5 August – West Hale Regatta: Family Fun Day. Saturday 12 August – Hale Summer Festival …*

'You haven't forgotten what day it is, have you?'

The sound of the voice startled me. My body gave a little jerk and I turned around to see Simon Reed standing at the entrance to the bus shelter clutching a long roll of drawing paper to his chest.

'The festival,' he explained, nodding at the poster.

'Oh … right,' I stammered. 'Yeah, no … no, I haven't forgotten. I was just … I'm waiting for Bill.'

'The bus has already gone, it went twenty minutes ago.'

'Yeah, I know.'

I saw him flick a glance at my legs, then he lowered his eyes and stared at the ground, unsure what to say. Simon is always unsure what to say. Simon Reed … Weedy Reedy they used to call him. Or Simple Simon. Or just Weird. He's always been a slightly detached kind of boy. Even when he was at infant school he never mixed very well with the other children. The only person he ever seemed happy with was his older brother, Harry, a big lunk of a boy with a ruddy face and a permanent beaming smile. Simon was ten when Harry was killed in a farming accident, and after that he became even more remote, spending most of his time just drifting around the island on his own, studying plants, watching birds, barely talking to anyone. I'd got to know him quite well through helping out with the local RSPCA group his mum ran. I'm not usually that keen on getting involved with groups, and I'd only got mixed up with this one by mistake. The year before, Bill had gone through a short-lived *eco-warrior* phase. She goes through these phases at the rate of about one every two weeks – grunge-girl, hippy-chick, earth-child, ladette ... none of them ever last. Anyway, during her eco-phase she'd developed a huge crush on Simon, and she'd sneakily persuaded me to join her in volunteering our services to the RSPCA as a way of getting into his good books. The crush, of course, lasted all of a week, and when it came to actually *doing* some volunteer work Bill didn't want to know. 'Get out of it,' were her exact words. 'I'm not poncing around all weekend selling pictures of dead whales.' I was too much of a coward to back out though, so I'd stuck at it, and after a while I started to enjoy it. So I carried on. Simon and I met up now and then to arrange stuff for RSPCA stalls at fetes and local shows, designing posters, badges, local information, that kind of thing. That's what he'd meant about the festival. We'd been working on some ideas for a stall at the Summer Festival – in fact, he was coming round to my place next Friday to show me some posters he'd designed. We usually met at my house. Sometimes his mum would come round and pick me up and take me out to the small farm in the middle of the island where they lived, but more often than not he walked over to my house. That's why Dominic liked to pretend he was my boyfriend. That's why ... well, anyway, he wasn't my boyfriend. He was just a nice, quiet, slightly odd-looking boy who happened to be my friend.

I looked at him now. Shortish, kind of lean, with a long face and dark eyes and a shock of jet black hair that flopped down over his brow, causing him to continually brush it back with his hand. Although he lived on a farm, he had the complexion of someone who never went out in the sun. A pale, almost unhealthy look. This wasn't helped by the fact that, whatever the weather, he always wore a long black coat, a long-sleeved work shirt, and dusty old corduroy trousers – never shorts. But despite all that – or maybe *because* of it – there was something intriguing about him ... a prettiness, I suppose. But a certain kind of prettiness. The kind of prettiness that most girls reject, and other boys fear. And, of course, what they fear – or don't understand – they hate. So, all in all, Simon wasn't the most popular of boys.

I went over and stood next to him. He smiled nervously and started swinging the roll of paper against his leg.

'Is that for the posters?' I asked.

'Yeah. It's only rough stuff, it's the best I could do. I was going to get some proper stuff in town—'

'That's where I'm going. I could get some. There's that art shop down by the library – what do I ask for?'

'A1 cartridge paper, it's quite expensive—' He started digging in his pockets, looking for money.

'It's all right,' I said, 'I'll get it. What is it – sheets or a pad?'

'Well, if you can get about half a dozen sheets ...'

'White?'

'Yeah, thanks.'

'That's OK.'

He nodded again, then turned his attention back to the pavement. An awkward silence hung in the air. I thought about asking him if he wanted to come in to town with us. I knew he wouldn't, but I wondered if he'd appreciate me asking. Would I, I thought, if I was him?

Probably not.

'Are you going to the regatta next Saturday?' I asked him.

'I don't think so.'

'Why not?'

'I don't know ... it's not really my kind of thing.'

'You could come with us if you want. We usually watch it from that little cliff over the bay. It's quiet there.'

'Well, maybe.'

'It's just me and Dad ... and Deefer.'

'What about your brother?'

I laughed. 'I doubt if he'll be with us.'

'Well, I don't know ...'

'Go on, it'll be fun—' And then I stopped, realising that I sounded just like Bill when she was trying to persuade *me* to have a good time.

'What?' Simon asked.

'Nothing, it doesn't matter.' I changed the subject. 'What time are you coming round on Friday?'

'Uh ... about ... six o'clock? Is that all right? I could make it earlier if—'

'No, that's fine ... I got that information about the bird sanctuary, by the way. They sent a pile of stuff – leaflets, badges ...'

'That's great,' he said. 'I thought we could—'

He stopped in mid-sentence and we both looked up as

a bright green hatchback pulled up at the side of the road with the engine revving and bass beats booming from the open windows. The driver was a fat young man in a sleeveless T-shirt and sunglasses who I recognised as Robbie Dean. The girl beside him in the passenger seat, chewing gum, was his younger sister, Angel. Just as I was thinking to myself – oh God, what do *they* want? – Bill leaned out of the back window with a huge grin on her face.

'Hey, Cait!' she called out. 'Caity! Come on!'

I looked at her in disbelief. What the hell was she doing with the Deans? What was she *playing* at? I glanced with embarrassment at Simon. He'd shrunk into his coat and was doing his best not to look too uncomfortable. I wanted to say something to him, but I couldn't think what.

'Come *on*, Cait!' Bill yelled, swinging open the car door. 'Move your ass, girl!'

'I'd better go,' I mumbled to Simon. 'I'll see you on Friday, OK?'

His eyes remained fixed to the pavement as I walked across to the booming car, took a deep breath, and got in.

'Better than the bus, eh?' said Bill, lighting up.

We were racing across the Stand in a choking haze of cigarette smoke and perfume and deafening drum beats.

'What?' I shouted.

'Better than the bus!' she shouted back.

'Yeah ... great.'

She offered me a cigarette. 'Want one?'

'No, thanks.'

'What do you think?'

'What?'

She turned to face me, hands on hip, striking a pose.

'What do you think? Do you like it?'

It was a tight red strapless top, an unbelievably short two-tone skirt, and a pair of metallic grey ankle-strap shoes with three-inch platforms. With her streaky-blonde hair slicked with gel, crimson lipstick, and full-on eyes, she looked like an eighteen-year-old princess on a girls' night out.

'Very nice,' I told her.

She slapped my thigh. 'I see you made an effort – hey, Angel, didn't I tell you? Angel?'

The girl in the passenger seat turned to face us, snapping her gum and looking me up and down with a cold stare. She was sixteen, going on twenty-one. Curly peroxide hair, painted blue eyes, with lips like Madonna and an attitude to match. 'Yeah,' she said, fingering the top of her sheer white sun dress. 'Very sweet. They go for that.'

I lurched to one side as the car swung out to pass a stream of traffic on a narrow hill, then lurched back again as Robbie pulled over just in time to miss a double decker bus trundling down the hill on the other side. Tyres squealed. Horns hooted. Robbie grinned and stuck a finger out the window, shouting, 'Up yours!'

Angel laughed, then leaned across and whispered something in his ear. Robbie grunted, and I saw him adjust his sunglasses and glance at me in the rear-view mirror. I looked at Bill for support. She was checking her lipstick, brushing cigarette ash from her skirt, rolling her head to the beat of the music. She winked at me.

I settled back and stared out of the window, consoling myself with the thought that the journey wouldn't last for ever.

As we approached the roundabout at the edge of town, the

traffic got heavier and the car slowed to a crawl. For the last few minutes Angel had been fiddling around with a packet of cigarettes and a jigsaw of cigarette papers, and now she'd lit the joint and was leaning back with one arm dangling from the open window, sucking the smoke down into her lungs. Why she'd waited until we reached town, and why she was making such a big deal out of it, I didn't know. I assumed it was meant to impress me. After a few more puffs, she twisted round in her seat, wiggling her bum all over the place, and passed me the joint.

'No, thanks,' I said.

''S all right,' she sneered, 'it's only a bit of blow.'

'I know what it is – I don't smoke.'

'It's *grass*, girl. It won't kill you.'

She was leaning over the back seat with her bum sticking up in the air. I looked her in the eye, trying to see beyond the pose, trying to imagine what she was like when she was alone ... but I couldn't see it. That sort of girl is never alone, because without other people they have to be themselves, and they can't stand themselves.

'Your brother smokes,' she said, passing the joint to Bill.

'I expect he does,' I said.

She curled her lip. 'And your old man.'

'So?'

She seemed taken aback for a moment, as if she'd expected me to be shocked. Her lips tightened and her eyes narrowed, and then Robbie slapped her on the backside and said, 'Which way, Ange?' and she took the opportunity to wriggle back into her seat and regain her bad-girl composure.

'Multi-storey in Crown Street,' she hissed. 'And if you slap my arse again I'll break your bleedin' neck.'

Bill, meanwhile, was coughing to death on the joint.

'Having a good time?' I asked her.

'*Whoof*,' she said, with tears streaming down her cheeks.

With the car parked, and Angel and Robbie scuttling off into the spiral gloom of the multi-storey walkways, I finally had the chance to ask Bill what on earth she thought she was doing.

'What do you mean?' she said, walking off with an innocent giggle. 'It saved us a couple of quid bus fare, didn't it?'

'Oh, come on Bill ... Angel Dean, for God's sake—'

'Angel's all right, she's a good laugh.'

'No she's not.'

'You have to get to know her, that's all.'

'And you do, I suppose?'

She stumbled over a kerb and started giggling again, then skipped over and slung her arm around my shoulder. 'Oh, Caity ... matey ... you're not jealous, are you? You know you'll *always* be the only one for me ...'

'Yeah, yeah ... will you get off?'

I watched her as she bent down and checked her make-up in the wing-mirror of a parked car, and I watched the way a passing group of thirty-year-old men in football shirts nudged each other, eyeing her up. God ... I was really getting sick of the whole thing, the whole weekend, everything. I felt as if I'd been plucked out of nowhere and dropped smack in the middle of some tacky Australian soap, where everyone and everything revolved around tits and bums and sex. I was tired of it. If I'd known what was coming I would have turned around and gone home right then. But I didn't know what was coming. And Bill was my best friend. And I didn't want to appear un*friendly*, did I?

So I just followed her out of the car park and onto the bridge that spans the dual-carriageway, shaking my head as she hitched herself over the railings and gobbed at the passing traffic.

'Where are we going?' I asked wearily. 'Town's the other way.'

'Ah ...' she said, wiggling her eyebrows. 'Come this way, my pretty. A surprise awaits thee ...'

The surprise was having to spend the rest of the afternoon in a pub called The Cavern at the other end of the bridge with two of the lamest young men I've ever come across. They were waiting for us in a balcony garden at the rear of the pub, sitting at a plastic table in the shade of a plastic umbrella. Traffic groaned up and down the dual-carriageway below, almost drowning out the sound of the jukebox, and a stale odour of beer and cigarette smoke drifted out from the dim interior of the bar. Bill introduced the boys as Trevor and Malc.

'They're starting at the sixth-form college next year,' she explained proudly, crossing her legs and pouting as she sat down next to the one called Trevor. He was thin, with tinted glasses and a short-sleeved button-down shirt. The other one was even thinner, in white shorts and a beige-and-white-striped polo shirt. He had a face like a lizard.

'Hi, Kay,' he said. 'What are you drinking?'

I can hardly bear to describe the rest of the afternoon. In short, it was awful. A daze of giggling, drinking, grinning, smoking, bragging about cars, crappy jokes and beer-mat tricks, crisps, traffic fumes, flies, spiked drinks, sly looks and suggestions, and then, as the drinks took hold, red-faced slurs and scratches and winks, burps and farts, dirty stares, shuffling chairs and loose hands, with Bill flashing her knickers around like a drunk old granny at Christmas, and Trevor pawing her under the table, and Malc just sitting there like a sick little boy after I'd kicked him in the knee for trying to stick his damn tongue in my ear.

When Bill and Trevor sloped off to a corner of the balcony to get some more groping in, I just couldn't stand it any more. I took myself off to the Ladies, locked myself in a cubicle, and just sat there, praying for the day to end.

I didn't have *that* much to drink, but it wasn't possible to sit there all afternoon without drinking *something*, if only to dull the pain. And I'm sure Talcy Malcy slipped a few vodkas into my cider at the bar. And I hadn't eaten much. And I was tired. And we'd been sitting out in the sun all afternoon ... So, all in all, by the time we left the pub I have to admit I was pretty drunk. I don't quite remember walking back to the car park, but somewhere along the way we lost Trevor and Malcolm and were re-united with Angel and Robbie. They were with a man I'd seen around the island called Lee Brendell. I didn't know where they'd been, or what he was doing with them, and I didn't really care. I was just glad to get in the back of the car and sit back as Robbie drove out of the car park, swung across the roundabout and headed out of town.

After fiddling around with a pile of shopping bags and re-doing her lipstick, Angel swivelled around in her seat and lit a cigarette. She couldn't stop grinning at Bill, who was slopped in the corner with her eyes half-closed and an unlit cigarette hanging from her mouth. Lee Brendell had squeezed in the back and was sitting sullenly between me and Bill with his legs splayed wide and his eyes blank.

Robbie, meanwhile, had obviously taken something. His bug eyes were shining like black saucers and he couldn't stop talking and waving his hands about. He was driving even crazier than before. Cutting up cars, swerving all over the place, racing the engine ... it was scary.

I opened the window to let some air in.

'Want some sounds, Bren?' Robbie shouted, jerking his head around. 'Eh? What d'you want? Bit o' boom? You want some boo-oom!'

Brendell just looked at him. He was a big man, in his late twenties or early thirties, dressed in a faded grey T-shirt and dusty jeans, with a raw-looking face and large, weathered hands which he held flat on his knees. All I really knew about him was that he lived on a houseboat on the west of the island and that he wasn't a man to be messed with. He smelled of chemicals and sweat.

Robbie turned and grinned at him again. 'Say what? Wanna smoke? Whooo! Smokeen Joanna! You want some boom-boom? Ange'll get—'

'Just drive the car,' Brendell said quietly.

'Okey dokey, Bren,' Robbie replied happily. 'Okey bloody dokey.'

The outskirts of town blurred past and before I knew it we were heading out along the country lanes back to the island. Although I was still feeling a bit whoozy, the air rushing in through the open window was beginning to clear my head and I was starting to feel a little better.

Bill, though – well, Bill was suffering. Slumped against the window, with her head in her hands and her skirt all rucked up and mascara smudged around her eyes, she looked a complete mess. I didn't feel much sympathy for her. In fact, I didn't feel any. At that moment, I hated her guts.

But still ... she was my best friend. I couldn't just leave her, could I?

I leaned across Brendell and took hold of her hand. 'Bill? Bill, are you all right?'

'Nn nuh,' she said, slapping at my hand. 'Fug 'em, bassa ...'

'Come on, Bill, it's me, Cait.'

'Lemme 'lone, gwan ...'

Brendell turned his head and looked at me, his face utterly devoid of expression. He didn't say anything, didn't move a muscle, just stared at me like I was something in a cage, then slowly looked away. I pulled Bill's skirt down as far it would go, which wasn't far, then shuffled back to my side of the car.

Angel had resumed her bum-in-the-air position and was watching me with a mocking gleam in her eyes. With Brendell seemingly non-existent, Bill semi-conscious, and Robbie lost in a daze of speeding cars, Angel and I were as good as alone. We both knew it. She bent a stick of gum into her mouth and winked at me.

'Welcome to the world, darling,' she said. When I didn't answer she gave me a long hard stare, making a big deal of chewing her gum, and then she snapped the gum and sneered, 'You like to think you're something special, don't you? Something *special*. Clean and white, Caity McCann ... beach baby ... little Caity McCann ... isn't that what he calls you?'

'Who?'

'*Who*, she says ... shit – how many *are* there?'

'I don't know what you're talking about.'

'Course you don't – you don't know squat, do you? You just walk on the beach with your dog, looking at the sky ...' She leaned towards me and her voice took on a vicious tone. 'Listen, girl,' she hissed, 'just keep your hands off my boy.'

'*What?*'

'Don't touch what you can't handle, all right?'

I shook my head. She was crazy. What boy? Who the hell was she talking about? Malcolm? Talcy Malcy? Simon? Did she mean Simon ...? No, she wouldn't look twice at Simon. Then it struck me – *little Caity McCann*. That's what Jamie Tait had called me on the beach. *Well, if it isn't little Caity McCann* ... Was that who she meant? Jamie Tait? But that was ridiculous. Angel had nothing to do with him. She wasn't his girlfriend. Sara Toms was his girlfriend – his fiancée, in fact. But then, I thought, it's not as if Jamie's likely to be the most faithful partner in the world is it? But even so – Angel Dean? With Jamie? Surely not ... And anyway, even if she *is* talking about Jamie, how does she know what happened? He must have told her, he must have lied to her ...

A terrible groan interrupted my thoughts. I looked over and saw Bill clutching a hand to her mouth, her face as pale as a sheet.

'Pull over, Robbie,' Angel said. 'The little bitch is gonna throw up.'

Robbie swore and slid the car to a stop. 'Get her out! Quick, get her out! I only had it cleaned this morning.'

Bill started gagging, big lurching humps that started in her belly and snaked up into her throat. Angel just sat there, laughing. She wasn't going to lift a finger. And Brendell couldn't give a damn. So while Robbie was having a mental breakdown, swearing and spluttering and tugging at his door, trying to unlock it, I opened my door and hurried round to the other side. I got Bill out and helped her onto the verge. After a couple of steps her legs gave way and she sank to her knees and threw up in the grass. From the car I could hear Angel cheering and clapping, 'Yeah! Go on, girl, let it all out! Ha ha!'

This is it, I thought, this is *it*. It can't get any worse. I looked at Bill, coughing and retching in the grass, and Robbie, who'd finally got his door open and was now walking up and down sucking hard on a cigarette, mumbling to himself and manically clicking his fingers, and I looked at Angel, leering out of the car window, a crazy girl who just minutes ago had warned me to keep my hands off a man who less than twenty-four hours ago had virtually assaulted me ...

I couldn't believe what was happening.

How did I get here?

What was I *doing* here?

I looked around and suddenly realised where we were. The Stand. We were parked at the side of the road, about a quarter of the way across. It was almost too much to bear. All this – this car, these people, the sound of Bill gagging herself to death – all this muck and small-time horror didn't belong here ... not *here*.

I went over and stood by the railings, trying to control myself, trying to distance myself from the dirt. The tide was in, just about to turn. It was as high as it gets without flooding. The clear silver water was almost motionless, like a mirror, just a gentle lapping against the reeds and a hazy blue swirl way out in the middle of the estuary. It was beautiful. For a few seconds I forgot about everything else, it all just faded into the background as I stared into the calming silence of the water.

And then, with a guttural oath and a splash, the silence was shattered.

'Yay! Got 'im!'

I looked across and saw Robbie leaning over the railings hurling rocks at something on the bank, flinging them with all his strength, his face screwed up into a mask of spite.

'What are you *doing*?' I yelled.

He ignored me and bent down to dig out more stones from the verge. 'Hey, Ange,' he shouted. 'Come here, see this.'

Angel got out of the car and sashayed over to the railings, arriving at the same time as me.

'Look,' said Robbie, heaving another rock. 'Shit! There he goes, bastard.'

I looked over, expecting to see an injured bird or something, but it wasn't a bird – it was a boy. *The* Boy, the boy in green. He was about twenty metres down river, struggling up the bank with a fishing cane in one hand and his canvas bag in the other. The hair on the back of his head was matted with blood where a stone had found its target.

'Oh, God,' I whispered.

Angel had climbed up on the railings and was urging her brother on. 'Get him, Rob, go on, he's getting away. Get him!'

As Robbie grinned and went to launch another rock, I grabbed his arm and pulled him off balance. He swung out and shoved me away, then fired the stone with sickening force into the Boy's back. The Boy stumbled again and half-slipped down the bank, then steadied himself and leapt across a narrow gully before melting into a tangle of tall reeds. Just as he was disappearing from view he glanced over his shoulder and looked at us. From someone in his position I would have expected a look of fear, or anger, pain, or even bewilderment, but his face showed nothing at all. Absolutely nothing. It was the emotionless look of an animal, a look of pure instinct.

A look that had seen me.

'Dirty gyppos,' Robbie spat, lighting a cigarette.

'What?' I said.

'Gyppos, travellers – hey, what's your bloody game, anyway? Whose side are you on?'

'Yeah,' said Angel, coming up beside me. 'Whose side are you on, baby?'

I could hardly speak. 'Side?' I spluttered. 'Gyppos? What's the *matter* with you? You're all mad.'

'He another one, then, is he?' Angel smirked. 'Christ, you put it around, girl. Students, weirdos, rich kids, gyppos ... can't you say no to *anything*?'

'Don't forget the dawg,' Robbie snorted.

A surge of anger welled up inside me. I saw their mocking faces, teeth, lips, burning eyes, and the air around them tainted with cruelty, and it hurt so much I wanted to scream. But I knew it was pointless. It would always be the same. There was nothing I could do to change it. So I just turned around and started walking.

'Say hello to Big Dom,' Angel called out after me. 'Tell him Angel sends her love ... d'you hear me? Little Angel sends her *lurve* ...' Her laughing voice drifted away on the breeze.

Bill was sitting on the verge with her head between her knees, still groaning. As I passed by she looked up at me through bleary eyes. 'Cait? Wass goin' on? Wass 'iss? Where y'goin'?'

I walked past without saying anything and headed home.

The thing that upset me most about the whole day wasn't anything to do with Bill, it wasn't her stupidity or the pub or the idiot boys, it wasn't even the spiteful rantings of Angel and Robbie. No, what upset me most was imagining what the Boy must think of me. As I walked the long walk home, fighting back the tears, mumbling useless curses to myself, staggering every now and then from the last remaining effects of the drink, a single ugly thought kept nagging away in my mind: God, what must he think I *am*? A tarty little brat with noxious friends who vomit in public and throw rocks at strangers ... a thoughtless bigot ... just another teenage fool ...

I know it sounds incredibly arrogant and selfish of me, but I just couldn't help it. I couldn't get the idea out of my head. I imagined the Boy sitting quietly in a little hideaway somewhere, dabbing gently at his cut head, visualising me and the others laughing and pelting him with rocks. I felt so ashamed.

Of course, I was concerned for *him*, as well. That goes without saying. A terrible sickening feeling swirled in the pit of my stomach, a hollow rage that I hadn't felt since I'd tried to stop a bunch of kids torturing a cat a couple of years ago. It was bonfire night. They'd tied a rocket to the cat's tail and the poor thing was running around screaming in pain and panic and the kids were all laughing like lunatics. I *tried* to help, but the cat ran off and disappeared into some wasteground and the kids started laughing at me. I couldn't do anything. There were too many of them. I felt so helpless ... and that's how I felt now. Helpless. Sickened. I was worried about the Boy. I wanted him to be all right, I wanted him ...

The truth is, I wanted him to know that I cared.

Dad's always telling me not to worry what other people think of me, or what I *think* they think of me. 'Just be yourself,' he says. 'If it's good enough for you, it's good enough.' I know he's right, but sometimes it's easier said than done. With people like Angel and Robbie, I can just about manage it. I can say to myself – it doesn't matter what they think, their opinions are worthless. Let them think what they like – what do I care? I can *say* that to myself. It doesn't always work, but at least I can say it. But when it comes to people whose opinions I value – well, that's different. That's when it's hard. When someone you respect, or admire, or love, thinks badly of you, then it's *not* good enough to just be yourself. Because if you're being yourself and they still think badly of you, then either they're wrong, or you are.

The way I saw it, the Boy was bound to think badly of me, but he was wrong. Or, at least, he was mistaken. It wasn't his fault he was wrong. If anything, it was mine. But he was still wrong. That was straightforward enough. What I couldn't understand was why it seemed to matter to me. I didn't know the first thing about him. Why should I care what he thought of me? Why should I value his opinion? Did I respect him? How could I? Admire him? For what? I didn't love him ... I didn't even *know* him – so why did I care what he thought of me?

I thought about it all the way home, but I still couldn't work it out. My head hurt. My mouth was dry. I was too hot to think. In the end I just gave up.

After a cold shower and a change of clothes and a couple of cups of strong black coffee, I still felt lousy. It was only early evening, about eight o'clock, but I felt as if I'd been up for days. My head was all muzzy and I felt exhausted. I didn't want to go to bed, though. I didn't really want to talk to anyone, either. And the idea of watching Saturday night television was too depressing to think about. Of course, what I really wanted to do was go for a walk on the beach. I knew it was the only place that would get rid of all the crap in my head, but I wasn't quite sure if I was ready to face it yet. The memory of Jamie Tait was still too fresh in my mind. The trouble was, the longer I avoided the beach, the more tainted it would become, and the more tainted it became, the harder the memory would be to overcome. The beach didn't deserve that, and neither did I.

But it was hard. Especially after what had happened that afternoon. Too hard. And as I sat in the kitchen looking out of the window, I knew I wasn't going to make it that night.

I was still sitting there half asleep when Dominic came back.

'Hey, stranger,' he said, breezing into the kitchen. 'What are you doing sitting in the dark?'

'Nothing,' I said, rubbing sleep from my eyes. 'What time is it?'

'I don't know, eleven-thirty, twelve – where's Dad?'

'Working.'

'Makes a change.' He went over to the fridge and helped himself to a can of beer, popped it open and joined me at the table. 'You been out?' he asked, lighting a cigarette.

'No, not really—'

'I thought you were meeting Bill?'

'We just went into town ...'

He grinned. 'Living it up?'

'Something like that.'

I watched him as he drank from the can. I hadn't really seen him since he'd got back, I hadn't had a chance to see what he looked like. Now, in the semi-dark of the mid-night kitchen, I could see that he resembled someone who used to be my brother. The same quietly handsome face, the same delicate mouth and wood-brown eyes, the same mischievous energy ... only now it was all pinched and dull, the skin toneless and flat as if sealed beneath a sheet of clingfilm.

He drank some more beer and tapped ash into the ash-tray. 'Do you know what this reminds me of?'

'What?'

'That scene in *The Catcher in the Rye*, the one where Holden creeps back into his parents' house to see his kid sister – what's her name?'

'Phoebe.'

'Yeah, right, Phoebe. He creeps home and wakes her up in the middle of the night—'

'She's just a little kid.'

'I know.'

'She's only about eight or something.'

'Yeah, I *know*—'

'I'm fifteen, Dominic.'

'I know how old you are. I didn't mean you were *like* what's-her-name—'

'Phoebe.'

'Phoebe, right. I didn't mean you were like her, I just meant ...'

'What?'

'Nothing, it doesn't matter. Forget it.'

'I was only saying—'

'Yeah, I know.' His voice hardened. 'You're not a little kid and I'm nothing like Holden Caulfield and this isn't New York, it's Hale bloody Island.' He drained his beer and fetched another. From the way he slammed the fridge door and moodily lit another cigarette, I thought he'd gone all sulky on me, but when he sat back down at the table he had a big fat grin on his face. 'So,' he said, drumming his fingers on the table. 'This crocodile goes into a pub—'

'Look, Dominic, I'm not really in the mood—'

'No, listen. This crocodile goes into a pub. He goes up to the bar and orders a beer. The bartender pours his drink, then looks at him and says, "Hey, what's with the long face?"'

I forced a smile. 'Very good.'

He sipped from his can and looked at me. 'So?'

'What?'

'What's with the long face?'

I shrugged. 'I'm just a bit tired.'

'Come on, Cait, I'm only trying to help. What is it? Boyfriend trouble? Is Simon still playing hard to get?'

'Give it a rest.'

He grinned. 'I could have a quiet word with him, if you like. Next time he comes round—'

'It's all just a stupid game to you, isn't it?'

'What?' he said innocently.

'You *know* what. I mean it, Dom, I'm not in the mood. I've had it up to here with all this Simon crap. Just leave it, all right?'

He was quiet for a minute or two. Supping his beer, looking out of the window, tugging idly at his unshaven chin. There was something bothering him. I could tell by the way he was jiggling his foot up and down. It's a family trait. We all jiggle our feet up and down when we're bothered. I got the feeling there was something he wanted to talk about, but he didn't know how to begin. That was his trouble. He couldn't just come out and say what he wanted to say, he always had to poke and niggle at things until eventually the truth was forced out.

'It's Dad, isn't it?' he said after a while. 'He's giving you a hard time.'

I sighed. 'No, of course he's not—'

'What's the matter with him, anyway? He gave me a right bollocking about last night.'

'There's nothing the *matter* with him. He's fine—'

'It's probably this new book he's working on, got him all razzed up—'

'He's not *razzed up* about anything, Dominic. He was just annoyed with you for waking us up and acting like an idiot—'

'*Christ!*' he said. 'You're worse than *him*. I don't *believe* this place. It's like living with a couple of bloody nuns—'

'Stop *swearing* all the time, will you? It sounds horrible.'

'Oh, for God's *sake*,' he snapped, getting up and stomping over to the window, flicking ash all over the floor. As he stood there tipping beer down his throat and smoking angrily, I couldn't help thinking how ridiculous he looked, like a spoilt little boy. Just like all the rest of them ...

That was it, really. That was the heart of it. He'd become just like all the rest of them.

'Look, Dom,' I said. 'It wasn't just the noise that Dad was upset about—'

'No?' He turned from the window. 'What was it then? Don't tell me *Daddy* was annoyed because his precious son got a teeny bit drunk? Because I'm not having that, not from him. Shit! Talk about the pot calling the kettle black ... he's been half-drunk ever since Mum died.'

I looked at him. 'I can't believe you said that.'

'Yeah, well,' he said, lowering his eyes. 'It's true, isn't it?'

'I've had enough of this,' I sighed. 'I'm going to bed.'

I was halfway to the door when Dominic stopped me,

putting his hand on my shoulder. 'Come on, Cait,' he said. 'All I did was go out for a few drinks with some friends. All right, so we were a bit rowdy when we got back—'

'You just don't get it, do you?' I spat.

'Get *what*?'

I glared at him, my lips quivering. 'You ... you and your so-called *friends* ...' My voice trailed off. I couldn't speak. I couldn't find the words.

'What about them?' he said.

'Nothing – it doesn't matter. Just leave me alone.'

'Cait—'

'Get your hands *off*.'

He backed away, bemused. 'All right, all right, keep your voice down. Listen, I'm sorry. I didn't mean anything ... I know I shouldn't have said that about Dad—'

'No, you shouldn't.'

'But I didn't mean—'

'Forget it.'

'All I meant was—'

'Yeah, I know what you meant.' I stopped in the doorway and looked him in the eye, searching for a trace of the old Dominic, *my* Dominic ... but I couldn't find it.

'What?' he said, unsettled by my gaze.

'Nothing. Don't worry about it.' I turned to go. 'Oh, and by the way, Angel sends her love.'

He licked his lips. 'Who?'

'Angel Dean,' I repeated.

'What? ... when did—'

'Goodnight, Dominic.'

He was nine when Mum died. I was five. Dad was thirty-four. I suppose it affected us all in different ways.

* * *

That night I dreamed about the Boy. It was raining. He was running on the beach and people were chasing him, throwing stones at him and calling him names. *Gyppo! Thief! Dirty pervert!* There were hundreds of them, brandishing sticks and bits of piping, shovels and rocks, whatever they could lay their hands on, their nightmare faces gripped with hate and streaked with tears of rain. *Dirty gyppo! Dirty bastard!* Jamie Tait was there, oiled, in his too-tight swimming trunks. Angel and Robbie were there. Lee Brendell, Bill, Dominic, Deefer, Simon, Dad, everyone from the island was there, all storming across the beach screaming out for blood ... and I was there, too. I was with them. I was running with the mob. I could feel the wet sand beneath my feet, the rain in my hair, the weight of the rock in my hand. I could feel my heart pounding with fear and excitement as I raced along the shore, past the pillbox, heading for the Point. The Boy had stopped running and was standing at the edge of the mud flats. All around him the air shimmered with unseen colours. He glanced over his shoulder, looking at me with beseeching eyes, pleading for help. But what could I do? I couldn't do anything. There were too many of them. It was too late. *DON'T STOP!* a voice cried out. It was mine. *DON'T DO IT! DON'T STOP! KEEP RUNNING! DON'T GIVE UP! JUST RUN! RUN FOR EVER ...*

three

Over the next few days the weather never settled. In the space of a single day we'd have bright sunshine in the morning, followed by cloudy skies and a light summer shower in the afternoon, then another brief spell of baking heat, before the clouds built up again and the rain poured down in torrents. It was like watching one of those speeded up films of the passing seasons. In the evenings a cool wind breezed in from the sea scattering clouds of dust and sand to the air, and as the light on the horizon filtered through the haze, the skies took on the pastel colours of autumn. Then at night the air turned hot and sticky, and sometimes I could hear thunder rumbling faintly in the distance, like the mutterings of a disgruntled bully.

They were unsettled times.

I stayed at home as much as possible. I'd had enough of other people for a while. I didn't want to talk to anybody and I didn't want to think about anything. I just wanted to sit around and do nothing.

But it wasn't easy.

Do you know how it feels when you don't know how to feel? When your mind keeps slipping from one thing to another, when you can't relax, when you know you've got an itch but you don't know where to scratch it? That's how I felt after the events of the weekend. I just didn't know how to feel about anything: me, Dad, Bill, Jamie, Dominic, Angel, the beach, the Boy ... everything kept going round and round in circles in my head. It was as if someone had opened up a conjurer's box and a dozen grinning jack-in-the-boxes were waving their heads and screaming questions at me – what do you think of Simon? you like him, don't you? *how* do you like him? and what about the Boy? the dream? what does *that* mean? and what's up with Dominic? why's he hanging around with Jamie? is he seeing Bill? or Angel? do you care? do you *want* to care ...?

I wished I knew.

I wished ... yeah, I wished.

At least the weekend was over. It had been a long one – long, chaotic, and disturbing. Awful. Probably the worst few days of my life. But it was over now, I kept telling myself. It was over. Things would soon get back to normal. The skies would clear and I could settle down to a quiet summer of long hot days with nothing to do and nothing to think about. Just blue skies, good books, cold drinks, and cool nights. No more surprises, no more horror, no more crap.

That was it.

That's what I wanted.

Nothing to do.

Nothing to think about.

No more crap.

Fat chance.

On Tuesday afternoon I bumped into Bill in the village. I was with Dad. I hadn't really wanted to go with him, because whenever we go into the village together it always feels like one of those scenes from an old cowboy movie, when the homesteaders who won't sell out to the cattle baron ride into town in their cronky old wagon and all the gunslingers and tough guys are lounging around giving them dirty looks ...

That's how it feels to me, anyway.

It's not that the locals dislike Dad. They might be a bit suspicious of him, I suppose. A bit wary, a bit stand-offish ... but I'm sure they don't *dislike* him. Well, maybe some of them do. They probably think he's a bit weird. A bit scruffy. A bit *distasteful*. He drinks, you know. Smokes pot. Writes books. And, worst of all, he's not an islander. He might have lived on Hale for over fifteen years, but he wasn't *born* here. He's still an outsider. He's still *Irish*.

So, anyway, I wasn't that keen when he asked me to go with him, but he'd run out of whiskey, and he wanted to go to the library, and if I didn't go with him he'd have to walk ... and he was feeling a bit down ... and I didn't really have anything else to do anyway ... so what else could I do? I fixed a smile to my face, fixed up my hair, and off we went.

When we got to the village, we parked in the square and headed down the High Street towards the library. There weren't that many people about – one or two old folks lazing about on benches, young mothers with Jeeps full of kids, a couple of fishermen clomping about in waders with roll-ups dangling from their lips. There were a few bikers moping around by the bus stop giving us dirty looks, and a bunch of kids from school were hanging around outside the newsagent, but none of them saw me, and I was happy to leave it at that.

The library is a nice old place at the end of the High Street, with crumbly stone pillars guarding the entrance and high windows that glaze the interior with a cooling light. Although it's small, with only a limited selection of books, it's got a reasonably good reference section and it's always nice and quiet, the way libraries should be.

Dad needed to photocopy something from a reference book, but the copier was playing up, so while he waited patiently as the ancient librarian fiddled around hopelessly inside the machine, I passed the time messing about on the library computer.

I'd logged on and was checking out the RSPCA website when someone tapped me on the shoulder.

'Looking for porn, girl?'

I turned around to see Bill, chewing on a wad of gum, looking down at me.

'Oh, hello,' I said.

'What are you doing?'

'Nothing. Just browsing, you know.' I looked around. 'Are you on your own?'

She looked a little embarrassed. 'Angel's outside.'

I looked out through the door. Angel Dean was leaning in a doorway across the street talking to one of the bikers. She was wearing a skinny little vest and ripped denim shorts that were more rip than short. Her face was done up in goth lipstick and a ton of black eye-liner, and she was standing with her back arched and her hands hooked behind her head to show off her belly.

'Nice,' I said.

Bill shrugged.

'So what are you doing in here?' I asked.

'I saw you come in. I thought I'd say hello.'

I nodded, staring at the computer screen. I didn't know what to say.

'Look,' she said. 'About the other day—'

'Don't worry about it.'

'We're still friends, aren't we?'

I shrugged. 'I suppose.'

'It was only a bit of fun.'

'Right.'

'Come on, Cait ...'

She'd dyed her hair black and was wearing a short leather jacket and tight black leggings. With her mascara'd eyes and a cupid's bow of dark red lipstick, she looked like a 1950s motorcycle-slut. Not that there's anything wrong with that, in fact I thought she looked pretty cool. It just wasn't the Bill I *knew*.

She flicked at her hair and said, 'Hey, did you hear about the gyppo?'

'The *what*?'

'The kid we saw at the Stand.'

'He's not a *gypsy*, for God's sake. And you didn't see him anyway, you were puking your guts up at the side of the road—'

'*Sshhh!*' the librarian hissed, giving me a filthy look.

'Sorry,' I whispered.

Bill grinned. 'Old fart.'

I lowered my voice. 'What about him?'

'Who?'

'The *boy* ... the boy at the Stand.'

Bill smiled. 'Have you seen him? Sheesh! I wouldn't say no, even if he is—'

'What *about* him?' I interrupted. 'When did you see him?'

She leaned closer. 'Lee's got a friend with a powerboat. We were out on it last night, round the other side of the Point.'

'Who's *we*?'

'Lee, Angel, Robbie, a couple others—'

'What were you doing out at the Point?'

'Well, you know ...' She winked and touched the side of her nose. 'Anyway, we were drifting along with the engine off when Lee spots this *naked* guy in a pool at the edge of the woods across from the mud flats.' She laughed. 'It was him, the gyppo. Having a bath.'

'How do you know it was him?'

'Lee had a pair of binoculars. Angel recognised him from the Stand.'

'You watched him through *binoculars*?'

'You bet.'

I shook my head. It couldn't have been the Boy. The only way out to the woods is across the mud flats, and the only people who know the flats well enough to even *think* of crossing them are local. If you don't know what you're doing out there, you're dead in seconds.

'It must have been someone from the island,' I said.

'No way,' said Bill. 'If there was anyone round here who looked like that, I'd know about it.' She smirked. 'And if I didn't, Angel certainly would.'

I sighed. 'What happened? Did he see you?'

'Don't you want to know what *I* saw?'

'Just tell me what happened,' I said coldly. 'Did he see you?'

A look of annoyance crossed her face, and for a moment I thought she was going to tell me to stuff it. I wouldn't have blamed her. I was speaking to her as if she was dirt. But she's never been the sort of person to let annoyance get the better of her. And, anyway, the temptation to tell me about it was too great.

She squatted down beside me. 'It was really weird, Cait. I was watching him through these binoculars – I couldn't see *much* because the pool was sort of half-hidden behind some bushes.' She gave me a leery look. 'I could see enough, though, if you know what I mean.'

I ignored her nudging arm.

She went on. 'He was just standing there – totally naked – staring at something in the water. It was like he was in a trance or something. And then, as I was watching him, he suddenly turned his head and looked at me.' Her eyes narrowed at the memory. 'It was really weird. I mean, he couldn't have known we were there. We weren't making any noise or anything and we were a fair distance away ... I don't know how he knew. I just remember these calm blue eyes staring at me through the binoculars ...' Her voice trailed off and she stared at the floor.

'What happened then?' I asked quietly.

She looked up. 'He just disappeared. It was *so* weird. I must have looked away for a second ... I'm sure I didn't ... but I suppose I must have. One second he was there – and the next he was gone.'

I was staring at the blank computer screen imagining the Boy's face – the eyes, the smile – and I remembered that ghostly silence when I saw him for the first time on the Stand, my skin tingling ...

'They reckon he's living rough,' Bill said, standing up.

'Who?'

'The gyppo.'

'Who's saying that?'

'I don't know, it's just what I heard. He's been seen around the village a couple of times. Bought a few things at the Paki shop – tobacco, matches, soap. Apparently he's done a bit of casual work for old Joe Rampton. Cleared out his chicken sheds, bit of painting ...' She laughed. 'Joe gave him a fiver for the day's work. Mind you, I've heard he's been nicking stuff, too ...'

Joe Rampton's farm is just across the fields from us.

You can't see it from our house, it's hidden behind a low hill, but if you're standing on the bridge over the creek you can just about see his farmhouse through the gaps in a spindly wood that cuts across from our lane to his ...

'... I mean, they're known for it, aren't they?'

'What?'

'Gyppos – they're always nicking stuff.'

'Are they?'

She didn't answer. She just chewed her gum and scratched her belly, looking around the library as if it was the most pathetic place in the world.

I hated her for that.

We used to come here together, me and Bill, when we were kids. We used to love it. Sometimes we'd spend hours in here, looking through all the books, talking quietly, giggling, enjoying ourselves ... God, we used to get really excited about our trips to the library ...

Was that so long ago?

I looked at her now. Yeah, I realised, it was. It was a lifetime ago.

'I've got to go,' I said, glancing across at Dad. He was waiting at the door, clutching his photocopies and gazing thoughtfully at the ceiling.

I stood up.

Bill said, 'Give me a ring sometime, yeah?'

I muttered something non-committal, and then left.

Dad told me once that there's magic in the wind, and that if you listen hard enough it'll tell you what you want to hear. I don't know if I believe in magic – I'm not even sure it's something you *can* believe in – but as I lay in bed that night I was willing to give it a try.

I closed my eyes, kept perfectly still, and listened. It was only a very light breeze, and at first it was hard to separate from all the other sounds of the night – the creaks and hums of the house, the occasional sound of a distant car, the faint roll of the sea. But the more I listened, the clearer it became, and after a while I could distinguish the different sounds coming from different trees – a dry rustling from the elm in the back garden, a leafy rush from the poplars along the lane, and from the ancient oak in the field at the back of the house, a tired groan, like the sound of an old man getting up from a chair. I even managed to work out the difference between the sound of the sea breeze and that of the wind coming in from the island. The sea breeze had a soft, effortless feel to it, something like the sound of the sea itself. Whereas the wind coming in from the island was more hurried, rushing through the trees as if it had somewhere important to go.

But no matter how hard I listened, how carefully I listened, the wind in the trees didn't tell me anything.

Maybe I'm just not magical enough?

I was still having trouble working up the courage to go back to the beach, and by Thursday it was really starting to get to me. There was a lot of friction in the house, mainly between Dominic and Dad. They hadn't stopped sniping at each other since the night Dom went out with Jamie Tait. Dirty looks, little digs, sarky comments, frosty silences ... and then on Wednesday they'd had a blazing row. I can't remember how it started, I can't even remember what it was about – although I'm pretty sure it had something to do with Dominic's habits. He was hardly ever at home now, and when he did show up, usually late at night, he barely spoke to anyone. He'd stopped shaving, he wore the same dirty clothes all the time, and his eyes were becoming pale and unfocused. He looked like something out of a Mad Max film.

The row started at the dinner table. Dad had been drinking, and Dominic was doing his best to catch up with him, working his way through a litre bottle of red wine as if it was Coke. They were both smoking like chimneys. A haze of cigarette smoke hung in the air and the table was strewn with overflowing ashtrays and unfinished plates of food. I was just sitting there, keeping my head down, pushing a piece of limp lettuce around my plate, when suddenly Dad and Dominic were on their feet shouting at each other.

'... you and Tait and the rest of that boatyard dross!'

'Oh, come on—'

'That's where you've been going, isn't it?

'Don't treat me like a kid—'

'Oh, I wouldn't *dream* of it. A fully grown man like you?'

'I don't have to listen to this. Why can't you just leave me alone? Let me enjoy myself, for Christ's sake.'

'Is that what you're doing? Enjoying yourself?'

'Shit – what would *you* know about enjoying yourself ...?'

And on and on and on ...

I hated it.

It reminded me of the bad times after Mum died, when Dad was close to losing it and Dom was struggling through puberty and I didn't understand what was going on. It reminded me of all the tears and raised voices, the accusations and recriminations, the constant bickering ... and deep down I couldn't help thinking it was all Dominic's fault, that if he'd never come back then everything would still be all right.

And thinking that only made me feel worse.

I needed to get out, to walk on the beach, to feel the sea breeze in my hair and hear the rush of the waves on the sand. I needed to look out at the horizon and wonder what lay beyond it, to watch the birds, to feel I was back where I belonged again.

But I couldn't.

I just couldn't face it.

Simon phoned on Thursday night. I was just getting into bed when I heard Dad calling up the stairs. 'Cait! Phone! I think it's Simon.' I was tired, and I didn't really want to talk to him, but when I crept out onto the landing to ask Dad to tell him I was asleep, I saw the phone dangling against the wall and Dad closing his study door.

I went downstairs and picked up the phone.

'Hello?'

'Cait? It's Simon. I didn't wake you up, did I?'

'No.'

'Are you sure?'

'Yeah. How are you?'

'I'm all right.'

'Good.'

I waited for him to say something else but the line stayed quiet. Simon is hard work sometimes.

'So what have you been doing?' I said.

'Not much ... helping my dad out, mostly. We spent most of the day picking up a load of bonemeal.'

'Bonemeal?'

'Well, guano, actually.'

'Bird shit?'

He laughed. 'Yeah – it's from the old lighthouse across the bay, the one they demolished last year. There's tons of it ... dead cheap, too. Dad uses it as fertiliser.'

'I bet that smells nice.'

'It's good stuff, full of nitrogen. And anyway, it's better than dumping a load of chemicals in the field. Do you know how long chemical fertiliser stays in the food chain?'

I sighed. I didn't mean to be rude, but I really didn't feel like talking about the rights and wrongs of chemical fertilisers. 'Listen,' I said, 'I can't talk too long – my dad's waiting for a phone call.'

'Oh, right ... OK.'

The line went quiet again. I imagined Simon at home in his draughty old cottage, sitting on the bench in his gloomy hallway, winding the telephone cord round and round his fingers, his hair flopping over his eyes, his mother listening in from the kitchen ...

I heard him clearing his throat. 'Are you still there?'

'Yeah ... sorry. I was just thinking ...'

'What about?'

'Nothing.'

'Oh.'

Deefer came over and sat down beside me. I scratched his head and he flopped down heavily on the floor. On the phone I could hear Simon clearing his throat again, then sniffing, tapping his fingers against the mouthpiece.

'Umm,' he said hesitantly. 'Is it still OK for tomorrow?'

'Sorry?'

'The posters and stuff – for the festival. I was going to come round, remember?'

'Oh, yeah, right. Six o'clock.'

'I'll bring those designs I was telling you about.'

'OK.'

'Did you get the paper?'

'What paper?'

'You were going to get some A1 cartridge paper.'

'Yeah, sorry ... I didn't get round to it. I meant to—'

'That's all right, I'll bring some other stuff.'

'Sorry.'

'It doesn't matter – really.'

'OK ... well, I'll see you tomorrow then.'

'About six?'

'Yeah.'

'You sure?'

'Yeah, fine. Six o'clock, tomorrow.'

'OK ... well, I'll see you then.'

'OK.'

'Six.'

'Yep.'

'Six o'clock.'

'Six o'clock.'

'OK – bye.'

'Bye.'

I hung up the phone and went into the kitchen. The floor was cool beneath my feet. The refrigerator hummed. Through the window I could see a flicker of blood-red light on the horizon, a faint glow reflecting from the sea. The moon was down. It was dark. I didn't know what the flickering light could be – a ship, perhaps? Something in the sea, plankton, fish ...? As I stood there gazing out through the window, the light slowly faded away into darkness.

It must have been my imagination.

I thought about Simon.

(... about the Boy)

I thought about Simon.

(... about the Boy)

I thought about Simon.

Whenever he asked to see me, it was always the same – there always had to be a *reason* for it: posters, badges, newsletters, petitions about oil-tankers or caravan parks or whatever. He could never simply come out and say – Cait, I'd like to see you.

It should have bothered me, I suppose. Well, maybe not *bothered* me, exactly, but it should have meant something. I should have at least felt *something* about it – annoyance, frustration, anger, sadness – but I didn't. Because, right then, as I stood at the kitchen window gazing out at the night, all I could really think about was the Boy. The boy from nowhere, the boy I'd never spoken to, the boy I knew nothing about ...

The Boy.

four

I don't think courage is anything to be particularly proud of. It's usually just a case of doing something you don't want to do in order to avoid something else that you don't want to do even more. In my case, I realised that if I didn't make myself go back to the beach I'd have to stay at home for the rest of the summer waiting for my head to explode. So, on Friday afternoon, after a couple of hours staring out of the bedroom window, psyching myself up, I went downstairs, called Deefer, and set about exorcising the memory of Jamie Tait.

It was four o'clock.

As I walked down the lane I could feel a knot of anxiety growing inside me, and the closer I got to the beach, the more nervous I felt. I knew it was irrational, that there was nothing to be scared of, but that didn't make any difference. A sick fluttery sensation tingled in my stomach, and I had that strange feeling you get when you walk a familiar route and everything around you seems unfamiliar. You don't know what it is that's different, you can't quite put your finger on it, but you know that *something* isn't quite right. It's like one of those science-fiction stories when someone goes back in time and steps on an ant or a butterfly or something, and when they come back to the present everything has changed. The changes are so subtle that at first they don't realise anything has changed – but they're still aware that *something* isn't quite right.

There's something *spooo*-ky in the air.

That's how it felt that afternoon. It wasn't exactly spooky, but it wasn't quite right, either. There was a strange scent to the air, that fine metallic smell of rain on a dry pavement. The trees were unnaturally still. The ground beneath my feet felt too hard and too far away. Even Deefer was acting out of character. Instead of running around like a crazed wolf he was just ambling along beside me, barely bothering to sniff at anything, and all the time his eyes were darting around looking at things as if he'd never seen them before.

It was a weird feeling, and I knew there was more to it than just fear. It was the kind of feeling you get when you know that something is about to happen, something you've been longing for, only now that it's finally within your reach, you're suddenly not so sure ...

When I got to the bridge over the creek I paused for a while to settle myself. Deefer sat beside me sniffing gently at the air while I took a good long look around, making sure the coast was clear. The air was warm and sticky, and as I scanned the area around the pillbox and then looked out across the sea, I fanned myself with the front of my vest, sighing at the cool breeze on my skin. The beach was deserted and the sea was flat and empty. No movement, no swimmers, just an endless stretch of rippled blue water flecked with jewels of sunlight.

Sometimes, when the sea is so calm, it has a depth to it that makes me think of for ever.

I turned my gaze to the beach.

Away to the west, it was a colourful sight: the red of the cliffs melting into the sky, distant kites flying high above the country park, the lush green of the surrounding fields, the pastel yellow of the sands. The outlying saltmarshes looked dull and barren in the heat, but there was colour there, too. Thousands of tiny flowers were beginning to bloom, forming a mist of pink that seemed to float in the air above the marshes.

To the east was a different picture.

Here the colours were primitive and hard: the cold grey of the Point, the eternal brown of the mud flats, and beyond the mud flats the twisted darkness of the woods, a lightless thicket of blackened umber and ghost-green. The mud flats shimmered eerily in the sunlight, giving off a dull gleam that stilled the air. They looked almost harmless. And that's why they're so dangerous. To the unwary, they're just a vast stretch of sticky brown ooze. Something to avoid, perhaps. A bit unpleasant ... a bit messy. But they're much more than that – they're deadly. One foot in the wrong place and a body will sink down into the airless depths, never to be seen again.

Deefer nuzzled my leg and whined.

'All right, boy,' I said. 'We're going.'

We headed off towards the Point and then followed it round to the shallow bay that lies beside the mud flats. The bay rises gently to a broad bank of shell-dappled silt, and beyond the bank the shore is edged with a trail of muddy tracks that wind through dunes and gorse and swathes of marram grass before eventually leading back to the bridge at the creek.

Deefer bounded off along one of the tracks, and I followed him.

Even when the weather is fine, the pathways are difficult to follow. The muddy surface is slippy and sticky, and the dunes and grasses play games with your sense of direction. There are numerous dead ends where the tracks just peter out, or get swallowed up in the grasses, or blocked by unexpected tide pools. It's not the easiest of walks, nor the cleanest, but it's still a nice way to go.

I walked slowly, soaking up the sun and the silence, stopping every now and then to gaze into the tide pools or watch small birds as they flitted around in the gorse. Rabbits were scuttling about in the dunes, trying to keep out of Deefer's way, and when the pathway rose above the dunes I could see cormorants perching on the buoys in the bay, stretching their wings in the sun.

It was wonderful.

I could feel my head emptying.

I could feel my unwanted thoughts and fears drifting away into the air.

Then I saw him.

He was standing barefoot by a tide pool with a crab in one hand and a length of twine in the other. The twine was tied at one end with a small lump of meat, and as I turned the corner of the muddy track he was swinging the weighted twine in a graceful loop, preparing to cast the meat into the centre of the pool.

I stopped and stared.

Deefer stopped and stared.

The sun was directly behind him, silhouetting his figure in a halo of pure white light, and as I stood there my mind flipped and for the briefest of moments I was a five-year-old girl sitting on my dad's knee looking through the pages of an old-fashioned picture book, looking at pictures of angels.

The crab bait dropped into the pool with a gentle plop and the Boy turned towards me with a calmness that slowed the air. A slight movement of his head caught the sun and his silhouette disappeared along with my memory. He was a flesh and blood boy.

And I was a fifteen-year-old girl with a gormless look on her face.

'Hello,' he said, smiling.

Without taking his eyes off me he slipped the crab in his bag and checked his line, winding the twine around his fingers. His clothes, which were weather-faded but clean, hung loosely from his frame. They were the same clothes he'd been wearing when I'd first seen him on the Stand: green canvas trousers, a drab green T-shirt, and a green army jacket tied around his waist. His boots and his canvas bag lay at his feet. The sun had bleached his tousled mop of blond hair, lightening the edges to a fine golden yellow.

'It's Cait, isn't it?' he said softly.

For a terrible moment I thought I'd lost the ability to speak. All I could do was stand there with my mouth hanging open like an idiot. God, I thought, how embarrassing is *this*? The moment probably only lasted a second or two, but it felt a *lot* longer. Eventually I managed to get some air into my lungs.

'How do you know my name?' I asked.

It came out all wrong. What I'd meant to say was, 'How do you know my *name*?' in a kind of light-hearted, curious manner. But what I actually said was, 'How do *you* know my name?' as if I was accusing him of some horrendous crime.

But he didn't seem to notice.

'Joe told me,' he said simply.

Somewhat to my surprise, I found myself walking towards him. It seemed a natural thing to do. As I approached, his eyes never left mine. His gaze was refreshingly open, almost naive in its honesty. It was like being watched by a child.

I stopped a few metres away from him. 'Joe Rampton?'

He nodded. 'I was doing a bit of work for him the other day. He pointed you out at the creek.' His face broke into a smile. '"See that girl, yonder?" he said. "That's Cait McCann. Her daddy writes books."'

I laughed.

'I hope you don't mind,' he said.

'No,' I told him. 'I don't mind.'

Up close I could see that his teeth were as white as milk. I could see that his skin was lightly tanned. I could see droplets of sweat glistening on his forehead.

'I've read your father's books,' he said. 'He must be an interesting man.'

'You could say that.'

He looked away, tugging lightly on his crab line, then looked back again. 'My name's Lucas, by the way,' he said.

I smiled. 'Pleased to meet you, Lucas.'

He nodded, glancing down at my side. I didn't know what he was looking at for a moment. Then I looked down and saw Deefer. I'd forgotten all about him. Normally, when Deefer meets strangers he does one of two things. He either runs up and slobbers all over them, or he stiffens and keeps his distance, growling quietly in the back of his throat. That day he did neither. He just sat there, silent and serene, like a Buddha-dog, staring at Lucas. I'd never seen him like that before.

'This is Deefer,' I said to Lucas. 'He's not usually so timid. Are you Deef?'

Lucas just smiled. Deefer got up and walked towards him, his big tail wagging slowly from side to side. When he reached Lucas he half-circled once around his legs and then sat down next to him. I couldn't believe it. It was like watching a different dog. A well-behaved, calm, obedient dog. He raised his heavy head to look adoringly at his new best friend and Lucas gave him a casual scratch just behind his right ear ... exactly where he likes it.

'He's a fine dog,' said Lucas.

He removed his hand to check his line again and Deefer lay down at his feet, resting his head on his paws.

The three of us were silent for a while.

Lucas pulled in his line and re-tied the bait then looped it under his arm and cast it back into the pool. Deefer raised his eyes at the sound of the plop, but apart from that he didn't move. I would have at least expected him to sniff at the meat, but no, not a flicker. If ever a dog looked at one with the world, it was Deefer.

I wiped the sweat from my brow.

The silence was surprisingly comfortable. I didn't feel the need to say anything, to fill the gap, to make small talk ... I was quite happy just standing there in the heat of the evening sun watching Lucas fish for crabs. I liked the way he moved. Everything was slow and smooth, no sudden movements. It was simple, too. Nothing fancy. Nothing elaborate.

Yeah, I liked that.

His voice didn't have any trace of an accent, not that I recognised anyway. It certainly wasn't local. It was just nice and quiet, clear and precise, without being clipped. It was a *nice* voice, calm and relaxing. Simple. Nothing fancy. Nothing elaborate.

I liked that, too.

I remembered thinking about him that first day, when I was walking on the beach, just before my encounter with Jamie Tait. I remembered picturing his face and trying to guess how old he was. Thirteen? Eighteen, nineteen, twenty ...? Now that I could see him at close quarters, it still wasn't easy. He *looked* quite young. That boyish face with its smooth, beardless skin. Those innocent eyes. That lean, almost underdeveloped frame ...

Yes, he looked quite young. But he didn't act like any young boy I'd ever come across. There was no awkwardness, no arrogance, no overbearing self-consciousness. There was no preening or pouting. There was no indication that he felt the need to *act* at all. He was just himself, take it or leave it. And despite his somewhat frail physique I got the impression that he was perfectly capable of looking after himself ... perfectly capable.

So how old was he?

About sixteen, at a guess. Maybe younger.

Not that it mattered.

I moved over and sat down on a sandy bank beside the tide pool. The pool was about four metres long and two metres wide, with steep, almost vertical banks. The water was deep and clear. At the bottom I could make out several large rocks resting on the bed of silt. That's where the crabs would be.

Lucas was standing above me on the adjacent bank.

'What are you using for bait?' I asked him.

'Chicken.'

'One of Joe's?'

He smiled. 'He couldn't spare any bacon.'

I watched him cast the line, aiming for the shadows of the rocks.

'Is bacon better?'

'Sometimes,' he said. 'It depends on the crab. Some of them are picky. I tried them on fishheads yesterday but they didn't want to know.'

'I don't blame them.'

He pulled on the line and I watched the bait edge slowly past the rock. He let it rest for a second then gave the twine a slight tug. Something moved beneath the rock, a rapid scything motion that stirred up a small cloud of silt, and then it settled again.

Lucas laughed, reeling in the line. 'He's smart, this one. He remembers what happened to his friend.'

As he concentrated on the tide pool, the colour of his eyes seemed to waver in the reflected light. I watched, fascinated, as they faded from the pale blue of flax to an almost transparent tone, as faint as the blue of a single drop of water. Then, as he cast the line and the sunlight rippled the surface of the water, the colour of his eyes intensified, brightening back through the shades to a stunning sapphire blue.

He began the process again, pulling on the line, letting it rest, a slight tug, a pull, another rest ...

It was cool beside the tide pool. We were in a slight shallow, shaded by gorse-laden dunes and marram grass. Although the sun was still high, the ground all around us had a fresh, moist feel to it. Gorse flowers sweetened the air with a faint smell of coconut. I could smell the seaweed in the pool, the earthiness of the mud, the sand, the salt in the air. From the shore I could hear the plaintive cry of a curlew.

Lucas was still fishing.

'What kind of crabs are you after?' I asked him.

'Edible crabs.'

'Those dull red ones?'

He nodded.

'Do you eat them?' I asked.

He looked at me with an amused smile.

'Stupid question,' I said, embarrassed.

He was silent for a while, dragging the line round the

rock. Then he said, 'You have to be careful not to eat the head or the green parts. Apart from that they're tasty enough. Have you ever eaten one?'

I shrugged. 'Only in a restaurant.'

He nodded.

I asked, 'How do you cook them?'

'In a pot. Over a fire.'

'Right, I see.' I looked at the canvas bag at his feet, imagining the crab inside, wondering if it was still alive, and if it was ...

'Boiling water,' he said, reading my mind.

I shuddered slightly. 'Isn't that cruel?'

He thought about it for a second, then simply nodded. 'I suppose so.'

It was then I remembered that Saturday afternoon at the Stand ... the look on his face as he fled from Robbie Dean, leaping across a narrow gully before melting into a tangle of tall reeds ... the hair on the back of his head matted with blood ... and the expression on his face as he glanced over his shoulder and looked at us ... looked at me ... the emotionless look of an animal, a look of pure instinct – that was the look on his face now.

Cruelty? Cruelty was a fact of life.

Did he remember me? I wondered. Did he recognise me?

Without thinking I glanced at the back of his head. There was no sign of any injury.

I looked away, suddenly feeling ashamed of myself. I felt like an impostor. A liar. A cheat.

Lucas spoke quietly. 'It probably looked a lot worse than it was.'

'Sorry?'

He touched the back of his head. 'It was only a small

cut. Once I'd washed the blood away there was nothing to it.' He smiled. 'It's the blond hair – it shows up the blood.'

I looked at him. There was no anger or mockery in his eyes, just genuine amusement.

'I don't know what to say ...' I stammered. 'I feel so—'

'You didn't do anything,' he said.

'I know, but—'

'You tried to stop him.'

'Yeah, and a lot of good that did.'

'You tried, though.' He started winding in his line. 'I appreciate that. Thank you.' The twine whirred around his fingers and the line slid from the pool with a gentle hissing sound. He untied the bait and threw it back into the pool, then knotted the twine and slipped it in his pocket.

He looked at me. 'Those people you were with ...'

I shook my head with embarrassment. 'It was a mistake ... well, it wasn't a *mistake*, but—'

'You don't have to explain,' he said. 'I've been in the same position myself.'

'Have you?'

He nodded. 'It's not always easy to avoid the bad things. Sometimes you have no choice. You just have to do what you think is best.' He stepped down from the bank and pulled a water bottle from his bag. It was one of those army-type water bottles – green metal with a drinking cap and a leather strap. It looked old and well-used. He poured some water into the cap and placed it on the ground. Deefer lapped it up. Lucas passed me the bottle. 'It's a bit warm, I'm afraid.'

As I took the bottle from his hand I caught a faint drift of leather from the bracelet tied at his wrist. There was another smell, too. A barely noticeable scent of fresh soil and fish. Not the pungent smell of dead fish, but the sleek and silvery tang of the ocean, the smell of the living animal.

I drank from the water bottle.

Lucas sat down on a flat rock and rolled a cigarette. He kept his tobacco in a small leather pouch. I watched as he scattered the tobacco on a cigarette paper and rolled it up into a thin tube, then popped it in his mouth and lit it with a battered old brass lighter. The smoke whipped away in the breeze.

He was sitting quite close to me. Close enough to talk but not *too* close ... and I wondered if he'd done it on purpose. So the smoke wouldn't bother me. Or just because it was the right thing to do.

Deefer ambled over and lay down beside him. Lucas had a casual way of ignoring him without being dismissive. It was if they'd known each other for years and didn't need the constant reassurance of contact.

It was astonishing, really.

I capped the water bottle and stood it in the sand.

Lucas was looking thoughtfully at me. 'The girl in the white dress,' he said. 'The one with the cold eyes ...?'

'Angel,' I said. 'Her name's Angel Dean.'

He nodded. 'Is she the speed-freak's sister?'

'Speed-freak? You mean Robbie?'

'The stone-thrower.'

'Yes, Angel's his sister.' I was puzzled. 'What do you know about Robbie?'

'Robbie's not the one you have to worry about,' he said distantly. 'Angel's the one.'

As he spoke I felt a strange feeling in the back of my throat, a cold, coppery taste, like old coins. It reminded me of when I was young. Dad used to keep a jar of old pennies on his desk, those big old pennies from years ago, and for some reason I used to find them irresistible. I was always dipping into the jar and taking them out and sucking them. I don't know why. That's what kids do, I suppose. They put things in their mouths. Dad was always telling me off – *take it out of your mouth, Cait, it's dirty, you don't know where it's been ...*

That's what the taste in the back of my throat reminded me of – dirty old pennies.

I swallowed, but the taste remained.

Angel's the one?

I looked at Lucas. 'What do you mean?'

He didn't answer for a moment. He took a final puff from his cigarette then carefully pinched it out and buried it in the sand. He brushed the sand from his hands and looked up. 'Is she ill, do you know?'

'Ill? What do you mean?'

'Is there anything wrong with her?'

I laughed. 'Not physically, no. Why?'

He picked up a small stone and tossed it in his hand. 'I thought I noticed something when she was on the bridge.'

'What?'

'Nothing.'

'Tell me,' I said. 'Tell me what you saw.'

He lowered his eyes. 'That's it – nothing. That's what I saw.' He looked up. 'She didn't have a face.'

I don't think he was trying to frighten me, or impress me, or spook me ... I don't think he was trying to do anything except tell me what he'd seen, or what he thought he'd seen. It was a feeling. He'd had a feeling about something, and he'd learned over the years not to ignore his feelings, whether he understood them or not. I've come to think of it since as the same kind of feeling that animals have –

when birds know it's time to migrate, when dogs know a thunderstorm is coming, when ants know it's the right time to fly. They don't know *how* they know these things, and they don't know what they mean. All they know is that when you get the feeling you have to act upon it.

Lucas was just trying to warn me, that's all.

But I think he knew it wouldn't make any difference. The future's already there, it can't be changed.

'I'm sorry,' he said. 'I shouldn't have told you that.'

'Why not?'

'Some things are best left unsaid. I'm sorry.'

A sadness had darkened his face, a look that reminded me of Dad. It was that unmasked look of sadness, the look of someone who thinks they're alone. I didn't like it – it fit him too well.

'What about me?' I said. 'Did I have a face?'

He looked at me. 'Oh, yes. Yours was angry and miserable. And confused.'

'Yeah?' I grinned. I don't know why I grinned. What he'd told me about Angel was genuinely scary, scary enough to sadden him to hell and back, and there I was grinning like a fool.

Very mature.

Lucas didn't seem to mind, though. At least he didn't seem so sad any more.

'So,' I said lightly, 'what else do you know, Mystery Man? What did I have for breakfast that day?'

'From where I was, it smelled like cider.'

I stared at him. 'You're just guessing, aren't you? You probably saw Bill being sick – yeah, that's it. You saw Bill throwing up, you guessed she was drunk and you assumed I must have had a drink as well. That's it, isn't it?'

He smiled. 'Ah, but how did I know you'd been drinking *cider*?'

'That's what girls drink. It's obvious. Everyone knows that.'

He laughed. It was a soft, easy laugh.

The sadness had gone.

I reached for the water bottle and took another drink. The coppery taste in the back of my throat had gone, too. It was hard to believe it had ever been there.

Lucas put his boots on, then got up and walked over to a sand bank on the other side of the pool. He stepped up and looked out over the beach, his arms crossed loosely behind his back. A light breeze ruffled his hair. The evening was beginning to cool. One or two pale clouds had appeared in the distance, scudding along the skyline like white tumbleweed.

'This thing about Angel,' I said. 'What do you think it means?'

'Probably nothing,' he said, stepping down from the bank. 'It might be an idea to be careful, that's all. Keep your distance, keep your eyes open.' He crossed over to the tide pool and picked up his bag. 'You don't like her, do you?'

'Who – Angel?'

He nodded.

'I can't stand her,' I said.

'So it wouldn't be a problem to keep away from her?'

'Not at all.'

He shouldered his bag. 'Right,' he said. 'Well, that's OK.'

I stood up. 'Are you going?'

'I have some things to do.'

Deefer was sitting by the pool. He looked at Lucas.

Lucas made a tiny sideways movement with his head and Deefer stood up and padded over to me, wagging his tail as if he hadn't seen me for a week.

'Hello, stranger,' I said.

He gave me a baleful look.

Lucas said, 'Well, it was nice meeting you, Cait.'

'Yes,' I said. 'Yes ... thanks.'

With a final nod and a smile he started off along a track I didn't even know existed.

I should have just left it at that. I should have kept my mouth shut and watched him go, but of course I couldn't.

I called out after him. 'Are you staying long?'

He stopped and looked back at me.

I felt myself blushing. 'Here on the island, I mean ... are you staying ...?'

'I hadn't really thought about it.'

'Well, if you're still around tomorrow ... and if you've nothing else to do ... there's always the regatta ...'

'Regatta?'

I smiled. 'The West Hale Regatta. Fun for all the family. Yachting, raft races, tea and scones ... it's all free. Apart from the tea and scones, of course.'

'It sounds unmissable.'

'It is!'

'Well, if I'm still around ... and I've nothing else to do ...'

'There's a little cliff above the bay,' I told him. 'It's got steps cut into the side ... we usually watch the boats from there. Me and my dad ...' I suddenly realised I was probably making a fool of myself, yammering away like an over-excited child. I took a breath and calmed myself, thinking cool thoughts, thinking cool ...

'So, you know,' I said – cool as hell. 'If you're around ...'

He smiled again. 'I'll look out for you.'

'OK.'

He waved and turned down the path, and this time I let him go.

There are all kinds of feelings. There's the feeling you get when you're walking home in the evening sun with your head in the clouds and your feet floating over the ground, and your stomach is fluttering so hard you don't think you can stand it any more. When everything looks bright and clear and everything smells brand new. When the freshness of the air tingles on your skin and it feels like something alive, and you can't stop smiling, and the sand beneath your feet is so soft you want to take off your shoes and spin round and round and round ... and you know you look like a fool but you don't care ...

There's that.

And there's also the feeling you get when you take a moment to pause, to sit down beside a creek and think about things.

I sat down.

The creek was quiet, just the soft ripple of the water flowing under the bridge and the faint rustle of the wind in the grass. The water looked cool and dark in the evening light. It flowed slowly, rich with peat and sediment carried down from the rise of woodland hills at the heart of the island. Rain, wood, rotting leaves, long-dead animals, minerals, soil ... I imagined the elements working their way down from the hills into the creek and finally out into the open sea, where eventually they'd merge with the ocean or evaporate into the clouds, to fall again as rain on some other woodland hills ...

And what about me?

What was I?

Well, I was thinking, for one thing. I was thinking about the creek, the hills, the woods, the water ... how everything goes round and round and never really changes. How life recycles everything it uses. How the end product of one process becomes the starting point of another, how each generation of living things depends on the chemicals released by the generations that have preceded it ...

Yeah, I was thinking about that.

I don't know *why* I was thinking about it. It just seemed to occur to me.

I was also thinking about crabs. I was wondering if they *did* have a memory, as Lucas had suggested. And if they did, what did they remember? Did they remember their childhood, their baby-crabhood? Did they remember themselves as tiny little things scuttling about in the sand trying to avoid being eaten by fish and other crabs and just about anything else that was bigger than them? Did they think about that, scratching their bony heads with their claws? Did they remember yesterday? Or did they just remember ten minutes ago? Five minutes ago?

And I was still wondering what it must be like to be dropped into a pot full of boiling water ...

I was thinking about all these things and more, but I wasn't really thinking about them at all. They were just there, floating around in the back of my mind, thinking about themselves.

What I was *really* thinking about, of course, was Lucas.

And as I sat there gazing out over the creek, it dawned on me that I still didn't know anything about him. I knew his name, but that was about it. Even then I didn't know if it was his first or second name. He could be Lucas Grimes, Lucas Higginbotham, John Lucas, Jimmy Lucas ... I smiled to myself ... he could be a Wayne or a Darren for all I knew.

I didn't know where he came from or what he was doing here or how old he was. I didn't know what he kept in his canvas bag (apart from crabs and a water bottle). I didn't know where he'd gone to school, if he'd gone to school. I didn't know anything about his parents. I didn't know if he had any brothers or sisters. I didn't know what he liked or what he didn't like or what he thought about girls who wore their hair in *plumes* ...

But it didn't seem to matter.

It didn't seem to matter at all.

There are all kinds of feelings. There's the feeling you get when you walk into your house and you're feeling so good you don't think anything could possibly get you down, but then your dad pops his head round his study door and says, 'Simon was looking for you.'

Damn. I'd forgotten all about him.

Six o'clock, he'd said.

'What's the time now,' I gasped.

Dad shrugged. 'Seven, seven-thirty.'

'*What?*' I couldn't believe it. I'd been out for over three hours. 'Has he gone?'

Dad nodded. 'Left about ten minutes ago. I told him I didn't think you'd be much longer, but he'd already been waiting an hour. Where've you *been*?'

I shook my head. 'Just out for a walk with Deefer ... I must have lost track of the time.'

Dad grinned. 'Perhaps you ought to get a watch?'

'It's not *funny*.'

'Not for Simon, it isn't.'

I sighed. 'How was he? Was he angry?'

'Well, it's hard to tell with Simon, isn't it? He's not the most expressive person I've ever met.'

'Did he say anything?'

Dad shrugged. 'Not really ...'

'Did you talk to him?'

'He didn't come round to talk to me.'

'You could have *talked* to him, Dad. He's shy. You could have at least made him feel welcome.'

'I *did*. I made him a cup of tea, asked him how he was ... hey, what am *I* apologising for? You're the one who stood him up, not me.'

'I didn't stand him *up* ... it wasn't a date or anything ... anyway, I just forgot what the time was—'

He smiled. 'Like I said, get a watch.'

'Yeah, yeah ...'

I rang Simon later but his mother said he was out. She said he'd gone to visit a friend. Friend? I thought. Some bloody friend.

I felt pretty bad about it, especially at first. I imagined how Simon must have felt as he sat there waiting for me – embarrassed, uncomfortable, self-conscious, humiliated ...

If that was me, I thought, I'd have felt like hell.

But the funny thing was, although I felt bad about it, I didn't feel *that* bad about it. I mean, I didn't beat myself up over it or anything.

I went to sleep that night with a smile on my face.

Maybe that was wrong.

I don't know.

There are all kinds of feelings: love, hate, bitterness, joy, sadness, excitement, confusion, fear, anger, desire, guilt, shame, remorse, regret ...

And you can't control a single one of them.

five

I've never really understood what happened at the regatta that day. It was such a strange mixture of things that I tend to remember it as a bad dream, a dream that swings from joy to despair and back again in the space of a few moments. I can remember everything that happened quite clearly, sometimes too clearly. I can remember the events, and how I felt about them, and what they meant to me at the time. But, although I've learned a lot since, I still don't really understand what happened.

And I don't think I ever will.

I suppose, in a way, it was the start of everything.

The beginning of the end.

We set off at about ten-thirty in the morning. Me, Dad, and Deefer. Although the sky was beginning to cloud over, it was still warm enough to walk the beach in T-shirts and shorts, but we had a change of clothing in Dad's rucksack just in case. We also had a pile of sandwiches and cakes, a bottle of Coke, water for Deefer, a towel, a pair of binoculars, and four cans of Guinness.

A hip flask bulged in Dad's back pocket.

I'd phoned Simon again before we left but there'd been no answer. I didn't expect to see him at the regatta, but then I never really had. Like he said, it wasn't really his kind of thing. Lucas, though ... well, I just didn't know about Lucas. I was half-hoping he would show up, and half-hoping he wouldn't. Of course, I *wanted* to see him again. I wanted to ask him all the questions I hadn't thought of asking him before. I wanted to know who he was and where he came from. I wanted to know what he'd really meant about Angel ... what he kept in his canvas bag ... where he'd learned to fish for crabs ...

Yeah, I wanted to see him again.

But I wasn't so sure I wanted to see him with other people around. Not for any underhand reason, I hasten to add, and not because I didn't want anyone else to know about him, either. Admittedly, I *didn't* want anyone else to know about him. But that wasn't the main reason. The main reason I didn't want anyone else around when I saw Lucas was that I wanted to keep it pure. What *it* was – a friendship, a kinship, a likeness of minds – I had no idea. It didn't matter. Whatever it was, I didn't want to see it polluted.

It was me, Lucas, and maybe Deefer. And that was it. No one else.

As we crossed the creek and turned along the path, I glanced over my shoulder at the mud flats and the woods. Dark clouds were gathering in the distance, dimming the sky above the woods in an ugly yellow wash that blurred the trees to a witch forest.

'Come on,' Dad said. 'We want to get there before it rains.'

We moved on, and I turned my mind back to Lucas. What if he *does* turn up at the regatta, I thought. What are you going to do? You can't just ignore him, can you? You can't pretend you don't know him. All right, so there'll be other people around – so what? Is that so bad? Think about it. You never know, it might even be quite nice ...

'Hey.'

I looked up at the sound of Dad's voice. He'd stopped on the path and was peering at me with amused eyes.

'What?' I said.

'You're talking to yourself.'

'Am I?'

He nodded, smiling. 'I'd watch it if I were you – one of these days you might embarrass yourself.'

I felt myself blushing.

'Luckily for you,' he added, 'I never listen to a word you say. So whatever wickedness you were mumbling about, I'm none the wiser. But others might not be so ignorant.'

'Ignorant?'

'There's ignorant and there's ignorant.'

'What's that supposed to mean?'

'It means – keep your mind open and your mouth shut, the world's full of beaky fools. Now come on, let's get going.'

He turned around and strode off along the path.

Considering all the grief he was having with Dominic, he was in a fairly good mood. Mind you, he looked pretty rough. He was wearing his old khaki shorts tied with a long leather belt, a battered straw hat, and a pair of dirty old sandals. His beard needed trimming and his eyes were tired and bloodshot.

I caught up with him and walked at his side.

'Dad?' I said quietly.

'Hmm?'

'Have you spoken to Dominic since the other day?'

'When?'

'You know when. In the kitchen – that row you had.'

He sighed heavily and looked at me. 'I made a complete arse of myself there, didn't I?'

I smiled. 'Yep.'

'I couldn't help it,' he said. 'I tried keeping my mouth shut, but he's so bloody *infuriating* at times.'

'I know.'

'It's not as if he's an idiot or anything. He knows what he's doing.'

I looked at him. 'What do you mean?'

'Hanging round with Tait and the others ... I saw him at Brendell's, you know.'

'Lee Brendell?'

He nodded. 'Dom was on his boat. There was some kind of party going on.'

'When?'

'A couple of days ago ... I had to go into the village for something. Rita Gray gave me a lift.' He paused, thinking about it. 'They were all there – Dominic, Tait and his stuck-up girlfriend, the Deans, Bill, Mick Buck, Tully Jones, a load of bikers ... all strutting around like a bunch of bloody gangsters.' He shook his head at the memory. 'It's bad enough *Dominic* being mixed up with that lot ... but Bill and Angel Dean? They're just kids.' He looked at me. 'What's Bill playing at?'

'I don't know.'

'I thought she was supposed to be your best friend?'

I shrugged. 'We haven't seen that much of each other recently.'

He stared at me for a moment longer, then looked away, seemingly satisfied. He's never been that keen on Bill. Even when we were little kids I sometimes caught him watching her with a cold look in his eye. I think he thought she was a bad influence, or at least he thought she had the *potential* to be a bad influence. Outwardly, Dad might not be the most attentive of fathers, but in his own quiet way he doesn't miss very much.

He sighed again. 'It's not as if Dominic even *likes* that lot. He's only doing it to get my back up. He knows what I think of them, especially Tait. He's just doing it to spite me.'

'Have you talked to him about it?'

'Sort of.'

'What did he have to say?'

'Not much.'

We were nearing the country park. I could hear the sound of a brass band playing from the bandstand in the field. The forced jollity of the music had a mournful feel to it, like the upbeat dirge of a New Orleans funeral march. Small groups of people were milling around the field, some with ice creams and balloons, others standing in the shelter of trees watching a kite-flying display. There was a bouncy castle, a hot-dog stand, a beer tent. The car park was about half full with visitors from Moulton who'd come down to watch the regatta, but most of the revellers were locals. Some had even dressed up for the occasion. I saw long dresses, fancy hats, pirates, a couple of clowns, a man on stilts.

The wind was getting up now and the kite-flyers were struggling to control their kites. It was supposed to be a display of synchronised kite-flying, but the two brightly coloured dots swooping and flapping high in the sky didn't look that synchronised to me.

Although the rain was holding off, the sky looked ominous. There was a gloomy feel to the air, and while it was still quite warm the heat was thick and heavy with moisture. It was turning out to be one of those days when the weather comes down and casts a shroud over everything.

The sea looked like thunder.

Dad had gone quiet.

'He must have said something,' I said.

'Who?'

'Dominic. He must have said something about the party on Brendell's boat.'

Dad flicked at a swarm of midges. 'It was nothing, according to him. Just a party. He didn't know who was going to be there ... it wasn't his fault a bunch of young girls turned up, was it? What was he meant to do? Call the NSPCC?'

'I suppose he's got a point.'

'He's always got a point.'

I got the feeling that Dad didn't want to talk about it any more. Neither did I, really. The whole thing was just too depressing. Dominic and Bill, Bill and Angel, Angel and Jamie, Jamie and Dominic ... it was tacky and twisted and all mixed up.

'Do you want to go through the park?' Dad asked.

I looked out over the field. A bunch of people in animal costumes were running around shaking buckets of coins at passers-by. The band were playing a barely recognisable version of 'I Should Be So Lucky.'

'No,' I said. 'Let's go along the beach.'

To the west of the park the beach is overlooked by a bank of cliffs that gradually descend to the bay. Paths and steps are cut into the cliffs from the park at the top, but you can also reach the cliffs by cutting along the sea wall below the park and following the beach for about a kilometre until you come to a natural gap in the cliff wall. From there it's just a short climb up a clay bank and you're onto the main cliff trail that leads around to the bay. It's a longer way round, but quieter. There was less chance of us bumping into anyone we didn't want to bump into.

Unfortunately, less chance doesn't mean no chance, and as we were crossing the sea wall an unwelcome voice called down from above.

'Hey, what are you doing down there? You're missing all the fun.'

We both looked up to see Jamie Tait and Sara Toms leaning over the railings at the top of the four-metre wall. Jamie was dressed casually in a V-necked jumper and jeans, but Sara had thrown herself into the costume spirit and was dolled up like something from the cover of a glossy magazine: tight black dress, stockings, heels, black lace gloves, pearls, and a chic black hat with a veil. I wasn't sure what she was supposed to *be*, exactly, and I don't think she knew, either – but whatever it was, it suited her. She wore the darkness well. As she stood there looking down at us, the scent of her perfume drifted on the breeze: Chanel No. 5 – the smell of money.

Lee Brendell was off to one side, smoking a cigarette and gazing sullenly out to sea, and in the background I could see Sara's mum and dad talking with a couple of old ladies sitting on a bench. Bob Toms, Sara's dad, was dressed in his full police uniform, all shiny buttons and ribbons.

Jamie was slurping on an ice cream cone and his face was flushed. I think he was a bit drunk.

'Come on up, Johnny,' he grinned at Dad. 'They've got it all up here – ice creams, fancy dress, candyfloss, cold beers – everything a fun-loving man could wish for.' He looked at me. 'You want me to get you some candyfloss, Cait?'

Sara gave him a dirty smile, then looked down and gave me a dirty look. She was good at dirty looks. She had the face for it: high forehead, long black shiny hair, a hard, lipsticked mouth, porcelain skin, and acid green eyes. Her face was so beautiful it was almost ugly.

'Come on, Cait,' Dad said quietly.

He took me by the arm and started to lead me away.

Jamie called down after him. 'Hey, Mac – where's Dominic? Where's the boy?'

Dad paused. I could feel him stiffening.

Sara laughed – a horrible plummy sound – and said, 'He's probably locked away in his bedroom for being a naughty boy.'

'Knowing Dom, he'll be locked in *someone's* bedroom,' added Jamie.

Dad didn't say anything, he just looked at them. They stared back with mocking seriousness. Sara lifted a cigarette to her lips, took a scornful puff, then hooked her hand into the back of Jamie's belt. She's one of those clingy types who display their affection – or their ownership – by constantly groping their boyfriends. Jamie seemed to enjoy it. As they stood there leering down at us, a pair of heavily browed eyes and a severe peaked cap appeared beside them.

'Good afternoon, John,' Bob Toms said. 'Hello, Cait.' He gazed at the sky and rubbed his hands. 'Doesn't look too good, does it?'

'Not from here,' replied Dad.

Toms smiled tightly. 'It's good to see you out and about for a change. You should do it more often.'

Dad nodded. 'I see *you've* made an effort.'

'I'm sorry?'

'The fancy dress ... that's the best Heinrich Himmler I've seen in a long while.'

Toms looked down at his police uniform. 'Very funny.'

Dad glanced at Brendell and Tait. 'And you've even

taken the trouble to bring along a couple of stormtroopers for added authenticity. Now there's thoroughness for you.'

'Still the joker, I see.'

'Who's joking?'

While this was going on Brendell had turned his attention from the sea and was staring down at me with the pale vacancy of a corpse. A string of faded tattoos discoloured his neck, a crescent of crudely drawn stars, and I wondered what they were supposed to be. Something nautical? A sign? A constellation? I decided they weren't supposed to be anything – they were just tattoos. He was a big man, and from down here he looked even bigger. Heavy hands, broad shoulders, and a huge square head with battle-scarred features. He looked as if he'd been hit in the face with a shovel. Flat nose, flat lips, bruised yellow eyes ... and without taking those eyes off me he plucked his cigarette from his lips, leaned over the railings and spat. The gob of spit landed next to my feet with a flat splat. I looked down at it. It was brown and stringy and it made me feel sick.

Dad stopped talking, glanced at me, then slowly looked up at Brendell. Brendell fixed the cigarette in his mouth and stared back, his eyes full of nothing. Deefer started growling. Dad, too.

'It's all right, Dad,' I whispered. 'Please, just leave it. It's all right.'

I don't think he heard me. Brendell was making a big show of clearing his throat and hawking loudly into a handkerchief, never taking his eyes off Dad. Dad's jaw tightened and his eyes burned as Brendell grinned and folded the handkerchief into his pocket, then casually carried on smoking. In the background Jamie and Sara were looking on with cruel amusement. Sara, in particular, had a crazed gleam in her eyes. It was a look that reminded me of a picture I'd once seen of a face in the crowd at a cock-fight – a look of bloodlust.

Surprisingly, the silence was broken by Bob Toms. 'That's dis*gusting*, Lee.'

Brendell slowly turned his head. A thin smile cracked his lips as he said, in a low and lispy voice, 'I got a fly in my mouth, Mr Toms. What you want I should do? Swallow it?'

Toms shook his head. 'There's no need for that.'

'What?' said Lee.

'I think you ought to apologise.'

'Oh, come on, Dad,' Sara said, stepping up. 'Don't make such a fuss.' She smiled down at me, all icy lips and perfect teeth. 'I'm sure Lee didn't mean anything. Little Caity's all right – aren't you, dear?' She glanced disdainfully at Dad. 'And, anyway, I'm sure she's seen worse.'

Toms ignored her, watching Dad with anxious eyes. 'Now then, John,' he said, raising his hands in a placatory gesture. 'Let's not do anything silly. I'm sure Sara's right—'

'Don't worry, Bob,' Dad said coolly, still staring at Brendell. 'I'll not be ruining your day.' Brendell just sniffed and looked away. Dad looked at Toms. 'Thanks for your concern, though. It's good to know there's a bobby around when you need one.'

'Listen, John ...' Toms began.

But Dad had already turned away and was heading down the sea wall towards the beach. I called Deefer and we started after him.

The brass band was playing the theme tune from *Animal Hospital*.

It was raining.

The charity raft race starts at the boatyard and follows a series of buoys around the bay to a halfway point at the base of the cliffs where the rafts negotiate another marker buoy before doubling back along the same route. It's one of the high points of the whole day, and there's usually a fair-sized crowd along the route to cheer on the competitors. But as the morning went on and the weather worsened, the crowds dwindled, and by one o'clock there was probably no more than forty or fifty people left, spread out thinly over the beach and cliffs, half-heartedly cheering on the rafts. Most of those watching from the beach were visitors, while those on and around the cliffs were locals.

As usual, the rafts were a motley collection of lashed-together boards and oildrums and wobbly masts and sheet-sails. Some of them had the skull-and-crossbones flying.

Each year, one or two of the rafts fall apart, or capsize, or simply sink, and although the currents in the bay aren't usually dangerous, volunteer life-guards are positioned around the bay and the cliffs to keep an eye on things.

This year, though, there'd been a mix up with the timetable.

At one-thirty, when the storm began to break, and the rafts were approaching the halfway point, the volunteer life-guard who should have been on duty at the base of the cliffs was sitting in the Dog and Pheasant washing down a steak-and-kidney pie with a pint of cider and blackcurrant.

Dad and I were watching the rafts from a gently sloping field at the top of the cliff overlooking the bay. It's a hard place to get to – you have to scramble around over streams and ditches and squeeze through a couple of wire fences –

but it's worth it in the end, because no one else bothers to make the effort so you get the place all to yourself. It's got a great view, too. You can see the marker buoy where the rafts turn, you can see all along the beach, and – best of all – you can see the rest of the spectators scattered down below. Most of them, or most of what was left of them, were lined along the various cliff paths, but there was a small group of locals gathered on a flat ledge at the base of the cliffs directly beneath us.

I was watching them through the binoculars.

I was watching Jamie Tait and Sara Toms sitting on a rock laughing about something.

I was watching Lee Brendell talking to Angel Dean.

I was watching Bill Gray standing off to one side on her own. I wondered if she was waiting for Dominic.

They all looked rather forlorn in the rain. Sara in her posh frock and funeral hat, Brendell with his thin hair plastered like wet cotton to his skull, Bill in her leather gear, and Angel ... Angel was wearing nothing but a black bra-top and a pair of skin-tight jeans. She looked frozen stiff. But that didn't stop her casting sultry looks in Jamie's direction every two minutes.

As I adjusted the focus on the binoculars, I caught a close-up of Jamie smiling over his shoulder at Angel when he thought that Sara was looking elsewhere. But she wasn't. In one swift movement she threw a murderous look at Angel, whispered something in Jamie's ear, then flicked him hard in the groin with the back of her hand.

From the look on his face, it hurt. Good, I thought.

'You're supposed to be watching the boats,' Dad said.

He was lying on his back staring up into the rain. We'd had our food and changed into our wet weather gear of rain hats and capes. Dad had sunk a couple of cans of

Guinness and taken a good few slugs from his flask when he thought I wasn't looking. He seemed to have forgotten about the episode at the park. At least, he'd forgotten about it for now.

I said, 'They're not boats, they're rafts.'

'Rafts, boats ...' he muttered. 'They're all a bunch of arseholes.'

'Dad!'

'Well ...' He sat up. 'I mean, look at them. What do they think they're doing? It's pouring with rain and blowing a gale and they're paddling around the bay on a load of bloody *planks*.'

'And we're sitting up here in the rain watching them.'

He grinned at me. 'Ah, but we're not in danger of drowning, are we?' He looked around. 'Where's the dog?'

'Over there.' I pointed towards the edge of the clifftop where Deefer was sitting like a sentinel staring down at the beach. He'd been sitting there for about twenty minutes, hardly moving. Just staring.

'What's he doing?' Dad said.

'Don't ask me.'

Dad wiped a sheen of rain from his brow and popped another can. He looked up at the rolling skies. 'There's nothing like a good picnic, is there?'

'Yeah, and this is nothing—'

'—like a good picnic.'

He lay back in the grass.

I put the binoculars to my eyes.

The rain was getting heavier. The wind was starting to bite. The sea was turning rough. Along the base of the cliffs, the waves were crashing into jagged rocks, sending up fountains of dirty white spray.

The leading rafts were turning round the marker buoy when the little girl went overboard. From where I was watching it didn't look too bad – not at first, anyway. It was almost comical, the kind of thing you see on *You've Been Framed* ... if that's your idea of comical. I almost missed it. I'd put the binoculars down and was only half-watching the rafts when she went in. All I really saw was a small figure tumbling off a distant raft. There was no great splash or anything, no shouting, no screams, nothing to indicate that anything was seriously *wrong*. I thought at first that it was a woman. I think I must have subconsciously noted the bikini, that familiar bikini-shape, and just assumed that it was a young woman. But when I put the binoculars to my eyes, expecting to see a smiling face swimming back to the raft to be helped aboard by laughing friends, I saw instead the petrified face of a ten-year-old girl floundering alone in the waves.

'Dad,' I said urgently. 'There's a girl in the sea. She's fallen in.'

He sat up quickly. 'Where?'

I passed him the binoculars. 'By the buoy,' I said. 'She was on that raft with the blue flag ... why isn't it stopping?'

Dad stood up to get a better look.

I stood up as well. I could see the girl flapping around in a panic, her arms flailing as the waves ducked her under the water. The current was dragging her away from the rafts towards the cliff.

'Why aren't they *stopping*, Dad?'

'I don't know,' he said. 'Maybe they haven't seen her.'

She was heading for the rocks. The rain was lashing down and churning up the sea, and the sky was black and heavy. I suddenly realised how dark it was. As Dad and I hurried to the edge of the cliff to get a better view, the sky rumbled and a crack of thunder shook the air.

The girl was managing to keep herself afloat by flapping her arms like windmills, but I could see she was beginning to tire. Every time a big wave broke, her head went under. I looked down at the people on the beach and the cliffs. They were all just standing around watching.

'Why aren't they *doing* anything?' I cried.

Dad put his hands to his mouth and hollered. '*Hey! Help her! She needs help! She can't swim. Hey! HEY!*'

His words were drowned out by the roar of the wind and the sea. The people below just carried on watching, some of them casually pointing out to sea as if it was all just part of the show.

Meanwhile the girl was being swept towards the rocks.

I've thought about it a lot since, and I still haven't figured out why they didn't do anything. Maybe things looked different from down there. Maybe they thought she was all right, she was fine, she was just messing around. Maybe they didn't want to make fools of themselves – diving in to save a little girl when all the time she was perfectly OK ... how embarrassing would *that* be? Maybe they were scared. Maybe they were waiting for the lifeguard. Or maybe they just didn't care.

I don't know.

Another roll of thunder rocked the sky. Dad yelled again, trying to make his voice heard above the wind, but it was hopeless. I ran over to the right-hand side of the cliff and peered down through the rain at the rocky ledge where Tait and the others were gathered. Jamie's a good swimmer, I was thinking, he could help her. And when I saw him standing at the edge of the rock peeling off his jumper, I felt a surge of relief. At last, someone was going to do something.

The girl was getting close to the rocks now. I could see her face quite clearly. It was pale and struck with terror. Even if she avoided the rocks, the current was going to drag her down into one of the whirlpools that were forming in the deep pools beneath the cliffs.

I looked at Jamie again. He hadn't moved. Sara was standing beside him with a strange, icy look on her face. I could have sworn she was laughing at him.

I called down. 'What are you *waiting* for!'

Whether it was because the cliff was slightly lower on that side, or because my voice is higher pitched than Dad's, or because the wind had dropped for a moment ... I don't know. But Jamie heard me. I don't think he recognised my voice, he just heard a shout and looked up. And as he did, I knew immediately why he hadn't moved – he was scared stiff. Petrified. His eyes were wide open and his face was white. My heart sank. He wasn't going to do anything. He couldn't move. With a glazed look he turned back to the sea. He wasn't going in there. Not in a thousand years. It was too rough, too unpredictable. It was too much ...

In the distance the flotilla of rafts had rounded the buoy and were heading back towards the bay. The storm was keeping them close to the shore. Several competitors had decided to call it a day and were dragging their rafts up the beach.

Dad was still yelling but his voice was getting weak and the wind was getting louder. The people down below couldn't hear him. Jamie Tait couldn't hear him. Not that it would have made any difference. He was dead to the world, just standing on the rim of the ledge, bare-chested and helpless, with an embarrassed grin on his face. Behind him, Sara looked on, calmly smoking a cigarette.

The girl was almost on the rocks, now. She'd stopped struggling and was just half-floating in the sea like a sodden ragdoll. The current had dragged her around to the left of the ledge where vicious eddies swirled in the midst of the rocks.

I'd given up hope. All I could do was stand there and watch as the whirlpools sucked her down.

Then I heard a single bark from Deefer. Through all the thunder and yelling and running around, he hadn't moved. He was still sitting rigidly at the left-hand edge of the clifftop staring down at the beach. I know most of his barks – the warning bark, the happy bark, the angry bark, the rabbit bark – but I'd never heard this one before. It was an odd sound – not loud, but stunningly clear, almost prescient. There was something in it that lifted my spirits.

As the single bark echoed around the cliff I looked down and saw a blur of green racing across the beach.

'*Lucas!*' I gasped.

Dad looked at me.

'There,' I pointed. 'It's Lucas.'

He was up over the rocks at the base of the cliff, leaping from boulder to boulder like a mountain goat, veering round beneath the rocky ledge and bearing down on the sea. I'd never seen anyone move so fast. Barefoot, his clothes soaked and his hair slicked back in the rain, he looked and moved like something from a different world.

I was half aware of heads turning and fingers pointing. I heard Dad say, 'What the hell ...?' And then Lucas was diving off the base of the cliff and swimming towards the girl, cutting through the waves like a torpedo. It seemed to take no time at all. From the moment I saw him to the moment he reached the girl, it couldn't have been more than twenty seconds. It was all so easy, so smooth. Without stopping he just swept the girl under his arm, turned on his side, and swam one-handed for the shore, heading for a small sandy cove to the right of the ledge.

'Jesus ...' said Dad, shaking his head in admiration.

I looked at him. 'His name's Lucas.'

'Lucas?'

'The fine-looking boy on the bridge ... remember?'

We looked at each other for a moment. There were a hundred questions in Dad's eyes, but we both knew it wasn't the time for questions. We turned our attention back to the beach where Lucas was striding from the waves with the girl in his arms. The storm had died quite suddenly. It was still raining, but the howling wind had dropped and the air was calm. People had gathered on the ledge above the beach and were looking on with stunned expressions on their faces – *who is he? where did he come from? what's he doing?*

Lucas didn't seem to notice them. He laid the girl in the sand and knelt down beside her. She looked pale and weak, but her eyes were open and I could see her head moving. The sad little black bikini she was wearing had been pulled all over the place by the waves. The top was skewed over one shoulder and the bottom was halfway down her thighs.

Perhaps if she'd been in a worse state, not breathing or badly injured, Lucas wouldn't have bothered trying to make her decent. He'd have just got her into the safe position and started artificial respiration. But she *was* breathing, and she wasn't choking or vomiting, and there were people looking on, so what harm could it do to cover her up, to make her look respectable?

What harm could it do?

Probably none – if the girl's mother hadn't appeared on the beach at the very moment he was gently rearranging her clothes.

Her voice rang out in anger. *'What are you doing! Get away from her! GET AWAY FROM MY DAUGHTER!'*

six

At the sound of the voice, Lucas looked up. The woman was bearing down on him across the sand, her eyes bulging, her lank hair blowing in the wind, and her face twisted with rage. She was brandishing a rolled-up regatta programme in her hand and screaming like a banshee.

'*YOU PERVERT! ... GET AWAY! ... GO ON! ...*'

Lucas was too shocked to move. Soaked to the skin, with the little girl shivering beside him and the storm raging all around, he stared at the woman with a dazed look of confused innocence on his face ... what? what's happening? what have I done? what's *wrong*?

The woman was closing. 'Get away, Kylie ... you get away from him *NOW!*'

The girl was still groggy and frightened, and the sudden shriek of her mother's voice made her shrink into Lucas's arms. Lucas responded instinctively with a gentle hug and a reassuring smile – and then the woman whacked him across the head with her rolled-up programme.

'*Leave her ALONE!*' she hissed in his face.

On the ledge, someone laughed nervously.

Lucas stood up and backed away.

'I wasn't hurting her,' he said simply.

The woman whacked him again, then yanked her daughter's bikini into shape and started dragging her up the beach, her cold eyes fixed on Lucas. 'You – I know what you are. You dirty little *bastard!*'

Lucas was speechless. He looked around open-mouthed at the people on the ledge. They looked back at him, dead-eyed, saying nothing. They didn't want to know. It was nothing to do with them.

While all this was happening I just stood there looking down, too numb to do anything. A sense of unreality had gripped me, removing me from the moment. It was as if I was watching a film or a play. It was happening, it was there, but I wasn't part of it. I couldn't participate. I was too far away. All I could do was look down in disbelief as the nightmare scene unfolded on the beach.

The woman had made her retreat and was standing her ground at the top of the beach, breathless and wild-eyed. Her daughter was standing beside her, sobbing and shaking, pulling pathetically at the straps of her bikini. The people on the ledge were beginning to murmur among themselves. There were about twenty or thirty of them now. I couldn't see Angel or Brendell or Bill, but I could see Jamie and Sara standing at the back. Jamie had put his jumper back on and seemed to have regained his poise. He was in control of himself again, talking calmly to a young couple from the village, pointing at the beach, explaining something, shaking his head with concern. Meanwhile, Sara had separated herself and was standing to one side studying the crowd. Her face was gripped with that strange emotionless passion I'd noticed earlier, like it was all just a game to her, a distant game. The game of the crowd, the dynamics of the crowd ...

The crowd ...

Crowds are strange things. A crowd has a collective mind of its own, a mind that ignores the sense of its constituent parts and thrives on the lowest passions. The crowd had seen what had happened, they'd seen Lucas diving in to save the girl, they knew the truth – but the truth to a crowd is soon forgotten. The passion of the woman's actions had set doubts in their mind. The collective mind was taking over. I could see it turning. I could see the way they were looking at Lucas, and I could imagine their thoughts – *well, he must have done* something *wrong. Why else would the kid's mother be so angry? Look at him, look at his eyes – he's scared. The boy's scared. If he didn't do anything, why's he so scared? Yeah, he must have done something wrong ...*

Lucas was beginning to move away, backing off towards the rocks, and that only made it worse – an admission of his guilt. The crowd seemed to sense it, gathering a voice, and this gave the girl's mother more confidence and she started yelling again. 'Don't think you'll get away with this, you dirty little *perv*. I seen you, we all seen what you was doing – I'm getting the police on to you. Yeah – go on, that's it, run away. Not so *big*, now, are you?' She spat in the sand. 'God, people like you make me *sick*. I'm getting the police ...'

The wind had started up again. Gusts of sand and rain were swirling in the air, turning the sky grey. I looked down through the mist and saw Lucas quietly melting away into the rocks at the base of the cliff. The woman was still calling after him. The crowd was still looking on. But at least no one was going after him.

At least no one was going after him ...?

I couldn't believe what I was thinking. He'd saved the girl's life while everyone else did nothing. He'd saved her *life* ... and now I was breathing a sigh of relief because *no one was going after him.*

It was unbelievable.

'I have to talk to him,' I said, turning to go.

Dad grabbed my arm. 'Whoa – not so fast.'

'I have to talk to him, Dad. You saw what happened—'

'Hold on, Cait. Calm down.'

'But I have to go after him—'

He looked me in the eye. 'Just calm down a minute. Look at me ...' His voice was quiet. Rain dripped from his brow. 'Cait ... look at me. You're not going anywhere until you tell me what's going on.'

'Nothing's going on.'

'How do you know this boy?'

'There isn't *time*, Dad—'

'Make time,' he said calmly.

I looked into his eyes and sighed. 'I met him yesterday on the beach. We talked ... we just talked about things. He's a good person, Dad. It's not fair—'

'Whereabouts on the beach?'

'Round by the bay at the Point ... he was fishing for crabs.'

'Crabs?'

'We just talked about things ... he's just like ...'

'Just like what?'

I was going to say – he's just like you. But that felt wrong, so I didn't. I said, 'You'd like him if you met him. He's good, Dad. Honestly. You saw what he did. That little girl would have died if it wasn't for him. No one else was going to do anything. And then that stupid woman comes along—'

'You can't blame her, Cait. She was only trying to protect her girl.'

'But Lucas didn't do anything—'

'I know, love.' He squeezed my hand. 'Look, don't worry – I'll have a word with her. I'll explain what happened. I'm sure she'll understand.'

'Will you talk to her now?'

He thought about it for a moment, then nodded.

I looked at him. 'I have to go after him, Dad. Before it's too late ...'

'Too late for what?'

I gazed out over the beach. The rain was coming down in billowing sheets that merged the landscape to a colourless blur. I could just make out the darkened outline of the cliffs, but everything else was a blanket of grey. No perspective, no height, no distance, no sky, no sea, no solid ground ... just a shifting wall of rain.

'Where will he go?' Dad asked.

'I don't know,' I admitted. 'The woods, probably.'

'Across from the Point?'

I nodded.

He shook his head. 'You're not going there.'

'If I go now, I can catch him up on the beach.'

Dad looked hesitant.

'Please,' I begged. 'I only want to talk to him ... it won't take long. I just want to make sure he's all right. Please ...?'

Thinking back on it now, I realise how difficult a decision it was for Dad. Logically, he should have said no. All his instincts must have been telling him to say no. Why on earth should he let his fifteen-year-old daughter go running off after a strange young man in the middle of a storm? Why should he trust her?

Why?

Because he loved her.

'Go on, then,' he said at last. There was a touch of sadness in his voice, and for a moment it crossed my mind not to go. It was reckless, it was unfair, it was stupid and selfish ... but then Dad wiped a drop of rain from my cheek and smiled. 'Don't let me down, Cait. I'm putting more faith in you than I can afford to lose.'

'Don't worry, Dad.' I kissed him. 'Thanks.'

'Right, well I'd better go and have a word with the mad lady. You take the dog with you. I'll see you back at the house ... if you're not back by six ...'

But I couldn't hear him, I was already halfway across the field.

There's something exhilarating about a storm-drenched beach, and despite all the mixed-up emotions that churned inside me I couldn't help smiling as I ran along the sand with Deefer beside me, with the waves crashing on the shore and the song of the wind howling in the rain. It was energising, it made me want to shout and fly. The beach was raw and deserted, and it wasn't hard to imagine myself the only person in the world, running on the only beach in the world, beneath the only cliffs, next to the only sea ... This is how it must have been a hundred thousand years ago, I thought. No people, no cars, no brass bands, no games, no hate, no twisted hearts ... just this, the seasons and the skies and the rain and wind and tides ... things without grown spirit. Nothing to remember or want. Light. Darkness. A heartbeat. No words to think. No unnatural emotion. Nothing but cold and hunger to avoid. No tomorrow. No names, no history, nowhere to go. Nothing to do.

Nothing to do but run.

I ran.

Down the cliff path, through the fences and streams, along the west beach beneath the height of the cliffs, then across the sea wall and out onto the east side of the beach where the sand turned to shingle that crunched satisfyingly beneath my feet.

Now I felt at home.

This was my world, my beach, my island.

This was my time.

I slowed to a walk, edging up to the higher ground near the saltmarshes where the going was easier. Deefer followed me. His coat had fluffed up and darkened in the rain, and as he loped across the strandline, with his tongue lolling out and his eyes wild in the wind, he looked like a primitive beast.

Halfway along the beach I paused to wipe the moisture from my face. I couldn't tell if it was rain or sweat.

The storm was easing off a little. Although it was still raining hard, the sky had lifted enough to let me see where I was going. I looked out across the beach. Tall grasses waved in the wind and the sand was shifting close to the ground. Specks of debris were tumbling around on the strandline – discarded floats, bits of plastic and cardboard, the empty husks of whelk's eggs.

There was no sign of Lucas. No visible sign, anyway.

This might sound stupid, but I could sense his presence. There was an invisible – yet perceivable – trail in the air. Like a transparent tunnel, or the wake of a fish in the sea. I could see it, and yet I couldn't see it. I could sense it. It followed the shoreline, just beyond the reach of the waves, looping and swerving here and there to avoid rocky outcrops and sandbanks, before disappearing into the gloom, heading in the direction of the Point.

I cut down to the shoreline and followed the trail. Even when I couldn't see it – and sometimes I couldn't – Deefer could. He trotted along the invisible tunnel with his head held high and his tail wagging, and I jogged along behind him.

As we passed along it, the trail folded in on itself and faded away, its purpose served.

I was rounding the Point when I heard Deefer bark. It was that strange new bark of his, the one from the clifftop, but now I knew what it meant. I looked up and saw Lucas about fifty metres ahead of us, just beginning to cross the mud flats. In the haze of rain and misted sea, it looked for a moment as if he was walking on water.

I called out, 'Lucas! Hey, Lucas!'

He turned and peered through the rain. I waved, but he didn't wave back. It's the rain hat and cape, I thought. He doesn't recognise me.

'It's Cait,' I shouted. 'Cait McCann.'

He still didn't make any acknowledgement. He just stood there, a distant green statue in the rain. It was then I started thinking that perhaps I was making a huge mistake, that I was making a fool of myself. I mean, what was I *thinking*? Why on earth would he want to talk to *me*? What was I to him? I was nobody, just some stupid girl he met on the beach, another dumb islander. I was no better than the rest of them ... hell, he probably didn't even remember me.

But then I saw him smile, and he raised his hand and beckoned me over.

As I made my way across the Point I could hear a tiny voice whispering in the back of my mind. *Is this what it's supposed to be like? Is this how it's supposed to feel? Like a roller-coaster? Like a lifetime's emotions squeezed into a single minute? Like heaven and hell, sweet and sour, light and dark ...? Like losing your mind?*

I was having a bit of trouble walking. My feet seemed to have doubled in size and I kept stumbling in the shingle. Deefer, though, was prancing about like a puppy. He ran up to Lucas and stopped in front of him, then shook himself so hard he almost fell over.

'Hey, dog,' Lucas said.

Deefer rolled his eyes like a love-struck sap, then shook himself again and sat down. Lucas rested a hand on his head and the two of them watched me as I blundered up the beach.

'That's a nice cape,' Lucas said as I stopped in front of him.

'It's not a cape,' I panted. 'It's an all-weather poncho.'

He smiled. 'It's very yellow.'

'There's nothing wrong with yellow.'

'That's true,' he agreed.

Water dripped from his rain-darkened hair and his clothes were heavy with moisture. The sodden cloth clung to the shape of his body. As he gazed quietly at me, I rubbed some non-existent sand from my eyes and looked around. The rain was splattering down on the mud flats behind him, making a dull popping sound in the soft black ooze and filling the air with a faint whiff of decay. Beyond the mud flats, the woods were shrouded in a gloom of mist.

It ought to have felt odd, I suppose. Standing on a deserted beach in the rain, dressed in a rain hat and a ridiculous yellow cape, talking casually to a strange young boy who was soaked to the skin – but it didn't. It didn't feel odd, at all. In fact, it felt pretty good. I didn't understand any of it, and I wasn't sure why it felt good, but that didn't seem to matter.

But then, just as I was starting to enjoy the feeling, the rollercoaster roared and I remembered what I was supposed to be doing here – the little girl, her mad mother, the crowd – and the good feeling died.

'I saw what happened at the cliffs,' I started to explain. 'I was there with my dad. We saw the whole thing. It was terrible ... I don't mean what you did, that was fantastic, but what happened afterwards with that woman—'

'Come on,' Lucas said. 'Let's get out of this rain.'

'My dad said he's going to sort it out—'

'We can talk about it later. Right now I need to get into some dry clothes.'

'Oh ... yes, of course.' I looked around. 'Where—'

'Follow me,' he said.

He turned towards the mud flats.

Maybe it's because I don't have a mother, or maybe it's just because I'm a bit of wimp, but I don't like doing things that I know would upset Dad. It's not that I'm afraid of him finding out and punishing me, because I know he wouldn't punish me. He never has. He doesn't need to. His disappointment is punishment enough. And if that sounds too good to be true, well that's tough. That's just the way it is.

When I'm doing something I know I shouldn't be doing, I feel sick inside.

And that's how I felt as I followed Lucas to the mud flats. My stomach was fluttering, my heart was beating like a drum, and Dad's voice was echoing in my head. *You're not going there ... don't let me down, Cait. I'm putting more faith in you than I can afford to lose ... don't let me down ...*

I didn't want to let him down, he didn't deserve to be let down. But sometimes a higher power takes control, something that lies deep within you, beyond your conscious self, and you find yourself doing things you'd never normally do. You can make all the excuses you want – I didn't say I *wouldn't* go to the woods, I didn't *promise* anything, did I? – but you know in your heart you're just kidding yourself. It's wrong, but you're doing it anyway.

So just do it.

We stopped at the edge of the mud flats. I'd never been so close to them before and my senses were stirred by their morbid beauty. The smell of decay was stronger now. It was the odour of stagnant ponds, the sour smell of age-old blackened mud. The rain had stopped and a pale sun was fighting through the clouds. The shifting ooze of the flats lay stretched out before us, all the way across to the woods, a slimy brown plateau glistening dully in the tired light. Faint bubbling noises drifted from the surface. Drips, clicks, and watery pops, the sound of worms and molluscs going about their muddy business, just as they had for millions of years. This is how it must have been, I thought. Nothing to remember or want. Light. Darkness. No words to think. No tomorrow. No names, no history ...

'You'll need to take your shoes and socks off,' Lucas said.

I started untying my laces.

'I'll go first,' he explained, taking off his boots. 'You follow in my footsteps.' He looked at me. 'You follow them precisely, OK? Not an inch either side.'

I nodded, glancing doubtfully across the mud.

'Don't look so worried,' he said. 'It's a piece of cake.'

'But how do you know where you're going?'

He cocked his head to one side. 'It's easy, you can see the solid ground. Look.' He waved his hand, indicating a non-existent trail. 'See how it colours the air?'

All I could see was mud. I angled my head to one side like Lucas, but I still couldn't see anything. I thought of the invisible tunnel on the beach, trying to recall how I'd managed to see it, but I couldn't remember what it looked like any more. I couldn't remember it at all.

'What about Deefer?' I asked.

Lucas hung his boots around his neck. 'He's a dog,' he shrugged. 'Dogs see what they need to see. Are you ready?'

I stuffed my shoes and socks in my pockets, took a final look at the mud, then nodded.

And off we went.

It felt like stepping off the edge of a cliff.

After the first few tentative steps I started breathing again. It wasn't so bad. The surface mud was slick and oily, and I didn't like the way it oozed between my toes and sucked at my feet, but the ground underneath felt safe enough. It still didn't *look* very safe. It looked like I was walking across the surface of a thick brown soup. But the further I went without sinking, the easier it was to ignore what my eyes were telling me and listen instead to my feet. My feet were saying – this is OK. It's not the greatest feeling in the world ... but it's OK.

Lucas walked slowly, carefully planting one foot in front of the other, leaving nice clear footprints for me to follow. As soon as he lifted his feet, the prints filled with grainy black water. The water was cold, like cold grease.

'Are you all right?' he asked.

'Fine,' I said, trying to sound relaxed.

'Tell me if I'm going too fast.'

'Yeah, no problem ...'

Every now and then he'd stop, study the ground, then veer off to the left or the right. Each time we changed direction he glanced over his shoulder and spoke a few words.

'Turning left, now.'

'Right here for about ten paces.'

'Sharp left in a minute ...'

Deefer trotted along beside him. Once in a while Lucas would touch him lightly on the head or whisper a quiet word and Deefer would drop back and follow in single file for a few metres. Then, as the hidden trail widened again, he'd catch up and resume his position at Lucas's side.

By the time we were halfway across I felt confident enough to keep moving without staring at the ground. As long as I followed Lucas I knew I'd be all right. I raised my head and looked around. To the right, the open sea was calming itself after the storm. Murky brown waves lapped wearily against the shore, while further out the ocean rolled drunkenly against the sky, and rain shadows slanted down from dark clouds on the horizon. The shallow bay to our left had flooded its banks. I could see water filling the muddy trails through the gorse. The water would drain into the tide pools and soon the paths would be clear again, but not soon enough for me. I wouldn't be going home that way today.

Ahead of us the woods were becoming clearer. Clearer, but darker. The tangled thickets were black with rain and the trees were twisted into brooding shapes that seemed to defy the laws of nature. Loops and bowls fringed with hanging roots, jutting limbs, buckled trunks, strange spirals where branches had joined together like coiled snakes ...

'Have you seen this?'

Lucas had stopped by the remains of an old wooden boat. There wasn't much left of it – half a dozen blackened joists sticking up through the mud, thin slivers of rotted planking, one or two curls of rusted metal.

'It's an oyster boat,' I told him. 'They used to fish for

oysters all around here, across the bay, round the Point—'

'Oysters?'

I nodded. 'They're all gone now.'

'What happened to them?'

'Fished out, I suppose. Like everything else. One or two of the old boys still go out now and then, but these days there's barely enough to fill a basket. It's sad, really.'

'Why?'

I looked at him. 'Well ... it's not right, is it?'

'We've got to eat.'

'But we don't have to strip every single oyster from the sea, do we? If people hadn't been so greedy there'd still be some left.'

He picked a shard of damp wood from the wrecked boat and crumbled it in his fingers. 'Left for who?'

'What?'

'Who would they be left *for*?'

'Well ... for others, for us, for themselves ... I don't know. You know what I mean.'

He wiped his hands on his shirt. 'What do you think happened to the men in this boat?'

'Drowned, I suppose.'

He nodded thoughtfully, gazing past the wreck into the depths of mud. 'They'll all be down there, won't they?' he said quietly. 'The fishermen, the oysters ... they'll all be the same now ...' His words trailed off as he stared blindly into the mud, and just for a moment everything was silent. The air was still. Nothing moved. No birds, no wind, no waves. I looked at Lucas. I saw his skin, his clothes, his hair, his body, his pale blue eyes, his sad smile, his fleeting presence ... and then the air started moving again. A quiet wind whistled across the flats, feathering the pools of surface water, revealing countless tiny seashells dotted in the mud.

Pink and white, like tiny painted fingernails, they glimmered in the afternoon light.

I shivered.

It was suddenly getting cold.

Lucas snapped out of his trance. 'Come on, let's get out of here.'

'You first,' I said.

'You're all right, it's safe all the way from here. Look.' He pointed at Deefer who was running around in the mud shaking a clump of seaweed in his mouth. 'It's solid ground all the way.'

I looked towards the woods. We were closer than I thought. Twenty metres away the mud merged into a narrow beach of dark scrubby sand, and beyond that lay a line of stunted trees, waving us on with their misformed fingers.

'Don't worry,' Lucas grinned. 'It's nicer than it looks.'

It'd better be, I thought, as we slopped across the mud. I was beginning to get a bit fed up with the cold and the wet and the confusion of it all. I could do with a bit of nice.

I realise it was a foolish thing to do. Following someone I hardly knew into the midst of an isolated wood, on my own, with no way out, and with no one knowing where I was ... God, it was unbelievably stupid. It was just asking for trouble. I can see that now. But at the time it seemed fine. And it was fine. No, it was more than fine, it was wonderful. Apart from that odd little incident at the boat when Lucas seemed to go into a trance for a while, I'd never felt more relaxed in my life. And this was after a day of being spat at, humiliated, terrified, angered, soaked, frozen, and rollercoastered.

Yes, it was a foolish thing to do. But we all have to be fools every so often, don't we?

* * *

Rain dripped softly from the trees as I followed Lucas along a sun-dappled path through the woods. Although the air and the surrounding vegetation was steeped in moisture, the ground was remarkably dry. It was soft and springy, covered with a carpet of waxy leaves, and it gave off a sweet smell of rich, dark earth. The air was humid and still. Close up, the trees weren't as weird as they'd first seemed – but they were still fairly odd. I'm pretty good with trees, I know most of the familiar species, but these were new to me. Some were short and squat, with stunted branches growing directly from the trunk, while others were whip-like and twisted, or pale and bare, as if their bark had been stripped by some ravenous beast.

We walked in single file along the narrow path. Lucas led the way, walking with the quiet confidence of someone who knows exactly where they're going. Deefer ran around sniffing everything in sight, and I just plodded along behind in awed silence. I'd never been in such a strangely beautiful place. It was so quiet, so still. It felt like the loneliest place in the world.

Through the tangled undergrowth I caught occasional glimpses of the inlet on the other side of the woods. Against the darkness of the dense vegetation, the blue of the estuary shone like sapphire. I remembered Bill telling me how she'd spied on Lucas from a boat out there ... *we were drifting along with the engine off when Lee spots this naked guy in a pool at the edge of the woods ... it was him, the gyppo. Having a bath ...* I put the memory from my mind. I was here now. I was *here*. I didn't want to think about Bill and the others, that was out *there*. I didn't want to think about out there.

Ahead of me, Lucas stopped beside a slender tree with a fringe of hanging branches. It looked a bit like a weeping willow, only darker, and heavier, with broad leaves and odd little woody nodules spaced along the length of each limb. Lucas pulled aside the curtain of branches to reveal a small crescent-shaped clearing bathed in pale sunlight.

'After you,' he said.

I looked at him for a moment then stepped through into the clearing. It was a sheltered glade about the size of a small front garden, hemmed in by rhododendron bushes and raggedy clumps of trees, and spread with a carpet of bright green mossy grass. The grass looked as if no one had ever walked upon it. At the edge of the clearing a freshwater stream flowed gently over a bed of pale pebbles. I moved further in, walking gently, enjoying the softness of the mossy grass beneath my bare feet. The damp moss was jewelled with tiny blue flowers and pearls of rain.

Immediately to my right a length of khaki blanket was draped between the branches of two trees, the trees about three metres apart. Coils of twine and lengths of reed were hanging on a line suspended between another two branches, and an assortment of fishing poles and sharpened sticks were propped against one of the trees.

As I stood there taking it all in, Lucas stepped around me and pulled back the blanket to reveal a cosy little shelter cut into the heart of the trees. It was roofed with plastic sheeting interlaced with branches, and walled with a mixture of mud and reeds. I stepped closer and looked inside. At the front of the shelter I could see the remains of a fire on a blackened slab of rock. There was a tree stump for sitting on, and at the back I could see a bed of ferns.

'It's wonderful,' I said.

Lucas went in and fumbled around in a black bin liner, fishing out some dry clothes. They looked exactly the same as the clothes he was already wearing – only drier, of course.

He smiled awkwardly at me and gestured at the den. 'Make yourself comfortable, I'll be back in a minute.' He disappeared around the back of the shelter to get changed.

I sat down on the tree stump and gazed around the interior of the den. It was quite dark, but not gloomy, like the inside of a tent. The air smelled pleasantly of damp vegetation. I imagined Lucas sitting in here, all snug and warm, with the rain ticking on the plastic sheeting, a wood fire smouldering, the smell of the smoke drifting in the rain ... and I was reminded of a book I'd read when I was a kid – *My Side of the Mountain* by Jean George. It's the story of a young boy called Sam Gribley who runs away from his New York home to live in the burnt-out trunk of a hemlock tree in the Catskill Mountains. He learns to live off the land, eating berries and roots, trapping deer and rabbits ... he even tames a young falcon to help him hunt. There's a scene in the book where Sam's sitting inside his hemlock tree in the middle of the forest on a cold winter's night. It's snowing. It's quiet. He's lonely. He looks at the falcon on its perch, preening and wiping its beak, and he wonders to himself – what makes a bird a bird, and a boy a boy?

I always liked that bit. *What makes a bird a bird, and a boy a boy?*

I can't remember how the story ends ...

Yes, I can.

The boy's loneliness gets the better of him and he leaves the forest and goes back to live with his family in New York.

I never liked that ending.

As my eyes adjusted to the dim light of the shelter, I

began to notice more detail: a small pile of tattered books in the corner; a candle stub in an empty crab shell; bunches of dried herbs; a notebook and pen by the bed; and on the wall, a faded photograph in a small wooden frame. I got up to take a closer look. It was a picture of a pretty young woman sitting cross-legged on the floor of a sparsely furnished room. She was slim, about twenty years old, with spiky blonde hair, sad eyes, and pale red lips. She was wearing a plain white cotton dress strung with bits of ribbon and leather and beads, and blood-red Doc Marten boots. The smile on her face was remote.

I heard footsteps outside and turned away from the wall. Lucas came in with Deefer trailing along behind him. He'd changed into fresh clothes and scrubbed his hair dry. He glanced at the photo on the wall, then at me.

'She's pretty,' I said. 'Is she your girlfriend?'

He laughed. 'Not exactly, no.'

He knelt down by the blackened rock at the front of the shelter and started making a fire. His hands moved quickly, gathering up kindling from a pile by the wall, then adding small sticks and logs to form a neat little wigwam on the rock. As he worked I noticed a whitened scar on the inside of his left wrist – a faint puckered line, the size and shape of a shallow smile. It looked old. It looked part of him.

'It's my mother,' he explained, nodding at the photo on the wall. 'That was taken about fifteen years ago.' He struck his lighter and touched the flame to the base of the fire. A wisp of smoke emerged, the kindling crackled, and pale flames began licking at the twigs. Lucas watched the flames for a while, making sure they caught, then pocketed his lighter and stood up. He looked at the photo again. His face was expressionless. I looked at the picture of the young woman. I could see the resemblance now. The inner sadness, the remoteness, the quality of being somewhere else ...

'Where is she now?' I asked.

'I don't know,' he replied, looking away. 'I think she's probably dead.'

'Don't you know?'

He shook his head. 'I never knew her. When I was born she couldn't look after me ... she had a lot of personal problems. She wasn't well.' He ran his fingers through his hair and looked at me. 'Are you all right? I've got a jumper somewhere if you're still cold—'

'No, I'm fine.'

I wanted to ask him more about his mother, but I didn't know where to start. Instead, I took off my hat and cape and warmed myself at the fire. It was burning nicely now. The smoke drifted upwards and disappeared through a flap in the roof, leaving behind a sweet smell of wood ash.

'My mother's dead,' I told him, surprising myself. 'She died when I was five.'

Lucas nodded. 'That must have been hard.'

'Not really. Not for me, anyway. I was too young to understand. I can't remember very much about it. I just remember her not being there ... one day she was there, the next day she was gone. I suppose when you're five years old it's easier to accept the things you don't understand. You're used to it. You don't understand most things. It was incredibly hard for Dad, though ... he's never really got over it. I think he still blames himself.'

'What happened?'

I sat down. 'They were coming back from a party in London to celebrate the publication of his first book. It was late at night and the roads were icy. Dad had been drinking, so Mum was driving ... I've never had the guts to ask if she was drunk, too, but from what I know of her, I think she probably was. She liked a drink as much as Dad.' I looked down at the floor. I could feel the sting of tears in my eyes. I'd never told anyone about this before, and I didn't know why I was telling it now. I took a deep breath and carried on. 'There's a lonely stretch of road about three miles from the island that cuts through a forest on a hill. You probably walked past it if you came here from Moulton.'

Lucas nodded. 'A pine forest?'

'That's it. There's a sharp corner at the bottom of the hill ... they must have been going too fast or something, or maybe they hit a patch of black ice ... nobody really knows ... anyway, they lost control and went off the road, flew over a bank and smashed into a brick wall. Mum died instantly.'

'What about your dad?'

'Well, he's never really talked about it, but my brother told me that because of the bad weather and the remoteness of the location, no one called an ambulance until about an hour after the crash. A passing motorist just happened to stop for a wee or something. He saw the wreck of the car and dialled 999. When the ambulance finally arrived Dad was still sitting in the passenger seat holding Mum's hand. His head was all cut to pieces and the blood had dried on his skin. When one of the paramedics asked if he was all right, Dad just looked at him and said, "I've killed her. God help me, I've killed her."'

The fire crackled and a glowing ember spat from the flames. Lucas nudged it back with his foot.

He said, 'It's always hard to lose somebody. It leaves a hole in your heart that never grows back.'

I couldn't speak for a while. Deefer was lying on the ground beside me and I busied myself stroking the heavy grey hairs on his head. They were wet and glossy, the texture of fine wire. As I preened him, his eyes gradually closed. I felt a little dozy myself.

'Do you want something to eat?' Lucas asked after a while.

'I can't really stay long—'

'It won't take a minute.'

Before I could say anything else he'd fished out a couple of battered old pans and was fixing them up over the fire on a contraption of wires and sticks. A tied leather bag appeared from somewhere, a wooden spoon, the canteen of drinking water, and he was away, cooking up a meal of secret goodies. As I watched him I thought of all the questions I'd wanted to ask, but just then they didn't seem to matter. They had no relevance to anything. The only things that mattered were the simple things – heat, cold, wind, rain, food – and even they didn't seem to matter *that* much. As long as the world kept turning we'd be all right.

'Your brother,' said Lucas, stirring his pots. 'Is he the one with the dyed blond hair?'

'Yes,' I said. 'How do you know? Have you met him?'

'No, I've seen him around, that's all. I thought he looked something like you.'

'Thanks a lot.'

'No, I didn't mean he looked *like* you ... you know what I mean.'

'Yeah, well ... just as long as you don't think I'm anything like *him*.'

'Why? Don't you get on?'

'Not at the moment, no.'

'Why not?'

'It's a long story.'

He adjusted something on the fire, then sat to one side and rolled a cigarette. He took his time, concentrating on the tobacco and paper, getting it shaped just right, and then he placed it in his mouth, plucked a taper from the fire, and lit it.

'This long story,' he said, blowing out smoke. 'It wouldn't have anything to do with that muscle man at the cliffs, would it?'

'Muscle man?'

'The well-bred hunk with the broad shoulders—'

'Jamie Tait?' I said, shocked.

He grinned. 'That sounds about right.'

'What do you know about him?'

'Not much. I've seen him on the beach a couple of times—'

'When?'

'Late at night, mostly, hanging around with the rest of them.'

'Who?'

He shrugged. 'The rich girlfriend, the stone-thrower and his sister, your brother, a bunch of others – bikers, young girls, hangers-on ...' He looked at me. 'It's none of my business, Cait, but they're not the nicest people in the world.'

'I know.'

'They've got spite in their blood, especially Tait and his girlfriend. They're sick with it.' He looked at me. 'The blonde girl I asked you about before, the faceless one—'

'Angel?'

He nodded, gazing deep into the fire. 'She's looking for things she shouldn't be looking for ... not with them.

They'll take her down, Cait. They'll bury her. And they'll take your brother down, too, if he's not careful.'

I looked at him. 'What do they do on the beach at night?'

He looked back at me, tapping ash from his cigarette. 'They ruin each other.'

It was a strange way of putting it – kind of old-fashioned, especially for a young boy – but somehow it sounded just right.

'How do you know all this?' I asked.

He just shrugged.

'I don't know what Dominic's playing at,' I said. 'Hanging around with people like that ... it's like he's suddenly become a different person. You're sure it was him?'

'Cropped blond hair, brown eyes, medium height ...'

I shook my head and sighed. 'He's so *stupid*.'

Lucas just shrugged again. 'We all do stupid things now and then.'

Yeah, I thought, it must run in the family. First Lucas sees *me* with a gang of morons, and now he's having to warn me about *Dominic's* unsavoury friends. He must think we're dysfunctional or something.

Lucas put out his cigarette and smiled at me. 'I shouldn't worry about it too much. I'm sure your brother's got enough sense to keep out of trouble. He'll probably get fed up with them sooner or later, anyway. In the meantime, I'll keep an eye on things. If anything starts getting out of hand, I'll sort it out.'

'How?'

'I don't know,' he smiled. 'I'll think of something.' He got up and went over to the fire to check on the food.

I said, 'Why are you doing this?'

'What – cooking?'

'No – I mean, why should you want to help my brother? What's he ever done for you?'

'Nothing, as far as I know.'

'So why help him?'

'Why did you help me at the bridge when the others were throwing stones at me? What have I ever done for you?'

'Well, nothing ... but—'

'Just a minute.' He spooned some meat from the pan, blew on it, then popped a piece in his mouth and chewed. 'I think this is just about ready.'

I looked at him.

'Are you hungry?' he asked.

I nodded.

He smiled. 'OK. So let's eat.'

Over a surprisingly tasty meal of crab, boiled potatoes, stale crackers and black tea, we finally got round to discussing what happened at the raft race.

'I was on the cliff with Dad and Deefer,' I told him. 'We saw the whole thing. It was incredible.'

Lucas didn't say anything, just nodded slowly and concentrated on his food. There was only one plate, a battered old tin thing that Lucas had insisted on giving to me, so he was eating straight from the pan. He picked out a chunk of meat and gave it to Deefer, who took it with uncharacteristic grace.

'It was a good job you were there,' I said. 'If it hadn't been for you, that little girl would have drowned. No one else was going to do anything. I couldn't believe it. I don't know what was the matter with them.'

'It's just one of those days.'

'What?'

'Sometimes you get a day when all the lights go out, and everyone you meet is cold and bitter. They don't care about anything. Today's been one of those days. Didn't you feel it?'

I thought of Tait and Sara Toms and Lee Brendell at the sea wall ... the dirty looks, the mocking laughter ... but then, I thought, they're *always* cold and bitter. I knew what he meant, though. There'd been a sour taste to the air all day.

'What about you?' I asked. 'How come *your* lights weren't out?'

'They were – that's why the lady thought I was harming her daughter.'

'But you *weren't*.'

He shrugged. 'She was only doing what she thought right.'

'Well, anyway, Dad's going to have a word with her. That's why I came after you, to let you know it's going to be all right. He's going to explain what happened – in fact, he'll have already done it by now. So there's nothing to worry about. She won't be calling the police or anything.'

'Thanks, that's kind of you. Tell your dad I appreciate it.' He sipped tea from a tin mug and gazed out at the glade. The sun was out now. Pale light was filtering through the trees casting rippled shadows across the grass, and small birds were twittering in the sunlit bushes. The darkness of the day seemed to be lifting. But not for Lucas. From the look on his face, he didn't seem to share my opinion that everything was going to be all right.

'I'm sure it'll be fine,' I said, trying to reassure him.

'I'm sorry,' he said, turning to face me. 'Please don't think I'm being ungrateful, it's just that these things have a tendency to stick, whatever happens.' He wiped his mouth with his hand. 'No matter what your dad says, the police are still going to want to talk to me. They've already been sniffing around.'

'Why? You haven't done anything.'

He smiled knowingly. 'People don't like it when they don't know what you are. They don't like things that don't fit. It frightens them. They'd rather have a monster they know than a mystery they don't. In a place like this, the fear takes hold and spreads. It feeds on itself. Pretty soon the police are going to start asking me lots of questions, and then the rumours will start—'

'But Dad and I can tell everyone what happened—'

'It won't make any difference. I've been here before. I know how it works.' He started clearing away the pans. 'That's why it's always best to keep moving.'

'What do you mean? Are you leaving?'

'Not immediately. But it's going to start getting uncomfortable in a few days—'

'It might not.'

'It will, believe me.'

'But what about Dominic? You said you'd keep an eye on him—'

'I will.'

'For how long?'

'As long as it takes – a day or two, maybe a bit longer. Look, I'll make sure he's all right – don't worry about it.'

I wasn't worried about it – not just then, anyway. For all I cared, Dominic could go to hell. I just didn't want Lucas to go. But what could I say? I couldn't tell him how I felt. I couldn't *beg* him to stay, could I? He'd think I was an idiot.

'Why don't you stay until next Saturday?' I suggested.

'What's next Saturday?'

'The Summer Festival ... it's really good. Stalls, bric-à-brac, music ...' I paused, looking at the smile on his face. 'What?'

'It sounds quite similar to the regatta.'

'No, no, it's a lot better than the regatta. Honestly, you'd enjoy it.'

'Is there a raft race?'

'No, definitely not. No races. I'm running the RSPCA stall – well, I'm not actually *running* it, but I'll be there. You could come and say hello ...' I hesitated. 'I mean, if you're still here ... I could show you around, if you wanted ...'

He smiled again. 'Will you buy me an ice cream?'

'I might.'

'It's tempting ...'

'I think it'd be nice. You could meet my dad.'

'I'd like that.'

'So, you'll think about it?'

'I'll think about it.'

He got up and piled the pans and things outside the shelter, then he wiped his hands in the moist grass and dried them on his trousers. I went outside and joined him. Although I felt embarrassed by my behaviour, I was glad that I'd made the effort to persuade him to stay until Saturday. I would have felt worse than embarrassed if I hadn't. Lucas seemed happier, too. The troubled look had faded from his eyes.

As we stood in the warming sunlight watching Deefer jumping around in the stream, with the birds singing in the background and the smell of wood smoke drifting in a light breeze, I would have done almost anything to freeze the moment for ever. It was so quiet and peaceful, so simple, so serene.

I turned to see Lucas looking at me. His eyes shone with a savage sweet clarity that took my breath away.

'Where will you go?' I asked him.

'I don't know ... along the south coast, probably. There's some nice places in Dorset and Devon. I've always wanted to take a look at the moors.' He smiled. 'I'll send you a postcard.'

We stood there for a while longer, neither of us knowing what to say. Part of me wished I knew what he was thinking, but another part – the more astute part – was glad that I didn't. Sometimes it's best to rely on your imagination. Facts can let you down, but your mind will always look after you.

'I'd better get going,' I said eventually. 'Dad'll be waiting for me.'

'What are you going to tell him?' Lucas asked.

'About what?'

'Me.'

His honesty shocked me for a moment. It was the kind of question people *want* to ask but rarely do.

'I'll just tell him the truth,' I said.

Lucas looked at me and nodded. 'One day you will.'

I wasn't quite sure what he meant, if he meant anything at all ... but I didn't dwell on it.

I went back into the shelter to get my hat and coat. On the way out I noticed a row of small wooden figures lodged in the reeds of the wall above Lucas's bed. I knelt down for a closer look. They were crude, but remarkably beautiful, carvings of animals. No bigger than a finger, and carved out of driftwood, there were about a dozen of them. Dogs, fish, birds, a seal, cows, a horse ... there was only minimal detail in the carving, but each little animal had a character that stood out a mile. Beside the figures, hanging by a leather strap on the wall, was a bone-handled knife with a seven-inch blade. The blade was heavy and broad at the base, tapering to a razor-sharp point. It was hard to believe those wonderful little figures could be fashioned with such a deadly-looking tool.

Without thinking I reached across and picked out one of the figures, a familiar-looking dog.

'What do you think?'

The sound of Lucas's voice startled me and I jerked round, fumbling the little figure in my fingers. 'Oh ... I'm sorry – I was just looking—'

'It's all right,' he said, smiling. 'What do you think? Have I captured his soul?'

I looked at the carving in my hand. Of course – it was Deefer. It *was* Deefer. The look on his face, his head, the way he held his tail, everything. A miniature wooden Deefer.

I laughed. 'It's perfect ... it's *just* like him. How did you do it?'

'I just found a bit of wood and cut away all the bits that weren't Deefer.'

I nodded vaguely, not sure if he was joking or not.

'You can keep it, if you like,' he said.

'Are you sure?'

'He's your dog.'

'Thank you,' I said, rubbing my thumb over the carving. It felt smooth and warm, almost alive. I stood there for a moment, trying to think of something else to say, but I couldn't find the words to express myself. So I just thanked him again and slipped the carving in my pocket. 'I really do have to go, now. Dad's going to start worrying if I don't get back soon.'

'I'm ready when you are,' Lucas said.

With a final glance around, I put my hat on, slung my cape over my shoulder, and followed him out of the woods.

* * *

If I'd known then that I'd never see the shelter or the glade again, I might have taken a little more time. I might have allowed myself a longer goodbye, soaking up every little detail until the memory was firmly lodged in my mind for ever. The soft babble of the stream, the rhododendrons and the sun-dappled trees, that unforgettable lawn of jewels ...

But that's not how it works, is it? And maybe it's better that way. Because some things are never meant to be anything more than a moment. And that was one of them.

seven

Dad was waiting in the kitchen when I got back. He was sitting at the table with a glass of whiskey and a cigarette, reading a dog-eared copy of *Ulysses*.

'Did you catch him?' he asked casually as I wandered in.

My heart was beating fast as I quickly explained how I'd caught up with Lucas at the Point, that we'd had a chat, and that he'd asked me to pass on his thanks. Then, before Dad had a chance to interrogate me, I asked him how it had gone with the woman at the cliffs.

'Not too well, I'm afraid. Her name's Ellen Coombe. She's one of those people who can't see the truth even when it's poking them in the eyes. I *told* her what happened, but she just wouldn't listen. She wouldn't even listen to her own damn child.'

'How is she – the little girl?'

'A bit shaken up, but she's all right. Her name's Kylie.' He stubbed out his cigarette. 'She kept telling her mum – *he saved me, the boy saved me* – but her mum didn't want to know. I don't think she cared, to be honest. She never asked the kid if she was all right or anything, she even yelled at her when she started blaming someone called Derek. I think he was the one in charge of the raft. Poor bloody kid ... all that woman seems to care about is making trouble.'

'Will she call the police, do you think?'

Dad nodded. 'I've already spoken to Lenny about it. I rang him up and explained everything. I told him we're willing to make a statement. He said he'll get it sorted out, it shouldn't be a problem.'

Lenny Craine is the local police sergeant. He's been a sergeant on the island for as long as anyone can remember. He was here when Mum and Dad first arrived, and he's about the closest thing to a friend Dad has on the island. He helped out a lot after Mum died ... mostly by keeping Dad out of trouble. The two of them meet up occasionally for a quiet drink or two, or maybe three, and now and then they go out fishing together. At least that's what they call it. As far as I can tell, all they do is sit in a boat all day drinking beer.

'What about the others?' I said.

'What others?'

'The other witnesses. Will Lenny have to take statements from them?'

'I don't know. I suppose it depends on Mrs Coombe, whether she wants to press charges or not.'

'Press *charges*?'

'Hey, don't worry. It'll be all right. Lenny's a good man, he'll keep things under control.'

I shook my head. Lucas was right, I could sense the rumours starting already.

'Anyway,' Dad said, swallowing a mouthful of whisky, 'let's get back to you and this Wonder Boy.'

'He's just a *boy*, Dad ...'

He smiled thoughtfully. 'Tell me about him.'

'What do you want to know?'

'Where's he from?'

'I don't know.'

'How old is he?'

'Fifteen or sixteen, I think.'

'What's he doing on the island?'

'I don't know ... nothing, really. He does a bit of work now and then ... he's just passing through.'

'A drifter?'

'I suppose.'

'An honest-to-goodness tramp?'

'He's not a *tramp*. He's clean, he's intelligent—'

'Did I say there was anything wrong with tramps? I *like* tramps.'

'Well, he's not a tramp.'

'So what is he?'

I sighed. 'He's just a person.'

'All right, fair enough.' He lit a cigarette, eyeing me through the smoke. 'And what do you think of this person?'

'He's interesting.'

'In what way?'

'I don't know – he just is. Look—' I dug the carving from my pocket and passed it over. 'He did that.'

Dad studied the figure carefully, looking at it from different angles, rubbing his thumb over the surface, just as I had. After a while he said, 'Is this who I think it is?'

I nodded. 'It's good, isn't it?'

'Very good ... very good, indeed.' He passed it back. 'Lucas just happened to have it with him, did he?'

'Well – yes.'

'I see.'

'He's read your books—'

'Don't change the subject.'

'What? I'm not ... I was just telling you—'

'There's no need to fret. I'm only doing my father bit. I am your father, you know. I'm supposed to ask awkward questions – it's part of the job.'

'I'm not fretting.'

'You could have fooled me.'

'Well, all these questions – it's embarrassing.'

'It's meant to be. Now – let me get this straight. You're telling me that you spent the last—' he looked at his watch '—the last three hours standing around on the beach talking to Lucas?'

'We were sitting down.'

'For three hours?'

I shrugged. 'We were talking.'

He looked at me for a long time. It wasn't a threatening look, it wasn't even a questioning look, it was a look that said – *this is us, this is me and you, this is all we've got. You don't have to lie to me.*

I didn't like lying to him, I hated myself for it. But I didn't seem to have any choice. And besides, I could hear the echo of Lucas's voice in my head:

What are you going to tell him?

About what?

Me.

I'll just tell him the truth.

One day you will ...

I didn't know what he'd meant at the time, but I think I do now. I think he meant this – this story. This is my 'one day'. This is my truth. I think I knew, even then, that it would always come out, and that when it did Dad would understand. And I think he knew it, too.

'OK,' he said, with a smile. 'I won't embarrass you any more.' He drained the whiskey from his glass. 'Just be careful, Cait. All right? Please, be very careful.'

I nodded. My throat was too tight to speak.

Dad got up and rinsed his glass in the sink. With his

back to me, he said, 'There's plenty of hot water if you want a bath.'

'I had a bath this morning.'

'Your hair didn't smell of wood smoke this morning.'

The next day I finally got hold of Simon on the phone and apologised for missing him on Friday. He seemed all right about it, although I sensed a slightly wary tone to his voice. That wasn't surprising, really. I'd let him down, I'd humiliated him, he had a right to be wary.

We talked about this and that for a while, mostly RSPCA stuff. I did my best to sound interested, but Simon isn't the most gripping of story-tellers, and as he mumbled on about the latest developments with the oil-tankers and the caravan park, my mind drifted back to what Lucas had said when I'd told him that if people hadn't been so greedy there'd still be some oysters left. *Left for who?* he'd asked. I'd thought it was a flippant remark at the time, but now I wasn't so sure. Those three little words had set me thinking, and I was beginning to ask myself questions that I'd never even thought of before: who *are* we trying to save the planet for? for ourselves? for our children? for our children's children? isn't that unbelievably selfish? self-important? self-gratifying? and if we're *not* trying to save the planet for our own sake, then what *are* we doing? what right do we have to decide the fate of any given thing? who are we to say that a whale has more value than a mosquito? a gorilla more importance than a fly? a panda more worth than a rat? why *does* it matter if we strip every single oyster from the sea? they're all going to die anyway, aren't they? doesn't everything go round and round, never really changing ...?

They were just questions. I didn't have any answers.

Simon had heard about the incident at the cliffs. His dad had heard from someone at the pub – who'd heard from someone whose brother knew someone who'd actually *been* there – that young Kylie Coombe had dived from the raft in an effort to impress some boys on the beach.

'That's rubbish,' I said. 'She fell off the raft. I was there, Simon, I saw it happen. She slipped and fell, that's all.'

'What about this gypsy boy?'

'Oh, Christ! Not you, too?'

'What?'

'He's not a *gypsy*. Why does everyone think he's a gypsy? He's just a boy. And even if he *was* a gypsy ... I mean, so what? What's wrong with gypsies? They're not monsters, are they? God! What's the matter with people around here? It's like living with a bunch of damn hill-billies.'

The line was quiet.

'I didn't mean you,' I sighed. 'Simon?'

'I was only asking.'

'I know ... I'm sorry. It just annoys me when people make stupid assumptions about things they don't under-stand. What did you hear about Luc—' I stopped myself just in time. 'What did you hear about this boy? What are they saying about him?'

He hesitated. I think my outburst had frightened him a little. 'It depends who you listen to,' he said cautiously. 'According to some, Kylie was in trouble. The sea was a bit rough and she was heading for the rocks when the boy dived in and pulled her out.'

'And according to others?'

He lowered his voice. 'Ellen's saying that he was ... you know ... that he was messing around with her. She says she's got witnesses to back her up.'

'Who?'

'I don't know – I'm only telling you what I've heard.'

I took a deep breath, calming myself. 'Listen, Simon,' I said. 'You tell your dad, and anyone else who wants to know, that Ellen Coombe is a liar. I was there, I saw the whole thing. Kylie was drowning. While everyone else was standing around doing nothing, Lucas dived in and saved her. He didn't touch her, he didn't hurt her, he didn't do anything wrong. All right? He didn't do *anything* wrong.'

'OK,' he said defensively.

'Look, I'm not having a go at you or your dad. I know it's not your fault. I'm just telling you what happened.'

There was a short silence. Then Simon said, 'How do you know his name?'

'What?'

'You called him Lucas.'

'Did I?'

'Yes.'

Barely pausing to think, I said, 'Joe Rampton told me. Lucas did some work for him. That's what he said his name was ... Lucas ... Old Joe told me.'

'I see.'

He didn't sound too convinced – but, frankly, I wasn't that bothered. Why should I be? I had my own life to lead, didn't I? I didn't have to tell Simon everything. I mean, it wasn't as if he was my *boyfriend* or anything. And even if he was ... well, he wasn't. He was just a friend. If I didn't want him to know about Lucas ... well, so what?

The more you lie, the easier it gets.

The only trouble is, after a while you end up lying to yourself.

Anyway, I arranged to meet with Simon on Wednesday to finalise our arrangements for the festival. I didn't feel too enthusiastic about it, and I suppose – if I'm honest – I was just trying to make amends for letting him down on Friday. It was a bit awkward at first. I didn't know how he'd react if I suggested he come over here, but I didn't really want to meet him at his house, either. It was hard to find the right words. He wasn't much help, he just kept humming and ha-ing while I jabbered away like a fool. In the end I simply said, 'All right, I'll see you here at six. OK?'

'At your house?'

'Yes. Wednesday. Six o'clock.'

'Uh ... right, OK.'

'And don't worry,' I said, trying to make a joke of it. 'I'll be here. I promise. I'll be waiting at the door ... if I'm not ...' I tried to think of something funny to say, some hilarious forfeit I'd make if I broke my word. But I couldn't think of a damn thing. So I just said, 'I'll be here. Trust me.'

'OK,' he mumbled.

Afterwards I went upstairs and wrote *SIMON – WED @ 6* on a dozen large Post-it notes, and stuck the notes all around my room. On the walls, on the clock, on the ceiling above my bed, on the mirror, I even stuck one in my knicker drawer.

It was all very well trying to kid myself that I didn't care, that I wasn't bothered, that I had my own life to lead ... but I still had a conscience. My heart might not care, but my head knew better.

I spent the rest of the day sitting around in my room doing nothing – reading, thinking, staring out of the window – just waiting for the hours to pass. I didn't know what I was waiting for. I didn't really care.

The house had a strange feel to it. It felt cold and clammy, like a house that's been empty for a long time. Windows rattled in the wind. Floorboards creaked. The air sighed in the weary light. I lay on my bed and stared at the ceiling. I could hear the water tank dripping in the attic – *tack, tock, tock ... tack, tock, tock ... tack, tock, tock* – like a hesitant clock. It was a strangely hypnotic sound, and as I listened to it my mind drifted up through the ceiling and I imagined the draught of cold attic air and the smell of soot and old wood. In my mind I could see the dark beams and the scarred rafters and the light of the sky glinting through the cracked slate tiles. I could hear the rain ticking on the roof and birds scratching in the eaves ... and I was there. I was a child again, playing alone in my attic world. It was a world of dusty things hanging from beams: coils of rope, shapeless bags, old coats, cardboard boxes, bits of wood, rolls of carpet, tins of paint, broken suitcases, stacks of yellowed newspapers tied with string ... it was a world that was anything I wanted it to be. I could make a den out of an old piece of sheet draped over the beams and pretend I was marooned on a desert island, or lost in the woods ...

A door slammed downstairs, and the memory vanished.

I was back in my room again. I wasn't a child. I was fifteen years old. In less than a year I'd be old enough to get married and have a child of my own. The thought sent a shiver down my spine.

eight

Tuesday started off dull and cold, but as the day wore on the sun rose through a haze of mist and the overcast sky gradually blossomed into a glorious sheen of blue. By mid-afternoon the air was filled with a sweltering heat that turned your limbs to lead. It was almost too hot to move. Even the sea seemed to be suffering. It just lay there, barely stirring in the heat, too breathless to raise a breeze.

Dad and I drove into the village to pick up some groceries and a couple of magazines. We got the groceries from the village store. It's more expensive than Sainsbury's or Tesco's on the mainland, but Dad has a friendly arrangement with the man who runs the store – Shev Patel. Dad buys his groceries from Shev, and Shev keeps a supply of Irish whiskey for him. They both cheat, of course. Dad gets Rita Gray to buy him stuff from Sainsbury's whenever she goes, and Shev overcharges Dad for the whiskey. But neither of them seems to mind.

When we got back to the house there was a police car parked in the yard and Lenny Craine was sitting on the front step mopping his brow. He's a big man, with one of those big men's bellies that seem to start at the neck and continue down to the knees. He's scruffy, too. His tunic was undone, his shirt unbuttoned, and his face was glistening red. Dad parked the car and Lenny came over and helped us inside with the shopping.

In the kitchen, Dad got cold beers for himself and Lenny, and a Coke for me, and we all sat down at the table. Lenny had to pull the chair away from the table to make room for his belly. A slight groan escaped from his lips as he lowered himself into the chair, a mixture of tiredness and the strain of being overweight. He popped his beer, took a long drink, then wiped the froth from his mouth. He looked worn out. Dark circles ringed his eyes and his skin was sallow. His sparse hair had that lustreless look that comes from working too hard.

Dad was obviously of the same opinion. 'I hope you don't mind me saying, Len, but you look like crap.'

Lenny smiled. 'Thanks.' He sipped his beer and looked at me. 'And how are you, Caitlin? Still keeping your old dad on the straight and narrow?' His tone was cheery but I could sense the concern in his eyes. He really cared about Dad.

'I'm fine,' I said. 'Everything's fine.'

'Good,' he said. 'I hear Dom's back?'

'Not so you'd notice,' Dad said sourly.

He offered Lenny a cigarette.

Lenny shook his head and pulled some papers from his pocket. He laid them out on the table. 'I need to take your statements about what happened at the regatta.'

'Is Ellen Coombe still pressing charges?' Dad asked.

Lenny sighed. 'I don't think she knows *what* she's doing. One minute she's ranting and raving about having the boy locked up, the next she's complaining about police harassment. I think she just enjoys being in the limelight.'

'So why don't you tell her to get lost? You know it's all bullshit.'

Lenny looked hesitant. 'It's a bit more complicated than that.'

'What do you mean?'

Lenny stared at the table for a moment without answering. Eventually he said, 'Look, we have to be extremely careful with this kind of thing. You know what it's been like with all the recent media coverage. We have to make sure that every angle is covered, we have to be thorough.'

'So?' said Dad.

Lenny went on. 'I've talked to everyone who was on the cliffs that day, at least everyone who admits to being there. And I've also spoken at length with the boy.'

'You've interviewed Lucas?' I said.

Lenny nodded. 'I had to.'

'What did he say?'

He looked at me. 'How well do you know him?'

Suddenly, the room seemed very quiet. I could hear my heart beating. When I spoke I couldn't keep a tremor from my voice.

'I don't know him very well,' I said. 'I've met him on the beach a couple of times, that's all.'

Lenny nodded slowly. He looked at Dad. 'Mac?'

Dad shook his head. 'I've not had the pleasure.'

Lenny turned to me again. 'What do you think of him?'

I could feel myself blushing. 'I think ... well, I don't know ... I think he's nice. I know he wouldn't hurt anyone. He *didn't* hurt anyone.'

Lenny didn't say anything, he just looked at me. There was a strange look in his eye, a look that was almost fearful, but not quite. An odd mixture of curiosity, wariness, and uncertainty.

'Did he tell you anything about himself?' he asked me.

'Not really,' I said. 'What did he tell you?'

Lenny smiled. 'That's confidential, I'm afraid.'

'Ah, come on, Lenny,' Dad interrupted. 'This is *us*

you're talking to. You're not in the witness box now. Spill the beans, man.'

'I can't, John. It's not allowed.'

'And drinking on duty *is* allowed, is it?'

'That's different—'

Dad grinned. 'I'll tell you what – you tell us about the boy and we won't grass you up for drinking on duty. *And* I'll get you another cold one. How's that for a deal?'

Lenny smiled. 'You're an evil man, John McCann.'

''Tis an evil world, Lenny Craine,' Dad replied. 'Now, what about this boy?'

Lenny had gone looking for Lucas on the Sunday after the regatta. He hadn't known exactly where to find him, so he'd just set off along the beach with one of the island's two police constables, a young man called Pete Curtis. They'd heard that Lucas had done some work for Joe Rampton, and they'd also heard rumours about someone camping out in the woods, so their plan was to check along the beach, call in at Joe's, and then head on out to the Point. But they'd barely started walking when Pete Curtis nudged Lenny and said, 'Is that him?'

Lenny had looked up to see Lucas walking towards them along the beach.

'He didn't seem too bothered about anything,' Lenny told us. 'He just walked up with a smile on his face, held out his hand, and said, "My name's Lucas. I expect you're looking for me."'

'How did he know where to find you?' Dad asked.

'I don't know,' Lenny said. 'It was a bit strange, to be honest.' There was a brief silence as Lenny gazed thought-fully out of the window, rubbing at the back of his neck, then he shook his head, breathed in, and went on with the story. 'We took him to the station, explained that a complaint had been made, and that we'd like to ask him some questions. He seemed happy enough with that. When we told him he wasn't under arrest and that he was free to consult a solicitor, he just smiled and said that wouldn't be necessary. So, we sat him down and started with the usual things – name, age, address ... and that's when it all went a bit loopy.'

'Loopy?' I said.

Lenny frowned. 'He told us his name was Lucas. When I asked if that was his first or last name, he just looked at me and said, "Neither. It's just Lucas." I said, "What do you mean? You can't have just *one* name." And he said, "It's not a crime, is it?"'

Dad laughed. 'Well, is it?'

Lenny shook his head. 'I don't know. I've got someone looking into it.'

'Didn't he have any ID?' Dad asked.

'Nothing. No birth certificate, no driving licence, no medical card, not a thing. All he had in his pockets was a penknife and some tobacco.'

I said, 'Can't you trace him on your computer records?'

'Not with just the one name, no.'

Dad said, 'Didn't you ask him to explain *why* he's only got one name?'

'Of course I did. I spent the best part of an hour on it. All I got out of him was that he didn't know when or where he was born, that he was an orphan, and that he couldn't remember the names or whereabouts of any of the homes he'd been brought up in.'

I remembered the photograph on the wall in Lucas's den, the pretty young woman with the spiky blonde hair and dark eyes. And I remembered Lucas saying – *It's my mother. That was taken about fifteen years ago ... I think she's probably dead ...*

'What about his age?' I said. 'Did he say how old he was?'

'Sixteen,' Lenny replied. 'Which, if it's true, means he's free to live how and where he likes. Which is exactly what he's doing.'

'How do you mean?' asked Dad.

'He just drifts around from place to place. He does a bit of work now and then if he needs the money, but most of the time he seems to make do by living off the land. Fishing, rabbits, wild fruits, berries ...'

'A regular Robinson Crusoe,' Dad said.

'Looks like it.'

'Well, good for him.'

Lenny shook his head. 'I don't know, Mac. It doesn't seem right.'

'Why?'

'Well, firstly, I'm not sure if I believe him. All this mystery stuff about who he is and where he comes from ... it's a fair bet he's wanted for something somewhere, and he knows that if he gives us his real name he's going to be locked up or sent back to wherever he came from.'

'Is that what you really think?' I asked.

He looked at me. 'It's what my experience tells me, Cait.'

'But what do you *think*?'

He paused for a while, then said, 'I honestly don't know. Even if it is true, even if he is some kind of harmless nomad, just wandering around all over the place, I'm not sure I like it.'

'Why not?' Dad asked.

'He's just a kid, Mac. He should have someone looking after him. It's not a nice world out there ... I mean, look at this mess he's got himself into now.'

'What *mess*?' Dad said. 'He saved a girl from drowning – where's the mess in that?'

Lenny looked uncomfortable. 'There are conflicting reports as to what actually happened.'

Dad frowned. 'I *told* you what happened. The girl was drowning, Lenny. Lucas dived in and pulled her out. It's as simple as that.'

'Not according to other witnesses.'

'Like who?'

'Ellen Coombe, for one.'

'But she didn't *see* anything. She only turned up after Lucas had pulled Kylie from the sea. She saw him with her daughter, she saw the state she was in, and she jumped to the wrong conclusion. All he was doing was trying to make the girl look decent.'

Lenny took a sip of beer and looked at me. 'Is that how you saw it, too?'

'That's how it *was*,' I told him.

Dad sighed. 'I don't see what the problem is, Len.'

'The problem is, I've got half a dozen witnesses who back up Ellen's version of events.'

'Well, they're lying,' Dad said simply. 'Either that, or they're blind. Who are they?'

Lenny didn't answer immediately. He took a deep breath and rolled his head back to stare at the ceiling. I knew what was coming, but even so, when he finally breathed out and began to speak, I was still shocked to hear the names.

'Jamie Tait,' he said. 'Bill Gray, Robbie and Angel Dean, Sara Toms ...'

'Oh, for Christ's *sake*,' Dad said angrily.

'They were there, Mac. I've confirmed it. They saw what happened.'

'I *know* they were there,' Dad spat. 'They were hanging around on the rocks pissing in the wind while Kylie Coombe was drowning—'

'John—'

'Tait's a natural born liar, Lenny. Same as his father. They all are. You *know* that.'

'Just calm down, John. Take it easy.'

Dad glared at him. His face was tight and his eyes were on fire. I thought for a moment he was going to crack up, but after a while his face relaxed and I saw the anger fading from his eyes. He breathed out slowly and lit a cigarette.

'All right,' he said calmly. 'What's *their* story?'

Lenny looked embarrassed. 'Well ... the way they saw it, Kylie *dived* off the raft when it reached the buoy. She wasn't drowning, she was just swimming.' He coughed nervously. 'They're saying the boy went in after her and dragged her onto the beach—'

'That's crap,' said Dad.

'Mr Hanson has confirmed she dived in. So have his two boys.'

'Who the hell's Mr Hanson?'

'Derek Hanson – a friend of Mrs Coombe. It was Derek's raft—'

'What kind of friend?'

'I don't know – Ellen's divorced. He's the boyfriend, I suppose.'

'He's bound to lie, then, isn't he?' Dad snorted. 'What about Kylie? What does she have to say?'

'She says she can't remember.'

Dad was getting irate again. 'It's *ridiculous*. Why the hell would anyone dive in and drag a girl from the sea and then *molest* her in front of fifty witnesses? It's a bloody ludicrous idea.'

'I know.'

'So why are you even *listening* to these idiots?'

Lenny didn't answer.

Dad said, 'What about all the others? What did they have to say?'

'Not much. One or two tell it the same as you. Others go along with Tait and the rest. Most of them aren't willing to commit themselves. Either they didn't see anything, or it all happened too fast, or they can't remember ... you know how it is.'

'Yeah ... it's pathetic.'

I got up from the table and went over to the sink to wash my face. I was feeling hot all over. Hot and sweaty and fluttery. It was all turning to hell, just as Lucas said it would – *people don't like it when they don't know what you are. They don't like things that don't fit. It frightens them. They'd rather have a monster they know than a mystery they don't ...*

At the table Dad was still arguing with Lenny.

'You surely can't *believe* all this, can you? You met the boy. Did he act like a lunatic?'

'No.'

'Did he seem deranged?'

'No.'

'So why would he do something that only a madman would do?'

'I don't know ... why would half a dozen people lie about it? Tell me that, John. What have they got to gain by lying? What's in it for them?'

Pleasure, I thought to myself. They gain pleasure from the suffering of others. Particularly from others they perceive as a threat. Lucas is a threat to them because he's different, because he's unknown, because he does things that they don't understand. And that makes them feel bad.

And when something makes you feel bad, you either put up with it, learn to like it, or you get rid of it. If getting rid of it is the easiest option, or the most pleasurable, then that's the one you take.

Right or wrong, that's the way it is.

I filled a glass from the tap and took a long cool drink.

Dad and Lenny were still talking.

'... I wanted to keep him in for a while, at least until we'd done some more checking, but Toms told me to let him go.'

'I should think so,' said Dad.

Lenny lowered his voice. 'For God's sake, John. I didn't want to keep him in for *questioning*. I wanted to protect him. You can't keep this sort of thing quiet. What do you think's going to happen when the rumours start to spread? You know what people are like.'

'You think he's in danger?'

'I don't know ... but I think it's probably best if he doesn't hang around ...'

'Did you tell him that?'

Lenny nodded.

'And?' Dad asked. 'What did he say?'

A puzzled look creased Lenny's face. 'He said that he was content with what he was.'

Dad didn't speak for a moment. He just stared at the table, rubbing thoughtfully at his brow. Eventually he looked up and took a puff on his cigarette. 'Martial,' he said quietly.

'What?'

Dad smiled. 'It's a quote from a first-century Latin poet called Marcus Valerius Martialis. "Be content with what you are, and wish not change; nor dread your last day, nor long for it."'

nine

On Wednesday morning Dad went into Moulton with Bill's mum. He needed some stuff from the big stationery warehouse in town, and Rita needed someone to give her a hand with a pine cupboard she was buying.

'She'll probably want to buy me a burger on the way back,' Dad told me. 'But I shouldn't be too long.'

I gave his belly a squeeze. 'Take as long as you like. You never know – you might even enjoy yourself.'

He gave me a doubtful smile. 'Yeah.'

After he'd left, I had a bath and got dressed and then I went downstairs and made myself some breakfast. In all the turmoil of the last few days I'd forgotten how restful the house can be when it's empty, and it was a real pleasure to sit in the kitchen munching toast and drinking tea and gazing out of the window without having to talk to anyone. I wasn't completely alone, of course. Deefer was out in the garden, lying in the shade of a cherry tree, chewing lazily on a bit of old bone. I could hear the grinding chomp of his back teeth and the occasional sharp crack as the bone splintered in his mouth. He had the bone lodged between his two front paws, and as he chewed on it his eyes wandered casually around the garden, checking on this and that. Every now and then he'd pause in mid-chew to concentrate on the movements of a bird or an insect, and then, satisfied with what he'd seen, he'd start chomping again.

I sipped my tea and started thinking about the day ahead. It didn't take long. There was the washing up to do, a bit of hoovering ... Simon was coming round at six ... and that was about it.

It wasn't exactly Thrill City, but I didn't mind – I enjoy a bit of boredom now and then.

After I'd stacked the dishes in the sink, I started wandering around the house. As far as I was aware, there was no particular purpose to my wandering, I was just bumbling around, enjoying the solitude and the silence, getting to know the house again.

In the front room I tidied up a few magazines, straightened the cushions on the settee, clicked on the television, then clicked it off again. I browsed the bookshelves for a while, reminding myself of all the books I'd always meant to read but had never got round to – *To Kill a Mocking Bird, The Bell Jar, Mehalah, The Ballad of the Sad Café* – then I went over to the large bay window that looks out over the garden. In the distance the tide was going out and the receding sea looked flat and silver in the low light of the sun. Flickering rays fanned out across the water like the veins of a petal. I rubbed my eyes and ran my fingers through my hair. The house was quiet.

No one home.

Just me and Deefer.

I glanced up the lane, saw it was empty, and then I went upstairs and into Dominic's bedroom.

The curtains were closed and the light was off. I stepped over to the window and pulled back the curtains. Outside, the sky was clouding over and cold shadows were creeping across the yard. I turned to face the room. It looked a lot emptier than I remembered it. There was a bed, a bedside cabinet, a chest of drawers, a wicker chair by the window, and that was about it. Bare shelves, no ornaments, no pictures on the wall. No one lived here any more. It was just a drab and empty room. The bed was unmade and a pile of pillows lay scrunched up on the floor. Dirty clothes were scattered all over the place and a chaotic heap of belongings radiated out from an upturned rucksack in the middle of the floor. Books, magazines, disposable razors, a packet of cigarettes, letters, train tickets, chewing-gum wrappers, coins ...

I sat down on the edge of the bed and looked around.

I didn't know what I was doing in here. I didn't know what I was looking for, or why, or what I was going to do if I found anything. And even if I *did* find something, I knew it wouldn't change anything. It wouldn't solve any problems or make me feel any better. Worst of all, I knew in my heart that what I was doing was wrong. It was sneaky. Treacherous. Underhand.

It was stupid.

I started going through the drawers of the bedside cabinet.

In the top drawer I found a packet of cigarettes and a torn pack of cigarette papers with a scribbled note on the cover – *fr7br1k – 07712664150*. I stared at the note for a while, trying to work out what it could mean. The last bit was obviously a mobile telephone number, but the rest of it didn't make much sense. *fr* could be Friday, I thought, and *7* could be a date. But it was the ninth today, so that didn't fit. Unless it meant the 7th of *September*? I started counting out the days to see if the 7th of September was a Friday, but I kept getting lost, so I gave up. Maybe it meant seven o'clock? Or maybe it was a street number. *7br* ...? Seven something road? A road beginning with *b*?

It was impossible.

It could be in code. It could mean anything.

It probably meant nothing.

I dropped the packet of papers back in the drawer, closed it, and opened up the middle drawer.

There were a couple of magazines – *FHM* and *Loaded* – a train timetable, a packet of condoms, and, tucked away in the corner, a roll of £20 notes tied with an elastic band. I took out the money and counted it. Traces of fine white powder dusted some of the notes, and they showed signs of having being rolled into a tube. There were seventeen notes in all – £340. It was a hardly a fortune, but that wasn't the point. The point was, while Dad was working night and day just to keep us in food, Dominic had a bundle of dodgy cash squirreled away in his drawer. That's what sickened me.

With a heavy heart I put the money back and opened up the last drawer, the bottom one. At first glance the contents seemed quite harmless. There were no mysterious codes, no condoms, no money, just a row of balled-up socks and a couple of pairs of pants. I would have liked to have left it at that, to have simply accepted things as they were – nice and neat and normal – but I knew I couldn't. I reached inside the drawer and started checking through the socks and pants. My hands felt numb and unfamiliar, as if they belonged to someone else, someone with a cold and unforgiving heart.

I found the bottle of pills stuffed inside a pair of socks.

It was one of those brown plastic bottles you get from the chemist. The label was worn and smeared and the writing on it was illegible. I shook the bottle and held it up to the light. The tablets were small, white, and round. The bottle was about half full.

I tugged on the lid, trying to open it, but it wouldn't budge. I held it up to the light again and looked closer, realising with a shake of my head that it was a child-proof lid and I'd forgotten to line up the little arrows.

'Idiot,' I whispered to myself.

I lined up the arrows and got my thumbs under the rim of the lid. Then, just as I was popping it open, a sudden loud bark erupted from the garden. The sound shot through me like a jolt of electricity. My body jerked, my heart leapt, and the bottle of pills flew out of my hand and spilled all over the place. I cursed Deefer, then I cursed myself for reacting like a scared rabbit, and then I just cursed. The pills had scattered everywhere – on the bed, under the bed, on the bedside cabinet, on the floor. There seemed to be thousands of them. I looked around for the bottle, found it on the floor, and started picking up the pills. Outside, Deefer was still barking. It was his warning bark. He was telling me that someone was coming down the driveway.

I stopped picking up the pills and listened.

At first all I could hear was Deefer.

Maybe he's wrong, I thought. Maybe he heard someone up at Rita's, or Joe Rampton's. Or maybe it's just the wind ...

Then I heard it. A car, rumbling down the driveway. Faint at first, then louder ... and louder. For a moment I tried to convince myself that it was Rita's car, or Lenny's ... but I knew it wasn't. I knew whose car it was. I remembered the sound of it roaring down the lane and screeching into the yard in the early hours of the morning. I remembered the sound of laughter and drunken voices cracking the night – *yay, there! Dommo, Dommo ... watch it! ... woof! woof! ... can't get out, man ... hey, hey, Caity ...*

It was Jamie Tait's car.

And now it was turning into the yard, slowing, stopping ...

I jumped up off the bed and ran over to the window and peeked out through the gap in the curtains. A jet-black Jeep with bull-bars and tinted windows was parked in the middle of the yard. The top was down and dance music was blaring from a huge pair of speakers in the back. Jamie Tait was sitting in the driver's seat swigging from a can of beer, and Dominic was sitting next to him. They were both wearing sunglasses and smoking cig-arettes. As Deefer padded slowly across the yard to greet them, Jamie switched off the music and they both started to get out of the car.

I glanced over my shoulder at the pills scattered on the floor, then I looked out of the window again. Jamie and Dom were halfway across the yard. They were coming in. Once they were in, they were bound to come up here. And when they came in here and Dom saw the pills all over the place ...

My heart was thumping like a hammer, pumping adrenaline into my body, screaming at me to run – *get out of here, quick, before they catch you* – but my head was telling me different. *If you go now*, it was saying, *Dom's going to know you've been in here searching through his stuff ... so pick up the pills and* then *go.*

Heart: *there isn't time ...*

Head: *yes there is ...*

No there isn't ...

Yes there is ...

I looked out of the window again. They were at the front door. Dom was getting his keys out ...

There wasn't time to think any more.

I turned from the window and hurried across to the bed and started scooping up the pills into the plastic bottle. I got the ones off the bedside table first, then I turned to the bed. The duvet was white, the same colour as the tablets – I couldn't see the damn things. As I ran my hand over the duvet, feeling for the pills, I heard the front door opening downstairs. I paused, listening. Deep, muffled voices ... a laugh ... the door closing ... footsteps moving along the hallway. I breathed out. They were going into the kitchen. I carried on running my hands over the bed until I was sure I had all the pills, then I dropped them into the plastic bottle and turned to the floor. Christ, they were all *over* the place. Under the bed, against the skirting board, mixed in with Dom's dirty clothes ... As quietly as I could, I got down on my hands and knees and started crawling around picking them up, all the time keeping my ears open for footsteps on the stairs. I inched along the floor, scanning the carpet in front of me and grabbing up pills with both hands, and after a while I began to think I might just make it. I had a good rhythm going. The bottle was filling up. The pills on the floor were gradually disappearing. Faint sounds from the kitchen told me that Jamie and Dom were still downstairs. All I needed was another couple of minutes to get the last few tablets into the bottle, have a final look around, put the bottle back in the drawer, then I could get out and sneak along the landing into my bedroom ...

Then I heard them coming up the stairs.

I was at the door, picking out a pill that was stuck under the carpet. I dropped it in the bottle, jumped to my feet, and automatically reached for the door handle. But it was too late. I knew it. They were halfway up the stairs. I could hear them talking, grunting, laughing. Even if I went right now they'd see me.

I was trapped.

Breathing hard, I backed away from the door and

moved quickly across to the bed, looking around as I went to make sure I had all the pills. I didn't know what I was doing, or where I was going. Somewhere in the back of my mind I could see Dominic opening the door and asking me what the hell I was doing, and a stream of half-baked excuses were already running through my head – uh, I was just looking for something ... I thought I heard something ... I was just tidying things up ...

It was a waste of time. He'd know I was lying.

They were coming along the landing now, passing the bathroom ... and then they stopped. I heard someone tapping on a door, then Dominic calling out my name – 'Cait? Are you in there? Cait?' – and I realised they were outside my bedroom, checking to see if I was in. I heard Jamie say something, but I couldn't make out what it was, and then I heard someone open my bedroom door.

My skin felt icy cold.

I bent down and put the bottle of pills in the bedside drawer.

My hands were shaking.

I quietly shut the drawer.

I heard my bedroom door closing, more muffled voices, and then their footsteps moved along the hallway and stopped at Dom's room.

I couldn't move.

I stared, petrified, at the door handle.

Nothing happened for a moment. Maybe they've changed their minds, I thought. Maybe they've forgotten something, and they aren't coming in after all. Maybe they'll turn around and go back downstairs and everything will be all right ...

Then the handle turned and the door swung open.

* * *

It's amazing how fast you can move when your mind shuts down and your body takes over. It's the survival instinct, I suppose. The autonomic nervous system, primitive reflexes, fight or flight ... whatever. I don't know what it is or how it all works ... but I guess that's the whole point. If you knew how it worked, it wouldn't work. Conscious thinking is all well and good, but when you get right down to it, it's the not-knowing stuff that does the business.

I didn't know what I was doing as the door opened, but my body did. It buckled my knees, dropped me to the floor, stretched out my arms, and rolled me under the bed. It was all over before I knew it – bam bam bam. Half a second, tops. By the time my mind kicked in again I was lying on my back, staring up at the underside of Dominic's mattress, listening intently as the bedroom door slammed shut and voices filled the room.

'... probably at the beach or something. She might be at Reed's place. I don't know.'

'Did you see him?'

'Who?'

'Reed. Earlier on, poncing round the village in his stupid coat ...'

I could see two pairs of boots walking across the floor towards me. Two pairs of boots, two moving voices. From the way they were talking, I didn't think Jamie and Dom had seen me, but I was still pretty scared. I was breathing hard, almost panting. It sounded incredibly loud. Even if they hadn't seen me, I was sure they'd *hear* me. But as I lay there with my head pressed to the floor, they just carried on talking, and gradually my fears began to recede.

They were still talking about Simon.

'So he's the boyfriend, is he?' Jamie asked.

Dominic sat down in the wicker chair against the wall. 'No,' he said. 'Not really. I think they're just friends.'

Jamie laughed. 'The odd couple.'

Dominic laughed, too, but without any enthusiasm. 'Simon's all right. He's just a bit—'

'He's a tosser.'

Jamie dropped a six-pack of beer on the floor then plonked himself down on the bed. The bedsprings groaned and the mattress plummeted down to within an inch of my head. Bits of fluff and dust billowed up into my face and I had to pinch my nose to keep from sneezing.

Jamie's voice boomed out from above me. 'Does she do him?'

'For God's sake, Jamie! She's my *sister*. She's just a kid.'

'Yeah? Have you seen her recently?'

'Leave it out.'

'I wouldn't say no.'

'Christ!'

Jamie farted. The sound reverberated through the mattress and the smell seeped down like a cloud of poison gas. It was vile. I heard Jamie slurping from his beer can, then I heard a cigarette being lit. Across the room I could see Dom's legs in the wicker chair. His hand dropped into view, tightly gripping a burning cigarette. On the bed, Jamie adjusted his position and the mattress bounced and then sagged down again. I turned my head away from the sagging bit and listened to Jamie's voice. He was still talking about me.

'... she's the same age as Bill.'

'So?'

'You don't mind sniffing around *her*, do you?'

'She's the one does all the sniffing.'

Jamie laughed. 'So I've heard.'

I carefully picked a lump of fluff from my tongue.

Dominic said, 'Anyway, what's Cait got to do with anything? Why are you so interested in her?'

'Interested? What's there to be interested in?'

'You tell me. You're the one looking in her room, asking where she is, who's her boyfriend—'

'I was just asking, that's all. I like to know what's what. Besides, I'm already spoken for.'

Dominic let out a quiet snort. 'That's not what Angel thinks.'

'Angel doesn't have to think – not with that body. Did you *see* her last night? Jesus ...'

Above me, the bed vibrated.

'You're a sick man, Jamie.'

He laughed. 'Sick as a dog.'

'No, I mean it. Angel's just a kid. She's still at school, for Christ's sake. She doesn't know what she's doing.'

'You reckon?'

'Come on ... all that tarty stuff? It's just an act. It's a game. If anyone touched her she'd run a mile.'

There was an ugly silence for a moment. Then Jamie said, 'Yeah well ... we've all got to learn some time.'

Dominic sighed. 'And what if Sara finds out? You know what she's like. She'll go ballistic. Remember what she did to that girl in the pub, the one she caught you out the back with? Christ – if the landlord hadn't stepped in she would have killed her.'

Jamie laughed. 'It's all part of the fun, Dom. Bit of this, bit of that, bit of slap and whack ... there's nothing like a bit of slap for keeping things fresh. Know what I mean?'

'Not really.'

'No, I don't suppose you do.' He laughed again. 'You're too damn Irish, that's your trouble. You think with this—'

I heard him thump his heart '—when you should be thinking with this.'

The bed wobbled again, vibrating with Jamie's dirty laugh – *nyuh nyuh nyuh* – and for a moment I thought I was going to be sick. I'd never really heard boys talking about girls before, at least not when they thought they were alone. Although I had a good idea of *what* they talked about, I'd never really imagined the *way* they talked about it. It was so cold and nasty, so insecure, so *false*. It was nauseating. Of course, I knew it was wrong to judge others by Jamie Tait's standards, but I had a funny feeling he probably wasn't that much worse than most.

The bed bounced and Jamie's voice spoke up again. 'When's your old man getting back?'

'Bill said about four. Rita's taking him to Sloppy Joe's.'

'Good choice – you want another beer?'

'Yeah.'

Jamie's hand snaked down and he peeled a couple of cans from the pack on the floor. I heard him throw one over to Dom, then he lay back on the bed and popped open the other one. Meanwhile, Dominic had got out of the chair and walked over to the window. From where I was lying all I could see was his boots and the bottom half of his legs, but that was enough to tell me he wasn't very comfortable. Maybe I was just kidding myself, but I got the impression his heart wasn't in it – whatever *it* was. Being grown up, acting big, talking dirty ... it just didn't come naturally to him. He was having to work at it.

I heard him open his beer and take a sip. Then I heard the window opening, and a draught of air blew cigarette smoke across the room.

Jamie's voice piped up again. 'You had any of that stuff that Lee brought in?'

'Yeah,' said Dominic.

'Any good?'

'It's all right. A bit buzzy.'

'Tully said he was getting some more ...'

I didn't know what they were talking about, but I presumed it was smuggled booze or drugs or something. There's a lot of petty smuggling on the island – cigarettes, tobacco, beer, wine, a bit of cannabis now and then ... everyone does it, it's no big deal. Most people don't even bother talking about it, but I suppose Jamie and Dom thought it was cool. Stuff, gear, booze ... blah, blah, blah ... it all sounded pretty puerile to me, like two little kids talking about bloody Pokémon cards or something.

I tuned out for a while and looked around at my surroundings. I had to crane my neck and scrape my head against the floor. There wasn't a lot to see. Bedsprings, dust, bits of cotton, a paperclip, dog hairs, a grimy old 2p coin. The underside of the mattress was dotted with holes and mouldy-looking stains, and the joints of the bed frame were pitted with rust.

I turned my head and looked across the room.

That's when I saw the pill.

It was on the carpet on the far side of the bed, about an arm's length away from the edge. The carpet was dark grey, so the pill stood out like a snowball in an empty car park. I couldn't believe I'd missed it. Luckily, it was hidden from Dominic's view by the bed. But I was pretty sure that Jamie could see it. Unless he was facing the other way ... or maybe he *had* seen it but didn't think it was worth mentioning ...?

It didn't really matter.

I had to retrieve it.

Jamie and Dom were still talking, nattering away about

cars or boats or something, and they'd both started on another can of beer. I guessed that if they kept on slurping it wouldn't be long before one of them needed to use the bathroom, and when that happened there was a good chance that one of them would see the pill. So I didn't have a lot of time.

I started slithering across the floor, moving as fast as I could without stirring up the dust. There wasn't much room. I had to flex my legs, balance myself on my elbows and arch my back, then slide across the floor inch by inch. I couldn't help making a bit of noise, so I timed my movements to coincide with the sound of their voices. Every time they stopped talking, I lay still. Fortunately, they didn't stop talking very often, so it didn't take long to reach the edge of the bed. Then it was just a question of reaching out and grabbing the pill. But I still didn't know which way Jamie was facing. If he was looking this way, he'd see my hand. He'd have to be blind *not* to see it. I lay there for a while, staring at a rip in the mattress, trying to work out what to do, but nothing came to me. I couldn't think how to find out which way Jamie was facing. I couldn't think of a safe way of distracting him. And I couldn't think of any other way of retrieving the pill.

In the end I just took a deep breath, counted to three, then whipped out my hand and snatched the damn pill.

The talking suddenly stopped.

I held my breath.

Then I heard the click of a lighter and a sharp intake of breath as Jamie lit another cigarette, and I carefully breathed out again. The smell of cigarette smoke filled the room and I could hear Jamie making stupid little noises as he tried to animate some sordid joke he was telling Dom.

I backed away from the edge of the bed and lay still,

letting my heart settle down.

After the joke was finished, and Jamie had laughed himself stupid, I heard Dominic cross the room to fetch himself another beer. Then he went back over and sat down in the wicker chair. I heard Jamie sigh, and I felt him lie back on the bed.

It was quiet for a while.

I realised I was still gripping the pill in my hand. I could feel it, hard and round, in my palm. I'd been in such a hurry when I was picking up the pills that I'd never bothered checking to see what they were. Not that it mattered. But now I had time to spare, I was curious to find out. I lifted my hand to my face and uncurled my fingers. The light was dim under the bed, so I moved my hand right up close to my eyes and peered at the little white pill. I didn't really know what I was expecting to see. Ecstasy, maybe? Amphetamines? LSD? Nothing would have surprised me. But when I saw the familiarly simple design, and suddenly recognised it for what it was, I felt like screaming.

It was an aspirin.

After a while the effects of the beer took hold and Jamie and Dom started giggling like idiots. Their conversation descended into a series of garbled laughs, unfinished sentences, and irrelevant digressions. They sounded like a couple of over-excited eight-year-old boys, the sort of boys who don't know what they're talking about but are determined to talk about it anyway. I couldn't be bothered to listen any more. I'd had enough of it. So I just lay there with my eyes closed and my arms crossed over my chest, waiting for them to shut up and leave.

I felt like a corpse.

A corpse with an aching back and a numb backside.

I don't know how long I lay there. It was probably no more than an hour or so, but it felt like a month. Jamie kept talking, they both kept drinking and smoking, and after a while the room got muggy with smoke and beer fumes and I started feeling a bit drowsy. To avoid dozing off, I thought of the beach, imagining the breeze on my skin and the smell of the sea air ... but it didn't do any good. I stifled a yawn. My head felt thick and my body was numb. I was falling asleep.

Just as I was drifting off, I heard someone say *Lucas*. At first I thought I'd imagined it, but then I heard it again. It was Jamie's voice. Suddenly I was wide awake.

'... Sara told me,' he was saying. 'Craine took him in for questioning on Sunday.'

'What for?'

'They were asking him about Kylie Coombe. Her mother still thinks he molested her. Stupid bitch.'

'I thought you said he *did*?'

'Of course he didn't. The little cow was drowning – I was just about to dive in and get her myself when the gyppo jumped in.'

'So why are you backing up Ellen's claim?'

Jamie didn't answer.

Dom said, 'He's not doing any harm—'

'No? Have you ever *seen* a gypsy camp? Crap all over the place, dogs, horses, nicked cars, lorry-loads of scrap-metal and tarmac ...'

'Don't be ridiculous.'

'Don't be *what*?'

'I didn't mean—'

'You think I'm being *ridiculous*?'

'No ... I just meant ...'

'What?'

'Well, he's on his own, isn't he? He's not part of some travelling tribe or anything. He's not even a gypsy. He's just a kid.'

'I don't care what he is – the little bastard's not staying here.'

There was a brief silence then, and I realised I was holding my breath. I gently let it out and breathed in. My chest hurt. My head was still muzzy from all the smoke and I was finding it hard to take in what Jamie had said. I knew it meant trouble, but I wasn't sure why or how or when or where. It was like switching on the TV halfway through a soap that you never watch and trying to work out what's going on.

Jamie said, 'This is our island, McCann. We live here, most of us were *born* here. This is our home ... you don't let shit into your own home, do you? You keep it out – right?'

Dom mumbled something unintelligible.

Jamie continued, his voice sounding slightly deranged. 'Look, the gypsy's not going to be charged over this Kylie thing, he's not going down for it or anything, but the longer we keep it going the dirtier he looks, and the dirtier he looks the easier it'll be to get rid of him. Once he's got a name for himself, people will believe anything. A rumour here, a rumour there – you know how it is. Cars get broken into ... things get nicked ... some young girl might be walking on the beach ... someone waggles his todger at her ... she reports it to DI Toms ... these things happen.'

'Then what?'

'If he's got any sense, he'll leave before it gets any worse.'

'And if he doesn't?'

'He will. I've asked Lee to have a word with him. Lee

can be very persuasive when he wants to.'

'How's he going to find him?'

'Joe Rampton's offered him an afternoon's work tomorrow, clearing the hedges in the bottom field. He'll finish at six. Joe's going to pop down and pay him before he finishes so he won't have to walk up round the house. He'll cut down through the lane. We'll be waiting for him.'

'We?'

'Me and Lee – and you, of course.'

'Me?'

'Why not?' There was a mocking edge to his voice. 'It's about time you showed us what you're made of.'

Ten minutes later, after Dominic had rummaged around for a clean shirt while Jamie sat on the edge of the bed scratching at mosquito bites on his leg, they finally left. I listened to them stomping down the stairs, into the kitchen, then back out into the hallway. I heard Deefer's tail thumping against the wall as Dominic said something to him. And then, at last, I heard the front door open and close. I waited until I could hear their footsteps crossing the yard, then I rolled out from beneath the bed, brushed myself down, and hurried off to the bathroom.

From outside I could hear Jamie's Jeep starting up. He revved the engine, turned on the sound system, then swung the car around the yard, showering the lawn with gravel, and raced off up the lane in a swirl of thumping bass beats.

I sat there holding my head in my hands.

It was turning out to be one hell of a summer.

ten

When it comes to beliefs, I like to think I'm pretty level-headed. I don't believe in God and I don't believe in the Devil. I don't believe in Superman or Santa Claus, and I don't believe that characters in soap operas are real. I don't believe in these things because they don't make sense. I'm perfectly happy to accept that other people believe in them, and if God turned up one day I'd be more than happy to sit down and have a chat with him – but I'm not holding my breath.

Religion, astrology, UFOs, corn circles, ghosts, spoon-bending, faith-healing – none of these things make any sense, and that's why I don't believe in them. I know that strange things happen – like when the phone rings just as you're thinking about someone, and when you pick up the phone it's them – but that doesn't mean anything. It's just coincidence. How many times do you think of someone and the phone *doesn't* ring? Yes, strange things happen. But it's a big world, there's a lot of stuff going on – it'd be strange if strange things *didn't* happen now and again.

The point is, although I don't believe in these things, that doesn't mean they don't believe in me. I'm not quite sure what that means, if anything, but I know what it feels like. Because, as I walked down the lane that afternoon after Dominic and Jamie had gone, I knew without a shadow of doubt that Lucas would be waiting for me at the creek. I *knew* it. It was there, in my mind. It was already a part of me. I didn't just picture him, he was there – like a memory of the future.

It didn't make sense.

How did he know I was looking for him?

How did he know I was coming?

How did I know he was there?

I didn't know.

I still don't know.

But I wasn't wrong.

He was sitting quietly on the bank, leaning back on one elbow and chewing on a blade of grass. The creek was almost still. The sun's reflection rippled on the surface and a pair of swans floated motionlessly at the water's edge, their necks upright and their eyes fixed on Lucas. I paused for a moment to take it all in. The hazy air, the mottled colours, the dappled light ... it was like a scene from an Impressionist painting.

The afternoon breeze ruffled my hair as I moved on down the lane.

Despite everything, I felt surprisingly calm. It was an odd sense of calmness, kind of dull and emotionless, and normally that would have worried me. I would have wanted to know *why* I wasn't feeling anything. Why *wasn't* I nervous, happy, sad, frightened, angry, excited ... what was the matter with me? Was I sick? Didn't I care? Was I fooling myself? It would have bothered me, and that would have made me feel even worse. But that afternoon I didn't give it a moment's thought. It just didn't seem to matter. It was almost as if I'd been here before, and whatever lay ahead had somehow already happened, so there was no *point* in being emotional about it. It was beyond emotion.

Lucas looked up as I approached. A depth of solitude showed briefly in his eyes – a lifetime of isolation – and then, as he recognised me, he removed the blade of grass from his mouth and his face broke into a warm smile.

'You look nice,' he said.

My legs went weak and I nearly fell over. I didn't know what to say. I just stood there looking at him. His hair was damp, and rings of sweat darkened the armpits of his T-shirt. He put the grass stem back in his mouth and turned his gaze back to the swans.

I sat down next to him.

We didn't speak for a while.

The creek was dark but clear, like liquid bronze. Sunlight filtered down through the water revealing flat stones and lumps of blackened bog-wood resting on the sand bed, and in the shallows small fish were darting around looking for flies on the surface. Quiet popping sounds punctuated the silence.

Lucas made himself a cigarette. When it was finished he sat there looking at it for a while, rolling it around his fingers, studying its shape, and then he reached up and stuck it behind his ear. He scratched idly at the scar on his wrist.

'I didn't mean to be creepy,' he said.

'Sorry?'

'What I said.'

'When?'

'Just now – when I said you looked nice. I didn't mean anything ... I just meant you look nice.'

'I know – it's all right. Thank you.'

He smiled. 'You're welcome.' He plucked the cigarette from behind his ear and lit it.

I don't really like smoking. I don't like the smell of it and I don't usually like the way it makes people look. It makes them look stupid. And the fact that they think it makes them look cool only makes them look even *more* stupid. But with Lucas it was different. I'm not sure why. It seemed more natural with him, as if he was doing it purely for his own pleasure. It wasn't an addiction. It wasn't an act or an affectation. It was just something he enjoyed now and then. I don't know why that should have made a difference, but it did. I didn't even mind the smell too much, either.

'No Deefer, today?' he asked.

'No.'

'Just walking?'

I looked at him. 'Actually, I was looking for you.'

His head nodded slightly but he didn't say anything. He carried on gazing at the swans in the creek. They hadn't moved since I'd first seen them. They were still at the water's edge, still motionless, and they were still staring at Lucas.

'They're beautiful, aren't they,' I said.

Lucas frowned. 'Do you think so?'

'They're so graceful.'

'I've never really liked them that much.'

'Why not? What's wrong with them?'

'There's nothing *wrong* with them, I just think they're a bit ugly, that's all. Stupid long necks, beady eyes, nasty-looking beaks ...' His mouth creased into a grin. 'When I was a kid I used to think the beaks were the dangerous bit. I'd read somewhere that swans can break your leg with a single blow of their wing, but somehow it got all muddled up in my mind and I ended up thinking they could break your leg with a single blow of their *nose*.'

I laughed.

Lucas looked at me, smiling. 'I sometimes get things muddled up.'

'It happens to the best of us.'

'I suppose so.' He re-lit his cigarette and blew smoke into the air. Then he glanced at the swans again. I saw him make a gentle jerking movement with his head, a sort of sideways nod, and at the same time he mumbled something under his breath. Down at the creek the two swans turned as one and glided off downstream.

I stared after them, quietly bemused. What I'd just seen, or thought I'd seen, didn't make sense. It wasn't natural. It wasn't ... it wasn't important. Strange things happen. It's a big world, there's a lot of stuff going on ...

I watched the swans as they drifted away into the distance.

When I eventually turned back to Lucas he was studying the end of his cigarette, gazing at the glowing tip as if it was the most fascinating thing in the world.

'I need to tell you something,' I said.

He looked at me, his blue eyes calm and clear.

'You have to leave,' I said.

'What – now?'

'No, I mean you have to leave the island. It's not safe.'

He laughed quietly.

'I'm serious,' I said. 'I overheard Jamie Tait talking about you. He doesn't think you should be here.'

'Really?'

I nodded. 'That's why they're all saying you messed around with the little girl you saved. They're trying to give you a bad name.'

He smiled. 'That shouldn't be too hard.'

I looked at him. Chewing on a piece of grass, idly flicking at flies – he didn't seem to have a care in the world. 'Look, Lucas,' I said. 'Jamie's not as stupid as he looks. If he wants to cause trouble for you, he can do it. And he'll get away with it, too. No one's going to touch him – his dad's an MP, his future father-in-law is a policeman—'

'I know.'

'Jamie's got some rough friends.'

Lucas shrugged.

'I think they might be planning to set you up.'

'For what?'

'I'm not sure – something to do with a girl on the beach, I think. Some kind of sex thing ...'

'Sex thing?'

I felt embarrassed. 'You know what I mean.'

He held my gaze for a moment, then lowered his eyes and looked away without saying anything. I stared at him, trying to read his thoughts, but his face gave nothing away.

I said, 'They're coming after you, Lucas.'

'Who?'

'Jamie Tait and Lee Brendell. Tomorrow evening, after you've finished work at Joe's place. They're going to be waiting for you in the lane. I think my brother might be there, too.'

He nodded thoughtfully. 'I wondered why Joe was so insistent on giving me some work.'

'Jamie's father owns his farm. I think they probably twisted his arm.'

'Or slipped him some cash.'

'Joe wouldn't have known what they wanted you for. I mean, he's not that bad ... I'll give him a ring and explain why you won't be coming. He'll understand.'

'You don't have to do that.'

'I don't mind.'

'I need the money, Cait.'

'What do you mean?'

He raised one leg in the air and waggled his foot. 'I

need new boots. Look—' He picked at a bit of loose leather. 'These are falling apart.'

'What? You're not still *going*, are you?'

'I need the cash.'

'But what about Tait and Brendell? It's not a game, Lucas. They're not just messing around. They're vicious, especially Brendell. You could end up in hospital.'

'We'll see.'

I frowned at him. 'What's the *matter* with you? You said you were leaving the island anyway. Why don't you just get out before it's too late?'

He looked at me. 'I thought you wanted me to come to the festival on Saturday?'

'Of course I do,' I said. 'But you won't be able to come with two broken legs, will you? Look, I can give you some money if you need new boots. I'll *buy* you some bloody boots.'

'You don't know my size.'

'Oh, for God's *sake* ...'

The emotion in my voice surprised me, and I think it surprised Lucas, too. He looked at me for a moment, opened his mouth as if to say something, then thought better of it and looked away. Suddenly the air seemed very still. I wanted to say something ... anything. But I couldn't. I could hardly breathe, let alone speak. The silence was suffocating.

'Look at me,' Lucas said eventually.

I looked at him.

He spoke quietly. 'They can't hurt me, Cait. It's as simple as that. They can't hurt me, so there's nothing to be afraid of.'

'I don't understand.'

'Just trust me. It'll be all right.'

I looked into his eyes. 'Why? Why can't they hurt you?'

'There's nothing to hurt.'

I couldn't think of an answer to that, so I just turned away and stared dismally at the ground. A small black beetle was scuttling around in the grass. I watched it, wondering what it was doing and where it was going. Did it have a plan? Did *it* know what it was doing? Was it thinking about anything? Was it aware of my attention? I doubted it.

'Don't be angry,' Lucas said quietly.

I breathed in slowly, still staring at the ground. I could smell the sweat from his skin. It was a nice smell. Nice and clean and earthy. I looked up. Lucas was smiling at me. He raised his hand to wipe his face, and just for a minute I thought he was going to reach out and touch me, just a friendly pat on the arm or something – but he didn't.

'I'd better go,' I said, getting to my feet. 'A friend's coming round to see me. I'm probably late.'

Lucas stood up.

I looked at him again, and for the first time I saw him for what he really was: a small and fragile young boy.

I said, 'You know what's going to happen tomorrow, don't you?'

He nodded.

'And you don't care?'

He shrugged. 'It's going to happen.'

'Take care, Lucas.'

'You too.'

We stood looking at each other for a moment, then I turned around and walked away.

eleven

When I got back, I just had time for a quick shower and a change of clothes before the doorbell rang. I pulled on a clean white T-shirt, hurried downstairs and opened the door. Simon was just reaching up to press the bell again. When he saw me he jerked his hand back and nearly fell off the steps. It was one of those hazy humid evenings when the heat makes the air almost too heavy to breathe, but Simon was dressed as if it was winter. Long black coat, a battered old trilby hat, and a worn-out rucksack slung over his shoulder. Rolls of drawing paper and RSPCA posters were poking out from the top of the rucksack. In the yard behind him, thousands of flying ants were crawling on the walls and launching themselves into the sky, only to be snatched up by clouds of hungry gulls and rooks swooping and circling in the air. I watched them, wondering how the ants knew it was the right day to fly. Was it the heat? The light? The humidity? How did they *know*? And what would happen if they waited all summer and the right day never arrived?

Simon cleared his throat.

'Sorry,' I said, looking at him. 'I was miles away.'

I stepped back and we went inside.

'Aren't you too hot in that?' I said, nodding at his coat.

'Not really,' he mumbled.

I led him into the kitchen.

'Do you want something to eat?'

'No thanks.'

'Do you mind if I do? I'm starving.'

I fixed myself a bowl of salad and some bread and cold chicken, sat down at the table and started scoffing it down. Simon stood there watching me.

'Thure you don't want thome?' I said through a mouthful of bread.

'No, thanks.'

'Thuit yourthelf.'

I spent the rest of the evening being equally loathsome. Poor Simon, he did his best – showing me his poster designs, sketching a plan for the stall, talking to me about what we should and shouldn't sell at the festival – but my heart wasn't in it. Whenever he tried to get me involved I either said something stupid or I didn't say anything at all. I was angry, I suppose – angry, confused, and worried. Worried about Lucas, confused about Lucas, angry with Lucas ... I know it wasn't fair to take it out on Simon, and I didn't really *mean* to, but I did it anyway. The way I was behaving, it would have been subtler to hang a banner round my neck saying *Go Away*.

After an hour or so, Simon eventually got the message and started packing away the festival stuff in his rucksack.

'I'll get the rest of it sorted out later,' he said, with an embarrassed smile.

'Right,' I said.

After all I'd put him through, I was confidently expecting him to say goodbye and head straight for the front door, so it came as a bit of a shock when he didn't. Instead, he plonked his rucksack down on the floor and then just stood there looking at me, kind of shuffling around with a bashful grin on his face. I stared at him, thinking to myself – go home, Simon ... please ... for your own sake ... just go home, *now*, before I get any worse ...

But he had no intention of leaving.

I should have taken that as a compliment, I suppose, but I wasn't in the mood for compliments. I wasn't in the mood for anything.

The rest of the night went from bad to worse.

We watched television together in bored silence. I sent him out to make me some tea. I showed him photographs of Mum and snapped at him when he asked me about one of her poems. I made him listen to music I knew he didn't like. And when we went out for a walk in the dark, I pushed him away when he tried to hold my hand.

I was the Girl from Hell.

I hated myself for doing it, but I just couldn't help it. It was as if there was someone else inside me controlling everything I did, someone who didn't give a damn about anything. I don't know where the real me went. Every now and then I heard a voice calling out from somewhere, begging me to think about what I was doing, but it was too far away to have any impact. It was too weak. All I had to do was tell it to shut up and off it went, scuttling back into its hole with its tail between its legs.

The nastier I got, the humbler Simon became – thanking me, apologising to me, being *nice* to me ... and I just lapped it all up. It was almost as if I was trying to see how far I could go, baiting him, seeing how hard I could push him before he snapped.

God ... I was terrible.

Thinking about it now makes me cringe with shame.

Why did I *do* it?

How could I be such a cow?

I don't know.

I wish I could say that I didn't know what I was doing, but I did – I knew exactly what I was doing. And that's what made it so awful.

I'm sorry, Simon.

twelve

It thundered during the night. Mostly it rumbled away in the distance, but occasionally it drifted in close and ripped through the sky with a great black roar that shook the walls of the house. The air was hot and heavy, charged with electricity, and my sleep was ravaged with dreams. In one of them there was a room, an enormous bedroom, like a vast and dirty warehouse, with curtained windows and mattresses on the ceiling and a carpet made of pills, and in this gigantic bedroom there was a party going on. Thunderous dance music was blaring out from wall-to-wall speakers and everybody was drinking and smoking and laughing like lunatics. Bright lights were flashing and the whole room was shaking to the music. I was standing alone in the middle of the room looking around at what was going on. In one corner I could see Simon cavorting with Bill and Angel. He was wearing his battered old hat and his long black coat, but underneath the coat he was naked. Bill and Angel were both dolled up in high-heeled boots and sexy underwear and they were crawling all over him, pouting their big red lips as they stroked his hair and pulled at the buttons of his coat. He was pretending to shoo them away, but I could tell he was enjoying it. He kept looking at me, making sure I was watching him. Over by the wall there was a beach area, a stretch of sand that faded away into the wall ... but the wall was somehow the sea. It rippled with the movement of waves, and in the distance a bright green powerboat was racing silently across the horizon. Down on the sand a group of young girls in skimpy bikinis were standing round in a semi-circle clapping their hands and laughing at something. I moved to one side to get a better view. I saw two men, both dressed in boots and baggy shorts. One of them was Jamie Tait and the other one was Dominic. Dominic was lying face down in the sand and Jamie was sitting on his head. Dominic's head was half-buried in the sand and his eyes were white.

Then I saw the swans.

There were two of them. They were walking towards me, each as big as a man, with soleless boots flapping on their too-long legs, and cigarettes held in the tips of their wings. Each had a man's head bobbing on top of their long white necks, and each of the heads was Lucas. I thought at first they were twins, and I wondered for a moment if that's why he was here, to look for his long-lost twin brother. Then I realised they were both the same person. They were joined in the middle. They only had one pair of wings between them. They were both Lucas. He had two heads. One of them was smiling, but the other one had no mouth at all, just a thin white scar running horizontally beneath his nose ... or where his nose should be. For there was no nose, just a bone-black empty socket. And there were no eyes, either. No mouth, no nose, no eyes – just a skin-covered skull.

He was dead.

That's why they can't hurt him, I thought. He's already dead.

And with that thought, the room, and everything in it, disappeared.

I saw a lot of things that night. Some of them I can't remember and some of them I can't forget, but all of them are too painful to think about.

By morning the thunder had moved on, leaving the air stale and exhausted. The day felt hungover. Irritable and sluggish. It didn't want to get going. It was tired. Restless. It had a headache. The sun was out, but its light was cautiously shrouded in mist, and the birds seemed wary of making too much noise. I imagined them tiptoeing around in the trees, whistling quietly among themselves, like little children trying to keep out of their father's way on the morning after the night before.

I got out of bed and went to the bathroom.

The house felt depressed.

I felt depressed.

There's nothing worse than realising you've done something shameful and knowing there's nothing you can do about it. I'd treated Simon disgracefully. I'd belittled him, snubbed him, I'd taken his friendship and thrown it in his face. I couldn't have *been* more vile. And it didn't matter how much I regretted it, or how much I apologised for it, nothing could change the fact that I'd done it. My cruelty was indelible. I'd done it. It was done. There was no going back. No going back ...

Damn it.

I slammed open the bathroom door and marched inside, stopping suddenly at the sight of Dominic. He was sitting on the lavatory, holding his head in his hands, dressed in nothing but a pair of grey boxer shorts. My anger turned to embarrassment and I let out a quiet yelp of surprise. Dominic looked up. His eyes were teary and bloodshot.

'I'm sorry,' I said, backing out. 'I didn't know you were in here.'

'It's all right,' he said. 'I wasn't doing anything.'

I turned to go.

'Cait?'

I stopped, but didn't turn around.

'You don't have to go, ' he said. 'I'm finished. I was just going.'

The lifelessness of his voice was painful to hear. It pulled at me, reminding me of what he was and what we used to be – brother and sister. I tried to resist it, I wanted to resist it, but I couldn't. I turned around. He'd slipped a hooded sweatshirt on and was standing with his back to the sink. His head was bowed and he was toying with the drawstring of the hood.

He couldn't look at me.

I let out a long sigh. 'It's all right,' I said. 'I'm not going to bite you.'

He didn't seem to hear me.

I moved a little closer. 'Dom?'

Wearily, he raised his eyes. His face was a picture of confusion: fear, pain, bitterness, pride ... It was the face of a child struggling to cope in a young man's body. Or was it the other way round?

He wiped his face and sighed. 'It's bloody hard, isn't it?'

'Yep.'

We stood there in a weight of silence. Me in my night-dress, Dominic in his sweatshirt and shorts, both of us desperate to pour out our troubles but neither of us will-ing or able to start. Dominic lowered his eyes and stared at the floor. I gazed around at the familiar bathroom clutter. Dusty bottles on dusty shelves, toothbrushes, a rusty radio, straggly geraniums in pots, a ceramic fish, a rubber crocodile, a plastic duck, a sponge sheep ... and then my eyes settled on the framed picture hanging above the cistern. It's been there for as long as I can remember. It shows a moose drinking from a sparkling blue lake, the lake surrounded by hills and dark pines. It's a nice enough picture, but there's always been something about it that bothers me. The moose has got his heavy head bowed down and he's dipping his snout into the ring-rippled surface of the water, and I'm always afraid that something's going to sneak up behind him while he's not looking and pounce on him, a wolf or a grizzly bear or something. I know it's stupid. I know it's only a picture, but every time I go into the bathroom I have to tell the moose to watch out. 'Watch out for them grizzlies, moose,' I say. It's like a prayer. I don't have to say it out loud, a whisper will do, or even just mouthing the words. I *know* it doesn't make sense. I know it's idiotic. But I don't really mind. The way I see it, feeling like a complete idiot is a small price to pay for saving a moose's life, even if it *is* only a picture moose.

I looked back at Dominic.

He looked at me.

The moment had passed.

We both knew it. If either of us had been meaning to say anything, it was too late now. We'd both had time to think, or not think, and we'd both found it too hard. There was too much at stake. Too many skeletons.

Dominic cleared his throat. 'Well ...' he said. 'I'd better get going.'

I grinned. 'Me too.'

He didn't get it at first, then the corners of his mouth pricked into a smile. It wasn't much of a smile, but it was better than nothing.

'Right,' he said, starting towards the door.

I watched him.

He walked heavily, with his shoulders stooped and his eyes down. As he passed me he hesitated, then stopped, and I felt his hand on my arm. The lightest of touches. I looked into his eyes. He held my gaze for a moment, then spoke in a broken whisper. 'None of it means anything, Cait.'

I shook my head. I wasn't sure what he meant, but I knew he was wrong. 'Don't do it, Dom,' I said. 'You know better.'

A flutter of concern showed briefly on his face, then he blinked and the lifelessness returned.

'I'll see you later,' he said.

He let go of my arm, turned around and walked out.

I listened to his bare feet padding along the landing, then I shut the door and sat down on the edge of the bath and looked up at the picture on the wall. The moose was still there, still drinking calmly from the lake. He was all right.

I wondered if moose-prayers worked on people.

The rest of the day was just a matter of waiting. Whether he believed it or not, Lucas was in trouble. At six o'clock, he'd finish work, cut down Joe Rampton's lane and come face to face with Tait and Lee Brendell. Big trouble. Someone had to help him. He wasn't going to help himself. I kept on running through the alternatives – telling Dad, telling Lenny Craine, I even thought of ringing Joe Rampton and telling him – but whichever way I looked at it, the end result was always the same.

It was up to me.

I tried to convince myself that I wasn't going to do anything stupid, but I knew in my heart that I was. Your future is set. Sometimes you can see it – you *know* it. You might not understand it, and you might not have any faith in it, but somewhere deep inside, in those unknown places that tell you what to do, you know where you're going. You know it all along.

I knew it.

Once I'd admitted that, all I had to do was wait.

So I waited.

Nothing happened to pass the time, it just crept along, getting slower and slower ... and slower ... and slower ... until the minutes turned into hours and the hours turned into days and I began to think that something was wrong. Either all the clocks were faulty, or it was just far too hot. The heat had melted time, turned it into tar or something ... made it too thick to flow ...

Melted my brain.

Around two o'clock I lay down on the settee in the front room and closed my eyes. I knew I wouldn't sleep, I was too wired, but I thought it might help to calm me down a little bit ...

I woke up with Deefer's wet snout in my face. For a second I didn't know where I was or what day it was, and then I remembered and started to panic. I pushed Deefer away, rubbed the sleep from my eyes and looked at the clock. It's a lumpy old thing with stubby hands and big fat roman numerals, and sometimes it's really hard to read. For a moment I thought it said twenty past twelve. Oh God, I thought, I've slept for ten hours ... then I realised I'd got the hands mixed up and it was actually four o'clock.

I let out a deep breath.

Four o'clock was close enough.

I set out for Joe Rampton's lane.

Sunlight was misting through the branches of the poplar trees along the lane, and as I headed down towards the creek I could feel the sweat glistening on my skin. Mosquitoes whined in the air, attracted by the heat of my body, and clouds of midges swarmed silently around my head.

I walked slowly, taking my time.

I didn't know what I was doing.

The only solid thought in my mind was to get to Joe Rampton's lane before anyone else did, find somewhere to hide, and then wait. After that ... I didn't want to think about it.

Joe's lane runs almost parallel to ours. It starts from his farm house, winds down through a patchwork of fields, then straightens out and heads off towards the beach, emerging at a shallow bend in the creek opposite the pillbox. Most of the land between the two lanes is taken up with fields, but three-quarters of the way down there's a narrow strip of woodland that stretches from one lane right across to the other. It's not much to look at, just a ragged spread of spindly trees, most of which look as if a puff of wind would blow them over. But if you need to get from one lane to the other without going down to the beach, it's perfect.

With the trees in sight, I clambered up the hedgebank, squeezed through a gap in the hedge, and dropped down into a cornfield on the other side. I made my way along the edge of the field to a barbed wire fence at the bottom, carefully straddled it, then slid down a dusty bank, and there I was – in the woods. It seemed like a different world. Although the trees weren't high enough to provide any shade, the light had dimmed and the air was suddenly cool. It was the kind of light you see in those scrubby little woods that run alongside motorways, a cold and forgotten light. It had no energy. It was almost as if it had given up trying, as if it had said to itself – what's the point? there's nothing here ... why shine when there's nothing to shine on?

I moved into the heart of the woods and started walking. There was no path, but the land was so sparse I didn't need one. Although Joe's lane wasn't visible, I could see his farm house in the distance, and over to the east I could see the sunlight reflecting on the bay, so all I had to do was head for a point halfway between the house and the bay and I knew I'd come out somewhere along the lane.

Beneath my feet the earth was dry and dusty. The air was cool and still and there were no midges or mosquitoes to bother me. There was no sign of life at all. No birds, no flowers, no nothing. The woods were stark and silent.

I walked on.

The lane wasn't far away, but it seemed to take a long time to get there. At one point the land sloped down into a marshy area full of rotten tree stumps and boggy pools, and I was forced to walk around in circles for a while to find a safe way through. When I eventually got back to dry land again I didn't know where I was. I scrambled up a small hillock and looked around, trying to work out where the lane was, but everything looked different. My perspective had changed. The trees looked taller, then smaller. The sky was greyer. The horizon was facing the wrong way ... then, just as I was beginning to think I was lost, everything suddenly clicked into place. It was like one of those magic-eye pictures. One second I was staring hopelessly at a blur of meaningless dots, and then, in an instant, the dots took shape and I was staring past the trees at a wooden gate set in an overgrown hedge about ten metres away. Beyond the gate I could see the welcoming lines of the lane.

Keeping my eyes fixed on the gate in case it disappeared again, I hurried on through the trees. The silence was fading now. I could hear farm sounds. The faint scrabble of chickens. A tractor away in the fields somewhere. And beyond that, a distant metallic hammering, as if someone was beating on a sheet of steel. I wondered if it was Lucas. What might he be doing? Fixing a barn roof? Putting in fence-posts? Whatever he was doing, I imagined he'd be hot. Hot and thirsty, tired and sweaty ...

I climbed the gate and dropped down into Joe's lane.

Now that I was out of the woods the light had brightened again and the lane was lush and colourful. Tall hedges either side of the lane were thick with flowers and berries, and the air was sweet with the smell of honeysuckle. Butterflies flitted around in the warm air. I used to visit the lane quite a lot when I was a kid, sometimes with Dad, sometimes with Bill, occasionally on my own. It was a nice place to walk, especially in summer when the butterflies were out, and I always felt at home there. But I hadn't been this way for some time, and the lay-out of the lane seemed to have changed. It was different. I'm not sure *how* it was different – maybe it was just the state of my mind – but everything seemed unfamiliar. The lane was narrower and more wiggly than I remembered, and the hedges were too high to see over, so it was almost impossible to judge exactly where I was. Not only that, but I didn't know where Jamie Tait and the others were planning on meeting Lucas.

I stood there for a moment, thinking.

They wouldn't come from the direction of the farm house, I was pretty sure of that. If they did, they'd run the risk of missing Lucas. Unless they came down our lane and cut through the woods, they'd have to come along the beach. And I couldn't see them cutting through the woods ... no, they'd come along the beach. They'd have to. It was the only way.

I went over to the gate and clambered up. By keeping close to the hedge and grabbing hold of a hawthorn branch for balance, I managed to get myself into a standing position on top of the gate. I didn't feel too safe, but at least I had a reasonable view of my surroundings. To my left, I could see the lane winding down towards the beach. I couldn't actually see the beach, nor where the lane came out, but I could tell that it wasn't too far away. In the other direction, I could see the distant outline of Joe's farmhouse surrounded by an assortment of barns and outbuildings, and from there I could follow the trail of the lane down through a maze of coloured fields. There were squares of bright yellow oilseed rape, the blue of borage, and golden corn ... but I couldn't see Lucas anywhere. I stretched up higher, standing on tiptoe, searching the fields ... then the gate started wobbling and I came to my senses and carefully climbed down.

I had what I needed.

The way I saw it, Jamie, Lee and Dom would come along the beach and then turn up the lane and wait for Lucas somewhere between the gate and the farmhouse. They couldn't afford to wait at the bottom of the lane in case Lucas turned off at the gate and went through the woods. Dom knew about the gate to the woods, and I was assuming that Jamie and Lee did too. But, even if they didn't, I guessed they'd want to meet Lucas somewhere quiet, somewhere they could get on with things without being disturbed.

I looked around. The lane here was narrow, hidden from view, no one ever came here ... it was as good a place as any.

I started looking around for a place to hide, walking down the lane for a bit, looking in the hedgerows, then back up again, towards the farmhouse. I didn't know exactly what I was looking for, and I thought it might take a while, but after a few minutes I found it. It was just past the gate on the right-hand side going up – an odd little place where the hedge had thinned and the bank was low enough to let me through to the field on the other side without too much trouble. I was only wearing a T-shirt and shorts, and by the time I'd squeezed through the hedge my arms and legs were covered in scratches. The field on the other side was filled with tall stalks of maize. I crossed over to the thickest part and crouched down among the stalks in line with the cut-away bank. It was perfect. I could see through to the lane, but no one could see me.

It was quiet. I could hear all the sounds you never normally hear – the rustle of unseen mice, insects calling, the sea breeze whispering in the air. It was comfortable, too. The ground was shady and soft, and the maize had a nice grainy smell to it. If the circumstances weren't so dire it would have been a pleasant spot to while away a few hours.

I got myself into an agreeable position, made sure I had a good view of the lane, then settled down to wait.

One of the things I find strange about characters in books and films is that they hardly ever need to use the lavatory. You see them doing all kinds of things – falling in love, having fights, driving cars, eating food, drinking whiskey, smoking cigarettes, having sex, taking drugs – but the only time you see them visiting the lavatory is when they need to escape from somebody by climbing out of a window, or else when they're going to get beaten up or stabbed or something. You never hear anyone say, Excuse me, I just need to go for a wee. Or if you do, you know they're not *really* going for a wee, they're going to climb out of the window or get beaten up or stabbed or something. I know it doesn't matter, but it just seems odd that something so fundamental, so universally essential, is almost completely ignored. I'm not saying I *want* to see actors in films going to the lavatory every ten minutes, it's just that when I'm watching a film or reading a book I can't help wondering every now and then if so-and-so needs a wee. I'll be watching Leonardo DiCaprio running around on a sinking boat, or Russell Crowe doing a bit of gladiating, and I'll suddenly find myself thinking – he hasn't had a wee for ages, he must be *bursting*.

Like I say, it doesn't really matter. I only mention it because as I was waiting there crouched in the maize I suddenly realised that *I* was bursting for a wee. I don't know where it came from ... maybe it was nerves ... it just crept up on me. One second I was sitting there nice and snug, the next I was fidgeting about trying to work out what to do about it. At first I kept telling myself to ignore it, hold it in, this isn't the time or place to be worrying about your bladder. But after a while I couldn't ignore it, I really *had* to go. Luckily, there was plenty of cover. I didn't want to pee where I was hiding, but I didn't want to lose sight of the lane either. So I crept out of my hiding place and scuttled over to the hedge where I found a spot just to the side of the gap where there was a stray little patch of maize. Although the hedge was dense, I was close enough to see through to the lane, and I was pretty sure that no one could see me. I paused for a moment, took a good look around, then lowered my shorts, squatted down and started to pee.

It was then I heard voices coming up the lane.

They were close, surprisingly close. I couldn't understand how they'd got so close without me hearing them. I could hear Jamie Tait booming away about something, and then Dominic, muttering in agreement. They were getting closer all the time. I stopped peeing and looked over my shoulder. They were right there – I could see them through the hedge; Jamie in front, Dom to one side, and Lee Brendell slumping along behind them. A half-empty bottle of whiskey was dangling from Jamie's hand and his shirt was hanging open. Lee Brendell had a big fat joint stuck in his mouth, and Dom looked totally fed up. Suddenly, I wasn't so sure that I couldn't be seen. If I could see *them* so clearly ...

Damn.

I shouldn't have panicked. I should have kept perfectly still and stayed where I was ... but I wasn't thinking. In hindsight, I hadn't been thinking all day. Right up to that moment I'd been kidding myself that nothing was going to happen. At worst, I was going to wait for an hour or so in the maize, meet Lucas, and somehow persuade him to go back the other way, or maybe hide in the maize with me ...

But now the stupid dream was over. And as the nightmare sank in, I panicked.

My first mistake was trying to pull up my shorts and run for cover at the same time. The combination of fear, vanity, and embarrassment, and a complete lack of thought, sent me tumbling to the ground with my shorts around my knees. My second mistake was grabbing at my shorts as I fell instead of putting out a hand to cushion my fall. If I'd put out a hand I probably wouldn't have caught my knee on a jagged piece of metal half-buried in the ground, and the jagged piece of metal wouldn't have sliced into my skin, and I wouldn't have let out a sharp cry of pain. And without that sharp cry of pain, no one would have known I was there, and I wouldn't have ended up lying half-undressed in a field of maize with Jamie Tait clambering through the hedge, leering at me with drunken eyes.

thirteen

I managed to get my shorts up before Jamie could get a good look, and then I scrambled to my feet. A sharp pain stabbed in my knee. I glanced down to see blood streaming from a deep gash. A drunken curse made me look up. Jamie was walking unsteadily towards me, swigging from the whiskey bottle and licking his lips. His feet stumbled in the dirt. His face was red from drinking and his eyes were shrunk to pin-holes. They fixed on me like laser beams.

'Look at this,' he said. 'Look at *this* ...'

'Stay there,' I told him, backing away.

He laughed. 'Why – what you gonna do? Set your dog on me? Woof woof ...' He stopped a short distance from me and took a swig from the bottle. Whiskey spilled from his mouth. 'Here,' he said, offering me the bottle. 'You wanna drink? Have a drink ... go on.'

I shook my head.

'What's the matter? Eh? Look at you ...' He wiped his mouth and looked me up and down, nodding at my knee. 'Nasty ... want me to kiss it better? Give it a suck?'

'Leave me alone,' I said.

He grinned and started edging towards me. My heart was pounding and my throat was dry. I'd never been so scared in my life. I backed away some more, wondering where the hell Dominic was. Over Jamie's shoulder I could see Lee Brendell watching idly through the gap in the hedge, but there was no sign of Dominic. Brendell kept glancing behind him, looking down at the ground, and I began to fear the worst.

'Dominic!' I called out. *'DOMINIC!'*

Jamie stopped in his tracks. 'Shut up,' he said quietly.

I started to shout again – 'Domin—' but before I could finish Jamie stepped forward and slapped me hard across the face. It didn't hurt that much, but the shock of it was absolutely stunning. He hit me. He actually *hit* me. I couldn't believe it. No one had *ever* hit me. A surge of ice-cold rage shot through my veins and without thinking I started lunging towards him. He didn't move. He simply stared at me, daring me to try it. The look in his eyes drained the life out of me. As I cowered away, I heard Dom's voice calling out weakly from behind the hedge.

'Cait ... Cait?'

Jamie turned and called out to Lee. 'Put him *out*, chrissake.'

Brendell disappeared from view. I heard a scuffle, then a dull thump, followed by a groan ... and another dull thump ... and then it was quiet. Brendell sauntered back to the gap in the hedge and nodded at Jamie. Jamie turned back to me. The grin was gone. His eyes were cold and dull.

'Come here,' he said.

I shook my head.

Without a word he reached out and grabbed me by the arm and began dragging me across to the hedge. I struggled at first, but the more I pulled the tighter he gripped me, digging his fingernails into my skin. I gave up struggling and stumbled along beside him. He wasn't talking any more. His face was set in a trance-like gaze and he was continually licking his lips and wiping his mouth with the back of his hand. Up close, he smelled disgusting – a foul mixture of whiskey, cigarette smoke, and sweaty after-shave.

As we approached the hedge, Brendell lit a cigarette and blew smoke into the air. He ogled me for a moment then spoke to Jamie.

'There's no time for that,' he said.

'Shut up. Where's McCann?'

Brendell shrugged. 'Sleeping.'

Jamie shoved me towards the hedge. 'Go on.'

I looked at him.

'*Move,*' he hissed.

I climbed through the gap in the hedge. Brendell took hold of my arm and dragged me to one side. Across the lane, Dominic was lying in the verge with his knees tucked up into his chest. Blood was dribbling from his mouth and an ugly bruise was already beginning to colour the side of his head. I started pulling towards him, but Brendell just flicked his wrist and tugged me back. The strength in his arm was incredible.

'What have you done to him?' I cried.

Brendell ignored me.

'What have you *done*?'

He tightened his grip and a blinding pain creased my arm. When I yelped he glanced at me. His eyes were blank holes.

'He's breathing,' he said, glancing at Dom.

Simple as that.

Meanwhile, Jamie had squeezed through the gate and was taking a long swig from the whiskey bottle. Brendell just watched him. When Jamie had finished drinking he took a deep breath and looked around. His feet were steady on the ground but his upper body was circling.

'What's the time?' he said.

Brendell looked at his watch. 'Six – just gone.'

Jamie belched and spat on the ground. He looked up the lane. 'Where the hell is he?'

'He'll be here,' Brendell said calmly.

Jamie turned his eyes on me. I couldn't stand the way he was looking at me and I had to lower my eyes to the ground. It was quiet for a minute. I looked over at Dominic. The blood had stopped running from his mouth. He still wasn't moving, but I could see his chest rising, and I thought I could see a faint fluttering movement of his lips. I heard Jamie sigh and start towards me.

'It's no good, Lee,' he said. 'I got it good for this one. You'll have to take the gyppo on your own.'

I heard Brendell mutter something under his breath. Then he said, 'Not now, Jamie. Save it.'

'Can't,' he said.

I was still looking at the ground when I felt Jamie's hand on my neck. I flinched and ducked away. He grabbed me by the hair and pulled me towards him. Brendell let go of my arm. Jamie jerked my head, making me look at him. His jaw was set tight and his eyes were out of control.

'Time for a walk in the woods,' he said, letting go of my hair and grabbing my hand. He started pulling me towards the gate. I dug my feet in and resisted. He stopped and stared at me.

'You might as well make it easy on yourself,' he said.

'My dad's going to tear you apart,' I said quietly.

He smiled. 'Probably – but that's not going to help you much now, is it?'

The cold truth of his words momentarily sapped my strength, and as he tightened his grip on my arm and dragged me off towards the gate, I let myself go limp.

Struggling then was pointless, a waste of energy. Physical strength wasn't going to get me anywhere, he was far too strong for that. I had to use my head, think clearly, slow things down, wait for the right time, wait for the opportunity to surprise him.

As he yanked my arm again, pulling me upright, I glanced around. In the distance the woods spread out like a dark and dirty blanket tossed on the ground. I shuddered, imagining the stark trees and the barren earth and that cold, forgotten light ...

Don't give up, I thought.

Never give up.

We were nearly at the gate now. Jamie was tugging me along at a frenzied pace, jerking on my arm, whipping it like I was a dog on a lead. He was breathing heavily. I looked over my shoulder at Brendell, hoping desperately that he might take pity on me. But he wasn't even looking. He was peeing in the hedge.

Jamie tugged my arm again and swung me round in front of the gate. I looked down into the woods. This is it, I thought. Last chance. If you go down there it won't be worth coming back.

As Jamie took a drink from the bottle, I studied the gate. It was an old wooden thing, about shoulder height. I couldn't be sure, but I reckoned he'd have to let go of my arm to get over it. Even if it was only for a second, that was enough. It had to be. I thought it through. Either he'd go over the gate first, in which case I'd run down the lane and head for the beach, or else he'd make me go over first ... which meant running for the woods. That didn't exactly fill me with confidence – but it was a whole lot better than nothing.

'You ready?' Jamie slurred. I looked at him. The bottle

in his hand was almost empty. He could hardly stand up. He rolled his head and looked at the gate, lurched to one side, then looked back at me. 'I know what you're thinking,' he said. Then, with a loopy grin, he spun round and launched a kick at the gate. The hinges cracked, the gatepost split, and the whole thing toppled over and fell to the ground.

Jamie turned to me and winked, and with a sunken heart I bowed my head and said goodbye to my sanity.

I felt his hand tighten on my arm, and I bent my elbow to lessen the shock of another sharp yank – but it never came. I waited a few seconds and then eventually looked up, expecting to see him drinking again, or leering at me, but he wasn't. He was looking back up the lane. His eyes were suddenly sharp.

The next few minutes passed in a blur. At the time, it all happened so quickly that I couldn't take it in, but whenever I think about it now – and I think about it a lot – I can remember every little detail. I can remember the flash of the pale blue sky against the green of the hedges as I turned my head and looked up the lane, and I can remember the flood of emotions that flowed through my body as I saw Lucas striding down the lane. I can feel them right now, an intoxicating blend of ecstasy, fear, relief, hope, love – and loathing. For the first time in my life I wanted to see someone hurt.

Brendell lumbered into the middle of the lane to block Lucas's way. Standing tall, with his legs slightly apart and his hands hanging down at his sides, he looked enormous. In comparison, Lucas looked frail. But that didn't seem to bother him. He just walked directly at Brendell, never wavering and never taking his eyes off him. The closer he got, the less confident Brendell looked. His feet started fidgeting. He scratched his head. He hunched his shoulders. I heard him say something, but Lucas said nothing. He just kept walking.

It was if Brendell didn't exist.

Lucas closed rapidly, walking like a man possessed. Brendell waited until he was less than a metre away, and then he made his move. For a big man, he was surprisingly fast, and as he steadied his feet and then suddenly lunged forward, I held my breath, expecting the worst. But Lucas was faster. The instant Brendell moved, he dodged to the left and then flashed to the right and snatched up a two-foot log from the hedgerow. It happened so fast that Brendell was still stumbling after thin air as Lucas rounded on him and hammered the log into the back of his head. A bone-shattering *whump* rang out and Brendell fell heavily to the ground. As he lay there, with one leg twitching in the dirt, Lucas stepped up, raised the log in both hands and brought it down on his head again.

'*Jesus*,' whispered Jamie.

I'd forgotten he was there.

Lucas dropped the log and turned to face us. He was about thirty metres away, but I could see the look in his eyes. The savagery of it was frightening. As he started towards us, Jamie swung me round and grabbed me round the neck, holding me in front of him. I could feel the tension in his body. I could hear his terrified breathing in my ear. I could smell the panic in his sweat. He started dragging me towards the broken gate, and I thought for a minute he was going to run for it, but at the gate he stopped. I could sense him looking around, and I wondered what he was looking for. His arm was so tight around my neck I could hardly breathe. I tried telling him to loosen his grip, but all that came out was a throaty squeak. Then he moved again, pulling me over to the broken gatepost with a strange grunting noise. His grip tightened, I felt a sudden movement behind me, and then I heard the hollow crash of breaking glass.

The next thing I knew he was holding the broken bottle to my face.

His hand was shaking and I could feel the jagged glass brushing against my cheek. I knew that if I looked at it I'd probably die of fright, so I kept my head still and focused on Lucas. He was coming towards us, walking down the lane with the same primitive determination as before – eyes fixed, face set, his body primed for action.

Sweat dripped into my eyes.

I could smell whiskey from the broken bottle.

As Lucas closed, Jamie dragged me away from the gate into the middle of the lane. His breathing was harsh and rapid now, as if he couldn't get any air into his lungs, and his skin was drenched in sweat. It smelled sour.

Lucas was almost upon us.

Jamie held me tighter. I felt the broken bottle press against my skin, and then his voice rasped in my ear. 'That's far enough,' he warned Lucas. 'Come any closer and I'll cut her face off.'

Lucas slowed and stopped. He was about a metre away. He didn't say anything. He didn't even look at me. He just kept his eyes fixed on Jamie as he reached behind him and pulled out a knife. Sunlight glinted on the wicked-looking blade. I recognised it as the one I'd seen hanging on the wall in his den.

Jamie stiffened and his arm tightened around my neck.

'Drop it,' he said. 'Drop it or I'll cut the bitch.'

'Then what?'

Jamie hesitated. 'You think I'm joking?'

Lucas shrugged. 'I don't really care. I'm going to stick you anyway.' He raised the knife and held it balanced lightly in his hand.

Jamie was trembling now. His voice caught in his throat as he spoke. 'Listen ... if anything happens to me—'

'Do you want to live?'

'What?'

Lucas stepped forward and raised the knife, levelling it at Jamie's eyes. It was no more than an inch from my face. Lucas still hadn't looked at me. His face was blank and cold, emotionless. He spoke quietly. 'Lose the bottle or I'll take your eyes out.'

'You wouldn't—'

'Do it.' The knife edged past me. 'Now.'

The next few seconds lasted for ever. No one spoke. The heat bore down and the air was thick with the smell of honeysuckle and sweat. The background was a non-existent blur. All I could see was Lucas. His hand, gripping the bone-handled knife. His face, his eyes, the pores of his skin. The lane was deathly quiet, interrupted only by the sound of Jamie's terrified breathing. He knew as well as I did that Lucas meant what he said. It wasn't a threat, it was a fact. Plain and simple. If he didn't drop the bottle and let me go, Lucas would use the knife. Jamie only had one option, and eventually he took it. With a strange little whimpering sound he relaxed his grip on my neck and stepped back. Seconds later I heard the broken bottle drop to the ground. I felt my knees go weak, and I thought for a moment I was going fall, but I managed to steady myself. Lucas hadn't moved a muscle. He still had the knife in his hand and he was still staring at Jamie.

'Are you hurt?' he asked me.

'I don't think so.'

'Come here.'

I stepped towards him.

He said, 'Move out of the way.'

'What—'

'Get behind me. Now.'

I stepped to one side and moved behind him. When I turned around I could see Jamie standing in front of us. His face was drawn and pale, he was shaking from head to toe, and his eyes were white with fear. It's hard to believe, but I almost felt sorry for him.

Lucas wasn't quite so sympathetic.

The moment I was safely out of the way, his knife hand lowered and he moved towards Jamie. Jamie barely had time to raise his hands in meek surrender before Lucas swung to one side and kicked him hard in the belly. As Jamie groaned and doubled over, Lucas grabbed him by the hair and brought his knee up into his face. Jamie's nose broke with a sickening crack and he slumped to the ground with blood pouring from his face.

I thought that was it. Enough. But I was wrong. Lucas hadn't finished. He hadn't even started.

As Jamie writhed on the ground holding his face in his hands, Lucas stepped over him and squatted down on his chest then pinned his arms to the ground with his knees and held the knife to his throat. Jamie coughed, spluttering up blood. Lucas stared at him for a moment then leaned forward and whispered something in his ear. Jamie's eyes widened and he started sobbing – *No! Please! No!* – and the next thing I knew Lucas had twisted round with the knife between his teeth and was unbuckling Jamie's trousers. Jamie was screaming and writhing in panic but Lucas had his arms pinned down with his feet and there was nothing he could do.

I was stunned for a moment.

I thought – he's not, is he? Surely he's not ...?

Jesus Christ!

I screamed – 'Lucas! No! *LUCAS!*' – but he didn't take any notice. He had the belt undone now and was taking the knife from his mouth. 'LUCAS!' I yelled. 'PUT THE KNIFE DOWN! *PUT IT DOWN!*' This time he seemed to hear me. I saw him pause. He looked at the knife in his hand, then looked up at me.

'Don't do it, Lucas,' I said, breathing hard. 'Please – put the knife away.'

He stared at me. There was no anger in his eyes, not a trace of viciousness. He looked as docile as a puppy. As I flicked a glance at the knife in his hand I noticed a dark stain on Jamie's dishevelled trousers. He'd peed himself. I looked into Lucas's eyes.

'That's enough,' I said gently.

He looked over his shoulder at Jamie. I looked at him too. He was a mess. His nose was red and swollen, his face was covered in blood, and a jagged bit of broken tooth was stuck to his lip. His eyes focused on me and he tried to say something, but all that came out was, 'N ... nuuh ...'

Lucas looked at me. 'You know, it'd save everyone a lot of bother if I cut him up and buried him in the woods.'

'For God's *sake*, Lucas ...'

I stopped when I realised he was smiling at me.

As we walked back up the lane to check on Dominic, I couldn't stop thinking about what I'd just witnessed. I'd never experienced any real violence before, and now that I had I didn't know what to think about it. Of course, I was glad that I was safe, and I can't pretend that I didn't enjoy seeing Jamie Tait suffer ... but whatever sense of relief I had was completely outweighed by my reaction to the violence itself. Its sheer power, its brutal simplicity, the way it cut straight to the heart of things – it was breathtaking. Up until then I'd always gone along with the idea that violence never solves anything ... but now, I wasn't so sure. I was beginning to realise that violence *can* be a legitimate answer. It *can* solve things. And I wasn't sure I liked that.

I glanced at Lucas, walking calmly beside me. He had the face of a young boy again. It was almost impossible to believe that a few moments ago he'd nearly committed an act of atrocity. If I hadn't stopped him when I did ...

I looked over my shoulder. Jamie had got to his knees and was throwing up at the side of the lane.

'Would you really have done it?' I asked Lucas.

'Done what?'

'You know ... cut off his thing.'

He looked at me, his face a picture of innocence. 'What do you think I am – some kind of animal?'

Dominic was still out cold. Lucas knelt down and checked him over. First he examined his head, looking in his mouth and his eyes, then he ran his hands over his body, and finally he checked his pulse.

'He's all right,' he said, standing up. 'He'll come round in a minute. Get him on his side and loosen his clothing.' He looked down the lane, watching Jamie as he staggered off into the distance, and then he turned back to me. 'He's gone. I'm just going to check on the other one.'

I watched him walk over and squat down beside Brendell, and then I tended to Dominic. His skin was pale and cold to the touch and his breathing was still quite shallow. I got him into the recovery position. His eyes started fluttering and a faint groan sounded in the back of his throat.

I pulled a handkerchief from my pocket, spat on it, and dabbed at the egg-sized swelling on the side of his head.

After a while I heard Lucas come up behind me.

I looked up at him. 'How's Brendell?'

'He'll live.'

I wiped a smear of dirt from Dominic's face. Lucas crouched down beside me with a wad of crushed dock leaves in his hand. He put a hand on my leg and told me to hold still, then gently cleaned the cut on my knee. The crushed leaves felt cool and refreshing on my skin.

'Thanks,' I said.

He smiled.

'I mean, for everything. If you hadn't come along when you did ...' My voice started trembling and my whole body began to shake. 'Oh, Lucas ... he was going to ...'

Lucas took my hand and helped me to my feet. 'It's over,' he said. 'You're safe. They won't bother you again.'

I shook my head. 'It'll never be over ...'

And then I broke down and cried. I wept so hard I thought I was going to die. The tears welled up from somewhere deep inside, wracking my body with a violent trembling that sucked the air from my lungs and had me gasping for breath. God, it hurt so much ... everything hurt. And that just made me cry even harder. Lucas stepped forward and took me in his arms. I held him tight and let the tears flood out.

'It's all right,' he whispered. 'It's all right ...'

But I knew it wasn't.

When I finally stopped crying, I felt drained, sick, and ugly. My eyes were swollen, my chest ached, my neck hurt, and my face was caked in snot and tears. Also, my fingers hurt from clinging so hard to Lucas. As I sniffed and reached for my handkerchief, he gently prised himself away.

'Your brother,' he said.

'What?'

He nodded at Dominic. I looked down to see him getting gingerly to his feet, holding his head and groaning.

'What the hell's going on?' he mumbled, swaying from side to side and blinking at the sunlight. 'Cait? What are you doing here? What happened?' He squinted at Lucas, then his eyes widened and he took a step back. 'Hey – what are you ...?' He groaned again and put his hand to his head. 'God – who hit me? Did you hit me? Where's Jamie ...?'

'Shut up, Dom,' I said.

'What—'

'Just shut up and listen.'

We sat him down and explained everything ... well, almost everything. I toned down Jamie's intentions and left out a few unnecessary details, but I told him as much as he needed to know. I think he was suffering from a slight concussion. At first, he didn't seem to understand what I was saying, he just sat there with a dazed look on his face. Then all at once he jumped to his feet and started ranting and raving, saying he was going to kill Jamie, kill Brendell ...

'For God's sake,' I sighed.

'I'll bloody *kill* him—'

'Shut *UP*!'

He stared at me, all hurt and offended. 'What? What's the matter? I was only—'

'Don't,' I snapped, close to tears. 'Just don't say another word.'

His mouth opened and he started to say something, but when he saw the look on my face he changed his mind.

He couldn't keep it up for long, though, and within a couple of seconds he'd turned his attention to Lucas.

'Yeah?' he said. 'What are you looking at?'

Lucas smiled. 'I think it's time we had a little chat.'

After double-checking that Jamie had gone and Brendell was still unconscious, Lucas walked Dominic up the lane and spent a couple of minutes talking to him. There were no wagging fingers, no raised voices, they just stood there facing each other like a couple of old ladies having a natter. When they came back Dominic was quiet and thoughtful and he couldn't look me in the eye.

I don't know what Lucas said to him – I've never asked, and Dominic's never told me – but as the three of us headed back through the woods I began to think I might have a brother again.

After all I'd been through, it was about as much consolation as a £10 lottery win the day after your house burns down.

We walked in silence, like weary soldiers returning from the battlefield, all lost in our own troubled minds. Come to think of it, we probably looked like soldiers, too. Dominic with his battered head, me with my wounded knee, and Lucas in his green fatigues with a knife stuck down his belt. It was a hard journey, both mentally and physically, and by the time we reached the cornfield at the edge of the woods, my mind and my knee were both beginning to throb.

Lucas, who was leading the way, stopped and turned around. Me and Dominic shuffled to a halt in front of him.

'Right,' he said, looking at both of us. 'You'd better start thinking about what you're going to tell your dad. Truth or lies? You can't just go home looking like that and hope he won't notice anything.'

I looked at Dominic to see if he had any ideas, but he still wasn't ready to talk. There was a blank, almost drugged look on his face. I don't know if it was self-pity or guilt or what, but whatever it was, it was starting to get on my nerves.

I said to Lucas, 'I don't think I can tell Dad the truth – not yet, anyway. It's too complicated. I need some time to think about things.'

'You'll have to tell him something,' Lucas said.

'If I can get in the house without him seeing me, I think it'll be all right. As long as I don't wear shorts, he won't notice the cut on my knee.'

'You'd better cover up your arms, too,' Lucas suggested.

I looked down. There was a hand-sized bruise on my elbow where Jamie had grabbed me. 'What about my neck,' I said. 'It feels a bit sore.'

Lucas gently lifted my chin with his finger and took a close look. 'No, it's all right. Just a bit red. You can hardly see it.' He smiled at me, then his eyes hardened and he turned to Dominic. 'What about you?'

Dom blinked. 'Uh?'

Lucas moved towards him. 'Come on, snap out of it. There'll be plenty of time for feeling sorry for yourself later. Right now you've got to help your sister.'

Dom glanced at me and nodded.

Lucas said, 'Right. Start thinking. Give me some lies. What happened to your head?'

Dom licked his lips. 'Uh ... I was drunk.'

'Where?'

'Brendell's boat?'

'Good. What happened?'

'He hit me with a pool cue.'

'Who did?'

'Brendell.'

'Why?'

'He likes hitting people.'

Lucas nodded. 'That'll do. It's stupid enough to make sense. When you get home, you go in first and find your father. Tell him what you just told me. Then, when he starts giving you hell, Cait can sneak in without being seen. Have you got that?'

Dom nodded again.

Lucas looked at him. 'Well – what are you waiting for?'

'Aren't you coming?'

'I want a word with Cait. It won't take long. Go and wait for her in the lane.'

Dom hesitated, looking at me.

'It's all right,' I told him.

He thought about it for a moment, looking hard at Lucas, then he climbed the bank into the cornfield and headed towards the lane. I waited until he was out of sight and then I moved towards Lucas. I didn't think about it. It just happened. It seemed the most natural thing in the world. But when I reached him and went to hold him, an embarrassed look crossed his face and he took a step back.

'What's the matter?' I said.

'Cait ...'

'What?'

Without saying anything, he looked me in the eye. I looked back. He didn't *have* to say anything, his eyes said it all. I knew what he meant.

I stepped back, feeling a bit foolish. 'Sorry.'

Lucas grinned. 'Me too.'

'It's been a funny old day, as my dad would say.'

'That's the truth of it.'

Just for a moment I felt as if I'd been here before ... only it wasn't here, it was somewhere else. And Lucas was some*one* else, someone familiar, and we were talking about secrets ...

I'm not a child.

'Cait?' said Lucas

I looked at him. 'I'm not ...'

'You're not what?'

I shook my head. 'Nothing. I was just ... it's nothing.' I stretched my neck and looked up at the sky, then breathed in deeply and looked down at the ground. The light was greying and the evening shadows were lengthening. Strangely enough, the woods looked lighter than they had this afternoon.

'What are you going to do?' I asked Lucas.

'About what?'

'Come on – you *know* what. Jamie Tait's not going to forget what you did to him.'

'I know.'

'There's going to be a lot of people looking for you.'

'I know.'

I looked at him. 'You're leaving, aren't you?'

'I always was.'

'When?'

'Sunday, probably.'

'Sunday?'

He shrugged. 'I've managed to avoid getting my legs broken so far. I think I can probably last another couple of days. Besides, I've got a festival to go to ...'

I laughed. 'And some new boots to buy.'

'I thought you were buying them?'

'I don't know your size.'

We smiled at each other. It was an awkward moment, with all sorts of unspoken things bubbling away beneath the surface, and after a while we both looked away.

That was us, I realise now. Us – a moment. That was what we were: a moment. No past, no future, nothing beyond the present. It was almost as if we were different people when we were together, people who only existed in the present. And in its own way, that was perfect. It's just that it would have been nice to be somewhere else once in a while.

'You'd better go,' Lucas said. 'Your brother'll be wondering what's going on.'

'Let him wonder. What are you going to do for the next couple of days?'

'Hide, mostly.'

'Good.'

'I don't know what time I'll get there on Saturday—'

'Don't worry. I'll be there all day.'

He looked at me. 'Don't be too hard on your brother. And try not to worry. I'll always be close.'

Before I could ask what he meant, he came over and kissed me on the cheek, then turned around and headed off into the woods. I was so surprised I couldn't move for a moment. As I watched him merge silently into the dark of the woods, I touched my cheek and put my hand to my mouth.

His kiss tasted of sweet tobacco.

fourteen

I haven't been back to Joe Rampton's lane since that day, and I don't think I ever will. It's a shame because I always used to like it there. The leafy hedgerows, the warm summer shadows, the smell of maize and honeysuckle ... it was a special kind of place.

Now it's just a sick memory.

I try not to think about it too much, but sometimes it's hard not to, especially at night when the air is thick and hot, or when I catch the smell of certain things, like whiskey or glass or stale aftershave, or sometimes even when I'm just having a wee. Then it all comes flooding back – the drunken menace, the violence, the heat, the disabling sense of fear ...

I suppose it would have helped to tell someone about it. As Dad said, it probably wouldn't have made me feel any better, it might even have made things worse for a while, but at least it might have given the pain some life. Maybe that's why I'm telling it now, to relieve the pain ... or maybe not. I don't know. Things are different now. My outlook has changed. I'm older, things have moved on ...

Things are different.

Back then there didn't seem much point in talking about it. It was over, it was done. Talking wouldn't have changed anything. It was just like before – I knew I ought to tell someone about it, but I couldn't think who. If I'd told Dad, he would have gone crazy and probably ended up killing someone, and that wouldn't have done either of us any good. And if I'd told the police ... well, what was there to tell? What had *actually* happened? Not much. A bit of manhandling, a slap, some verbal assault, veiled threats ... all impossible to prove. I'd have had to explain what I was doing there, and what happened afterwards, and then Lucas would have got dragged into it, and he was in enough trouble already ...

There was no point.

Of course, if I'd thought about it a little less selfishly, things might not have turned out as they did. But I wasn't to know that then.

When I went downstairs the following morning I was surprised to see Dominic and Dad sitting together at the kitchen table. They weren't arguing, they weren't even frowning at each other, they were just sitting there quietly smoking cigarettes and sipping from mugs of steaming hot coffee. The swelling on Dom's head had gone down a little, but the bruising had spread right across his face. From beneath his eye to behind his ear, his skin was a hideous blend of purple, black, crimson and blue.

Dad smiled. 'Pretty, isn't it?'

Of course, he didn't know that I already knew about it, and as he looked at me I tried to give the impression that I was shocked. It wasn't that hard – I *was* shocked. Not by the bruise, obviously, but simply because Dad looked so damn happy about it. The night before, as Lucas had suggested, Dominic had gone in first and I'd sneaked in a few minutes later. By then the shouting had already started. As I went upstairs to shower and change I could hear Dad yelling at Dominic in the front room. It went on for hours – screaming and swearing, slamming doors, kicking the walls. They were still at it when I made myself some cocoa and climbed into bed.

And now, here they were, all sweetness and light.

It baffled me.

'What happened?' I said, putting on my best puzzled face.

Dad smiled again. 'Someone beat some sense into him.'

I looked at Dom. An embarrassed grin crossed his face.

'It's nothing,' he said. 'It looks worse than it is. I'll tell you about it later. Do you want some coffee?'

After a moment's hesitation, I joined them at the table. As Dom poured me a cup of coffee he gave me a quick glance and a sly nod of his head. I took that to mean that everything was all right. He'd sorted things out with Dad, he'd lied successfully. He'd been beaten unconscious and I'd almost been raped – and we'd got away with it. Yeah, everything was just fine.

I sipped my coffee. It tasted bitter.

Dad said, 'Sorry about all the noise last night. We had a few things to iron out – things got a bit fraught.'

'You seem all right now,' I said.

He looked at Dom. 'I think we're getting there.'

'Well, that's good.' I turned to Dom. 'You've seen the light, have you?'

He looked uncomfortable. 'I wouldn't put it like that.'

'How *would* you put it?'

'Look,' he said. 'I'm sorry if I've been a pain in the arse—'

'Sorry?'

His face was serious. 'Yeah – I'm sorry.'

I knew he meant it, but just then I didn't care. The way I saw it, sorry didn't change anything. It didn't undo what I felt or what I'd been through. Nothing could do that.

Not now, not ever. He'd hurt me. He probably hadn't meant to, and it probably would have happened anyway, but he was my brother. Brothers aren't supposed to hurt you.

I got up from the table and turned to go.

'Hold on, Cait,' Dominic said. 'Just a minute—'

'I have to go,' I said. 'I'll see you later.'

As I went out the door I heard Dad call my name. There was quiet concern in his voice, and I suddenly felt sorry for him. He finally gets his son back ... everything's fine ... and then his uptight daughter goes all moody on him. I nearly turned round and went back, but I knew if I did I'd start feeling sorry for Dominic, too, and then I'd start to think about forgiving him, and I didn't *want* to forgive him.

So I called Deefer and stomped off down the lane, and I didn't slow down until I'd made myself good and angry again.

The trouble was, as soon as the woods came in sight the anger turned to trepidation and I couldn't bring myself to go any further. I tried, but each time I got to the gap in the hedge my legs turned to jelly and I couldn't breathe properly. When I turned back, I felt all right again. But I didn't *want* to go back. In the end I just sat on a rotten log for the best part of an hour while Deefer stared at me and whined.

The rest of the day passed fairly quietly. Dad got on with his writing, Dominic stayed in his room, and I just pottered about trying to make myself feel normal again. At first, I didn't think it was possible. There were just too many things going on in my head, things I didn't know how to deal with: there was Lucas, Jamie, Simon, Bill, Dominic, Dad; there were confused feelings of desire, hate, pain, ignorance and doubt; there were memories of the past and fears for the future; and then there was me. Caitlin McCann. What was I? What was I doing? Where was I going? Was I innocent? guilty? foolish? gullible? Was I true to myself ...?

All these things were connected, but at the same time they didn't fit together. They were out of sync. It was like one of those puzzles where you have to slide the little tiles around to make a picture. All the bits are there, but until you get them in the right order you can't see what the picture is supposed to be. So that's what I tried to do – get the bits in order.

As the afternoon wore on I just kept moving all the bits around in my head, trying to fit them together. But, unlike a plastic puzzle, these bits didn't keep still. They kept shifting around and changing shape. I'd work on two or three bits, get them sorted out, fix them together, and then I'd leave them for a while to go off and look at some other bits. But by the time I'd sorted *those* bits out, the original bits didn't fit any more. They'd become something else. And then, when I went back to working on *them* again, the other bits started to change.

It was infuriating.

I kept at it, though, and by early evening I was pretty sure I'd got everything as clear as I was going to get it. It was still a bit shaky, a bit out of focus, but all the bits were in place and I could finally see the whole picture. The only thing was, it was an abstract picture, and no matter how hard I looked I still couldn't work out what it was supposed to be.

Later that night, around ten o'clock, Lenny Craine came round. I was in the bath when he arrived. The radio was playing quietly and the bathroom was filled with steam. I heard Dad open the door, I heard them go into the sitting room, and then I heard Dominic going downstairs to join them. The sitting room is directly beneath the bathroom, so I turned off the radio and lay still, trying to hear what they were talking about. But all I could hear was a chink of glasses and a low muffled mumbling through the floor-boards.

I turned the radio back on and sank my head beneath the water.

Forget it, I told myself. Ignore them. What do you care what they're talking about? It's probably nothing, anyway. It's just Lenny popping round for a quick drink ... maybe a few quick drinks ... a quiet chat ... it's nothing ... nothing to do with you ...

I sat up and rinsed soap from my hair.

... and even if it *is* something to do with you, you don't really want to know right now, do you? Let it wait. Go to bed. You're tired. Tomorrow's Saturday. You've got to get up early in the morning for the festival. You don't want to go downstairs ... imagine it ... they'll all be sitting around smoking cigarettes and drinking beer and talking about fishing or books or something ... Dominic, Dad and Lenny ... having a laugh ...

What do you want with that?

I got out of the bath and stood in front of the mirror and told myself to shut up. Then I quickly dried my hair and put on a dressing gown and went downstairs.

In the sitting room the curtains were open and a full moon was shining brightly through the window. It was a tidal moon, hanging low in the sky, as bright and clear as a pale white sun. Dad was standing at the window, Dominic was in the armchair, and Lenny was slumped heavily on the settee. Everyone had drinks in their hands and serious looks on their faces.

The room was heavy with silence.

Dad turned from the window and smiled at me. It was a good effort – but it didn't fool me. The biggest smile in the world wouldn't have been enough to hide the tension in his eyes.

'Do you want a glass of wine?' he asked.

I nodded.

'Dom?' he said.

'I'll get it,' said Dominic.

I went over and sat next to Lenny. He was out of uniform, dressed in a loose khaki shirt and baggy old trousers.

'Hello, Cait,' he said. 'Looking forward to the festival?'

His voice had that forced chirpiness that usually means bad news.

I nodded. 'Are you going?'

'Of course,' he grinned. 'Someone's got to keep the peace. You know what these environmental terrorists are like when they get out of hand. The RSPCA, Cats Protection League, the Women's Institute ...'

I smiled as best as I could.

Dominic came over with another beer for Lenny and a glass of wine for me. As he passed it over he gave me a 'be careful' look. Seeing as I didn't have a clue what I was supposed to be careful *about*, I thought it was a pretty stupid thing to do. I kept my eye on him as he sat down in the armchair and lit a cigarette, hoping he might give me a hint, but his face was expressionless. I took a sip of wine and looked at Dad. He was standing at the window sipping his whiskey and watching me like a hawk.

'Where did you get that?' he said suddenly.

'What?'

He nodded. 'That cut on your knee.'

I looked down. The hem of my dressing gown had slipped to one side revealing the bruised gash on my knee. 'On the beach,' I said quickly. 'I slipped over – there was a metal stake or something buried in the sand ...'

Dad stared at me. 'When?'

'I can't remember ... yesterday, I think.'

'Why didn't you tell me?'

I shrugged. 'It's just a cut.'

He gave me a long, hard look. 'Is there anything else you haven't told me?'

'About what?'

'Lucas.'

I glanced at Dominic. He was staring into thin air. I looked back at Dad. 'What's this all about?' I said.

'You tell me.'

'There's nothing to tell.'

'When did you last see him?'

'I don't know ... a couple of days ago. I saw him down at the creek. Why?'

Dad took a drink of whiskey and Lenny took over the questioning. 'When exactly was this, Cait?'

'I just said – a couple of days ago.'

'Wednesday? Thursday ...?'

I looked at him, then at Dad.

Dad said, 'Just tell him what day it was, Cait.'

I had to think about it. We were sitting at the creek, the creek was almost still. The sun's reflection was rippling on the surface and a pair of swans floated motionlessly at the water's edge ... it seemed a long time ago.

'Wednesday,' I said.

'Are you sure?'

'It was Wednesday.'

'What was he doing?'

'Nothing ... I just bumped into him at the creek. He wasn't doing anything.'

'Did you talk to him?'

'Yes.'

'What about?'

'I can't remember ... just stuff, you know. Nothing important.'

Lenny rubbed his mouth. 'Did anything happen?'

'Like what?'

'Did he ...'

'Did he *what*?'

Dad came over and knelt down in front of me. 'Did he touch you, love?'

'*What?* What do you mean – *touch me*? What the hell are you talking about?'

Lenny said, 'I'm sorry, Cait. We have to ask—'

'Why?' I snapped. 'What's it got to do with you?'

Dad put his hand on my knee. 'All right, Cait—'

'No,' I said angrily. 'It's not *all right*. What's going on? Why are you asking me all these stupid questions?'

Lenny answered. 'There's been another complaint about Lucas.' I turned to look at him, knowing what he was going to say before he said it. He went on. 'A young girl was indecently assaulted near the cliffs this afternoon. She's given us a fairly good description of her attacker ...'

'And you think it was Lucas?'

Lenny nodded. 'Young boy, short to medium height, blond hair, green clothes, carrying a canvas bag ...'

'This girl,' I said. 'Who was it?'

Lenny looked at Dad.

Dad said, 'Angel Dean.'

I laughed, I couldn't help it. *'Angel Dean?'*

Dad frowned at me. 'It's not funny, Cait. He had a knife. She said he threatened her—'

'She would.'

'Pardon?'

I sighed. 'She's lying, Dad. She's making it up. Lucas didn't do anything to her. He wouldn't go anywhere *near* her. She's lying. It's obvious.'

Lenny said, 'Why would she do that?'

'Because ...' I suddenly realised that I couldn't tell them why. If I told them why, I'd have to tell them everything. And if I told them everything ... well, I'd have to tell them everything.

'When did this so-called assault take place?' I asked.

'About two o'clock,' Lenny said.

'Have you asked Lucas where he was?'

'We haven't been able to find him yet.'

I took a deep breath. 'He was with me.'

Two pairs of eyes bored into me.

I looked at Dad. 'When I went out with Deefer today ... you remember? We went down to the beach. We met Lucas and went for a walk. I was with him from about half past one until half past two.'

'Why didn't you say so earlier?' Dad asked.

I shrugged. 'I don't know.'

'You don't *know*?' Lenny said.

'I didn't feel like it.'

'Come on, Cait—'

'I was with him,' I said flatly. 'He couldn't have done it. I was with him.'

Lenny shook his head. 'We're still going to have to bring him in.'

'On what evidence? Have you got any evidence?'

Lenny looked at me. 'Angel told us who it was, Cait. She *described* him—'

'Any forensic evidence? Any injuries? Bruising, skin under her fingernails, blood, fluids ... anything like that?'

'Cait!' Dad exclaimed.

I kept my eyes on Lenny. 'Have you got anything?'

Lenny looked at me. 'Not yet.'

'Isn't that a bit odd?'

'Maybe ... it's not unheard of ...'

'But you'd expect to find something, wouldn't you?'

He nodded. 'Usually.'

'Maybe you ought to ask Angel for some more details,' I suggested. 'Examine her a bit more closely.'

'Listen, Cait, if you know something—'

'All I know is Lucas didn't do it. He *wouldn't* do it. Believe me – he's not like that. And anyway, like I said, he was with me. If you want me to make a statement, I'll make one. If you want me to testify, I will.' I looked at Dad. 'He didn't do it.'

They carried on asking me questions for a while but I didn't have anything else to say. No, I didn't know where Lucas was. No, I didn't know if he was still on the island. No, I didn't know where he'd go if he left the island ... I didn't know anything. Which was pretty much the truth. They weren't very happy about it, but then neither was I.

I figured that made us just about even.

Before he left, Lenny took me to one side and had a quiet word in my ear. 'Don't push your luck, Cait. I like you and I like your dad. You're good people. I'm glad to have you as friends. But I'm still a police officer. I've got a job to do. There's only so far I can go – do you understand?'

'You can go as far as you want,' I said.

He looked at me. Disappointment showed in his eyes. 'Ah, Cait,' he sighed. 'I thought you were one of the good ones.'

That surprised me. I don't suppose it should have, but it did. It hurt me, too. It wasn't fair. I *was* one of the good ones, that's why I was doing what I was doing. I was trying to do what was best ... I *was* good ...

Wasn't I?

I lowered my eyes and looked at the floor.

I just didn't know any more.

Dad showed Lenny to the door, leaving me alone with Dominic for a minute. As soon as I heard the front door open I leaned forward in my seat.

'Do they know anything?' I whispered.

'About what?' he said.

'Anything.'

He frowned. 'I don't think so.'

'Did Lenny say anything about Tait or Brendell?'

'Not to me ... I gave him the story about Brendell hitting me with a pool cue but he didn't seem too bothered about it.' He glanced nervously at the door. 'This thing with Angel and Lucas—'

'Tait set it up – didn't you know?'

He shook his head. 'I thought he was joking. I didn't think he'd—'

The front door slammed.

Dominic looked at me.

'Don't say anything,' I hissed. 'Just don't—'

Dad entered the room and stood in the doorway looking at us. There wasn't much affection his eyes. As I waited for him to say something my mind strayed back to the day before when I was alone with Lucas at the edge of the woods, when I'd felt as if I'd been there before and that

Lucas was someone else ... and as I thought about it the same strange feeling came over me again. Only this time it was even more mixed up. I couldn't tell if *this* was the moment I'd been thinking about then, and that Dad was the someone else, or if *then* was the moment I was thinking about now, and that Lucas was someone else ... someone familiar ... and we were talking about secrets ...

I'm not a child.

'Cait?' said Dad.

I looked at him. 'I'm not ...'

'You're not what?'

I shook my head. 'Nothing. I was just ... it's nothing.'

At a signal from Dad, Dominic got up and left the room. Dad watched him go, closed the door, then came over and sat down next to me. The settee sagged in the middle and drew us close together.

Dad put his hand on my knee. 'I think it's time we had a little chat.'

Now that we were alone I was afraid my instincts would take over and I'd break down and blurt out the truth. It was the natural thing for me to do, the way I'd always coped in the past, and I didn't think I was capable of resisting it. I didn't think I had the guts ... or the lack of them. But in the end it wasn't as hard as I thought.

Dad wasn't angry. Or, if he was, he didn't show it. Even when I didn't answer his questions he remained in control. He didn't shout, he didn't fume, he didn't go crazy. In fact, his eyes were so steady and his voice so calm, I almost had trouble staying awake. There were a lot of questions – questions about Lucas, questions about Dominic, questions about Angel. But mostly the questions were about me – what are you feeling? what are you thinking? what's wrong? why are you lying? why don't you trust me? what do you want? what do you want me to do? how can I help? are you sad? happy? ill? lonely? jealous? bored? angry? ... They were questions I'd been asking myself since I was old enough to think, and I couldn't have answered them even if I'd wanted to. So I did what a confused teenage daughter is supposed to do – I stared silently at the wall, distant and incapable, and wished that things were different.

I know I ought to have said *something*, if only to put Dad's mind at rest, but I just couldn't find it in me. I couldn't find the words. My mind kept drifting away. I don't know where it went. I don't even know what I was thinking about. I was too tired. I couldn't concentrate. My thoughts were vaporous and indistinct.

It must have been about midnight when I realised that Dad had stopped talking. He was just sitting there with his arm around me staring out of the window. The moon had moved on and the room was dark and quiet. I leaned against him and looked up into his eyes.

'I'm sorry,' I said.

He smiled. 'I know you are. We'll talk about it tomorrow. Right now, I think you'd better get some sleep.'

I kissed him goodnight and left him sitting alone in the dark.

fifteen

The next day I got up early and showered and then started getting ready for the festival. It was only about seven o'clock, but the heat of the sun was already fierce and it looked as if it meant to stay that way. The sky was high and blue and there was barely a breath of wind in the air. It was a day for shorts and a vest, but I was still conscious of the cut on my knee and the bruise on my arm, so I dressed in a pair of cropped trousers and a long-sleeved top. I started fiddling around with my hair, trying to do something a bit special with it, but after a while I got fed up looking at myself in the mirror and I gave up on it. I wasn't really in the mood for looking nice anyway. What was the point? Whatever I wore and whatever I did to my hair, I'd still be a sweaty mess by the end of the day. Besides, it was only a stupid little festival. It was nothing to get excited about. Nothing was going to happen.

Lucas wasn't going to be there.

He wasn't stupid. He'd know the police were looking for him, and he'd also know that that was the least of his worries. Angel's story would have got around by now, and with Jamie's help it would have grown from an unsubstantiated rumour into a stone-cold fact: Lucas was a pervert, a child molester, a rapist, and what's more he was a dirty thieving gyppo. If he showed his face anywhere near the festival, there'd be a riot.

No, Lucas wasn't going to be there. If he had any sense

he'd be miles away by now, heading for the south coast ...
there's some nice places in Dorset and Devon ... I've always want-
ed to take a look at the moors ... I'll send you a postcard ...

Great, I thought. A postcard ...

Wish you were here ...

I ran a comb through my hair, jammed a sun hat on my head, and told myself to forget it. He's gone. Forget it. It was nice while it lasted – whatever it was. But it's over now. It's done. Finished. It's time to move on ...

Crap, crap, all bloody crap.

It *was* nice, damn it. It was fun. It was exciting. It was miserable. It was hard. It was terrifying. It was heartbreaking. It was alive. It was true. It was all there was.

And now ...?

Now all I had to look forward to was a long hot day with Simon and his mum selling *Save the Beach* badges and drinking cans of warm Coke.

Do I really want that? I thought. Do I?

I stared at the mirror.

Does it make any difference what you want?

Does it mean anything?

The girl in the glass looked back at me with a blank face and empty eyes – she was no help at all.

I sat there for a couple of minutes feeling sorry for myself, then I went to the bathroom, had a quiet word with the moose, scooped all my RSPCA stuff into a carrier bag, and set off for the village.

The Hale Summer Festival is held every year on the second Saturday in August. It's not the most thrilling of events but it's always been a pretty good day. The main part of the village is closed to traffic and by nine o'clock the High Street and surrounding sidestreets are lined with all kinds of stalls: local charities, arts and crafts, tombolas, bric-à-brac, plants, clothes, jumble ... everything you'd expect from a small village festival. The pubs are open all day. There are ice cream vans, burger vans, vegetarian stalls, people selling home-made cakes and buns. There's usually a brass band somewhere, and a local pub group playing on the back of a lorry, one of those two- or three-piece bands with drums and an organ and a middle-aged woman singing lively old tunes that get the old folk clapping along when they've had a few drinks. And throughout the day the streets ring out to the sounds of jugglers and clowns and open-air theatre shows. It gets pretty busy, especially when the weather's fine. The local population is swelled by an influx of visitors from the mainland, and by the middle of the afternoon the streets are usually packed.

When I arrived it was still quite early and everyone was busy getting their stalls ready. I knew most of them, at least to say hello to, and as I headed up towards the RSPCA stall outside the library I was greeted with a chorus of friendly nods and waves that went some way towards lifting my spirits. The street was a hive of activity, with people bustling about unloading things from vans, laughing and shouting and singing along to radio music. There was an expectant buzz about the place. But there was also something else in the air, something unspoken. There was an edge to things. Narrowed eyes, frowns amid the smiles, furtive glances ...

It's Angel, I thought as I approached the RSPCA stall. Everyone's heard about poor little Angel and the monster who attacked her. First Kylie Coombe, and now this – what *is* the world coming to?

'Morning, Cait,' Mrs Reed said. 'Thanks for coming.'

I looked up and smiled.

Simon's mum is one of those women who don't care what they look like but who always look pretty good anyway. In her mid-forties, with shoulder-length pale blonde hair and a nice fresh face, she was wearing a plain white dress, no jewellery, no shoes, and no make-up. Her eyes shone like jewels.

'Here,' she said, reaching for my bag, 'let me take that. You look hot. Do you want a drink?'

She put my carrier bag on the counter and passed me a can of economy-brand Coke. I didn't really want it but I thanked her anyway. I looked over at Simon. He was stapling posters to the back wall.

'Hello, Simon,' I said.

He smiled at me. It was a genuine smile, and I was relieved to see it. After what happened the last time we met, I wouldn't have blamed him if he didn't want anything to do with me. He turned back to the poster and finished tacking it up, then put the staple gun in his pocket and spoke to his mum. 'Can you manage on your own for a couple of minutes? I want to have a word with Cait.'

'All right,' she said. 'Don't be long, though. There's a lot of work to do.'

'Five minutes,' he said, signalling for me to follow him.

We walked off down the High Street and turned into a quiet lane that leads up behind the library. I still had the unopened can of Coke in my hand. As we sat down on the kerb I offered it to Simon.

He wrinkled his nose. 'I don't know why she buys it. I can't stand the stuff.'

He was wearing a heavy black shirt with the sleeves rolled up, faded black trousers, and black boots. The darkness of his clothing accentuated the paleness of his skin. He looked almost anaemic. Apart from that, though, he seemed happy enough.

'Have you heard?' he asked.

'About what?'

'Angel Dean – someone attacked her.'

'Yeah, I know.'

'They think it was that boy, you know, the one who—'

'I don't want to talk about it.'

'There's a rumour going round that he's been seen in Moulton—'

'Simon,' I said, giving him an impatient look, 'I really don't want to talk about it. OK?'

He stared at me for a moment, looking a bit puzzled, then flicked at his fringe and lowered his eyes.

We sat there in silence for a while, just staring awkwardly at the ground. My mind wandered back to that Saturday afternoon two weeks ago when I was standing at the bus stop waiting for Bill, reading the Village Events poster. *Saturday 29 July – Jumble Sale in the Village Hall. Sunday 30 July – Free Concert in the Country Park, Brass Bands + Moulton Majorettes. Saturday 5 August – West Hale Regatta: Family Fun Day. Saturday 12 August – Hale Summer Festival* ...

It had all seemed so harmless then.

'We'd better be getting back,' Simon said.

'OK.'

As we headed back to the stall I tried to apologise for my behaviour on Wednesday, but Simon just brushed it off. He was either being kind or he really hadn't noticed how unpleasant I'd been. I preferred to think he was just being kind. Because if he wasn't, if he truly thought my behaviour was acceptable ... well, that was just too pitiful to think about.

By mid-morning the festival was in full swing. The band

had started up, jukeboxes blared from the pubs, and the streets were absolutely jam-packed. I'd never seen it so busy. We were rushed off our feet. It was incredibly hot, and as the day wore on the heat intensified. People stripped down to bare chests and bikinis and the air was thick with the smell of perfume and suntan lotion. I suppose it was the heat that brought out the crowds – that and all the juicy rumours flying around. Everyone had their opinion – customers, locals, stallholders, even people from the mainland – and as I worked I could hear a constant stream of mixed-up comments – *damn gypsies ... nearly killed her, apparently ... people like that need putting down ... mind you, they're used to it – it's the inbreeding, you know ... disgusting ...*

No one had anything *rational* to say about anything. It was as if the heat and the noise and the crowds had driven them all mad. Even people I knew to be level-headed and intelligent were suddenly talking absolute rubbish.

Hell is others, someone once said. I'm not sure who it was, but I bet he lived on an island.

Even though I knew he wouldn't show up, I kept my eyes open for Lucas. It was stupid, I know, but somewhere in the back of my mind a little voice wouldn't let go: *he could disguise himself ... he could send a message ... he might be watching from the cliffs ...*

Yeah, I thought, and he might come riding in on a big white horse and sweep me off to Wonderland.

But I kept a look-out anyway. Once or twice I even thought I saw him – a distant flash of green at the end of the street, a mop of blond hair moving in the crowd, a lone figure walking on the cliffs – but it was all in my imagination.

***

Around midday, I had a bit of trouble with a funny-looking kid in glasses who wanted to buy a poster of a starving dog. It wasn't for sale, of course, it was one of those pictures the RSPCA uses to show how people abuse their pets. But when I told the kid he couldn't have it, he started crying. I showed him some novelty erasers, trying to calm him down, but he didn't want to know. He kept pointing at the skinny old dog, going, 'That one, that one, that one ...'

Then someone said, 'Give him what he wants, for goodness sake.'

I looked around at the voice, about to lose my temper, only to see Dad standing there with a great big grin on his face. Dominic was standing to one side of him, and across the road I was surprised to see Rita and Bill Gray.

'Hello, John,' Mrs Reed said.

'Hello, Jenny,' Dad replied. 'How's it going?'

'Hectic. You wouldn't believe how busy it's been.' She smiled at me, then looked back at Dad. 'We couldn't have managed without Cait.'

'I hope you're working her hard,' Dad said.

'Well, it's all for a good cause.' She glanced at the kid I was serving. He was still crying. 'Simon,' she said. 'Why don't you look after this little chap. Cait can take a break while her family's here.'

'I don't mind—' I started to say.

'Don't be silly. Go on, off you go.'

As I went to leave, Simon reached up and started taking down the dog poster.

'You can't give him that,' I said.

'Why not? He wants it.'

'He's just a kid – it'll give him nightmares.'

'So?'

I shook my head and left him to it.

Outside the stall, Dad pushed through the crowd to meet me.

'How're you doing?' he asked. 'Everything OK?'

I nodded. 'I'm hot.'

'That'll be the sun,' he grinned. 'It'll do that to you.'

He put his arm round my shoulder and steered me across the road. 'We thought we'd go to the Dog and Pheasant. How does that sound?'

'Yeah ... fine.' I glanced across the road at Rita, Bill, and Dominic. 'Did you all come together?'

'Me and Dom were just leaving when Rita drove down and asked if we wanted a lift. You don't mind do you?'

'No – why should I?'

'God knows – I've given up trying to work out what's going on around here.'

We joined the others and headed off towards the pub.

Bill looked a lot different to the last time I'd seen her. Her hair was back to its natural colour and she was dressed quite simply in a summer skirt and a plain white vest. Apart from a light covering of lip gloss, she didn't seem to be wearing any make-up. Her eyes were hidden behind dark glasses and she looked tired, as if she'd been through a lot of sleepless nights. But at least it was a natural-looking tiredness.

At the pub, the others stayed inside with a tray full of beer and sandwiches while me and Bill took ice-cold Cokes out into the beer garden. It felt pretty strange being with her, kind of good and bad, easy and uneasy, all at the same time. I couldn't work out what I wanted. I wanted to talk to her ... I didn't want to talk to her. I wanted to go inside and talk to Dominic ... I didn't want to talk to Dominic. I wanted to know what was going on ... I didn't want to know. Most of all, I think, I wanted to see Lucas. But I wasn't even sure about that any more.

The beer garden was packed with lots of noisy drinkers and children chasing ducks around the pond, but we managed to find a relatively quiet spot at the end of the garden where a mossy old wooden bench overlooked a dried-up stream. We sat down and sipped our drinks, smiling awkwardly at each other. The sun was hotter than ever and the sounds of the festival drifted distantly in the air.

'So,' I said tentatively. 'How are you?'

Bill shrugged. 'I've been better. How about you?'

'Could be worse.'

She grinned. 'How's the stall going?'

'Hot. Busy.'

'Is Simon all right?'

I looked at her, searching for any sign of maliciousness in her face, but all I could see was a flicker of nervous tension.

'He's about the same as he usually is,' I said.

'Irritatingly nice?'

Without meaning to, I laughed. It wasn't much of a laugh, no more than a quick snort, but it left a dirty taste in my mouth. Christ, I thought to myself, why are you so damn *weak* all the time? Why can't you be a bit more unforgiving for once in your life? You're supposed to be angry with Bill. You're supposed to be avoiding her, not having a civilised chat and laughing about Simon with her.

What the hell's the matter with you?

I took a deep breath and tried to relax. The cool odour of beer wafted out from the bar, reminding me of the balcony garden at the rear of the town-centre pub ... the traffic groaning up and down the dual-carriageway below ... Trevor and Malcolm sitting at a plastic table in the shade of a plastic umbrella ...

'You think I've been a stupid little cow, don't you?' said Bill.

I looked at her. I didn't know what to say.

She sighed. 'You're probably right. I have been. But I'm not going to apologise for it.'

'It's up to you what you do,' I said.

'You don't know what I do.'

I shrugged.

'I'm not a tart, Cait. I just want a bit of fun now and then.'

'I know.'

'That's all it is – a bit of fun. There's all kinds of people out there and I want to see what they're like. I want to know what they're doing. I want to enjoy myself, that's all.'

'And are you?'

She flicked a mosquito from her face and stared into the distance. I sipped cold Coke and watched a dragonfly darting over the pond, its body flashing a sheen of metallic blue. It hovered for an instant on invisible wings then dipped its head and shot off silently across the pond like a strange and beautiful spacecraft.

I turned back to Bill. 'I hear you went to a party at Lee Brendell's?'

She shrugged. 'It wasn't really a party, just a bunch of people and a load of booze. I saw Dominic there ...'

'I know.' I looked at her. 'Are you and him ...'

'What?'

'You know ...'

'What – me and *Dominic*? You must be joking.'

'I thought—'

'Well, you thought wrong.' She shook her head. 'God, Cait, when are you going to grow up? There's a world of difference between flirting and fancying and actually doing anything about it. Just because I like someone doesn't mean I'm going to drop my knickers whenever I see them.'

'No?'

Her face broke into a grin. 'Well ... not unless I *really* like them.'

I couldn't help smiling. Bill shook her head again, still grinning, and we exchanged glances, neither of us quite sure if it was all right to be joking or not. It didn't feel right to me, but it didn't feel wrong, either. To hide my confusion, I reached for my Coke and took a long drink. Bill did the same.

'So,' I said, putting my glass down. 'This party on Brendell's boat – was it any good?'

She laughed. 'Not really. They're all the same, that lot. Once you've got over the initial excitement it's all pretty boring. Drugs and booze ... more drugs and more booze ...'

'Been there, done that,' I said sarcastically.

A look of anger flashed across her face. 'At least I'm making an *effort* to grow up. You can't learn *everything* from books, Cait. You can't wrap yourself up in cotton wool and pretend that everything's how it used to be. We're not little girls any more. Things change. Sometimes you've got to get out and do things for yourself.'

'Oh, right – slumming it with Jamie Tait and Lee Brendell, swanning around in Jeeps and speedboats, snorting coke and getting drunk ... that's growing up, is it?'

'*What?*'

'Have you got *any* idea what Jamie Tait is really like?'

'Yeah, I told you. He's boring. He's a stuck-up little prick—'

'And what about the rest of them? What about Angel?'

'What about her?'

I hesitated. 'Do you still think she's all right? You think she's a *good laugh*?'

Bill sniffed. 'That's not fair.'

'Why not?'

'Look, she might be a bit on the *easy* side, she might flash it around a bit, but underneath it all she's just the same as you or me.'

'Don't be ridiculous.'

'All right, so she's not *quite* the same. And maybe she gets a bit too close to the edge now and then. But that doesn't mean she deserved what happened to her. No one deserves that.'

'I didn't say she did. All I meant was, that's what can happen when you start messing around with the bad stuff, when you take your fun too far.'

'Oh, come on, Cait. How can you blame her? What happened to Angel could have happened to anyone. She was in the wrong place at the wrong time, that's all. If you're going to blame anyone, blame the ones who let him out in the first place.'

'Let who out?'

'The gypsy – who else? They had him, didn't they? The police already *had* him for what he did to Kylie Coombe, but then they let him go. If they hadn't let him out he wouldn't have attacked Angel.'

I looked at her. For a brief moment I couldn't tell which Bill I was looking at. Her face seemed to shimmer between two separate personalities: the old Bill, the one I used to know so well; and the new Bill, the one that repelled me. They were two distinct people, they were the same, they merged together, half and half, melting into each other and then melting apart again ...

I shook the illusion from my head.

'I don't understand you,' I said wearily. 'I really don't. One minute you're talking some kind of sense and the next you come out with stuff like that.'

'Like what?'

'You *saw* what happened at the regatta, Bill. You were there. You saw it with your own eyes. How can you lie to yourself?' I sighed. 'I think you've spent too much time with the wrong kind of people.'

'And you haven't, I suppose?'

'What's that supposed to mean?'

She lowered her eyes. 'Nothing.'

I was sick of it now. It was all too confusing, too non-sensical, too much love and hate, all mixed up. It was nauseating.

'I think I'd better go,' I said.

Bill didn't say anything as I got up and walked across the garden, but I could feel her watching me. I didn't know what I thought about that. I didn't have a clue what I thought about anything any more.

I took my empty glass back to the bar then went over to tell Dad I was going. He and Rita were sharing a bottle of wine and Dominic was sitting off to one side nursing half a pint of lager. A gauze patch was taped over the wound on his head.

'Did you have a nice chat?' Rita asked.

'Yeah, thanks ...' I turned to Dad. 'I have to get back now.'

'What time do you finish?'

'About six, I think.'

He looked at Rita. 'We'll still be here then, won't we?'

'I expect so.'

Dad turned back to me. 'We're parked behind the bank at the end of the High Street. If we don't meet you at the stall, we'll be in the car. OK?'

I nodded, then glanced at Dom. There was a look on his face I hadn't seen for a long time. A slightly worried, but calm and reassuring expression that reminded me of the old Dominic. It really felt good to see it, and I couldn't help smiling at him.

'Are you staying on?' I asked.

'Probably,' he said. 'I'll come round later, if you like. When it gets a bit quieter.'

'That'd be nice.'

He smiled. 'OK.'

Through the window I saw Bill crossing the garden. For a moment I felt an urge to go out and talk to her again, but I knew it wouldn't do any good, so I turned around and left.

sixteen

By mid-afternoon the sky had begun to cloud over and the air was thickening with the smell of the sea. A fine mist of silvery-white light filtered the glare of the sun, giving an impression of coolness, but that was about all. The heat burned down as strongly as ever. With the salty smell of the sea mingling with the odours of barbecued meat and beer, and the hot air sucking the atmosphere dry, there was a lot of drinking going on. Most of it was fairly harmless, but every now and then drunken shouts echoed in the streets, and there were reports of one or two scuffles breaking out. Normally it wouldn't have bothered me that much, but with all that had happened over the last few days I was feeling a bit jumpy. Also, there didn't seem to be any police around. I hadn't seen any sign of Lenny ... or anyone else come to that. I suppose they had more important things to do – like running around Moulton searching for imaginary maniacs. But still, you would have thought they'd send someone to keep an eye on things.

I was probably over-reacting, but I could feel a nasty edge creeping into the day and I didn't like it one bit.

Although Dominic had said he was coming to see me, I was still surprised when he showed up. It was about two o'clock. The stall was relatively quiet for a moment, so I asked Mrs Reed if I could take a quick break and then I signalled for Dom to meet me round the back.

He was smoking a cigarette and he looked hot. The gauze patch on his head was limp and sweaty.

'That looks nice,' I said.

He smiled sheepishly, dabbing at the dressing. 'Someone beat some sense into me.'

'Not before time.'

'Yeah ... I know.' His face saddened. 'I never was much good at judging people, was I?'

I looked at him. 'I don't suppose you want to talk about it?'

'Not really – maybe later.'

He puffed on his cigarette and glanced at a pretty girl who was walking past. She saw him watching and tried to look coy, flapping her eyes like Princess Diana used to, but it was all too obvious and it didn't quite work. She just looked as if she had something wrong with her eyes.

Dom looked at me. 'Have you heard from Lucas?'

'No – I think he's probably gone.'

'That's a shame – I never really got the chance to thank him.'

'Neither did I.'

'Maybe he'll come back when it's all died down.'

'I don't think so. He's not the sort of person who comes back to a place.'

'He might come back to a person, though.'

I'd had the same thought myself, but thinking about it had led me down into an uncomfortable world of self-delusion, and I didn't like that. It wasn't that I didn't rate myself, I was just being realistic. I'm OK, I'm all right, I'm quite nice – but I'm nothing special. Why the hell should someone special want to come back to *me*?

Dom lit another cigarette.

'You're smoking too much,' I told him.

'You sound just like—' His voice trailed off and his face dropped as Jamie Tait and Sara Toms suddenly appeared round the corner of the stall, walking arm in arm. My stomach turned over. It was inevitable I'd meet up with Jamie again sooner or later, and I'd tried to prepare for the occasion by telling myself to stay cool, keep calm, be brave, don't lose control ... but when I actually saw him, my brave heart just sank to the ground. Fear, shock, disgust, shame ... the weight of it all was more than I'd ever imagined. And, somehow, the sight of him with Sara, all cosy and civilised, made it even worse. Jamie was dressed in a Nike vest and swimshorts, and Sara was wearing a long wrap skirt over a low-cut one-piece swimsuit.

'Well, this is nice,' Jamie said with a slight lisp. 'How're you doing, McCann? How's your head?'

Dom looked at him. 'Better than yours, I expect.'

Jamie winced. His face was a mass of bruised flesh and stitches. An ugly gash split the side of his nose, and the nose itself was discoloured and swollen from when Lucas had kneed him in the face. His mouth, too, was swollen on one side, and when he smiled I could see a bit of tooth missing from the front. That would account for the lisp. I wondered what he'd told Sara about his injuries. Whatever it was, I was fairly sure it wasn't the truth.

He tried to make light of it, shrugging his shoulders and smiling crookedly. 'At least I'll have a face worth remembering when it heals.' He looked at me. 'You won't forget it, will you, Caity?'

'No,' I said, trying to steady my trembling voice. 'I don't *th*uppo*the* I will.'

His smile vanished and he stepped towards me. Sara pulled him back. 'Keep away from her, darling,' she told him, staring at me. 'You don't know where she's been.'

Jamie smiled, tonguing the gap in his teeth. Sara slipped her hand inside his vest and continued staring at me. Her eyes were like nothing I'd ever seen before: cold, emotionless, inhuman. It was frightening.

Dominic stepped up beside me. 'Just ignore her,' he whispered. 'She's unbalanced.' He raised his voice and spoke to Jamie. 'So, how's it going, Tait? Still keeping things fresh?'

The words were casual, but the tone of his voice was hard.

'Fresh enough,' Jamie replied.

'I expect you've heard about Angel.'

Jamie smiled coldly. 'Shocking, isn't it?'

'And now the boy's gone.'

'So they say.'

'Looks like you got what you wanted then.'

'I always do, McCann.'

'You don't let shit into your home, right?'

'You've got it.'

'What about me?'

'You got what you deserved.'

Dom sighed and shook his head. 'You like your little games, don't you?'

'Like I said, you got what you deserved.' He looked at me. 'You too. How are you sleeping, by the way?'

'Not too good,' I said. 'But at least I haven't wet myself lately.'

His face froze. Sara looked at him and Dominic looked at me, but for a brief moment neither of them existed. There was just me and Jamie Tait and the shared memory of him lying in the lane with his face covered in blood and his trousers soaked in urine. I wasn't proud of myself for reminding him, it was a pretty cheap thing to do, but as we stood there staring at each other I have to admit I enjoyed the humiliation on his face.

Sara shot me a murderous look then hissed in Jamie's ear, 'What's she talking about?'

He didn't answer, just carried on staring at me.

Sara shook him. *'Jamie!'*

'Shut up,' he snapped. 'We're going.'

'I want to know—'

'Shut it!' He started dragging her away then spun around and jabbed his finger at me. 'You – I'll be seeing you, you little bitch. And when I do you're going to wish you'd never stopped him. Think about it ... you think about *that*.' Then he turned on his heels and marched off down the street, with Sara scrabbling along behind him, throwing vicious glances over her shoulder at me.

Dominic watched them go.

I sighed heavily.

Simon popped his head out the back of the stall. 'What was all that about? Has he gone? Is everything all right?'

'Yeah ... everything's fine,' I said. 'I'll be back in a minute.' He looked concerned. 'Really,' I told him. 'There's nothing to worry about. He was a bit drunk, that's all. I just need a quick word with Dominic and then I'll be right back.'

He didn't look too happy about it, but then he never looked too happy about anything. He nodded slowly and disappeared back into the stall. When I turned around Dominic was watching me with a mixture of pride and confusion.

'Well,' he said. 'That was interesting.'

'You started it.'

He smiled. 'It looks like I missed out on the best bits, though. Are you going to tell me what that was all about?'

'You don't want to know.'

He looked at me with raised eyebrows.

'Look,' I said, 'I've got to get back. I'll talk to you later, all right? I'll tell you what I can.'

He nodded. 'I can hang around if you want. I don't think Jamie will try anything, but just in case he does—'

'No – thanks anyway. I'll be all right.'

'If you say so.'

He came over to me, took off my hat and ruffled my hair. I felt a lump rising in my throat.

I said, 'I'm still annoyed with you, Dom. I haven't forgiven you yet.'

'That's all right,' he replied, putting the hat back on my head and jamming it down over my eyes. 'I can wait.'

I pulled the hat from my eyes and watched him saunter off down the street with his hands in his pockets and his head in the air. I didn't know what to think. It seemed as if every time I lost something I found something else. I'd lost Bill, found Lucas. Lost Dominic, found Bill. Lost Bill again, found Dominic. Lost Lucas ... lost Lucas ...

I'd lost Lucas.

I swallowed hard and went back into the stall.

There wasn't really time to think about anything for the next hour or so. The festival got busier, the sun got hotter, and the people just kept on coming. It was incredible. I didn't get a minute's rest. As soon as I'd finished with one customer another one would take their place. *How much is this? What do you think about that? Why should I give money to the RSPCA when there are children dying all over the place? Why don't you do something about the seagulls? What do you think about fishing? Where's the toilets? What's that made of? Where's the best place to buy an owl?* ...

I was finding it really hard to cope. Too many stupid questions, too many people who couldn't be bothered to think for themselves, too many sun-burned, half-drunk faces ...

At one point, after a particularly unpleasant encounter with a local hunt supporter, I looked up to see the funny-looking kid who'd bought the poster of the starving dog. He was standing there with the rolled-up poster in his hand. His dad – who looked exactly like him – was standing beside him with a scowl on his face.

My heart sank and I looked towards Simon, but he was busy doing something else.

'What d'you think this is?' the kid's dad said.

I looked at him. 'I'm sorry?'

'This.' He grabbed the poster from his boy's hand and waved it at me. 'What the hell is this supposed to be?'

I looked at the boy. He was starting to cry again.

His father said, 'I could do you for this. I could set the whasnames on you, the trade descriptions. It's a bloody disgrace. Look at it. That's not a dog, it's a bloody carcass. Look, it's a sodding *skellington*. My boy's not putting that on the wall. I want my money back *and* an apology. I want – are you *listening*?'

I wasn't. I was staring off into the distance watching Jamie Tait as he disappeared down a secluded footpath at the end of the street heading for the beach. His face was shielded with the peak of a baseball cap, and the sun was shining in my eyes, but there was no doubt in my mind – it was him all right. And the girl in the bra-top with her arm round his waist – that was Angel Dean. As I leaned to one side and squinted through the glare, trying to get a better look, a white Mercedes with tinted windows rolled down the street and slowed at the entrance to the path, momentarily blocking my view. The car stopped for a couple of seconds then speeded up and purred away. I caught a quick glimpse of Jamie looking over his shoulder, and Angel reaching up and nuzzling his ear, and then they were gone, hurrying down through the shadows towards the beach. I kept my eyes on the path for a while, replaying the scene in my mind, trying to convince myself I'd made a mistake. But I knew I hadn't.

'Hey,' the angry man said, slamming the rolled-up poster on the counter. 'Hey! You, Missy—'

I tore my eyes from the path and looked at him. His face was bright red, his eyes were bulging, and his son was bawling his eyes out.

'Now you listen to me—' he began.

'I'm sorry,' I said. 'I'm not feeling well. If you'd like to wait there a minute I'll get someone to deal with you.'

I called Mrs Reed over, explained what had happened, then excused myself and stepped out the back of the stall and headed up a little alley where a Portaloo had been put in for the festival. I opened it up and went inside. It didn't smell too good, but at least it was cool and quiet. I sat down and waited for my head to stop spinning and then I tried to work out what to do. Jamie and Angel ... Jamie and Angel ... Jamie and Angel ... where were they going? what were they doing? did it mean anything? should I tell anyone? would it help Lucas if I told anyone? did it matter?

I couldn't think straight. There were too many unknowns, too many fears and ugly images to contend with. I just couldn't think things through. In the end I decided it was probably nothing. They were just sneaking off for a quick grope in the sand dunes. It was none of my business and the best thing to do was forget it.

Under the circumstances, I don't think it was a bad decision. It probably wasn't the most *objective* choice I've ever made, but I'd like to think that's understandable. Even so, I can't help feeling that if I'd been a bit more thoughtful I might have realised ... I might have done something else ... I might have changed things. If I'd known ... I would have tried to stop it ... I would have tried. But I didn't. I didn't know. How could I?

I just did what I thought was right.

I thought I was *right*.

As the festival drew to a close, I began to think the worst of the day was over. I certainly hoped so. I was hot and tired, my feet ached, my clothes were dirty and damp with sweat, and my emotions were so mixed up I'd forgotten what it was like to feel normal. I was hungry, too. All I'd had throughout the day was a couple of bags of crisps and about a dozen cans of cheap and gassy Coke. My mouth felt sweet and sticky and I had a belly full of wind. All in all, I felt like – and probably looked like – crap. Mrs Reed, on the other hand, was still as fresh as a daisy. Chatting away, smiling, humming and singing to herself, with her clothes clean and dry and her skin as cool as you like ... it was maddening. Simon was beginning to get on my nerves, as well. He'd hardly said a word since the incident with Jamie. He wasn't nasty or anything, just sulky. I didn't blame him for that. I expect he felt left out, cut off, perhaps even embarrassed. I just wished he'd *do* something about it instead of being so *meek* all the time. I wanted him to swear at me or give me a dirty look or something ... anything. But all he did was mope around with a hurt but inoffensive look on his face. It was driving me mad.

By about quarter to six, I'd just about had enough.

While Simon and Mrs Reed were busy trying to persuade a man with a beard that they didn't have anything against caravanning *per se*, I snuck off to the back of the stall and sat down on a stool, determined to stay there until the day was over. It wouldn't be long now. Everything was winding down. One or two vans had pulled up at the side of the road and the stall-holders were starting to pack up their stuff. There were empty boxes piled up on the pavement and the street was scattered with bits of food. Discarded litter was rustling in the evening breeze. Although most of the visitors had gone, there were still a few stragglers hanging around, looking tired and weary, some of them a bit drunk. But that was all right. Dad would be along soon. A short drive home, and then I could run a cool bath and lie there in peace. After that, something to eat, a tall glass of iced water, and then an early night. Cool, fresh sheets, a night breeze drifting in through the window, a nice long sleep and a lie-in in the morning. Bliss. Tomorrow was Sunday. There'd be plenty of time for talking to Dom and getting things sorted out with Dad. Plenty of time ...

The shouting came from the direction of the beach. At first I thought it was just some drunken yobs getting out of hand, and I didn't even bother looking up. I just sat there on my stool and kept my head down. I didn't want to know. But as the shouting became clearer I began to realise it was more than just high spirits. It was a lone voice, loud but clear, and although it sounded out of control I could tell it was perfectly sober. Sober but desperate.

Hey ... hey ... help me ... I need some help ... there's a girl ...

I raised my head and looked down the street. A skinny old man with a yellowing beard was running up from the direction of the beach. He was about sixty or sixty-five, wearing baggy trousers with the legs rolled up and a pair of sandals and no shirt. For some reason I remember him quite clearly – I can still picture his half-starved chest and his caved-in stomach, all bony and white, and his withered arms waving in the air as he ran and shouted.

Help ... please ... help ...

I stood up, my heart quickening. I could see the old man's eyes, wide and terrified, and I could hear the breathlessness in his voice.

For God's sake ... please ...

People were moving towards him now, the sound of footsteps and puzzled voices getting louder as everyone realised that something was seriously wrong.

'What is it?' Simon said. 'What's he saying?'

'Stay here,' Mrs Reed said. 'I'll go and see what's happening.'

As she started off, I followed her.

'You too, Cait,' she said. 'Stay here.'

I ignored her and began running.

'Cait!'

Up ahead the old man was bent over in the middle of the street with his hands on his knees, gasping for breath. He was surrounded by a growing circle of faces, with everyone firing questions at him – *what's up? are you all right? what's the matter?* Someone got him a chair and sat him down and someone else got him a glass of water. When I ran up to the crowd he was thirstily draining the glass and wiping the drips from his chin. I edged my way through to the front of the circle.

'There's a girl,' he was saying. 'There's a girl ...'

'Take it easy,' someone said. 'Get your breath back.'

He shook his head. 'There's a girl ... on the beach. A

young girl. I saw her. It was terrible ...'

A man in a white cap crouched down in front of him and spoke calmly. 'Take your time,' he said. 'What did you see?' I recognised the voice. It was Shev Patel from the village shop. He gently put his hand on the man's knee and looked in his eyes. 'Tell me what you saw,' he repeated.

The old man looked at him and shuddered. 'A girl ... all cut up ... I think she's dead.'

seventeen

No one spoke for a moment. Everyone just stood there looking down at the old man, not sure whether to believe him or not. I could see the doubts in their eyes – he's old, he's been out in the sun too long, he's probably just seeing things. The old man looked back at them, recognising their cynicism, and raised his hands, showing the dried blood on his palms.

'She's in the pillbox,' he said.

Someone said – *oh my God!* – and then everyone started bustling about, filling the air with a clamour of jostling footsteps and excitable voices – *what did he say? what's happened? a girl? who is it? where is she? is she dead?* Amid all the jabbering and head-shaking I caught the word 'gypsy' a couple of times, and I thought I heard someone say 'Lucas', but I couldn't be sure. A strange sense of detachment had come over me. I felt disconnected from everything, even myself. I didn't feel anything. I wasn't shocked. I wasn't scared. I had no emotions at all. I was there, but I wasn't *there*. As the initial panic subsided and everybody started *doing* things, all I could do was stand there motionless in the middle of the street watching them.

Shev Patel took charge. The first thing he did was whip out his mobile phone and dial 999. While he waited for an answer, he barked out a series of instructions. 'Everybody stay calm. Keep the noise down – get back, give him some room. You two—' this to some ladies from the Women's

Institute stall '—look after the old man. Get him some more water and cover him up with a blanket.' Then he called over to Mrs Reed. 'Jenny, find out exactly— hello?' As he started speaking into the phone, asking for police and an ambulance, Mrs Reed knelt down in front of the old man and spoke quietly to him. I couldn't hear what she was saying. The street was awash with noise.

I looked slowly around.

A group of young men had already got themselves organised and were starting off towards the beach carrying boards and blankets and first-aid equipment. One of them was also carrying a metal pole. There were people standing on the tops of vans scanning the beach with binoculars. Children were crying. I could hear people calling up friends on their mobiles to let them know that something was going on. Others were moving away: quiet couples, young women, families taking their children home. One or two solitary people were just standing around grimly enjoying the excitement.

Shev was still speaking into the phone. '—that's right, the pillbox by the Point. The man who found her is a Mr Willington, Stanley Willington.' Shev's eyes focused on someone up the street and he raised his hand and waved them over as he carried on talking into the phone. 'Mr Willington's being looked after. He's in the High Street. I'll take someone with me and meet you at the Point ... no, I know ... I won't touch anything ... OK ... whenever you can.' He clicked off the phone and looked up as Dad appeared through the crowd.

'Glad to see you, Mac,' Shev said. 'Just a minute.' He turned and shouted at the group of young men hurrying off towards the beach. 'Hey! Hold on! Wait a minute!'

The men didn't stop.

Dad glanced at me. 'What's going on, Cait? Are you all right?'

Before I could answer, Shev took him by the arm and led him off down the street, talking quickly to him as they went and glancing anxiously at the young men who were picking up pace and starting to run.

Someone from the crowd shouted out, 'Go get 'im! Get the dirty bastard!'

Someone else called out, 'Yeah! Teach 'im a lesson!', and then they all started, egging on the young men with snarling shouts and clenched fists waved in the air.

Shev looked angrily over his shoulder and the crowd momentarily quietened. He called back to one of the women looking after Mr Willington. 'There's a high tide coming in, Betty, so the police might be delayed. If they're not here in half an hour get Mr Willington inside the library, but make sure you leave someone out here to wait.' The woman called Betty raised her hand and nodded. Shev turned to the crowd. 'The rest of you – stay calm and keep out of it. And for God's sake keep away from the beach.'

With a final glare he turned back to Dad and the two of them hurried off after the others. As they moved out of earshot I heard someone say, 'Bloody Paki – who the hell does he think he is? He's only been here five minutes and he thinks he runs the sodding place.'

This was met with murmurs of agreement.

'That Paddy, too,' someone added.

'Yeah ...'

I had my eyes lowered, but I could feel people looking at me. I could feel the growing hysteria in their voices.

'Coming here and taking our jobs—'

'Scum!'

'It's our island—'

They were losing control.

'Get the van, Tully,' someone said. 'Let's find us a gyppo.'

Feet started moving, keys jangling, car doors opening.

Betty said, 'Now hold on, you heard Mr Patel. The police will be here soon—'

But no one was listening any more.

'Someone get up the Stand, block it off, make sure he don't get away.'

'Right.'

'Tide's coming up – get a boat out there.'

'Check the old woods, flush him out – get old Jack, he knows the flats.'

'Who's up for it?'

'Come on!'

The whirlpool raged around me and all I could do was hang my head and listen to its ugly roar. The sound of vans starting up, heavy feet running, the primitive rush of violent voices ...

It was beyond belief.

Within about ten minutes most of the men had gone and the street was quiet again. The wind was getting up, scattering litter around the half-empty roads, and the temperature was dropping quite rapidly. Dark clouds were looming in the distance and the air smelled of thunder.

I looked around at the people left behind. Some of the faces I didn't recognise, and I guessed these were people from the mainland hanging around to see what happened, but most of them were locals. Apart from a handful of youngsters they were mainly women and older men. Simon was there, standing with his mum. Betty and some others were still tending to Mr Willington. Dominic had turned up with Rita and Bill. And in the background the remaining stall-holders were shuffling back to their stalls to continue packing up. A cloud of shameful resignation darkened the street. It was everywhere. In the way people walked, the way they talked, the way they avoided making eye contact. Everyone had that 'nothing-to-do-with-me' look on their faces, the look of people who *know* that what they're witnessing is wrong, but are either too scared or too embarrassed to do anything about it.

It was an incredibly depressing sensation.

As the storm closed in and the first spots of rain began moistening the ground, Dominic walked up to me and put his arm round my shoulder.

'Come on,' he said softly. 'Let's go home.'

I shook my head. 'I'm staying here.'

'There's nothing you can do—'

'It's Angel,' I said.

'What?'

'The girl – it's Angel.'

'How do you know?'

I looked at him. 'I saw her with Jamie earlier on. They were heading for the beach – I *saw* them, Dom.'

'When?'

'I don't know – about an hour after we saw him with Sara. About three-thirty, I suppose. They went down the path at the end of the street.'

'Together?'

I nodded.

'Have you told anyone?'

'Who? There isn't anyone to tell.'

'Where's Lenny Craine?'

'In Moulton, probably, looking for Lucas.'

The rain was coming down quite heavily now and gusts of wind were flapping noisily in the canopies of stalls. People were putting on coats and struggling with umbrellas and some of the mainlanders were beginning to drift away. Mrs Reed was helping Betty with Mr Willington, getting him to his feet and into the shelter of a nearby shop, and I could see Simon and Bill standing together on the library steps.

Dominic looked up at the sky. 'We'd better go,' he said. 'Get Bill and I'll meet you at Rita's car.'

'But what about—'

'There nothing we can do here. I've got Shev's mobile number. When we get home I'll give him a ring and then I'll call Lenny and tell him about Tait.'

'What about all those people looking for Lucas?'

'Don't worry. I'll tell Lenny about them.'

'He won't do anything.'

'Yes, he will. Now go on.' He gave me a little shove. 'I'll meet you back at the car.'

As we pulled away from the village the skies opened up with a thundering crash and the rain came down in torrents. High winds buffeted the car and tore at the branches of roadside trees. The narrow lanes were rapidly flooding. Rita drove slowly, concentrating on keeping the car on the road. Her body was rigid and her face was taut as she peered intently through the waves of water gushing across the windscreen. The rest of us just sat there shivering in our wet clothes, listening to the sound of rain hammering hard on the roof. No one said anything. There wasn't anything to say.

There was quite a lot of traffic around, mostly festival traffic heading off the island, but I was surprised to see almost as much coming back the other way, towards the village. I thought at first they were gruesome sightseers coming from the mainland, drawn like flies to the scent of blood, but as we approached the junction at the Stand I realised I was wrong.

'Look at this,' murmured Rita, slowing the car.

I squinted through the windscreen at the queue of traffic stretching back from the Stand. It must have been half a kilometre long. The water level in the estuary was higher than I'd ever seen it, lapping up over the railings and still rising. The Stand was completely submerged beneath the storm-ravaged waters of a muddy-brown lake.

'Christ,' whispered Dom.

At the junction a white Transit van was parked across the Black Hill road, blocking the entrance to the east of the island. A rough-looking man smoking a cigarette was sitting in the driver's seat studying the cars as they approached the Stand. Three or four others were walking around directing traffic back to the village. As they leaned down to explain the situation to frustrated drivers I could see them surreptitiously checking inside the cars. It was like something out of a vigilante movie.

The queue of traffic inched forward as those up ahead turned around and drove back to the village. I could see the drivers shaking their heads in dismay.

'They won't be going home for a while,' Rita said.

'Neither will we at this rate,' Dom added.

Some of the cars were pulling out of the queue and turning back before they got to the Stand, but most of them just carried on queueing, either waiting to find out what was going on, or hoping against hope they'd be able to get through. It took us about twenty minutes to reach the junction. During this time a motorcycle roared past us and raced up to the white van where it skidded to a halt. The rider, a helmetless thug in a leather jacket, spoke to someone in the passenger seat of the van, then swung the bike around and sped off up Black Hill. I saw Dom watching with a worried look on his face.

'Do you know him?' I asked.

'Micky Buck,' he whispered. 'A friend of Brendell's.'

I started to say something else but Dom nudged me in the leg, nodded at Bill and Rita in the front of the car, and shook his head. I didn't quite understand what he meant, but I knew enough to shut up.

Rita put the car in gear and we edged up to the front of the queue. There was only one car ahead of us now and I had a clear view of the swollen estuary. Across the other side, cars were pulling up at the water's edge before turning round and heading back to the mainland. Out in the middle of the estuary a small rowing boat was bobbing up and down in the waves. There were two men in it, both of whom I recognised from the festival. They were peering over the side of the boat like drunken fishermen looking for sharks. It was hard to believe how stupid they were. Even if Lucas *was* still on the island, did they really think he'd try to escape by swimming across a well-guarded estuary in the middle of a storm? And how did they think they were going to stop him if he did? What were they going to do – harpoon him?

Idiots.

As I was watching, one of them looked up and pointed at the sky. The other one craned his neck and got to his feet, but the boat started wobbling and he quickly sat down again, still looking upwards. Then I heard it too, the whirring chop-chop of a helicopter. I leaned against the window and gazed up just in time to see a small yellow helicopter flying low over the estuary making a bee-line for the Point.

'Air ambulance,' said Dom. 'They're going to have trouble landing in this weather.'

'At least they're trying,' I said.

Dom looked at me. He was about to say something when someone rapped on the driver's window and a rain-soaked face appeared in the glass. Rita wound down the window and a stocky young man poked his head in, filling the car with a waft of beery breath.

'You gotta go back,' he said, glancing in the back. 'Tide's up, you can't get through.'

Rita glared at him. 'Do you mind getting your head out of my car?'

The man grinned. 'Only trying to help, love. You see, when the tide comes in—'

'We live here, you idiot. I've seen more high tides than you've got spots on your chin. Now get your head out of my car and get that bloody van moved. I want to go home.'

He wasn't grinning any more. He stared at Rita for a moment, shot another glance at me and Dom, then snapped his head back and called across to the van. 'Hey! Tully! This one says they live 'ere! Wants the van moved!'

The man in the van turned his head and spoke to someone in the passenger seat, then leaned out of the window and shouted something back through the howling rain.

The stocky man leaned down again and said, 'What's the name?'

'What the hell *is* this?' Rita fumed. 'I don't have to give my name to *you* – Jesus *Christ*! Get out of my way before I call the police.'

The man sniffed and spat on the ground. 'The police

are busy, lady. There's a killer on the loose—'

Rita shook her head and put the car in gear.

The man reached in and put his hand on the wheel. 'I wouldn't if I were you.'

Rita glared at him and thumped his hand. He swore at her and started reaching for the ignition keys. Dominic leaned across the seat and grabbed his wrist.

'Tell Tully it's McCann,' he said.

The young man looked at him.

Dom's eyes were hard. 'Tell him we're coming through and he'd better move the van right now.' He let go of his wrist and the man stepped back. Dom put his hand on Rita's shoulder. 'Are you all right?'

She nodded, glancing at the man. 'I will be once fatso moves his face.'

Dom looked at him. 'What are you waiting for?'

The man glared at Dom for a moment then spat again and started walking across to the van. Dom sank back into his seat. Aggression wasn't in his character, and he looked almost as shocked as I felt. His face was drained and his hands were shaking.

'Who's Tully?' I asked him.

'The one in the van. Tully Jones – one of Tait's lackeys. He's nothing without Jamie, same as the rest of them.'

Just then the car behind us sounded its horn. Rita turned around and gestured angrily through the back window. Bill, who hadn't said a word so far, told her to calm down, and then *they* started arguing.

Dom shook his head. 'Christ, I don't believe this. The whole thing's turning into a bloody nightmare.'

Meanwhile, over at the junction I saw the white van reversing halfway across the road.

'Let's get out of here,' I said.

Rita didn't hear me, she was too busy sniping at Bill. '... you're a *fine* one to talk, my girl. You're the one that's been hanging around with slobs like that, so don't you dare—'

'That's *enough*!' I cried.

Rita shut up and everyone looked at me.

'Can we *please* just go home,' I said.

There was a moment's stunned silence, then the car behind us sounded its horn again. This time, Rita ignored it. She wound up the window, put the car into gear, and pulled out across the junction towards Black Hill. A man in a long black raincoat had joined the stocky young man and they were both leaning against the van door watching us. Wet hair was plastered across their heads and rain dripped from their faces. As we approached the van Dominic told Rita to slow down.

'What for?' Rita said.

'Just pull in over there a minute.'

She steered the car across the road and stopped next to the van. Dominic wound down the window and leaned out. As rain gusted into the car I heard him speak to the man in the driver's seat.

'Hey, Tully,' he said.

The man stared slowly at him. He was lean and hard, with close-cropped hair, red-rimmed eyes, and bad skin. Just below his left eye three small letters were crudely tattooed in red ink. The letters read: *R. I. P.*

Dom said, 'Tell Buck if I see him anywhere near my house I'll break his neck. You got that?'

The man called Tully laughed. I saw him lean to one side and speak to someone in the passenger seat, and then I heard another laugh – *nyuh nyuh nyuh* – and a gasp of recognition caught in my throat.

Tully looked out of the window, saw me, then spoke to

his hidden companion again.

Dom said, 'OK, Rita. Let's go.'

As Rita put the car into reverse, Tully called down from the van. 'Hey, McCann – yours is that run-down place at the end of the lane, right? What's it like down there all on your own? Nice and quiet? Must get a bit lonely sometimes, eh? Especially at night.'

Dominic didn't say anything.

Tully flicked a burning cigarette end into the rain and laughed again. 'I'll be seeing you. Sleep tight.'

We drove off up Black Hill and the van moved back across the road. I looked back through the rear window trying to catch sight of the other man in the van, but all I could see through the pouring rain was a featureless head behind the glass. I looked at Dom. He was chewing a thumbnail and staring thoughtfully at nothing.

'That was him, wasn't it?' I whispered.

'Who?'

'You *know* who. The other one in the van – it was Jamie.'

He looked at me, then looked away. 'Maybe ... I don't know.'

'Yes you do.'

He shrugged, then forced a smile. 'Don't worry about it.'

'Don't *worry* about it?'

Dom looked across at me and I looked back. His lips started quivering, his mouth broke into a giggly smile, and then we both started laughing like idiots. Rita frowned at us in the rear-view mirror and Bill turned around with a puzzled look on her face.

'What's the matter with you two?' she said.

'Nothing,' Dom giggled. 'N-nothing ... don't worry about it ...'

It seems pretty stupid now, but at the time it was the funniest thing in the world.

It was getting on for eight o'clock when we drove down the lane and pulled into the yard. The gravel track was water-logged and the skies were so dark and rain-whipped I could hardly see the house. The car lurched to a halt and a roll of thunder split the sky. White lightning lit up the lane and just for a moment I could see the poplar trees thrashing in the wind, their shredded leaves cascading into the sky, and then it was dark again and all I could see was a wall of black rain.

'Do you want us to come in with you?' Rita asked.

'No thanks,' Dom replied. 'We'll be all right. You go on home. I'll ring you as soon as we hear anything.' He turned to me. 'Ready?'

I thanked Rita for the lift, said goodbye to Bill, then we got out of the car and ran through the rain to the house. It was only about twenty paces, but by the time we got to the door we were both soaked to the skin again. As Dom got his keys out, a great crash of thunder ripped through the air and another bolt of lightning lit up the sky. We both shuddered. I could see bits of broken roof-slate scattered on the step, and from inside the house I could hear Deefer barking and whining.

Dom fumbled with the keys.

'Come on,' I said. 'What are you doing?'

'My hands are cold.'

'Here, give me those.'

I snatched the keys from his hand and unlocked the door and we hurried inside. The house was cold and dark and it smelled of damp wood and dog. It smelled of home.

I switched on the hall light and headed for the stairs.

'Wait a minute,' Dom said, holding me back.

'I need a wee.'

'Just wait here a minute.'

'What for? I'm freezing—'

'I won't be long.'

He went down the hall and into the front room. I heard him turn on the light and close the curtains, then he came back out and went into the kitchen. After he'd checked all the rooms downstairs and turned on all the lights, he disappeared upstairs. I heard doors opening, lights being switched on, curtains closing. Then I heard him rummaging around in Dad's bedroom.

Deefer sat down beside me and rubbed his head against my leg.

'Yeah, I know,' I said. 'You'd tell us if anyone was here, wouldn't you? Dom's just double-checking, that's all.' I patted his head. 'Do you want to go outside?' I opened the front door. Deefer stood up, took one look at the rain, then sat down again. I shut the door.

After a couple of minutes Dom came downstairs. He'd changed out of his wet clothes and was carrying a baseball bat.

'It's Dad's,' he said in answer to my questioning look. 'He keeps it under his bed.'

'Do you think we're going to need it?'

He shrugged. 'Probably not.'

I tried to think of something funny to say, something to lighten the tone, but I couldn't think of anything.

Funny-time was over.

'I'm going to get out of these clothes,' I said.

Dom nodded. 'I'll light the fire then make some phone calls.'

* * *

I don't know if it was the effect of the storm, or just because I hadn't been alone with Dom for such a long time, but for some reason the house felt all wrong. The stairs seemed steeper than normal and the ceilings too high. The carpets felt thin and hard beneath my feet. The night was too dark, the lights too bright, the thunder too loud. The walls, the windows, the floor ... everything was slightly distorted, like visions in a dream that isn't a dream.

A spoken thought entered my head: *This is your world, Cait. It isn't a dream. A thousand miles and an inch* are *the same. This is it. The world grows elastic.*

I didn't know what it meant or where it came from, and I didn't really care. I'd given up trying to understand anything.

I went into my room and stripped off my soaking wet clothes. Gusts of rain were pounding against the window and I could feel a cold draught rippling through the curtains. I went over to check the window. It was closed. The wind was coming in through cracks in the frame. I tightened the latch then fetched a towel from the airing cupboard and dried myself off. I smelled of sweat. My skin was cold and wet and wrinkled and flecked with bits of damp fluff.

I went over to the chest of drawers to get some dry clothes – and that's when I saw the small wooden figure on the bed. It was the carving that Lucas had given me, the miniature Deefer. It was just lying there on top of the bed, bang in the middle, as if it had been placed there deliberately.

Had I put it there?

I sat down on the edge of the bed and tried to remember when I'd last been in here. This morning ... it was this morning. I'd got up early, had a shower, got dressed, got the RSPCA stuff ready ... had I looked at the carving? I couldn't remember. I kept it in the drawer of my bedside table, the drawer where I kept my underwear. Had I taken it out when I was getting dressed? I picked up the figure and turned it over in my hand, trying to jog my memory. From above, I could hear the water tank dripping in the attic – *tack, tock, tock ... tack, tock, tock ... tack, tock, tock* – like a hesitant clock. It was a strangely hypnotic sound, and as I listened to it and stared at the carving in my hand, my mind drifted up through the ceiling and I imagined the cold attic air and the smell of soot and old wood. I could see the dark beams and the scarred rafters and the flash of lightning glinting through the cracked slate tiles. I could hear the rain hammering on the roof and the wind in the eaves ... and I was there. I was a child again, playing alone in my attic world. It was a world of dusty things hanging from beams: coils of rope, shapeless bags, old coats, cardboard boxes, bits of wood, rolls of carpet, tins of paint, broken suitcases, stacks of yellowed newspapers tied with string ... it was a world that was anything I wanted it to be. I could make a den out of an old piece of sheet draped over the beams and pretend I was marooned on a desert island, or lost in the woods ...

The door slammed open and Dominic marched in.

'Do you *mind*?' I said, covering myself with the towel.

His face reddened and he backed out of the doorway. 'Sorry ... I was just checking. You seemed to be taking a long time, that's all. Sorry.'

'I'll be down in a minute.'

He shut the door.

I was back in my room again.

I was fifteen years old.

I was a child.

eighteen

When I went downstairs Dom was sitting in front of the fire with a tumbler of whiskey in one hand and a cigarette in the other. Soft light glowed from a pewter lampstand in the corner, casting long shadows that loomed on the wall. The heat of the fire crackled in the air. Dom was staring into the flames.

'Have you fed Deefer?' I asked him.

He nodded.

I sat down in the armchair and curled my feet under my body. I was wearing one of Dad's old cardigans with a pair of pyjama bottoms and thick woolly socks. Scratchy but warm. Dom took a mouthful of whiskey and puffed on his cigarette. The smoke folded in the air and curled away up the chimney. He took another drag then threw the cigarette into the fire and turned to face me.

'I couldn't get through to Shev,' he said. 'He must have his phone switched off.'

'Maybe it's the storm,' I suggested.

He shrugged.

'What about Lenny?' I asked.

'He's stuck in Moulton. He went down this morning with Bob Toms and Pete Curtis to look for Lucas. They had a tip-off he was hiding out in some woods by the river.' He looked at me. 'Anonymous phone call.'

I shook my head. 'It wasn't me.'

'Lenny sounded pretty pissed off about it.'

'Why?'

'I don't know – probably because he's been tramping around in the woods with Bob Toms all day.'

He drank more whiskey and lit another cigarette. The light of the fire seemed to age him, and for a brief moment he looked just like Dad. It was all there. The worried face. The voice – distant and emotionless. The way he looked at things. Even the way he sat – hunched over his cigarette, sipping whiskey and staring mournfully at the fire ... it was Dad all over.

'Did you tell Lenny I saw Jamie with Angel?' I asked him.

'I told him everything.'

'What's he going to do about it?'

'Well ... like I said, he's stuck in Moulton, but he's in touch with Bob Toms – Toms came back on the helicopter with the paramedics. They should be at the scene by now.'

'Has Lenny heard from them?'

'Not yet.'

'So we don't know if it *is* Angel?'

'Lenny doesn't know anything. Communications aren't too good, apparently.'

I was beginning to get a bad feeling about this. Things didn't feel right.

I said, 'Who else was in the helicopter?'

'Just Toms, the paramedics, and a CID sergeant from Moulton.'

'That's it?'

'There wasn't room for anyone else. Pete Curtis and the other constable – what's his name, the blond one?'

'Warren, I think. Jeff Warren.'

'Warren, that's it. Him and Pete are in a patrol car on the other side of the Stand. Until the tide goes down, there's nothing they can do.'

'They could row across, couldn't they?'

'Toms won't let them.'

'Why not?'

'He says it's too risky.'

'Too *risky*? We've got a girl who's probably dead, we've got gangs of thugs roaming the island looking for trouble, and he thinks it's too *risky* ...? What the hell's going on, Dom?'

'What do you mean?'

'Nothing makes sense. Why didn't Lenny take the CID sergeant's place in the helicopter? How come Toms can order his men not to cross the estuary but he can't let Lenny know what's going on? And what did *he* come back for, anyway? Bob Toms is a desk man. He doesn't know how to deal with something like this. Why didn't he send Lenny?'

Dom shook his head. 'I don't know.'

I looked at him. 'Does Toms know about Jamie and Angel?'

He didn't answer for a moment. He took a long drag on his cigarette and tapped ash into the fire. Outside, the night was black and the storm was still raging. I could hear the rain hammering on the lawn and the sound of leaves being torn from the elm tree in the garden.

Dom sighed. 'I don't know about Toms. He's pretty tight with the Taits, so I wouldn't be surprised if he knew that *something* was going on ... but I'm not really sure. To tell you the truth, I never really knew what was going on with that lot myself.' He looked embarrassed. 'I was just ... I don't know ... they're a weird bunch, Cait. Especially Jamie and Sara. I thought they were exciting at first, I thought they were just having a laugh, having some *fun*.

You know? I didn't think there was any harm in it. I should have known, I suppose ...' He shook his head. 'God ... how dumb can you get?'

I got up and went over to the window. I could feel Dom watching me, and I wondered what he wanted me to say – it's all right? we all make mistakes? I forgive you?

I pulled back the curtain and looked out at the yard. I could see my reflection shimmering in the window, and beyond that the white blur of Dad's car shivering in the rain. Everything else was lost in the storm. There was nothing to see, nothing to say, and nowhere to go. There was nothing to do but wait.

I dropped the curtain and went back to the armchair.

'Do you think he's out there?' Dom asked quietly.

'Lucas?'

He nodded.

I rubbed my thumb and forefinger together, imagining the feel of the wooden carving, and I remembered Lucas's voice – *Don't be too hard on your brother. And try not to worry. I'll always be close ...*

Was he still out there somewhere? On the beach, in the woods, cold and wet, tired and hungry, hiding in the dark like a hunted animal ...? For his sake, I *wanted* to hope that he wasn't, but deep down I couldn't help hoping he was. It was a selfish thing to want, I know – selfish, heartless, stupid, and cruel – but what could I do?

You can't stop yourself wanting something, can you?

The night dragged on and the storm showed no sign of easing. I don't know how long we sat there, hardly speaking, just waiting for something to happen, but it seemed to last for ever. Every now and then one of us would get up to go the bathroom, or make some coffee, or – in Dom's case – get another drink, and then whoever it was who'd gone would come back in and sit down again.

'Anyone call?'

'No.'

Dom tried Shev a couple more times but his phone was still switched off, and when he tried calling Lenny all he got was an automated message saying that all lines to the mainland were currently unavailable. Even Rita and Bill's phone was dead. We were on our own. Just me, Dom, Deefer, a thousand ugly thoughts, and the never-ending crash of thunder and rain.

It was after midnight when Deefer's ears pricked up and a growl rumbled in his throat. He swung his head round in the direction of the drive and let out a short, gruff bark. I knew it was coming but it still made me jump. Dom stood up and reached for the baseball bat that was leaning against the wall.

'It'll be Dad,' I told him.

He walked over to the window and drew back the curtain. Deefer climbed down from the settee and walked stiffly to the door, his throat grumbling and his hackles rising.

'Let him out,' Dom said.

I opened the door and let Deefer out into the hall. He started barking loudly at the door. I still couldn't hear anything above the storm, but through the frosted glass panels above the door I could see the twin beams of yellow headlights sweeping across the yard. After a few seconds the lights cut out and Deefer stopped barking.

'Who is it?' I called out to Dom. 'Is it Dad?'

'I can't see. It looks like a van ... you'd better come in here.'

I went back into the front room and joined Dom at the window. He was standing with his face pressed up to the glass and the baseball bat grasped behind his back. I cupped my hands to the window and peered out into the darkness. I could just make out the outline of a van-sized vehicle parked beside the Fiesta. Rain glinted on a darkened windscreen.

'Shit,' whispered Dominic. 'This is ridic—'

He stopped as a light went on inside the van. Dad's face appeared in the windscreen and we both sighed.

'Who's that with him?' I asked.

'I think it's Shev – it must be his van.'

We watched Dad shake Shev's hand, then he opened the door and hurried across the yard, glancing at the window as he went. Dom raised his hand and I went to open the front door. Deefer was barking again, but this time it was his 'welcome home' bark, and his heavy tail was wagging from side to side. I unlocked the door. It swung open in the wind and slammed against the wall, and then Dad bounded in, shaking the rain from his head. He looked terrible. His face was white and streaked with mud, his hair was a mess, his clothes were soaked and dishevelled, and he smelled atrocious.

I grabbed him round the waist and squeezed him tight.

'Hey ... hey ... it's all right,' he murmured, stroking my hair. 'Everything's all right.'

I buried my head in his chest.

After he'd had a quick shower and a change of clothes, Dad joined us in the front room. Dom poured him a big glass of whiskey and he slumped down in the armchair and drank down half of it in one go.

'That's better,' he sighed. 'God, what a day ... are you

two all right?'

We both nodded.

Dom said, 'I tried ringing Shev but his phone was off.'

'Dead battery,' Dad said, finishing the whiskey. He lit a cigarette. 'Has Lenny phoned?'

'No,' I said.

He shook his head. 'Christ, this is a mess. Did you see those bloody idiots at the Stand?'

'Tully Jones was there,' Dom said. 'And Mick Buck. Is the Stand still cut off?'

Dad nodded. 'If this storm keeps up, I can't see it going down until the morning. Maybe not even then. It's like a damn lake out there.' He stared into the distance and puffed thoughtfully on his cigarette.

'What happened, Dad?' I asked.

He looked at me with troubled eyes.

I said, 'Did you find her?'

He took a deep breath and let it out slowly. 'We found her.'

'Was it Angel?'

He stared at me for a long time. Eventually he said, 'How do you know?'

'Was it?'

He nodded gravely. 'You'd better tell me what you know.'

There was no reason to hide anything any more. No reason, no point, no sense in *not* telling him – in fact, I was finding it hard to remember why I hadn't told him everything in the first place – and as I opened my mouth and started to talk I had every intention of speaking the truth. But something happened. Something clicked in and overrode my intentions, and the words that came out weren't the words I meant to come out.

'Jamie Tait's been after Lucas,' I said. 'Jamie and Lee Brendell, some of the others, they wanted him off the island. That's why they all lied to the police about what happened with Kylie Coombe. They thought that if the police were after Lucas and everyone thought he was a pervert, he'd leave the island.'

'How do you know all this?' Dad asked.

'Lucas told me.'

He shook his head disapprovingly. 'All right ... we'll come back to that later. How does Angel Dean come into this?'

'You know what she's like, Dad. She's been chasing after Jamie for ages – hanging around him all the time, flirting, flashing herself about ...'

'So?'

'When Jamie found out Lucas hadn't been frightened off, he threatened him. He said if he didn't leave the island he'd find himself in big trouble. He didn't say what kind of trouble, but Lucas got the impression that he was going to set him up for something.'

'The attack on Angel?'

'Yes.'

'And Lucas told you all this?'

I nodded. 'He didn't do it, Dad. He wouldn't hurt anyone.'

'No?'

'This afternoon at the festival I saw Jamie and Angel heading for the beach. She had her arm around his waist.'

'When?'

'Three-thirty, maybe a bit later. Lenny knows. Dom told him. He said he was going to tell Bob Toms.'

Dad looked puzzled. He got up and refilled his glass then started pacing around the room, tugging at his beard.

He stopped at the window.

'What time did you get in touch with Lenny?' he asked.

'As soon as we got in,' Dom said. 'About half eight.'

'What's going on, Dad?' I said. 'What happened to Angel?'

He flashed a look at Dom, then sat down and looked at me. His face was drawn and his eyes were full of pain. He put his hand to his mouth and breathed out through his fingers.

'She was in the pillbox near the Point,' he said slowly. 'It was almost dark when we got there. Those damn boys were chasing around all over the place, kicking up hell, looking for someone to kill ...' He shook his head. 'They even started in on Shev. It must have taken us an hour to get rid of them. By the time we got to the pillbox the rain was coming down so hard we couldn't see more than three feet in front of us.' He paused and took a long drink of whiskey. 'I went down ...' He cleared his throat. 'I went down into the pillbox. It was pitch black. I had my lighter going ...' He flicked a glance at me, then lowered his eyes. 'Ah, God ... it was terrible. She was just lying there in the dirt ... all on her own. She looked so small ...' He sniffed and wiped his eyes. 'She was all cut up ... her face, everything. Cut to ribbons. Jesus ... there was blood all over the place. I thought she was dead.'

'Was she?' I asked quietly.

Dad shook his head. 'I think she'll probably pull through. She was unconscious and she'd lost a lot of blood, but she was still breathing when the paramedics arrived ...' He sighed heavily, his eyes brimming with anguish as he remembered the scene. 'Most of the cuts weren't too deep, thank God ... but there was a bad one in her leg, just here ...' He touched a spot on his upper thigh.

'Somehow she'd managed to strap a cloth to it and keep her leg raised ... God knows what might have happened if she hadn't – she probably would have bled to death.'

'I thought you said she was unconscious.'

He looked at me. 'She was.'

'So how did she manage to bandage her leg?'

He shrugged. 'I don't know ... she must have done it before she lost consciousness, I suppose.' He closed his eyes and wearily rubbed his brow. 'Jesus ... can you *imagine* how the poor girl must have felt?'

A long silence filled the room.

That cold, coppery taste had returned to the back of my throat, the taste of dirty old pennies. It brought with it a memory of Lucas, when I first met him at the tide pool and he told me about Angel. *Robbie's not the one you have to worry about ... Angel's the one.* I could see him sitting on a flat rock, the breeze ruffling his hair as he lowered his eyes. *That's it – nothing ... that's what I saw ... looking up at me ... she didn't have a face.*

Then, now.

The future was now.

I was dying inside.

I'd seen Jamie and Angel going off together. I'd *seen* them. I'd seen her smiling and nuzzling his ear ... and now she was lying in a dirty old pillbox with her face ripped up. I'd seen her ... I'd *seen* her with him ... and I'd let her go. I knew what he was like. I'd been in Joe Rampton's lane with him. I'd felt what she must have felt. I'd been there, I'd been there with Angel – and now she was ruined.

It could have been me.

God, it could have been me.

In the soundless room, it was too much to think about – too bad, too selfish, too many lies ...

It was too late.

Dom broke the silence. 'What's happening now, Dad? What's Toms doing?'

Dad shook his head. 'God knows. When the helicopter turned up they roped off the area and kicked us out. Toms wouldn't talk to us, all he cared about was getting the damn place sealed off and keeping his hair dry.'

'What about this CID sergeant?' Dom said.

'He was just as bad,' Dad sighed. 'One of those big nasty bastards who think they're in a cop show. I think he used to work with Toms when he was at Moulton. He took our details and then told us to go home.'

'What are they going to do?' I asked. 'Are they looking for Lucas?'

'I don't know, love. When I left they were still arguing with the pilot. The paramedics had got Angel into the helicopter, but the pilot refused to take off because of the weather. As far as I know, they're still there.'

'Shouldn't we do something? Tell someone about Jamie Tait?'

He looked at Dom. 'You told Lenny?'

Dom nodded. 'But I couldn't get through the last time I rang. The lines are down or something.'

'I'll try him again. Have you spoken to Rita?'

'Can't get through.'

'I'll nip up and see her later.' He drank off his whiskey. 'God, what a mess.' He turned to me. 'You should have told me this stuff about Lucas before, Cait.'

'I know – I'm sorry.'

'Do you know where he is?'

I shook my head. 'He said he was coming to the festival but he never showed up.'

'Is that the truth?'

'I swear – I don't know where he is. I haven't seen him since Thursday. I think he's probably miles away.'

'Let's hope so.'

'He didn't do anything, Dad. He's innocent.'

'No one's innocent.'

We eventually got to bed some time in the early morning. By then the rain had eased off a little and the thunder had faded into the distance. The wind was still blowing hard, though, gusting through the trees and rattling against the windows, and I couldn't sleep. I was so tired my body felt numb. I could feel a pulse thumping behind my eyes. It was fear, I suppose. I couldn't get the voice of the tattooed man out of my mind – *What's it like down there all on your own? Nice and quiet? Must get a bit lonely sometimes, eh? Especially at night* ... I knew the doors and windows were all double-locked, and I knew it was probably just an empty threat anyway, but that didn't help much. Fear doesn't listen to reason.

There were other things preying on my mind, too. The image of Angel cocooned in the pillbox, the pain she must have gone through, the terror, the loneliness, the injustice of everything, the confusion, the complexity, the sense that the world was coming apart ... and Lucas. Where was he? Was he safe? Was he frightened? Was he cold? Was he thinking of me? I pictured his face, his smile, his pale blue eyes ... and then suddenly his eyes iced over and I saw him squatting over Jamie Tait with a knife in his hand, and for the tiniest fraction of a second a terrible thought entered my mind: what if I was wrong about him? what if it *was* him that attacked Angel ...?

A groan of self-disgust choked in my throat. God ... how *could* I? How could I even *think* such a thing? It's sickening ...

You're tired, don't worry about it. Go to sleep.
I didn't mean to think it. I didn't mean it ...
I know.
I'm sorry.
Go to sleep.
I gripped the wooden figure in my hand and closed my eyes. The wind roared its wildness in the trees and I listened hard, searching for the magic. It was there. I knew it was there. In the elm in the back garden, in the poplars along the lane, in the ancient oak in the field at the back of the house ...

It was there.

It was close.

I could feel it coming.

nineteen

I can smell the sweat on his skin and the wet sand on his clothes. He smells of the sea. His hands are cold and wet, but soft. Soft and hard, just like his eyes. His eyes ... blue jewels burned with a heart of black, the heart that sees to the ends of the earth. I can smell his hair, too. Like earth, like the fur of a beast. Damp, but dry underneath. Dry and thick and warm. His mouth ... a crescent moon. His lips move, shaping the contours of his face, and he speaks with the silence of the night.

Caity ...

I feel his hand on my mouth.

Cait ... it's me ...

I taste the sweet rain on his skin.

Cait ... wake up ...

I open my eyes ... open myself ...

'Cait?'

'Lucas?'

'Shh ...'

The voice was real. The fingertips resting lightly on my lips were real. The face above me was real. It wasn't a dream. Lucas was standing beside my bed, leaning over me, his figure framed in the dim light. I could feel the touch of his breath on my skin.

'Wha—' I said.

'Shh ...' he whispered, looking over his shoulder. 'I don't want to wake anyone.' He slowly removed his fingers from my lips.

'What are you doing here?' I said. 'Are you all right? How did you get in?'

He smiled at me. 'That's a lot of questions.'

I sat up, covering myself with the duvet, and looked at the clock. It was three-fifteen. Rain was pattering steadily against the window and the room was cold. A pre-dawn silence stilled the air. Lucas stepped back from the bed and wiped rain from his face. Wet clothes clung to his skin and his hands and face were streaked with mud. He had his canvas bag with him, slung over his shoulder. He looked exhausted.

'I thought you'd gone,' I said. 'I thought you'd left the island.'

'Do you think I'd go without saying goodbye?'

'You didn't have to—'

'I know.' He cocked his head, listening to something, then went on. 'I meant to come to the festival but things got a bit awkward.'

'You know about Angel?'

He nodded.

'They're after you, Lucas. They think you did it.'

'I know. I've spent most of the night trying to avoid them. I thought I'd be safe in the woods, but an old man led a group of them across the mud flats. They found my place and smashed it up. They're everywhere, Cait. There's no way off the island.'

'You can stay here,' I said.

He shuffled his feet uncomfortably. 'I just need somewhere to hide until the tide goes down. Once it starts going out I can wade through the reeds and get past the mob on the bridge ...' He looked at me. 'I don't want to cause any trouble.'

'It's no troub—'

Suddenly the door swung open and a gowned figure stepped into the room. Lucas reacted instantly. I saw a blur of movement, a dull flash of metal, and the next thing I knew the gowned figure was pinned up against the wall with a knife to his throat.

'No!' I yelled at Lucas. 'It's my dad!'

Without lowering the knife, Lucas shot a glance at me, then his head snapped to one side as Dominic appeared in the doorway and turned on the light. The moment froze in the sudden glare: Lucas holding Dad against the wall with the point of the knife pressed to his throat; Dad staring wide-eyed at the blade; and Dominic standing in the doorway with his hand on the light switch and his mouth hanging open.

'Dad?' he said. 'What the—'

'It's all right,' I said. 'It's Lucas.'

'Christ – what's he doing?'

'Lucas,' I said. 'Lucas, listen to me ... it's all right. It's my dad. Put the knife down.'

Lucas looked at Dad.

Dad licked his lips and met his gaze. 'So you're Lucas?' he croaked, glancing at the knife. 'Nice to meet you.'

Lucas didn't move for a moment. His eyes drilled into Dad, cold and calculating, weighing up the situation, and then he slowly lowered the knife and stepped back. Dad breathed out and put his hand to his throat, wiping at a pin-prick of blood. He examined his hand then looked up at Lucas.

'Do you always greet people like that?'

'I'm sorry,' Lucas said. 'I didn't know who you were.'

'Who the hell were you expecting – King Kong?'

A hint of a smile flickered on Lucas's mouth. 'I'm a bit jumpy tonight.'

'Jumpy? Jesus Christ ...' Dad stepped away from the wall and looked around, his body swaying slightly with shock. A quick glance at me, then he turned his attention back to Lucas. 'How the hell did you get in here? The doors are locked ... where's the dog? If you've hurt him—'

Lucas nodded towards the door.

Dad looked round. Deefer was sitting calmly in the doorway, gazing adoringly at Lucas.

'You're supposed to *bark*,' Dad said to him. 'What's the matter with you?'

Deefer ignored him.

Dad turned to Lucas and looked him up and down. 'Put that away,' he said coldly, indicating the knife. Lucas slipped the knife in his belt. Dad stepped up to him. He wasn't shocked any more. He was just angry and tired. 'Listen, son,' he said quietly. 'I've heard a lot about you. Some of it I like, and some of it I don't. My daughter seems to trust you, and normally that's good enough for me. But this is different. This is as about as different as it gets. Do you understand what I'm saying?'

'I'm not your son,' Lucas said calmly, looking into his eyes.

Dad's face tightened. I thought for a moment he was going to hit him. But then he nodded slowly and said, 'All right. Fair point. I apologise. Now, tell me you understand what I'm saying.'

'I understand.'

'Good.' He looked at him for a moment then turned round and spoke to Dom. 'Go back to your room.'

'But I wanted—'

'Don't spoil it, Dom. Just go back to your room and get some sleep. You're probably going to need it.'

'OK.'

Dad watched him go, then turned back to Lucas. 'You go and wait outside.'

Lucas walked out without a word. He hadn't looked at me since the light came on, and he didn't look at me as he left.

Dad closed the door then came over and sat on the bed. 'Are you all right?'

I nodded.

'What's going on?' he said. 'What's he doing here?'

'They're after him, Dad ... he's got nowhere else to go.'

'How long has he been here?'

'A couple of minutes—'

'Are you sure?'

'I just woke up—'

'Did he try anything—'

'No! Of *course* he didn't. How could you—'

'I'm your father,' he said, as if that answered everything ... which I suppose it did. 'Listen to me, Cait,' he said. 'I know you've been keeping things to yourself recently – no, let me finish. I'm not having a go at you, I'm just telling you how it is. Please, listen a minute. It's important. OK?' I nodded and he carried on. 'It's all right to keep stuff from me, it's natural. I'm not saying I *like* it, because I don't, but I can live with it. I trust you – even when you're wrong. That's fine. It's OK to be wrong. But you mustn't be afraid of it. Just take it as it is – don't try to mend things, don't punish yourself, don't dwell on it. Just take it, use it, make it good and keep it pure. All that matters is knowing your own rules. Because if you don't know them, you won't know when you're breaking them.' He sat back and looked at the ceiling. Then he sniffed and looked at me. 'Does any of that make sense?'

'Not really.'

He smiled. 'I didn't think so.'

I held his hand. 'I'm trying to do what I think is right, Dad. But it keeps going wrong.'

'I know.'

'Do you?'

He picked up Lucas's carving from under the duvet and tapped it on the back of my hand. 'You're not the only one who's been listening to the wind, you know.' I stared at him. He stood up and tightened his dressing gown then tossed me a bath-robe from the back of the door. 'Put that on and then I'll call the Lone Ranger back in. We've got some serious talking to do.'

twenty

Fifteen minutes later Dad and I were sitting side by side on the bed while Lucas paced around the room with his hands cupped to a mug of strong black coffee. He'd refused any food or a change of clothing, but had gratefully accepted the coffee, asking with some embarrassment for three spoonfuls of sugar. Dad had dressed in a thick shirt and a pair of corduroy trousers. He was smoking a cigarette. The window was open to let the smoke out. The air was cold.

Lucas paused at the window, stared into the depths of his drink for a moment, then raised his head and continued pacing up and down, his boots creaking on the floorboards. The room ticked patiently in the dawn silence.

Dad watched him closely for a while, then said, 'Start talking, kiddo.'

Lucas talked.

First of all he told Dad that there were certain things he didn't have the right to divulge. Things about me.

'There's nothing to hide, Mr McCann. You have my word. But if I told you something your daughter hasn't told you, I'd be betraying her faith in me. And I can't do that.'

Dad studied him long and hard. Finally he said, 'OK. I'll buy that for now. But I want to know what happened on the beach today. No conditions, no rights, no bullshit. I want to know everything.'

Lucas nodded. 'OK. It started on Friday evening. I was looking for crabs across from the bay when I overheard a couple of teenagers talking about a girl who'd been attacked near the cliffs. They were a young couple, and they were a bit ... busy. They didn't know I was there, and as soon as I realised what they were up to I left them to it, but I heard enough to realise that the girl they were talking about was Angel Dean, and that the description she'd given the police was meant to be me.'

'And was it?' Dad asked.

'Dad!' I said. 'You can't—'

He held up his hand. 'Let him answer. Did you attack Angel Dean on Friday?'

'No.'

'Can you prove that?'

'No.'

'Where were you?'

'When?'

'In the afternoon.'

Lucas thought about it. 'I was in the woods until about three. I spent about an hour fishing at the bay. Then I went back to the woods.'

'Doing what?'

He shrugged. 'Nothing much. Eating, sleeping, reading, sitting around, thinking, watching things ...'

'You didn't go anywhere near the cliffs?'

'No.'

'OK – so what happened today.' He looked at the clock. 'I mean yesterday.'

Lucas finished his coffee and put the mug down on the bedside cabinet. 'Is it all right if I sit down?'

Dad indicated a chair by the window.

Lucas sat down. 'Do you mind if I smoke?'

Dad nodded.

Lucas started rolling a cigarette. 'Jamie Tait and Angel Dean rigged up a story to turn the island against me—'

'Why?' Dad interrupted.

Lucas glanced at me, then back at Dad. 'Several reasons.'

'Such as?'

'Tait's afraid of me.'

'Afraid of you? Why?'

'I'm different. He doesn't know what I am. He knows I'm not afraid of him. He knows I'd kill him if I had to. And he knows I'm better-looking than him.'

Dad grinned. 'You think so?'

Lucas lit his cigarette. 'I know so.'

There wasn't any arrogance in his voice. He wasn't boasting, he was simply stating a fact. He *was* better-looking than Jamie. He knew it. And he knew it meant something. Despite what everyone pretends to think, looks *are* important. *You* might not care what you look like, but others do, and little things like that can determine their reaction to you.

I think that's what he thought, anyway.

A cloud of smoke drifted from his mouth and snaked out through the window into the rain. The wind had dropped and the rain was coming down hard and straight. In the distance, way out over the sea, daylight was paling the sky.

'What about Angel?' Dad said. 'Why did she go along with Tait?'

'She wanted him.'

'How do you know?'

'I know desire when I see it.'

'Yes, but—'

'Please, Mr McCann – if you'd stop asking questions and let me carry on, it'll all become clear.'

A glare appeared in Dad's eyes, but it was a semi-respectful glare. 'Be my guest,' he said sarcastically. 'And stop calling me Mister. It makes me feel old. My name's John.'

'I thought they called you Mac?'

'My *friends* call me Mac.'

Lucas nodded and went on with his story. 'I would have left the island there and then, but I'd promised Cait I'd see her at the festival. I knew people would be looking for me, but I thought I'd be fairly safe in the woods. So I spent the night and most of Saturday holed up, and then I set off for the festival around four o'clock. I didn't know exactly what I was going to do when I got there, but with the festival going on I thought the beach would be quiet and I could work something out on the way.'

Dad said, 'Why didn't you work something out during the night?'

'I tried to. Nothing came to me.'

'But you were still prepared to risk it?'

'I would have thought of something.'

Dad lit another cigarette. As an afterthought he offered the packet to Lucas. Lucas was still smoking his roll-up. He shook his head and continued. 'The tide was coming in. The shoreline was narrow and I had a good view of the beach up ahead. There was an old man sitting at the sea's edge reading a book, but apart from that the beach was empty. I was keeping in close to the saltmarshes, following the strandline. That way, if I did come across anyone, I could either take off into the marshes or drop down and hide.'

'What about the path along the creek?' asked Dad.

'Anyone there?'

Lucas shook his head. 'Not then. Not that I could see.'

'OK. Go on.'

'As I approached the pillbox I heard faint voices coming from inside. A man and a girl, or a boy and a girl ... it was hard to tell. The concrete deadens the sound. They were just voices. I was on the marsh side of the pillbox, the entrance side.' He hesitated, looking at Dad. 'You know what goes on in there?'

Dad nodded. 'Do you?'

'Couples, men, junkies ...' He shrugged. 'Wherever you go there's always a place like that. I keep away. It's none of my business.'

'But you didn't keep away this time?'

'No ... something didn't feel right. I'm not sure what it was. The tone of the voices, maybe. A scent of fear in the air ... I don't know.'

'What did you do?'

Lucas pinched the end off his cigarette and dropped the stub in his pocket. 'There's a small window in the wall of the pillbox ... not a window, exactly – what do you call it? Like a slot, a hole in the wall ...'

'I know what you mean,' Dad said. 'Just tell us what happened.'

'I decided to take a look inside.' He paused, visualising the scene. 'The sun was high and facing me. I was in the shadows. I crept up quietly and squatted down beside the window. The sand was damp. The air smelled of waste. The voices were clearer, now. I recognised Tait's, but not the girl's. He was doing most of the talking. His voice was low and throaty and I couldn't make out what he was saying, but I could tell he was drunk. Not drunk enough to slur his words, but not far off.' He looked at Dad. 'You probably know what I mean.'

Dad nodded.

Lucas went on. 'The girl sounded drunk, too. And frightened. She was trying to hide it by laughing and swearing all the time but that only made it worse. I don't think she knew what to do with it.'

'With what?'

'Her fear. It embarrassed her. And the embarrassment surprised her. She wasn't used to it.' He got up and looked out of the window. 'After a couple of minutes I inched my head around and looked inside. There was a dirty old mattress on the floor surrounded by empty bottles and beer cans and all sorts of muck. They were sitting on the mattress with their backs to me. They couldn't see me, but I could see them. That's when I realised it was Angel Dean. Tait had his arm around her shoulder and was fiddling with her top. She was giggling and trying to pull it back up. Tait was swigging from a half-bottle of whiskey. He kept offering it to Angel, almost forcing it on her, and she kept taking it.' He stopped speaking and rolled another cigarette.

'Was she *with* him?' Dad asked. 'I mean, do you think she *wanted* to be there?'

Lucas lit his cigarette and turned from the window. 'I don't think she knew *what* she wanted. She probably knew what he was after, and she probably thought it might be fun. But then reality kicked in, and I think she realised it wasn't a game any more. It wasn't a photo-story. It wasn't a snog and a cuddle. It was something else, something cold and dirty and mean.' He drew cigarette smoke into his mouth and looked at Dad. 'She was scared.'

Dad couldn't think of anything to say.

Lucas blew out smoke and stared into the distance. The

air around him was charged with darkness and the room was filled with the same ghostly silence I'd sensed when I'd first set eyes on him. The wind had suddenly dropped and pale lights were shimmering in the morning sky. My skin was cold. I was there, on the beach, at the pillbox. I was there. In the dirty dark. I could smell it: stale beer, whiskey, urine, fear. I could feel the damp sand beneath my feet and I could see through Lucas's eyes. I could see skin, glass, cloth, hair, hands, fingers, contours, shivering flesh, opening mouths, a broken face rigid with need ...

Dad clicked his cigarette lighter and the vision dissolved. My sight came back to me. I was sitting on the edge of the bed staring at Lucas, and he was staring at Dad. I could see everything as it was. The boy, the man, the walls, the window, twisted leaves blowing in the wind. I could see what I could see, nothing else.

Dad spoke quietly. 'Time's getting on, Lucas. Tell me what happened.'

Lucas sat down wearily in the chair. He studied the glowing tip of his cigarette and his voice got cold. 'They started ... he got her down on the mattress and she closed her eyes. She wasn't struggling, she wasn't crying or anything. She wasn't *enjoying* it ... but ... I don't know. He didn't force her. Not physically. And she didn't say no ... not that he asked her ...' He lowered his head and stared at the floor. 'I couldn't watch any more. I moved back into the saltmarshes, crouched down, and waited. I couldn't think what else to do.' He paused again, scratching at the scar on his wrist, then carried on. 'It was quiet for a while. Then, after about ten minutes, I heard his voice again. Quiet at first, then louder, and then he was really yelling at her, calling her all kinds of dirty names. She started crying, he shouted some more, then I heard a slap and a sharp cry and it all went quiet again. I was just getting to my feet when I saw him come out. He was pulling on his shirt and stumbling all over the place. Red-faced, drunk, glazed eyes. I sank down and watched him go, then I went in to see how she was.'

'Which way did he go?' asked Dad.

'Along the beach.'

'This old man you saw sitting on the beach – would he have seen him?'

'Probably – he was down in that little sandy dip where the rock-pools are. Do you know where I mean?'

Dad nodded. 'So Tait would have passed him?'

'Unless he cut across the marshes to the creek.'

'What about *Angel*?' I said impatiently. 'Did you see her?'

Lucas nodded. 'Yeah, she was OK. Dishevelled. A bit drunk and teary, a bit sorry for herself, and very angry. But she was all right.'

'*What?* She wasn't—'

'Tait didn't hurt her ... not badly, anyway. He slapped her face, but he didn't cut her. I'm not sure he even ... you know. And even if he did, she didn't seem that bothered about it. At least, that's what she wanted me to think.'

'You spoke to her?'

'I asked her if she was all right.'

'What did she say?'

'She told me to go away.'

'Go away?'

'Something like that.'

'What did you do?'

'I went away.'

I looked at Dad, waiting for him to say something, but he remained silent. I looked at Lucas. He was staring intently through the window.

'Did you hear that?' he said suddenly.

'What?'

'Listen,' he whispered.

I couldn't hear anything.

'There's nothing—'

'Shhh!'

Downstairs, Deefer barked.

'There,' said Lucas. 'Did you hear that?'

'That was Deefer,' I said.

'Not that – there was something down the lane.' He peered out into the darkness. 'A metallic sound ...' He stared out into the night for a while then turned around and started talking. There was a fresh urgency to his voice. 'Anyway, after I'd spoken to Angel I left the pillbox and headed back to the woods. There was no point going to the festival any more. Angel would be getting back there soon enough and it wasn't hard to imagine what she'd have to say. She'd seen me at the pillbox, she had a slapped face, my footprints were all over the place. I wouldn't have lasted five minutes.' He looked over at me. His face appeared gaunt and old – the blue of his eyes was dying. He glanced out of the window again. 'I was about halfway across the mud flats when I looked around and saw someone crossing the marshes towards the pillbox. A young woman, a girl. Seventeen, maybe eighteen.'

'Do you know who it was?' asked Dad.

Lucas avoided the question. 'She had long black hair,' he said, 'wrap-around sunglasses, a confident walk. She was wearing a black swimming costume under a loose white shirt and she was carrying something, some kind of shoulder bag. She must have come along the creek path.'

'Did she see you?'

'I think so. She stopped for a moment and looked over in my direction and then she hurried on into the pillbox. I thought at first she might be a friend of Angel's, that maybe she'd been keeping an eye out for her or something ... but she didn't look the type. There was something about her ... something unsettling.' He nipped at the curtain and looked down the lane, then he turned around and faced us. 'I started back, but the tide was high and the mud flats were nearly waist deep, so it was slow going. By the time I was through them and onto the beach the girl in the swimsuit was already out of the pillbox and heading back along the creek path. When I reached the edge of the saltmarshes she was gone.' He stared at nothing. 'She did it. It wasn't Tait – it was her. She's the one that attacked Angel.'

'Are you sure?' Dad asked gently.

Lucas nodded. 'When I went down into the pillbox Angel was lying on the floor with her head in her hands ... she was covered in blood. I checked her over. She was drifting in and out of consciousness and her pulse was weak, but her breathing was OK. I cleared her mouth and got her into the recovery position then tried to stop the worst of the bleeding—'

'*You* fixed up her leg?' Dad said.

He nodded again. 'While I was working on it I heard someone sniffing around outside. I thought it was Tait for a minute, or the girl in the swimsuit, so I hid away in the shadows at the back of the pillbox. Then the old man from the beach poked his head through the slot in the wall. When he saw Angel he nearly died of shock.'

'Did he see you?'

Lucas shook his head. 'I don't think so. It was pretty dark in there and he didn't hang around. He came down into the pillbox and took a quick look at Angel, but as soon as he saw all the blood, he was away, rushing off towards the village.'

'What did you do then?'

He shrugged. 'Not much ... I did what I could for the girl – kept her warm, checked her pulse, slowed the bleeding – and then after a while I heard you and Mr Patel coming along the beach, arguing with a bunch of boys.' He looked at Dad, a hint of helplessness showing in his eyes. 'I had to leave then. Her blood was all over me, I had a knife in my belt ... I was already suspected of attacking her. No one would have believed what really happened. No one. I *had* to go ...'

'It's OK,' Dad said quietly. 'I understand.'

Lucas took a deep breath and slumped down into the chair. 'I went back to the woods and started getting my stuff together. I saw you going down into the pillbox ... then the helicopter arrived ... and that's about it, really. You know the rest.'

Dad stood up and walked over to him. He put his hand on his shoulder, gave it a squeeze, then moved off wearily to the window.

'It was Sara,' I said quietly.

Dad turned around. 'What?'

'The girl Lucas saw – it was Sara Toms. Jamie's girlfriend. When I saw Jamie and Angel heading off to the beach there was someone in a car watching them. A white Mercedes. Sara's got a white Mercedes.'

Dad stared at me, thinking it through. After a minute he turned to Lucas.

'Do you know Sara Toms?' he asked. 'Have you ever seen her?'

'From a distance.'

'Could it have been her?'

He nodded.

'How sure are you?'

'It was her.'

'Damn.'

Lucas grinned coldly. 'Makes it a bit complicated, doesn't it?'

'It does for you,' replied Dad. 'Christ ... no wonder Bob Toms was acting so strangely. How the hell did he know?'

'Did you smell the perfume in there?' Lucas asked.

Dad looked at him. 'Angel's?'

Lucas looked to me. 'Would Angel wear Chanel?'

'No chance.'

'Do you know anyone who does?'

I didn't have to answer.

Lucas turned to Dad. 'Does a father recognise his daughter's scent?'

'I wouldn't – but Bob Toms probably would. My God ... he must have known straight away. He must have guessed.'

'Exactly,' said Lucas. 'That's why I have to get off the island. Toms can probably cover up the forensics and fix an alibi for Sara, but I'm the one he really needs to fix.'

'No,' said Dad. 'I can't believe that. Bob Toms might be a lot of things – he *is* a lot of things – but I can't believe he'd go that far—'

'Of course he will,' Lucas said. 'He's already started.'

'No ... I'll talk to him—'

'Waste of time. This is his daughter he's trying to save. He's not going to listen to sense.' He looked at Dad. 'Imagine Cait had attacked someone with a knife and *you* had the power to blame it on a dirty little gypsy who everyone thinks is a pervert anyway. Don't tell me you wouldn't do it.'

'I wouldn't.'

Lucas smiled. 'You're a fine story-teller, John – but a hopeless liar.'

The room sank into silence.

I wished I was confused. I wished I didn't understand what was going on. I wished I could just get into bed and go to sleep and then wake up in the morning with everything back to normal. But I knew it wouldn't happen. I could see it all too clearly. Everything led to here. This was it. There was nowhere else to go.

It was a dead end.

Just then a loud metallic clink echoed out from the lane. We all heard it this time. Deefer barked and Dad and Lucas rushed to the window. As I followed them I heard the roar of a motorcycle starting up somewhere along the lane. Dad pulled Lucas away from the window.

'Get down!' he hissed.

Lucas sank to his knees and Dad flung open the curtains. Although dawn had broken, the light was dim and hazy and the sky was darkened with storm clouds. I could hear the sound of the motorcycle racing up the lane but I couldn't see anything.

'Where is it?' I said.

'He's got his lights off,' Dad replied. 'Wait a minute – there!' He pointed past the yard and I saw a flash of black against the grey of the hedge. I watched the blurred black shape speeding up the drive and crashing through the puddles, and then it faded from view. I heard the engine slow at the top of the drive, I heard it pull out onto the lane, and then I heard it race away into the morning gloom.

'Shit,' said Dad, dropping the curtain and turning to the doorway as Dominic came in. 'Did you see him?'

Dom nodded. 'Mick Buck.'

Lucas stood up. 'He must have been there all night waiting for me. He's gone to tell the others I'm here. I'm sorry, I should have known. I'll go.'

Dad took hold of him. 'You're not going anywhere, son.'

'I'm not—'

'Shut up and listen. You're exhausted. There's another storm on the way. You're staying here.'

'No, I can't—'

Dad pushed him gently but firmly into the chair. 'We've got about half an hour before they get here. An hour at the most. Dom, pop up to Rita's and let them know what's going on. They should be all right, but tell them to stay inside and keep everything locked. When you get back, take the car and park it across the driveway, about halfway up. Then get back in here.'

'OK.'

Dad turned to me. 'Get dressed and get Lucas up in the attic. I want you both to stay up there until I say otherwise. All right?'

I nodded.

He looked at Dom. 'Go.'

Dom left.

Dad looked at Lucas. 'Can I trust you to look after my daughter?'

'It'd be safer for all of you if I left. They're not going to leave if they know I'm here.'

'I asked you a question.'

Lucas looked at me, then at Dad. 'You can trust me.'

'Good. Well – what are you waiting for? The lady wants

to get dressed. Make yourself useful and get some coffee going.' He grinned. 'Do you know how to use a kettle?'

Lucas breathed in through his teeth and rolled his eyes. 'Well, I don't know about that ... is it one of them new-fangled electric ones?'

Dad smiled and opened the door. 'Out.'

They left together and I started getting dressed. As they went down the hall I could hear them talking. They sounded like old friends. Calm, quiet, perfectly at ease with each other. I listened hard, trying to hear what they were saying, but all I could hear was Dad's quiet laughter drifting away down the stairs.

twenty-one

I dressed quickly and started getting the ladder down from the attic. The storm was rising again. Driving rain was beginning to pound against the windows and the skies were rumbling. For just a moment I let myself think that if it got any worse it might dampen things down a bit. A cold wind, a good strong downpour ... maybe it would put the fire out ...

Yeah, I thought, just like it did yesterday.

The ladder trundled down and I automatically stepped to one side to avoid getting clonked on the head. The whirring sound was just as I remembered it – the sound of secrets and darkness. I began to climb the cold metal rungs, one at a time. I was halfway up when Lucas appeared on the landing carrying two mugs of coffee.

'Your dad says to hurry up,' he said.

'Just a minute.' I climbed up through the hatchway and felt the familiar seam of cold air cooling my face. I breathed in the smell of soot and old wood. Nothing had changed. I turned to Lucas. 'Come on then. Pass me those.'

He stepped on to the ladder and passed me the coffees. I placed them on the attic floor.

I said, 'Let me get in and then you can come up.' I hoisted myself into the attic, turned on the light, and sat cross-legged on the floor. 'OK,' I called down.

As Lucas climbed the ladder, I looked around the attic.

I could see the dark beams and the scarred rafters and the light of the sky glinting through the cracked slate tiles. I could hear the rain pattering on the roof and birds scratching in the eaves ... and I knew. I'd known all along that it was going to end here. Here, among the dusty things hanging from beams ... here was a world that was anything I wanted it to be. A desert island, the woods ...

Only now I wasn't alone.

Lucas's head appeared through the hatchway.

'Nice,' he said, gazing around.

'Yeah, it is. I like it.'

He pulled himself up and sat down next to me. I pressed a switch and the ladder started to trundle back up. Lucas watched it, fascinated.

'Electric,' I smiled.

'Ah ...'

The ladder's feet slid through the hatchway, the ladder clanked to a halt, and the hatch flapped shut behind it. I reached across and fastened the latch.

'Here,' I said, passing Lucas a coffee and waving my hand at the attic. 'Make yourself at home.'

He got up and began looking around, keeping his head down to avoid the beams.

'Is it safe?' he asked, looking at the floor.

'As long as you keep to the central walkway.'

'What happens if I don't?'

'You'll fall through the ceiling.'

While he carried on poking around, looking at this and that, studying the things hanging on the wall, examining the contents of boxes, I went over and sat in a battered old chair beside the water tank. Shadowed light fell from the bare lightbulb hanging from the rafters. It was only a weak light and the attic was still quite dark. Dark, but not gloomy, like the inside of a tent on a rainy day. Or the inside of a den, snug and warm, with the rain ticking on the plastic sheeting, a wood fire smouldering outside, the smell of the smoke drifting in the rain ...

'What's this?' asked Lucas.

I looked up. He was standing at the other end of the attic where an old piece of sheet was draped over the beams.

I smiled. 'I used to play in here when I was a kid. That was ... well, I don't know what it was exactly. My secret place.'

'Your hideaway?'

'Yeah.'

He grinned. 'What did you think about when you were up here? What did you wish for?'

'I don't know ... I just wanted to be on my own, I suppose. I wanted to get away from people.'

He nodded. 'It's good to get away.'

'Yeah ... I always came back, though.'

He looked at me. 'That's what you wanted.'

'I suppose so. What about you? Didn't you want to go back?'

He shook his head thoughtfully, gazing past me into the shadows. 'No ...' he said quietly. 'I didn't want to go back ...' His words trailed off as he stared blindly at the wall.

The wind whistled through the roof tiles and the light-bulb swung in the rafters, distorting the shadows.

I shivered. It was suddenly getting cold.

Lucas snapped out of his trance. 'Is there any way of looking out? Can we see the yard from up here?'

'Over here,' I told him.

He walked over to where I was sitting and I pointed out

a gap in the side of roof where the tiles were missing and the roofing felt was torn. 'If you lie down on that board and slither along you can see outside.' I rubbed soot from my hands. 'What's Dad doing?'

Lucas moved over to the gap in the roof. 'He's on the phone, trying to get through to Lenny. He didn't seem to be having much luck.' He lowered himself to the floor and slid along until he was close enough to the gap to look out. 'This is good,' he said.

'What do you think's going to happen?' I asked.

He adjusted his position, shuffling his legs about to make more room for himself. He said, 'In about ten minutes, a bunch of people are coming down your driveway looking for my blood. They'll probably be led by Tait and Brendell and Angel's brother, backed up by the boys from the Stand and whoever else fancies it. They'll be drunk and pumped up with coke and speed, and most of them will be out of their minds with hate. Bob Toms will be there, ostensibly to arrest me, but he won't do anything to stop any trouble. That old Fiesta of yours parked across the drive is going to hold them up for about two seconds. They're going to stream into the yard and your dad's going to go out and face them. He'll tell them I'm not here. He'll tell them I *was* here, because he knows they know it, but that I'm not here any more. I left half an hour ago, heading for the Stand.'

I got out of the chair and joined Lucas on the floor. As I wriggled up alongside him he moved over to make room for me.

'Then what?' I asked.

'Well according to your dad, they'll slap their thighs, turn around, and go chasing back to the Stand.'

'And according to you?'

He hesitated for a moment, shifting his head to let me see through the gap. I was right next to him now. I could smell him, his skin, his breath. I could feel the dampness of his clothing. We lay side by side and peered down at the yard below. It looked strange from up here. Cramped and unfamiliar. Too pale. Too flat. Its colour and dimensions distorted by the height.

'According to you?' I repeated.

'I don't know what's going to happen.'

'Yes you do.'

He turned his head and looked at me. I'd been close to him before, but not like this. I could see every line and every pore on his face, every little scar. I could see deep down into his eyes ...

'We'll soon find out,' he said calmly. 'It's happening now.'

I looked outside.

A convoy of vehicles was coming down the drive.

twenty-two

Lying side by side on the attic floor, we watched the trail of cars and vans rumbling down the driveway towards the yard. The groan of slow-moving engines shook the air, rattling the beams of the attic and showering us with dust. Thunder rolled in the distance, lightning flickered, and the rain-darkened driveway was ablaze with headlights. There must have been about a dozen vehicles in all. Jamie Tait's Jeep was in front, followed by the white van, then a ragbag assortment of cars, pick-up trucks, motorcycles ...

'This is unbelievable,' I whispered.

'Believe it,' said Lucas.

The black Jeep approached the spot where the Fiesta blocked the driveway. It slowed, pulled over to one side, and stopped. Jamie stood up in the driver's seat and gestured at the white van behind. He looked like a tinpot dictator directing a band of guerrillas. The van lurched forward, pulled out around the Jeep and accelerated towards the Fiesta. The tinny white car didn't stand a chance. A hollow crunch rang out as the speeding van slammed into it, and the Fiesta bounced across the drive and slid into the hedge with all the resistance of a broken ping-pong ball. Shattered windows sparkled in the rain and the bonnet flapped open with a rusty clank. Drunken cheers drifted in the wind. The van reversed, the Jeep took its place, and the convoy rumbled on.

'There's too many of them,' I said to Lucas. 'We don't

stand a chance. What are we going to do? We can't just—'

'Don't worry,' he said, touching my shoulder. 'There's always a way out. It's just a matter of finding it.'

I looked at him. He was barely aware of my presence. His face was dark and intense, his eyes fixed on the approaching vehicles like the eyes of a hunter. A hunted hunter.

'Wait and see,' he whispered to himself. 'Wait and see.'

The cars were turning into the yard now, their tyres crunching on the wet gravel as one by one they rolled to a stop, forming a ragged semi-circle facing the house. The engines ticked to silence and steam rose into the air. Headlights glared coldly in the rain. Car doors started opening and figures emerged. I could see their faces. I could put names to most of them. Jamie Tait and Robbie Dean in the Jeep. Lee Brendell and Tully Jones in the front of the van, another half dozen stumbling out of the back. Mick Buck, some local bikers, others I didn't recognise. Probably from Moulton. Faces from the village: trouble-makers, young lads, grown men who ought to know better. Women, even. Ellen Coombe, a handful of hard-faced mothers. Some of the men carried sticks, batons, bars, bottles. One of them had a machete. They were all high on something or other: drink, drugs, hate, excitement, twisted morality, the promise of blood.

My stomach churned.

At the back, keeping a low profile, I saw Bob Toms and a stony-faced man in a long black overcoat getting quietly out of a dark saloon.

A voice rang out through the rain. 'Hey! McCann! Get out here!'

I looked down and saw Jamie Tait standing at the front of the mob yelling up at the house. A black woollen cap was pulled down tight on his head and his black T-shirt and jeans were soaked to his skin. Brendell stood beside him, solid as a rock, and Robbie Dean stood on the other side, blank and emotionless, with a tyre-lever dangling from his hand.

Jamie cupped his hands to his mouth. 'McCann! We don't want you! Just the boy! Send him out! Hey! Are you *listening*, McCann—'

His voice stopped abruptly as the front door opened and Dad and Dominic walked out with Deefer beside them. Dominic was carrying the baseball bat.

Jamie grinned and took a step back, holding up one hand to quieten the murmuring crowd gathered behind him.

'Morning, Mac,' he said breezily. 'Dom.'

Dad ignored him, still scanning the crowd. 'Where's Toms? *Toms!*'

Jamie moved forward. 'Where's the gypsy, Mac?'

Dad looked at Robbie. 'Robbie – I'm sorry about your sister. It's a terrible thing—'

'*Where's the gyppo?*' someone shouted.

Dad looked up. 'He's not here. He didn't do it.'

Jamie laughed. 'Of course he didn't.'

Dad ignored him and spoke to Dean. 'Listen to me, Robbie. I know what happened to Angel. I know who did it. I can—'

A voice from the crowd drowned him out. '*Liar!*'

More shouts –

'*Bastard!*'

'*Get him!*'

'*Drag him out!*'

The voices rose to an incoherent swell and the mob began to move.

'No!' I whispered. 'No ...'

'It's all right,' Lucas said calmly. 'Tait wants to play it. Just wait.'

I saw Jamie turn and raise both hands, waving the crowd back. 'Hold on!' he called out. 'Just a minute! Just a *minute*!'

The crowd hesitated and the shouting faded to an angry murmur. As the rain hissed down and the wind howled around the yard, Jamie stood there with his eyes alight and his hands held out in supplication, like a preacher at the pulpit facing his congregation. He waited for the voices to fall and then he spoke. His voice echoed with madness. 'Listen to me! Listen! We're not *animals*. We're civilised people. We're not killers. All we want is justice. Let me talk to the man. Let me reason with him.'

'He's lost it,' Lucas said. 'He's flipped.' Then, under his breath, 'Watch the brother, John. The brother ...'

I looked down.

Jamie had turned to face Dad. Brendell hadn't moved. Dad was watching the crowd. Deefer was sitting beside him, rigid as a board, growling quietly. And Robbie Dean was staring murderously at the ground with the tyre-lever clutched in his hand.

Jamie's face burned with manic intensity. 'See, Mac?' he said. 'You see what you're up against? I can only do so much. I can't hold them for ever. So why don't you give them what they want? Send the boy out. I know he's in there. Just send him out. Then we can all go home and you and yours can get back to whatever it is you do. How about that? You can have another drink, write another story-book. Your pretty little daughter can dream her dreams. And you—' he grinned at Dom '—you can write yourself an essay.' He let out a strangled laugh and turned back to Dad. 'What do you say, Johnny?'

Dad spoke softly. 'I told you, boy. He's not here.'

Jamie's eyes narrowed. 'What do you think I am, McCann? You think I'm stupid? He's here. You know it. I know it. We all know it.'

'He *was* here,' Dad said. 'And now he's gone. He left about twenty minutes ago. He's probably halfway to Moulton by now.' He raised his voice, speaking to the crowd. 'Did you hear that? He's not here. He's gone. Now go, get off my property and go home.'

The crowd stirred and Jamie laughed again. 'Come on, man – do yourself a favour. Just send him out. The boy's an animal, a rapist. You don't want a thing like that in your house, do you? Think of your daughter. Is she in there with him now? Is she? You think she's safe with him? Did you *see* what he did to that girl? Jesus, what a mess—'

Without a word, Robbie Dean started walking towards Dad. His eyes were fixed on the ground and his body moved stiffly, like a zombie. The crowd hushed and Jamie looked on with an ugly smile. I heard Lucas catch his breath and I felt his body tense.

'Now hold on, Robbie,' Dad said. 'Robbie ... don't ...'

Robbie wasn't listening. I don't think he was capable of listening. He just kept on coming. As he neared Dad he raised his eyes and stared right through him. Deefer growled and Dominic raised the baseball bat, but Dad reached back and lowered Dom's arm.

'Robbie!' he snapped. 'Look at me! Look at me, Robbie!'

Robbie stopped and looked at him. There was no recognition in his eyes. He couldn't see. He couldn't think. He was a man without a soul.

Beside me, Lucas moved, sliding backwards along the floor.

'Wha— where are you going?' I said.

'It's not working,' he replied. 'Dean's the spark. It's about to explode.'

I grabbed hold of his leg and tried to pull him back. 'No, Lucas ... you have to stay here. Dad told you to stay here. You *promised*.'

He pulled his leg away and stood up. 'I said I'd look after you. That's what I'm doing.'

'But—'

'There's no time.' He stooped down and kissed my hand. 'It's been good, Caitlin McCann. Thank you.' He smiled at me, a flash of blue eyes, then he turned away and hurried across to the hatchway.

'Lucas—'

In one quick movement he smashed the hatch open with his booted foot, balanced momentarily on the ledge, then stepped into thin air and dropped out of sight. I closed my eyes and gritted my teeth, waiting for the sickening crash, but all I heard was a faint thump, the sound of a jumping cat, and then rapid bootsteps running along the hall and down the stairs.

For a moment I just sat there in the dust, stunned, rubbing the back of my hand and staring after him. A moment ... the moment.

My moment.

Gone.

With an emptying heart, I scrambled back to the gap in the roof and peered down at the yard. Nothing seemed to have changed. The rain, the dark skies, the cars, the ugly mass of people. Robbie Dean was still standing in front of Dad. Jamie Tait was still smiling his death smile. And Dad was still talking.

'... just you and me, Robbie. Come inside and have a quiet drink, a cup of tea. You can't think straight in all this noise. You need to rest—'

Then it exploded.

Someone – probably Jamie – shouted out, 'Time's up, Robbie! Angel's waiting! Take him out!'

It took a moment for the words to sink in, then Robbie's head jerked and his eyes bulged and he moved towards Dad with the tyre-lever raised. I don't think he knew what he was doing. He was simply reacting to the sound of his sister's name. The shouted words meant nothing to him. *Angel*, though ... *Angel* – that was all he needed to hear. With a pitiful groan he stepped up to Dad and swung the metal bar at his head. Dad didn't move until he had to. Even as the tyre-lever hissed through the air he was still hoping for another way out of it. He knew what was happening. He knew what it meant. I could see it in his eyes. *Oh God, please don't make me do this ...* At the very last moment he ducked to one side and the tyre-lever sliced through the air above his head. Robbie was carried forward by the momentum, and as he stumbled past, Dad raised his hand and clubbed him hard on the back of his neck. Robbie lurched forward, slammed head first into the door frame, and slumped to the ground. The tyre-lever fell from his hand and rattled loudly on the concrete step. In the shocked silence, the sound echoed around the yard like a ringing bell.

Dad gazed down at Robbie's crumpled body for a moment, then, with a dejected shake of his head, he turned around to face the crowd. As one disjointed organism, they stared back at him – fifty dead eyes burning through the rain. Dominic moved forward and stood beside Dad. The crowd-beast flicked its eyes – and then it moved. Crunch, crunch ... fifty legs and fifty arms, a thoughtless mass of flesh and bone moving to a stimulus.

Dad tried once more. 'Think about it!' he cried out. 'Stop and *think* ...' But his words were lost to the sound of the beast. Inhuman voices, groans, spits and growls, thoughtless feet crunching on gravel.

Dad gave up on reason and prepared to fight. His body slipped into a crouch and he stepped forward to meet the attack. Deefer bared his teeth and moved with him, guarding his flank, and Dominic moved to cover the other side. Dad's eyes scanned the approaching mass, trying to pick out the leaders. He knew it was his only chance – take out the leaders and the rest just might give up.

I searched with him. Jamie ... where's Jamie? There ... hanging back, just off the front, shielded by Brendell, goading the others on but keeping himself out of harm's way. Too smart. What about Toms? No ... no sign of him. No sign of his sergeant, either ...

I saw Dad's eyes settle on Tully Jones. Jones was at the front, moving fast and wielding a pick-axe handle.

My heart was bursting with fire. I was burning up. I felt so bad I can't even describe it. Everything all at once – paralysing fear, emptiness, panic, madness, rage ... my body screaming, burning, crying ... my head numbed, spinning, cold, overloaded with nothing and everything ...

I saw everything.

Tully Jones came on with a streetwise grin and feinted Dad with the pick-axe handle, raising it to strike then darting to one side. As Dad followed him round, two bikers sneaked up behind him. One was short and weaselly with a Stanley knife gripped behind his back, the other was a mountain man with stringy black hair and hands as big as shovels. Deefer got the weasel, bit him in the leg, and Dom went for the mountain man. The big biker just flicked him away like a bear swatting flies, and then he was on Dad from behind, pinning his arms to his side while Tully Jones came up from the front with drug-burned eyes and the pick-axe handle cocked over his shoulder.

I thought it was all over.

Then a bolt of lightning lit up the sky, cracking open the gloom, and Lucas flew out of the house with his knife in one hand and a whiskey bottle in the other. He moved fast and without a sound, cracking the bottle into Jones's face then spinning round and slashing the biker's arm with his knife. Jones crumpled to the ground and the biker screamed and grabbed at his bleeding arm. Then he screamed again as Deefer sank his teeth into his backside.

The rest of the mob were momentarily stunned.

Someone said, *'That's him!'*

Then, as one, they realised who it was.

'It's him!'

'The gypsy!'

'Get him!'

They started forward, but Lucas ignored them. Casually wiping a film of rain from his face, he dropped the bottle to the ground, sheathed his knife, and spoke quietly to Dad. I couldn't hear what he said, but Dad told me later that his voice was unforgettably clear. His exact words were: 'I've left my bag in your room. It's all in there. When I've gone give it to Craine.' Then he smiled and said, 'Maybe we'll talk again some time.'

The crowd was closing rapidly now, snapping and snarling like a pack of jackals, but Lucas didn't seem to care. With frightening calmness he shook Dad's hand and thanked him for everything, then he smiled and raised a farewell hand to me, and finally, with an almost arrogant weariness, he turned to face the approaching horde. His body stilled and his eyes emptied. The look of Lucas: no fear, no anger, no pain, no hate ... no nothing. Nothing at all, absolutely nothing. The emotionless look of an animal, a look of pure instinct.

They were almost on him now, and for one terrible moment I thought he'd given up. He was just going to stand there and take it. But then, just as the hands were reaching out and I thought it was too late, he swayed back, skipped delicately to one side, and took off into the rain.

My heart sang as I watched him run. His feet barely touched the ground. Round the edge of the yard, leaning into the wind, a quick dart across the lawn, then up and over the garden fence and he was away, flying down the lane towards the beach in all his ragged grace.

By the time the crowd realised what had happened, he was already out of sight.

I smiled through my tears.

False hope. That's all it was – false hope. He had nowhere to go. The island was still cut off. There was nowhere to run to. I knew it. He knew it. The crowd knew it. All he was doing was buying time, drawing them away from us. He might lead them a merry chase, he might hold out for a few hours, maybe even longer, but they'd get him in the end. They were always going to. It was written in his eyes. In the stars. He was born to it.

But you can still hope, can't you? Even when you know you're wasting your time, what harm can it do to hope?

The skies were darkening by the minute now. A driving wind swept in low to the ground then whipped up into the air and whirled around the yard, scattering rain in all directions. Thunder rolled and clouds flashed in the near distance.

Down in the yard Jamie Tait was barking out orders and the mob were spilling around and lumbering out into the lane after Lucas. The lane was too narrow for cars, but I saw some of the bikers running for their motorbikes ...

I crawled out from under the roof, hurried over to the hatchway and hit the button that operates the ladder. It groaned slowly into action. As it inched its way down through the hatch, I stepped cautiously up to the edge and gazed down at the hallway below. It was a long drop. God knows how Lucas managed it. If I jumped down there my legs would snap like matchsticks.

'Come *on*,' I said, whacking the ladder.

It carried on at the same speed ... very ... very ... slow ... ly ...

From outside I could hear the sound of the crowd jostling down the lane, fading into the distance. I could hear motorcycle engines, shouts, the wind and rain picking up strength.

The ladder was still only halfway down. If I waited much longer ...

I jumped onto the still-moving ladder. The sudden weight made the motor whine and half a second later something popped and the ladder dropped down and slammed into the floor. I don't know exactly what happened. All I can remember is a jarring pain in my back and then somehow I was on my feet and running downstairs and tearing out the front door into the yard.

A strong hand grabbed my arm and stopped me in my tracks. I whipped round and lashed out with my free hand, narrowly missing Dad's face.

'Whoah!' he said. 'It's me ... take it easy.'

I glanced quickly around. The mob had already disappeared down the lane, chasing after Lucas, and the yard was almost empty. Tully Jones was trying to get to his feet, holding a dirty rag to his face, while further on the two wounded bikers were helping each other across the yard towards their motorbikes.

I called Deefer and he sprang up from the shadows.

'See them?' I said, pointing out the bikers. *'Get 'em!'*

He set off in a loping run toward the two figures.

'What the hell—' said Dad. 'What are you *doing*?'

'It's all right – wait a minute.'

The two bikers turned suddenly at the sound of galloping paws. I saw their faces pale, their mouths drop, their eyes widen, and then I called out – *'Wait!'*

Deefer skidded to a halt in front of them.

'Sit!'

He sat, watching them with hungry eyes. They weren't going anywhere.

I turned to Dad. 'You can drive a motorbike, can't you?'

A minute later, after a little cajoling from Deefer, we had two sets of greasy keys for two greasy motorcycles. Dom got one going and Dad started the other. The powerful engines roared, headlights sliced through the rain, and black exhaust smoke billowed out into the wind. I climbed up on the pillion behind Dad and whacked him on the shoulder.

'OK,' I yelled. 'Let's go. Come on, Dad. *Go!'*

It was hard driving. With all the rain and the trampling feet, the lane was awash with deep puddles and long stretches of thick slimy mud. Too fast and the bikes would skid from under us, too slow and they'd stick in the mud. So we kept to a steady pace. It wasn't as fast as I would have liked, but it was fast enough. A strong cross-wind was blowing, battering the bikes from side to side, and the rain was lashing down hard, stinging my skin.

'Look!' shouted Dad.

I peered over his shoulder, feeling the full blast of the wind in my face. Up ahead two crashed motorcycles were sprawled across the lane and two mud-spattered bikers were sitting beside them. One of them was holding his head in his hands and the other was nursing a wounded leg.

Dad laughed. 'Looks like they caught up with Lucas!'

The wind was so cold my eyes were running with tears and I couldn't get enough air into my lungs to speak. I patted Dad on the shoulder to let him know I knew what he meant. He drove round the ambushed bikers, spattering them with more mud, then pressed on. I glanced over my shoulder. Dominic was close behind, riding hard, with his open shirt blowing in the wind and a crazy grin on his face, and further back I could see Deefer lolloping along through the mud. He looked as if he was enjoying himself, too.

I wasn't.

With every passing second my heart was getting heavier. On the horizon the aluminium grey of the sea was merging with the gloom of the sky to form an all-encompassing rise of dark air and water, like something primeval. It looked cold and hard. Like a place without air, without life, without hope. Like the end of something. That's where we're going, I thought. To the blackness, the darkness, to the place where there's nothing ...

I shook the doom from my head and reached for my hope.

Hope.

Hope.

Hope.

Dad swerved the motorbike and hit the horn, shouting into the wind. I couldn't make out what he was saying but when I leaned out I saw the smoking wreckage of two more motorcycles lying in the mud. Lucas had been busy. There was a half-buried body under one of the crashed bikes, a scabby young man in a filthy denim jacket and ripped leathers. His eyes were open, staring at the falling rain, but he wasn't moving. The other rider was kneeling in the rain beside him coughing up blood.

What's happening? I thought.

What's *happening*?

Dad rode on through the teeming rain, the engine shrieked, the skies above roared and flashed, the earth shook ... it was hopeless. I closed my eyes and prayed for a nightmare. You can wake up from a nightmare. I prayed for the rain I'd dreamed of, the dream of Lucas running on the beach with people chasing after him, throwing stones at him and calling him names. *Gyppo! Thief! Dirty pervert!* Hundreds of them, brandishing sticks and bits of piping, shovels and rocks, whatever they could lay their hands on, their nightmare faces gripped with hate and streaked with tears of rain. *Dirty gyppo! Dirty bastard!* Jamie Tait was there, oiled, in his too-tight swimming trunks. Angel and Robbie. Lee Brendell, Bill, Dominic, Deefer, Simon, Dad, everyone from the island storming across the beach screaming out for blood ... and I was there, too. I was with them. I was running with the mob. I could feel the wet sand beneath my feet, the rain in my hair, the weight of the rock in my hand, I could feel my heart pounding with fear and excitement as I raced along the shore, past the pillbox, heading for the Point. The boy had stopped running and was standing at the edge of the mud flats. All around him the air shimmered with unseen colours. He glanced over his shoulder, looking at me with beseeching eyes, pleading for help. But what could I do? I couldn't do anything. There were too many of them. It was too late. *DON'T STOP!* a voice cried out. It was mine. *DON'T DO IT! DON'T STOP! KEEP RUNNING! DON'T GIVE UP! JUST RUN! RUN FOR EVER ...*

The motorbike slid to a juddering halt and I opened my eyes. The nightmare wasn't a nightmare. There was no waking up this time. We were at the creek. The bridge was flooded. Beyond the saltmarshes I could see the crowd stretched out along the beach, a dark amorphous mass struggling across the sodden sands towards the Point, where Lucas was standing at the edge of the mud flats waiting in the dark light of the sky. He looked so small. Then I looked again and I saw him grow, rising out of the sands, and all around him the storm was dying and the sea was calm. Silent seabirds were circling in the air above his head. The tide had receded and the slimy brown plateau of mud stretched out in front of him. A breath of wind whistled quietly across the flats, then died. Pale sunlight broke from the clouds and glistened dully on the lights of tiny seashells.

I shivered.

Dominic pulled up beside us and raced his engine. 'What are you doing?' he shouted breathlessly. 'What are you waiting for?'

Dad indicated the flooded bridge. 'Too deep for the bikes.'

'So? Get *off*! What's the matter with you? *Come on!*'

Without stopping to turn off the engine he leapt off the

motorbike and started running. I snapped out of my trance and followed him. As we waded through the flooded banks of the bridge I heard Dad splashing around behind us.

'Cut across to the left!' he shouted. 'It's quicker.'

I emerged from the rainpool first and sprinted off across the sand with Dominic close behind. Up ahead I could see the crowd edging towards the Point. Those in front were slowing to let the others catch up. They could see Lucas waiting for them and they didn't want to face him alone. I was running faster than I'd ever run before. The ground disappeared beneath my feet and the beach passed by in a blur. I was vaguely aware of the rain falling and Dad shouting and Deefer barking, but it didn't mean anything to me. My senses were turned inside out. Nothing mattered, only running. The stormy smell of the sea, the sand, the strangely cool air – nothing. The pain in my legs and my aching lungs – nothing. The pillbox, a grey concrete lump fenced with blue and white tape, a flattened bowl of sand where the helicopter had landed ... the pillbox. A dirty darkness of stale beer, whiskey, urine, fear ... damp sand beneath my feet ... skin, glass, cloth, hair, hands, fingers, contours, shivering flesh, opening mouths, a broken face rigid with need ...

Nothing.

Run.

Around the edge of the bay, under the clouds, through the air, across the sand, running hard, down to the shore, down to the sea, down to the flats, where the world begins and ends ... and then I was there, breaking through a wall of people, shoving, pushing, shouting ...

'Get out of the way! Move! *MOVE!*'

They moved. Their bodies were soft and quiet. Eyes

blank, heads empty, they shuffled apart and let me through without caring who or what I was. They only had eyes for Lucas. And as I broke through to the front of the crowd and stumbled breathlessly to the edge of flats, I could see why. He was walking slowly across the mud flats towards the woods ... walking his walk, whispering secrets ... a walking dream. The rain had stopped and faint bubbling noises drifted from the surface of the mud. Drips, clicks, and watery pops, the sound of worms and molluscs going about their muddy business, just as they had for millions of years. This is how it is, I thought. Light, darkness, games of hate, twisted hearts ... things without grown spirit. No tomorrow. No history. A heartbeat ...

How do you know where you're going?

Lucas's voice whispered in the wind: *It's easy, you can see the solid ground. Look. See how it colours the air?*

I could see it now.

The coloured air.

Clear and bright.

Easy.

I stepped forward. A familiar voice called out my name. I think it was Dad's. I don't know. I wasn't there. I was stepping into the coloured air ...

And then it was gone.

The air was grey and the mud was brown and I didn't know where I was going. I never had. Something pulled me back from the edge. Something made me take a breath and raise my eyes ... and I looked out across the mud flats. The air was still and the sea was unnaturally quiet. Nothing moved. No birds, no wind, no waves.

The moment is eternal.

Lucas had stopped by the remains of the old wooden boat and was gazing across the mud towards the woods.

He was facing away from me, resting his hand on a black-ened joist sticking up through the mud. I couldn't see his face, but I didn't have to. His features were engraved in my mind – his pale blue eyes, his sad smile, his fleeting presence. The clouds parted and a pillar of sunlight fell from the sky and shrouded him in gold. I saw his skin, his clothes, his hair, his body ... I saw him pick a shard of damp wood from the wrecked boat and crumble it in his fingers. I saw him gaze past the wreck into the soul of the mud.

And then, in one simple movement, he stepped out of the sunlight and sank down into the airless depths.

twenty-three

Dad was right when he said that writing this wouldn't make me feel any better – it hasn't. It's straightened out a few things in my mind. It's taught me a little bit about myself. It's shown me what I am, or what I was, or what I thought I was. And, yes, it's given the sadness some life. But I don't think it's helped me to understand anything. It hasn't answered any questions. It hasn't changed anything.

But at least I've done it – I've cried myself a story.

And that's something, I suppose.

Now, as I sit here at my desk, looking into the faces I know, I'm wondering how it ends.

When Lucas stepped out of the sunlight and sank down into the mud, when I watched that mop of straw-blond hair being sucked down into the shimmering ooze ... that was the moment's end. He was gone. It was finished. Over. Done. I know it now, and I knew it then. Even as the mud settled and the bubbles stopped rising – I knew it. Even as I cried and screamed and launched myself into the mud – I knew it. Even as Dad and Dominic jumped in and dragged me out, clawing the mud from my mouth – I knew it. It was over. I knew it in my heart.

That was my end.

But the rest of it went on.

The world kept turning.

I have no conscious recollection of the immediate aftermath. I can vaguely remember being carried back to the house, kicking and wailing, screaming at the sky, hitting Dad, cursing him, cursing the world ... and I can remember the feel of the cold rain streaming down my face, mingling with the mud and tears, filling my mouth and the back of my throat with the grainy taste of salt and decay. Yes ... I remember that. I can taste it now – the taste of age-old blackened mud. But that's about all I can remember with any real clarity. The rest of it is just a blur. Dad must have carried me all the way back; across the beach, over the creek, up the lane, through the yard, and into the house. He must have helped me out of my mud-soaked clothes, washed me, dried me, got me into bed, settled me down, called the doctor ... but I don't remember anything about it. I wasn't there. I was disembodied, spiritless, lost in hell. My conscious mind had been ripped into a million pieces.

Over the next few days the outside world disappeared and I lived a dream of curtained light and muttered voices. I slept without sleeping, floating in a curious state somewhere between consciousness and unconsciousness. Strange things happened. The dimensions of my room lost control. The walls, the windows, the ceiling, the floor, everything shimmered like a dream. But it wasn't a dream. It was a fevered perception in which a thousand miles and an inch were the same. The world grew elastic. Angles and planes assumed alien qualities, turning themselves inside out. Colours formed and connected and then reformed in the shapeless light. I saw blood-reds and drifting greens and infinite blacks, shifting white flashes, searchlights, stars, and burning suns. I saw rogue shapes, shapes and colours that no one has ever seen. I saw kites of things in a ghost wind. My inner senses were deranged. The things that should have told me where I was and who I was stopped working. My limbs belonged to someone else, a long-armed giant, or a paralysed fool with giant fingers stretching up to the sky. I wasn't *me*. I was a little girl marooned on a desert island. I was a blood-drenched girl lying in a stone bunker. I was a teenage boy, a fisherman, scraping blindly through the underground mud looking for oysters. I was hot, cold, tired. I was ill. Sick. My body fought against me. It wouldn't do what it was told. Sometimes I couldn't move to save my life, and other times I couldn't *stop* moving; twisting, turning, crawling, twitching, wrapping myself in sweat-soaked sheets, crying, crying, crying ...

I don't know what it was.

It was senseless.

This went on for two, three, maybe four days, and then I gradually started coming back to myself. I slowly became aware of my surroundings. I recognised the people who came to see me. Dad, the doctor, Lenny, Dominic. Simon. Bill and Rita. I could hear what they were saying. I listened. I talked. I thought. And after a few more days in bed I realised that – physically – I was myself again. I was Caitlin McCann. I could get up in the morning, get dressed, eat, drink, breathe. I could walk, I could talk, I could see things and hear things and feel things and do things ... but that was all on the surface. In the place where it counts – my heart, my soul, my self – I was nowhere.

I didn't stop crying for a long time. Days, weeks, months ... time didn't have any meaning. Days came and went, the summer passed by, school started, Dominic went back to university, the leaves on the trees turned yellow, and all the time the tears kept flowing. Some days were better than others. School days, busy days, days when I didn't have time to think ... some days I hardly cried at all. But at night, alone in the silence of my bed, that's when it really hurt. When there was nowhere else to go and nowhere to hide, when the wind whispered in the trees and the breath of the sea hushed the night ...

When I cried the summer rain.

I cried so much ...

I didn't think I'd ever stop.

There was no reason to stop. There was nothing to look forward to, nothing to smile about, nothing to want or need, just long days and endless nights of pain and emptiness. Sometimes it got so bad I almost lost myself. Dark thoughts settled in my mind. Black questions: what kind of life is this? is it worth it? is it really worth living?

I didn't have any answers. I didn't know even where to look for them. Maybe there weren't any answers? Maybe that's why it hurt so much? I even started thinking about God. Maybe that's what he's for, I thought, to fill the gap when there *aren't* any answers, to ease the uneasable pain ...?

It still didn't make any sense.

One night, about a month after it all happened, Dad heard me crying and came into my room. It was about midnight. The window was open and the sky was bright with stars. A faint smell of gorse sweetened the air, bringing back bitter-sweet memories of a summer's day beside a tide pool, fishing for crabs. Me and Lucas ... we were in a slight shallow, shaded by gorse-laden dunes and marram grass. Although the sun was still high, the ground all around us had a fresh, moist feel to it, and the air was cool. I could smell the faint scent of coconut from the gorse flowers, the seaweed in the pool, the earthiness of the mud, the sand, the salt in the breeze, and from the shore I could hear the plaintive cry of a curlew. Lucas pulled on the line and I watched the bait edge slowly past the rock. He let it rest for a second then gave the twine a slight tug. Something moved beneath the rock, a rapid scything motion that stirred up a small cloud of silt, and then it settled again.

Lucas laughed, reeling in the line. 'He's smart, this one. He remembers what happened to his friend.'

As he concentrated on the tide pool the colour of his eyes seemed to waver in the reflected light. I watched, fascinated, as they faded from the pale blue of flax to an almost transparent tone, as faint as the blue of a single drop of water. Then, as he cast the line and the sunlight rippled the surface of the water, they darkened again. He began the process again, pulling on the line, letting it rest, a slight tug, pulling, a rest ...

When Dad knocked quietly on my door and asked if he could come in, the memory spiralled in on itself and scuttled away. I sat up and wiped my eyes and made room for Dad on the bed. He sat down gently and gazed out of the window.

'It's a lovely night ...'

He'd been drinking, but not much. His voice was clear, his eyes were tired but bright, and his breath carried just the faintest tang of good Irish whiskey. Since Lucas's death he'd cut down a lot on his drinking. He still drank regularly, but never enough to lose control. Just enough, I think, to soften the pain. He often came into my room at night. We didn't talk much. Most of the time we just sat together, being together, until one of us finally fell asleep. He listened if I wanted to talk, but I hardly ever did. We both knew there wasn't much to say.

But that night, after we'd been sitting together for a

while, breathing the night air, he told me something I've never forgotten. I'm not sure if it was meant to help or if it was just something he felt he had to say. And I'm still not sure what all of it means. But it stuck with me, and when something sticks with you it's usually worth remembering.

He told me that grief lasts for ever, that if it didn't last for ever then it wasn't true grief. He said, 'I know it sounds hard to believe, but once you stop fighting it and accept it as part of you, it's not such a bad thing. It'll still hurt, it'll still tear you apart, but in a different way. A more *intimate* way. You can use it. It's yours. It belongs to you. But the *pain* of grief ...' He hesitated. 'The pain you're feeling now doesn't last for ever, Cait. It can't. It hurts too much. You can't live with that much pain – not for ever. Your body can't take it. Your mind can't take it. It knows that if you don't get over it, it's going to kill you. And it doesn't want that. So it *makes* you get over it.'

'But I don't want to—'

'I know ... I know. But listen, getting over it doesn't mean forgetting it, it doesn't mean betraying your feelings, it just means reducing the pain to a tolerable level, a level that doesn't destroy you. I know that right now the idea of getting over it is unimaginable. It's impossible. Inconceivable. Unthinkable. You don't *want* to get over it. Why should you? It's all you've got. You don't want kind words, you don't *care* what other people think or say, you don't want to know how *they* felt when *they* lost someone. They're not *you*, are they? They can't feel what you feel. The only thing you want is the thing you can't have. It's gone. Never coming back. No one knows how that feels. No one knows what it's like to reach out and touch someone who isn't there and will never be there again. No one knows that unfillable emptiness. No one but you.' He looked at me, a single tear in his eye. 'You and me, love. We don't want anything. We want to die. But life won't let us. We're all it's got.'

After that I told him everything. I told him about meeting Jamie Tait at the beach. I told him what happened in Joe Rampton's lane. I told him how I felt about Lucas, about the day he took me to his place in the woods, about what he did to Jamie, and what he tried to do. Everything. I was surprised at how calmly Dad took it. He didn't shout or scream or threaten murder, he just held my hand and listened, nodding every now and then and comforting me when it got too much. And when it was all over, when I'd got it all out of my system, he sat quietly with me for an hour or so asking questions, clearing up a few little details, going over things he didn't quite understand, and then he started talking.

Apart from a daily trip to the beach, I hadn't been anywhere since Lucas's death. I hadn't been to the village, I hadn't talked to anyone. I didn't know what was happening elsewhere on the island. I didn't care. It didn't matter. I hadn't even talked to anyone about what happened to Lucas. Not Dad, not anyone. It was too painful. Lenny had come round a couple of times to ask me some questions, but we'd never gone into much detail. I think Dad had probably asked him to leave me alone as much as possible. I suppose I must have been aware that things were going on – investigations, news reports, that kind of thing – but none of it seemed to have any significance. It was all happening *out there* ... and *out there* was beyond my comprehension. It was nothing. Sounds, movement, words ... nothing. And while I knew I'd have to think about it some time, I also knew that *some time* wasn't now. Some time was always later; a time always on the horizon.

That night, as Dad started talking, the horizon came home.

'You don't have to worry about Jamie Tait any more,' he said. 'You don't have to worry about anything. Lucas left a full account of everything in a notebook in his bag. Dates, times, places, people—'

'Everything?' I said.

Dad nodded. 'After I brought you back from the beach that day, I found the bag in my room and hid it away. I was worried about the mob on the beach. I thought they might come back looking for more trouble ... I needn't have bothered, though. Most of them just wandered off along the beach back to the village. I saw Jamie and his boys coming up the lane about an hour or so later, but the fight had gone out of them. They'd lost interest.'

'They'd got what they wanted,' I said bitterly.

'I don't think they ever *knew* what they wanted. Maybe Jamie did in a twisted kind of way, and Sara, but the rest of them ...' He shook his head. 'I don't know. They just got in their cars and drove away. Didn't even glance at the house. They looked half dead. Confused. Shocked. Ashamed. As if they'd only just realised what they'd got themselves into ... as if they couldn't quite understand it.'

'What about Bob Toms?' I asked.

'I'll come to him in a minute.' He got up and went over to the window. He stood there for a while stroking his beard and gazing up at the stars, and then he started talking again. 'As soon as the storm died out and the Stand cleared, the place went crazy. There were police all over the island. Police, ambulances, helicopters, coastguards ... it was like something out of a disaster movie. Most of the police were from Moulton, and I didn't know if I could trust them or not, so I kept quiet about Lucas's bag until Lenny showed up later that night. I told him as much as I knew and I gave him the notebook and bag, and then I left him to it.' He turned from the window and looked at me. 'Jamie and Sara were arrested the next morning and Bob Toms was suspended from duty pending a full investigation.'

'What about the rest of them?' I asked. 'Lee Brendell, the bikers, Tully Jones and Mick Buck—'

'It's still going on. It's a complicated process, Cait. The entire Moulton police force are involved. There's a lot to sort out. Various charges of assault, attempted rape, deception, corruption, complicity ... I've been interviewed about a dozen times. Dominic's been interviewed. Bill, Rita, Shev ... the whole island's under investigation.'

'Good,' I said.

'The police want to talk to you, too.'

'What about?' I snapped.

He gave me a gentle look of admonishment, and for the first time in ages I felt the hint of a smile on my face. It *was* a pretty stupid question.

He came over and sat down next to me. 'It's good to see you smile again.'

I looked at him. 'It's all that talk of grief and dying – it's cheered me right up.'

He laughed quietly. 'I do my best.'

'I know – thanks.'

We sat in silence for a while. I gazed through the window at the night sky, wondering idly at all that space, all that blackness, all that nothing, and as I sat there looking up at the emptiness I began thinking about the creek, the hills, the woods, the water ... how everything goes round and round and never really changes. How life recycles everything it uses. How the end product of one process becomes the starting point of another, how each generation of living things depends on the chemicals released by the generations that have preceded it ...

I don't know *why* I was thinking about it. It just seemed to occur to me.

I was also thinking, curiously, about crabs. I was wondering if they *did* have a memory, as Lucas had suggested. And if they did, what did they remember? Did they remember their childhood, their baby-crabhood? Did they remember themselves as tiny little things scuttling about in the sand trying to avoid being eaten by fish and other crabs and just about anything else that was bigger than them? Did they think about that, scratching their bony heads with their claws? Did they remember yesterday? Or did they just remember ten minutes ago? Five minutes ago? And I was wondering what it must be like to be dropped into a pot full of boiling water ...

I was thinking about all these things and more, but I wasn't really thinking about them at all. They were just there, floating around in the back of my mind, thinking about themselves.

What I was *really* thinking about, of course, was Lucas.

'Why do you think he did it?' Dad asked in a near-whisper.

I looked at him. Beneath the beard and the weary eyes I saw the face of a child, a small child asking his mother to explain something. Something so simple it was bewildering – why? why did he kill himself?

'I don't know, Dad,' I said. 'I've thought about it so much I hardly even know what I'm thinking about any more.'

Dad nodded thoughtfully. 'Maybe it's best not to know.

He had his reasons, his secrets ... let him keep them. I think he deserves them.' He looked at me. 'We all deserve our secrets.'

'Yeah, I suppose ... it's hard not to wonder, though.'

'I know.' He gave me a long hard look, then patted my hand. 'Wait there – I've got something for you. I think you're ready for it now.' He got up and left the room. I heard him go into his bedroom, open a cupboard door, and then I heard his footsteps coming back along the hall-way. When he came back in he was holding Lucas's canvas bag.

'The police have finished with it,' he said, sitting down. 'They've kept the notebook for evidence but everything else is just as it was.' He passed it to me. 'Lenny thought you'd like it.'

I took the battered bag in my hands and felt the tears welling up. It smelled of Lucas. Sand, salt, sweat, crabs ... I gripped the rough green material in my hands and held it to my chest. I couldn't speak. I couldn't even cry.

Dad leaned over and kissed me on the cheek. 'Make it good,' he whispered. 'Make it part of you.'

Then he got up, said goodnight, and quietly walked out.

There wasn't much in the bag. Two green T-shirts, a pair of green trousers, pants, his water bottle, a length of twine, some fishhooks, a penknife, a handful of pebbles and seashells, and a small wooden carving wrapped in cloth. I suppose the rest of his stuff was in his pockets when he died, or got smashed up or stolen when his place in the woods was wrecked.

I keep his clothes in my wardrobe. The canvas bag hangs

on the back of my door. The rest of it is never far away. I can see it all now. As I sit here gazing out of my bedroom window, I can see the length of twine hanging from a pin on the wall, I can see the fish-hooks lined up in a row on my shelf, I can see the penknife resting in my pencil jar and the pebbles and shells sitting pretty in a clear glass jewellery box. And I can see the small wooden carving in my hand. I usually keep it on the bedside cabinet with the other one, the miniature Deefer, but I often find myself picking it up and holding it, not necessarily looking at it, just holding it comfortably in the palm of my hand. It helps me to think. It calms me. It's a carving of a face. Just like the one of Deefer, it's crude, but remarkably beautiful. No bigger than a finger, and carved out of driftwood, it feels smooth and warm, almost alive. I've spent many an hour studying it, staring at the face, the tiny eyes, the perfect nose, the beguiling mouth, and I'm still not sure what to make of it. It seems to change every time I look at it. Sometimes I'm sure it's meant to be me. It *is* me. And when I look at it, I see what I feel. If I'm happy, it's happy. If I'm sad, it's sad. If I'm lonely, it's lonely. But other times it doesn't look anything like me. It looks like Dad. And it mirrors *his* emotions, too. It's uncanny.

Sometimes, usually in the early hours of the morning, the carving takes on the appearance of Lucas. When the wind is blowing in the trees or the thunder is rumbling angrily in the distance, or when I just can't get to sleep for some reason, I wake up and look at the clock, and in the pale red light of the digital display I see Lucas's face gazing down at me from the cabinet. Unlike my face, or Dad's, Lucas's never changes. It's always the same: calm, peaceful, and beautifully sad.

Right now, as I hold the carving up to the light, I can

see all of three of us joined together. Three faces as one. I've never seen that before.

It looks nice.

Now it's late afternoon, about five-thirty. Mid-summer. Hot, but not too hot. Warm enough for shorts and a T-shirt. The sky is glowing with that wonderful silver light that lazes through to the early evening, and the house is quiet. Dominic is back from university again, taking a bath after a jog along the beach. I can hear the water tank dripping in the attic – *tack, tock, tock ... tack, tock, tock ... tack, tock, tock* – like a hesitant clock. Downstairs, I can hear Dad typing in his study. And from the garden I can hear Deefer chewing on a bone in the shade of the cherry tree.

Tomorrow is the first anniversary of Lucas's death.

I'll get up early and take a walk down to the beach and stand for a while looking out over the mud flats, just as I do every day. I'll probably say a few words and listen to the wind. I might even spend a few minutes searching for a glimpse of the coloured air, but I know I won't find it. I'll just stand there breathing in the smell of the sea and listening to the waves lapping gently on the shore, the wind in the air, the rustling sand, the seabirds ... and then I'll come back home again and get on with my life.

That's what happens.

You just get on with it.

There are no endings.

New from Kevin Brooks,
winner of the BRANFORD BOASE AWARD 2002,
shortlisted for the CILIP CARNEGIE AWARD 2002,
the GUARDIAN CHILDREN'S FICTION AWARD 2003
and the BOOKTRUST TEENAGE PRIZE 2003

*What do you do when all
you can do is wrong?
How do you choose between
bad and worse?*

Moo Nelson spends a
lot of time by himself.
Alone, avoiding the *rain*
– being pushed and
laughed at by others.
Every day he walks
through it all with his
eyes down, wishing
things were different.
But knowing they're
not.
Until the night he sees
a car chase – and a
murder . . . Or does he?
What is the truth and who wants to know? It seems a lot of
people do – the police, the lawyers, the bullies at school, and
one very bad guy indeed …

AVAILABLE NOW